CW01655744

The Purple Dolphin

M.S. Saxon

A critical parent with alcohol issues, a parrot with a knicker fetlsh and a mobster family who want to see hers dead. Catherine's life is stuck on a treadmill and something needs to change…

Statement of copyright

All characters within this publication are fictitious and have no connection with actual persons living or dead.

Contents

Table of contents

Dedications

For Jennifer and Alfie. My two greatest productions of all time.

Chapter one : The Christmas surprise

The plan was set to crumble even from the starting block. Fate had dragged Catherine Grimshaw by the sun lounger, right off that Corsican beach with all its perfectly toned attractions, only to dump her outside the doctor's surgery, far too close to home. It was ruthless, sadistic. And it was chucking it down.

Catherine's feet made squelching noises as she lowered herself onto a plastic chair near the toilets. Rain continued to hurl itself against the plate glass window as she glanced furtively around, hoping there were no familiar faces. Strangers of all varieties sat elbow to elbow in a contagious silence, except for the high-pitched nose blower buried in a crumpled hanky in a secluded corner of the room.

Looped over a fish tank, a child bandit poked the guppies on display with a Star Wars Lightsaber. Another swung his steel-capped boots into the back of Catherine's chair, setting in stone her general dislike of small humans and the clueless parents who spawned them. Maybe it was a sign from above that she was seeing this today, of all days.

In the next half hour a decision had to be made - and no easy one at that. But this time it would not be driven by the actions of family members.

Chapter one : The Christmas surprise

Catherine attacked her rain-frizzed hair with desperate palms but it would not be tamed. Her misted spectacles needed a wipe too. Ransacking the bag on her lap, fingers collided with the smooth bowl of Ted's favourite pipe. Its tag-along friend, the aroma of Captain Black seasoned the air with nostalgia. And the floodgates of memory threw themselves wide.

***

It was Christmas morning, 1961. Ted woke early, with bed springs poking him in the back and a throbbing head to remind him where he was and why. Twisting his weathered face, he peeled back the covers and shivered as bare feet met with the stone floor. Last night in The Fish Gutter's Arms he hadn't considered for long enough his reckless choice between a warm bed beside the missus and that extra pint of Brown Ale. Or was it two? And how was he to know some shifty geezer would burst his way through the clouds of stale cigarette smoke, selling all kinds from beneath a scruffy blanket? Ted was in a vulnerable state. The state of having too many notes in his pocket and a wish to make Molly happy. Egged on by side kick Sam, he staggered out of there with a live addition to the Grimshaw household, which seemed like the perfect gift at the time. This morning, not so much.

The house slept on as he quickened his pace down the garden path, tugging at his thin collar against the chill. For many months he'd watched with sadness as Molly flirted and fawned over fellow stall holder 'wide boy' Walter. But now,

Ted was convinced there'd been a parting of the ways, and today he planned to mend some bridges.

As Ted approached Sam's house the front door opened a crack, and a lavender strip of colour danced behind it. Sam hopped from one foot to the other, clutching a floral robe draped around his shoulders.

"Will you get in here before I bloody freeze to death?"

Ted strode up the path and leaped inside. "You're gettin' soft in yer old age Sam Wiggins. Try wakin' up with an icicle hangin' off yer nose." His brow furrowed as he clocked Sam's robe. "So you're finally on the turn then?"

Sam rolled his eyes. "It's the daughter's. And stop winding me up. Did Molly stick you in that bottom room again? You could keep a corpse fresh in there for weeks." Sam led the way to the kitchen.

"Aye, and that corpse may be mine when I give her this," said Ted, flicking his head at the dome shaped form on the kitchen floor.

"Talking of which," said Sam, ".... this little begger had the wife tossing and turning all night. Kept asking for Fred."

"The wife did? You might be in trouble there."

"You daft sod. Can you manage it on your own? I'm away back to bed for an hour."

"Aye. We'll see ourselves out."

Chapter one : The Christmas surprise

Ted lifted an edge of the cotton cover and peered inside the cage. Sleepy black eyes flashed him a do-not-disturb look. "It's alright young fella. You go back to dreamland. We'll be home soon."

***

Ted rounded the corner into Halfpenny Lane, as two local boys chased a football towards him. He thought of his son at the front window, making out like he wasn't bothered.

"Smashing Christmas present, lads," said Ted.

One boy looked up, while the other took a sneak shot between two rolled up jackets in the road. "And ... he scores!"

"I did loads better than Pete this year. He got some *terrible* short pants.

"Are there any other kind?" Ted winked, as he swept into his garden gate.

"What's under the blanket Mister Gee?" Pete shouted.

"Surprise for the missus. Pop round after dinner and you can see for yourself."

Stepping inside, a savoury blast of hot air perked up his taste buds, and festive songs played in the background, accompanied by the tearing of wrapping paper.

"Dad? Where've you been?" Steven's pubescent voice yo-yoed between mezzo soprano and baritone. Ted silenced a snigger and poked his head around the living room door.

"I've been out hunting - captured the most *amazing* creature."

Steven grinned from behind a coil of woolly scarf complete with price tag.

"You've never! So where's your spear then?"

Ted slapped his forehead with the palm of his hand. "Aw...I knew I'd forgotten something. And we can't eat him if he's still alive."

"What? Who's still alive?" Steven struggled to get up from the floor. The surgical boot was heavy, but a necessary evil to walk with his shorter leg.

"Take a guess, and you can have my last liquorice allsort."

Steven's smile got wider. "A jelly button or coconut roll?"

"You'll have to wait and see. Might be a triple pink sandwich."

"Umm, okay. So, can it swim?

"Do you know son, I haven't tested that possibility yet."

"So .... *not* a piranha then?"

Ted pushed a finger under his cap and scratched his head. "Not exactly. Is that what you were hoping for?"

"What's that smell? Is it a skunk?"

Chapter one : The Christmas surprise

Molly came out from the kitchen wearing a splattered apron and a disapproving face. She wiped her hands briskly on a towel.

"There'll be no talk of liquorice allsorts before dinner. You both know the rules. What have you done, Ted? Why aren't you coming in?"

At forty two, Molly still held onto the button nose and dimpled cheeks of her childhood. One or two greys had begun to show at her temples, multiplied by the odd splash of flour from the kitchen, her favourite place to be.

"Can't tell you yet. It's a surprise," he said.

"Say hello to Skipper." A rasping voice came from behind the door.

Ted turned towards the cage, still hidden from sight, and lifted the cover. "Oh, so you're talkin' now, are you?"

"Full of surprises. Full of surprises." Tiny feet pattered on wood.

Steven's boot squeaked as he limped across the room and pulled open the door, eyes wide.

"Woah! What kind is it, Dad?" He crouched awkwardly in front of the cage and the bird peered back at him, neck outstretched.

Molly scowled. "Ted Grimshaw, what am I supposed to do with that flaming thing? I thought you were bringing the ham. And look at the muck. Its cage is filthy."

"Sorry about the ham, love. But this little chap's got to be more entertaining. And if all else fails, you can serve him up on New Year's Day." Ted gave a mischievous grin, and Molly turned away with a sigh of impatience.

"Well, don't expect me to be doing the plucking," she said, strutting back to the kitchen.

"I was told," said Ted, hanging up his coat, ".... he's an African Grey."

"What does he eat? What should we call him?" Steven said.

"Skipper's a clever boy."

"Sounds like he already has a name. And there's a bag of his food in my jacket. Let's get Skipper inside and clear a spot on the sideboard."

As he positioned the cage, Ted stared at the couch. "Well, I never thought I'd see that..."

"See what?"

"A naked sofa. With a clear view of the skylarks. What happened to the plastic covers?"

"She took them off this morning. Just for today, she said."

"Well, can we sit on it or what?"

Molly reappeared at the kitchen door. "Of course you can sit on it. And they're *bluebirds* not skylarks." She looked him up and down. "So long as you change out of those trousers, and don't eat on it." Ted lifted an eyebrow, and left the room to find his best tweed turn ups. "... or fart on it for that matter," she called after him.

Steven's fascination with Skipper wrestled with his hunger, and he needed some persuading to join his father at the table. Then, with a sideways manoeuvre, Molly wobbled through the kitchen door under the weight of a large breasted turkey and set down the serving dish centre of table, humming along with the radio. Ted and Steven watched her adjusting the potatoes around it, standing back for a better view and humming louder.

"Where've you been hiding that Moll?" said Ted. "It's bigger than Australia."

Molly's brows came together and the humming stopped. A strand of hair sprang out from behind her ear and she dragged it back into line. "Is that all you've got to say? That it's *big*?"

Steven lowered his voice. "Don't let Skipper see what we're eating."

Ted picked up the carving knife. "Never thought of that, son. They could be distant cousins. Tell you what.... If it makes you feel better, I'll put him outside with those two mad cats from next door while we have our dinner."

Molly pressed her lips together and sat down. "Take no notice. Your father will do nowt of the sort. Anyway, I'll be sitting right in between. Ted, for God's sake take that bloody cap off. It's Christmas day."

Ted looked wounded. He was rather attached to his old cap. Steven waited for him to do the trick. As if on cue, Ted lifted his bushy brows, tipped his head, and the cap flopped into his waiting hand. He flashed Steven the briefest wink, laid the cap alongside the Brussels sprouts and smoothed his thinning hair.

"Thank you," she said. "It's bad enough we have to suffer that nasty pipe of yours." Ted reached up to his chest pocket and gave his pipe a defensive pat. If it wasn't there, it would be nestled in the gap between his bottom front teeth. Molly continued.

"Now stop waving that knife like it's a fairy wand and get the turkey sliced. I'm starved. How about you, our Steven?"

"Belly thinks me throat's been cut." Steven dug deep into every dish on the table with a shovel of a spoon, avoiding the green balls of hatred.

"Best change its mind quick then," said Ted, plating up turkey body parts before tucking in himself.

Awkward gaps in the conversation were not common at the Grimshaws', especially at meal times, yet seven minutes had gone by without a word. Ted gazed across at Molly, hesitating for a moment.

"Your sister couldn't make it then?" he said at last.

"I'll go and see her tomorrow. She likely has one of her headaches."

"It's time she saw a doctor about those. Invitations round here seem to trigger Joan's headaches....for some reason."

Molly shifted her eyes across the room, and pushed more food into her mouth.

"You two may as well be joined at the hip," he went on. "I wish you'd confide in me sometimes."

Steven's eyeballs flitted between the two, as his mother got up from the table, stone faced, and removed the empty plates.

"There's real brandy for the pudding, Dad," whispered Steven as Molly left the room. "I spied the bottle on the bench this morning."

Molly returned from the kitchen with a tray of dessert dishes, Christmas pudding and a steaming jug of custard but without a space on the table to place it. With purpose, she flattened Ted's cap beneath it.

"Hey Moll, if you'd asked, I would have moved that." Ted did not understand why she couldn't be happy, or at least make a show for Steven. Trying to second guess Molly every day should have made him an expert, but he was still at a loss. Although ... *he had* noticed there'd been no turnip on the plates lately, which was rather odd because she'd served it up every day for the last few months. Maybe that was significant.

"Can we set fire to it?" asked Steven.

Molly rubbed an eyebrow with one hand as she spooned the pudding into dishes with the other. "No ... we can't." She sat down. "We're out of brandy." Ted and Steven exchanged glances as she poured the custard, serving Steven first, then herself. She lifted her spoon and began eating. Ted helped himself to pudding, hoping to swallow his disappointment along with it. But just as he lifted the spoon to his mouth, Molly put hers down and fixed her eyes on the pepper pot. She clearly had something on her mind. Ted took a mouthful, watching her intently, while Steven scraped the last of his custard from the bottom of the dish.

"I'm having a baby, Ted," she announced. "And it's not yours."

Ted spluttered and coughed through his nose. He grabbed a napkin and pressed it against his face. Steven's gaze shifted faster from Ted to Molly, then back again.

"You choking? Dad?"

"…No, son … just ... swallowed a lucky sixpence," croaked his father.

"Not so lucky for you then," said Molly, tucking back into her pudding, job done. Steven sprang from the table and made for the door, overcome by giggles.

"Man overboard!" said Skipper.

As fate would have it, Ted's lucky coin was never seen again, and by the New Year, Walter had also vanished. In his place, a large man with carbuncles and halitosis had taken over the vegetable stall. Ted was thankful. He knew Molly wouldn't go there, big turnips or otherwise.

***

In early June when baby Catherine arrived, she came with a head full of ginger curls like Walter's, and a barrow load of baby blues for her mother. Molly's bonding instinct never showed its face, and Catherine was left to cry herself to sleep, deprived of cuddles, milk and a dry nappy. The medical profession, particularly those up north, trailed behind when it came to linking hormone deficiencies with mental health issues, and so Molly was advised by the family doctor to close her eyes for ten minutes in the afternoons and open her bowels every morning.

The market stall didn't seem to suffer without her. Steven was roped in to help, but in doing so had to give up his Saturday job at Smedley's garage, which he loved. Nevertheless, he took to market life like a dog to a lamp post, and Ted couldn't see the point of him wasting, as he saw it, even more time at school.

Molly's mood swings would unsettle the whole household, and Catherine still recalled the first scary incident, even thirty years on.

The preceding day, her mother remained in bed with a depression deeper than the bottom of her handbag, and Catherine steered clear of her room to avoid a tongue lashing and the odd flying missile. But by next evening, Molly had transformed into

Delia Smith on speed, with not enough hours in the day, nor flour in the cupboard to bake biscuits for the apparently starving neighbourhood. It took all of Ted's patience to get her into bed that night, even more to get her to sleep, but only when he heard her gentle snores did he drift off himself.

It was around two a.m. when he woke with a start to Molly's tone deaf singing downstairs and the smell of burning.

"Shit!" Ted said to himself as he flung back the bedcovers and ran down the stairs in long johns and vest. Standing in the kitchen doorway, it flashed through his mind he was having one of those weird nightmares that needed a Freudian translation. But that thought departed as fast as it came when the heat hit his face. The back door was ajar, and Molly stood over the cooker in her nightgown, singing 'Baby it's cold outside' to a stray fox cub she'd invited in from the garden, now cowering beneath the kitchen table. Crossing the threshold he saw flames climbing the curtains, and smoke, blackening the ceiling. He sprang across to the sink, grabbed a towel from the drainer and soaked it. Throwing it around his arm, he pulled down the curtains complete with rail, snatched open the back door, and flung the whole lot outside into the darkness. Seeing a means of escape, the fox cub followed, without its promised bacon treat, still smouldering on the grill pan.

"What the hell, Molly?" Ted gasped. "Are you determined to kill us all?" Molly stopped singing.

"Poor foxy was hungry. Who else is going to feed him?"

Ted reached across, dragged the pan from under the grill and blew hard on it. "His mother, for one. If you'd give her a chance."

"You're a bloody killjoy, Ted Grimshaw. Why can't you just have a bloody laugh? What's wrong with you?"

Watching from the doorway, Steven tugged nervously on his earlobe, while Cathy peered through his pyjama clad legs. Ted shook his head.

"This can't go on Molly. You'll have to see someone. There are two kids in this house that need a mother and this isn't fair."

"Just *one* kid, if you don't mind," said Steven.

"Calm yourself, grumpy drawers." Molly gave Ted's face an affectionate squeeze with one hand, slipped an arm around his waist and began to hum, swaying from side to side to the rhythm.

"Let's go dancing like we used to. Just the two of us, right now, hmm?" Her lashes fluttered in fly swatting mode. He unhooked her arms and placed them down by her side.

"Maybe not tonight love. It's late."

"I'll be allowed to drink beer pretty soon." Steven was determined to be heard.

Catherine stuck out her tongue. "Yeuck! Beer's nasty."

"How do *you* know, Pipsqueak?" asked Steven.

"It *smells* nasty. Anyway, Dad says so."

"And that's dead right, sweetheart," said Ted, as he secured the back door and turned off the cooker. "And I know you're dying to grow up our Steven, but you're still a kid to me, and I'll always want to protect the pair of you." He examined the plug holes where the curtain rail had been fixed and shook his head again.

"I must have a word with that handyman. Not very secure that rail, was it?"

"Um, I think that would be you, Dad," said Steven.

"Really?" Ted attempted surprise. "Then I'll have to shake the man's hand. He must have known it would need to come down in a hurry." With a glance at the clock on the wall, he slapped his palms together. "Now, let's get you lot upstairs."

"I love it when you're masterful," said Molly. "Play your cards right ....."

"*Don't...*" Ted cut her short, "..say those things .... not in front of these two."

"Was she trying to set fire to the house?" asked Steven as they headed upstairs.

"It wasn't *that* bad," insisted Molly. "Your father loves a bloody drama."

"Are you going to play cards, Dad? With Mam?" said Catherine.

"No, sweetheart, we're going to sleep like normal folk. Come on, up to bed with you."

After that, Ted worked fewer hours on the markets. Reluctant to leave Molly alone in the house, yet taking her to work was just as much a hazard. Steven returned to his part time job at Smedley's helping to service the vehicles. He'd missed it so much.

Chapter two : Peace and war

Cathy was still only six years old when Molly was admitted to Cherry Knowles hospital for a psychiatric assessment and stabilisation of her condition. She felt bad to think it, but those eight weeks without her mother were the most care free of her young life. Ted warned her about the gossips.

"Now listen, our Cathy..." he'd said. "When the nosy parkers round here ask where yer mother is...and they will....you just tell them to keep their big nebs out."

Of course Catherine wouldn't dream of saying any such thing, and no-one asked her outright, though she did see people whispering behind hands at the bus stop.

The long summer holiday had just started for Cathy, and she was excited to be the new recruit working on the stall with her dad and big brother. It was a fine, bright morning and she was finishing breakfast while the others loaded the van. She heard the van doors slam, and her dad came back into the kitchen.

"You ready love?"

Grabbing the last piece of toast from her plate, she snatched up her little bag and ran towards him.

"I've learned all the words, Dad," she said. "I even did them in my sleep."

"Good lass. You're gonna knock 'em dead."

As they pulled up at Oldcastle quayside, the place was already buzzing. Setting up and keeping pace with everyone else was always the hardest part for Steven, and those boxes of crockery had to be moved pretty sharpish.

"Well, look at you," came a voice from the next stall. Taffy Jones carried a huge box of doggy treats from the boot of his car.

"It's the Tupperware Trio." Taffy gave Catherine a big smile as he slapped the box down on his stall. "Are you helping your dad today, little one?"

"We've got a new act," said Cathy, arranging the crockery the way Steven had shown her, for maximum visibility.

"Oh yes? Has your dad been teaching you?"

Catherine nodded.

"Well, I'll be looking forward to that."

It was just gone nine thirty, and ambitious shoppers peered into lavishly dressed windows across the street before being tempted over to the market by mid morning. Ted stood by, pulling on his pipe while Steven opened the cab door of the van and took out a soft woven shopping bag and a flowery straw hat. He limped across to Catherine and placed the hat on her head. It was too big, and her red curls bounced beneath it.

"There you go, Pipsqueak. Keep this bag on your wrist, and wait for the crowd to gather. When I move this wooden box, I want you to stand on it. Then follow Dad's prompts."

Ted's sales banter began. "Gather round, you sorry folk. Grab a bargain, share a joke." Catherine listened for her cue, watching the crowd grow bigger. Ted chose a plate from Catherine's display. "So what could you serve on plates like these? Caviar? Or crackers and cheese? Rich or poor, the plates don't care. But *I'd kill* to be a millionaire." With gentle laughter from the crowd, Ted replaced the plate.

"Now folks, let's see how steady my hands are today." He held both arms out in front, fingers trembling. "Aw heck. Not so steady today then." Ted shook his head, picked up the tea plate again and threw it in the air. Someone gasped. He caught it in his opposite hand and picked up a second. Then, he began to juggle the pair. Steven stood by with a third, and Ted snatched it at just the right moment to throw into the sequence. All eyes were fixed on Ted and the flying crockery. Even those strolling past stopped in their tracks. Some feared the slip and the crash. Others, impatient for it.

"The missus told me I'd never manage the weight of three," he said.

"I told her, 'If I can juggle three of your fairy cakes, I can manage the weight of anything.'"

Laughter ran through the crowd. Catherine watched Steven lift the wooden box and come towards her. She stepped onto it, straightening her hat. Ted stopped juggling, and addressed the crowd with his full attention.

"Now then, can I interest any of you lovely ladies and gents in one of these genuinely fake Wedgewood dinner services?" He held a blue and white dinner plate aloft. "You've got six place settings here for when the mother in law comes to visit."

Men in the crowd groaned.

"Almost giving these away, I am. Cups and saucers are thrown in with it too."

Cathy raised her hand just above the heads of the crowd.

"I'll take one. But I don't want any broken cups young man, not when you're *throwing them in!*" She shouted in as grown up a voice as she could muster, and the row in front separated. Cathy and her wooden box were now centre stage, and Ted appeared to be insulted.

"Broken cups? I never break cups madam. The occasional heart, maybe..."

He winked at the crowd. "Will you give me ten quid madam? And I'll give you a matching casserole dish. A big family, have you madam?"

"That's none of your business, young man. And I'll give you a fiver. No more."

"Well, what do I say to that folks?" Ted asked the audience.

"Take the fiver," someone shouted. Ted poked his finger under his cap and scratched his head.

"Oh....I don't know about that."

"Take the fiver! Take the fiver!" shouted even more people.

Ted held up a hand. "Okay, okay, I know when I'm beaten. A fiver it is."

There was a round of applause, and Steven led Catherine to the front of the crowd where she took a bow as her hat fell off her head, to even more clapping.

***

As time passed, Molly's manic depression stabilised, and she was allowed home with prescribed medication, to be taken at the appropriate time each day. Eventually, she joined Ted and Steven on the market stall again and life seemed to settle back down until one busy day when they ran short of change.

Steven had a hangover that morning and stayed home, so without his help Ted and Molly were rushed off their feet. Waiting for a suitable lull, Ted asked Molly if she'd cope on her own for ten minutes while he went for some change. He'd been gone just a few moments when two spotty youths caught Molly's eye, hovering at a distance, more interested in her than the merchandise. She was serving someone who needed change of a twenty, and the lad directly across from her watched as she pulled a wad of notes from her waist pouch, peeling off a tenner. Within seconds his accomplice hooked an arm around her neck from behind and held a blade in front of her face.

"Give me the fucking money, bitch!"

The crowd scattered. Molly held on for seconds while he tugged hard. "Let ... fucking go!" She released her grip and he snatched it from her, his own force propelling him away. But he kept his footing and ran. His partner in crime sauntered off, disappearing into the crowd. Molly dropped to the cobble stoned ground, trembling. Blood ran down to her fingers, where he'd caught her with the blade. The customer she was serving came forward.

"Shall I find you a copper, love?" he asked. Then Ted arrived back, breathless.

"I saw the lad run off. Are you all right Moll?"

Molly couldn't speak. She stared at the blood running down her trembling arm.

"We're packing up now folks," shouted Ted, helping his wife up from the ground. She clung on to him and wept.

"The boy. I know him," she choked back sobs. "It was Tony Moretti's son."

Ted grimaced. He knew the Moretti family were bad news.

The police took a statement from Molly after she came home from having her hand stitched at the hospital. Molly's emotional state was still obvious, and although sympathetic, a knowing look between the two officers was noted by Ted.

As expected, the routine visit to Tony Moretti's home resulted in a solid alibi for both of his sons at the time of the robbery, and the case remained unsolved.

Molly's mental health plummeted following the attack. She missed taking her medication for days at a time and suffered more frequent manic episodes. Just as Catherine was getting to know her mother, the fragile bond unravelled again, and the feelings of rejection returned. Molly never went back to the market stall after that.

***

At the age of twenty three, Steven met a young woman and fell crazy in love. She was such a pretty thing that Steven thought he'd best grab her before she changed her mind, and in the weeks to come he could speak of little else. Catherine teased him, Ted would stuff socks in his ears, while Molly smiled, made gingerbread, and invited her to tea.

On that Sunday afternoon, Steven came through the back door clutching the hand of a petite, dark haired girl wearing an A line yellow dress and a broad smile. Catherine sat next to her dad at the kitchen table, wearing new eye glasses and catching up on her homework.

Ted stood up. "Come on in lass. Go through and sit yourself down."

Chapter two : Peace and war

The dining room table was laden with triangular sandwiches minus the crusts, fruit scones and chocolate cake. All on the best china.

"Is royalty coming then?" Steven said.

Molly appeared from the hallway wearing her posh frock.

"Hello love," she said to the girl. "Come, take a seat. Steven, where are your manners?"

"Mam, Dad, this is Wendy."

"Do you live round here Wendy?" asked Molly, moving a cushion so the guest could sit.

Catherine abandoned her homework for all of two minutes to peer round the door.

"Yeah we do. Next to the snooker hall on Bell End Road." Wendy smiled at Catherine. "Lovely glasses," she said. "They do suit you."

"I thought I knew all the families around here," Ted continued. "What's your surname, Wendy?"

Steven interrupted. "Don't bombard the poor lass with questions, Dad!"

But Wendy seemed happy to answer. "It's Moretti. My brothers are Tony and Joe. *Everyone* knows them. Tony, especially."

Molly's smile soon faded, and Ted's jaw dropped.

"Is the kettle on yet, Mam? We're parched." Steven stepped back into the kitchen to search for the kettle under a pile of sandwich making debris. “If I can find it, that is.”

“I can do it,” said Catherine, following behind.

Wendy threw Molly an awkward smile, and Ted went after Steven. Leaning over his son’s shoulder, he whispered.

“You do know who she is, don’t you?”

Steven sighed as he filled the kettle.

“I knew you’d be like this. That’s why I didn’t tell you.”

Ted persisted. “The Morettis are drug dealers. They’ve done time for burglary. Their father was connected to mobsters, and Tony’s sons robbed our stall.”

“We’ve only Mam’s word for that, and she’s hardly reliable. Anyway, it’s not drugs. Just a bit of weed. Everyone’s doing it.”

Catherine settled once more at the kitchen table. *Services not required.*

“Well *I’m* not!” said Ted. “And *you’re* not.... Are you? Flaming hell, this can’t be happening!”

Steven gave his earlobe a tug, frowning as he picked up the tea pot. “I need to get back in there. It’s gone quiet.”

Catherine drew stick men with angry faces in her homework book as Steven brushed past her chair.

"You won't get a gold star for doodles, Pipsqueak," he said.

She raised accusing eyes. "You told her to say that, didn't you?" said Catherine.

"Say what?" Stephen turned back.

"Something kind about my glasses?"

"Just take a compliment, will you? And those ears do a grand job of keeping them on your face by the way."

"So I've got big ears now? Thanks a bunch."

Steven gave her nose a gentle tweak, and grinned. "I'm off. Gotta keep my girl happy."

A grim faced Molly returned to the kitchen where Ted stood at the sink, squeezing a dish cloth inside a clenched fist.

"This can't last," she said, twirling the thin belt of her dress between her fingers.

"Keep your voice down," whispered Ted as he turned towards her.

"It can't last. We have to stop it." Her knuckles began to turn white.

Ted returned the cloth to its resting place and placed both hands over hers.

"You know, when he said she was pretty, God forgive me, but I wondered what she was doing with our Steven. I mean, he's kind hearted, but a girl like that?"

"But she can't get a normal fella, can she?"

"What makes you say that?"

"Some whispers ... *I might have* overheard at the hairdresser's. The lads round here won't go near her. Last one she had took a broken nose for his trouble. Those Moretti brothers are out of control."

Ted considered. "So our Steven gets to be the unlucky one twice over? First with the polio, and now the bonny lass with no other takers? Molly Grimshaw, you never cease to surprise me, with your common sense. And those elephant ears."

She gave a scornful look and overturned his backhanded compliment. "I've a bad feeling about this, Ted. And less of the *common* if you don't mind."

His face softened, and he drew her towards him.

"Like you say, it may not last."

Catherine looked up from her books. "At least her dress is nice. Don't you think?"

***

Molly was anxious about attending the wedding and coming face to face with her assailant, but Ted persuaded her that it was a long time ago, the boy had most likely regretted what he'd done, and whatever happened, he would stay by her side.

It was to be the first wedding Cathy had attended as a bridesmaid, let alone one of a pair dressed in puff-sleeved tangerine – with flounces that went way past their knees. However on the day, Francesca's hemline had been fashionably raised without consultation, and Catherine was more than peeved. As if the ginger hair didn't clash enough with the tangerine dream dress, she now felt the giant finger of ridicule pointing mercilessly at her from the sky. Okay, so Francesca was just that bit older than Cathy's ten years, and she was also a Moretti, so maybe there was some sort of entitlement status that no-one thought to explain? But silently debating both sides would get her nowhere this time. Cathy just had to get through the day by following the wiser, more confident one and all would be fine.

As it turned out, the church service went without a hitch, but the reception raised one or two red flags for the Grimshaws. Tony Moretti had his fully inflated ego out on display for all to admire as he played the role of best man, encouraged by a doting Rosa, who flapped around his coat tails like a mother hen.

It was a small venue with just one hireable reception room to hold around 40 guests. The Morettis and the Grimshaws sat at the top table with only the bride and groom in between. The close proximity of Tony Moretti's sons, amused at her distress, kept Molly topping up her own glass from a wine bottle she wouldn't share. Ted's gaze flitted from guest to guest when he noticed a secret exchange of glances between Tony and his brother's girlfriend, Gina. Especially since Tony's wife sat in ignorance by his side.

With the main meal over, Gina got up to visit the ladies' room, and Tony rose from the table, following in the same direction.

Joe watched his brother leave. "Where's he going?" He asked his mother.

"How should I know? Men's room, most likely."

Bridesmaid Francesca stood up from her seat, shuffled across to Catherine and whispered in her ear.

"Do you want to know a secret?"

"What kind of secret?"

"Sshh...come with me."

Catherine got up and followed her out of the room.

Joe still puzzled over his mother's dismissive response.

"But the Gent's is over there!" He indicated with a thrust of his head in a different direction. Rosa ignored him, took a mirror from her handbag and applied fresh lipstick to her non-existent lips.

While Wendy mingled among the guests, Steven attempted to start a conversation with his father.

"Wendy's gorgeous, don't you think, Dad? Maybe just a bit too perfect though?"

He looked at his father for some confirmation, but Ted was more aware of the surroundings and his uncomfortable suit.

"If she had a couple of webbed fingers ....or even a bit of a stutter ..... that would be enough. Heaven knows what she sees in me." But Steven's confidence sharing fell on deaf ears.

"What's up with you, Dad? What's so interesting?"

"Sorry son, I get the feeling something might kick off in a minute if we're not careful."

"Something like what?"

Ted looked ready for conflict. "I reckon it's time for the speeches."

Steven glanced at his watch and turned to Joe.

"Do you know where Tony's gone? He's supposed to be making his speech about now."

Joe shrugged. "Tony pleases himself. Does what he wants, wherever he wants."

Wendy returned to her seat and leaned across the table. "Joe, will you go and find him? He's been gone ages."

Joe stubbed out his cigarette and began to get up. "Okay, he can't be far."

Ted was already standing. "Stay there Joe. I'll go."

Joe shrugged again and sat back down as Ted headed in the direction he'd seen Tony go off in.

Meanwhile, Francesca turned the handle on the door of the ladies' powder room with caution, and peered inside. She beckoned to Cathy to follow behind, and crept into the room. There were soft grunting noises coming from one of the cubicles, which Catherine assumed was a guest having some sort of private difficulty. When Francesca grinned and moved closer to the toilet door to listen, Cathy was horrified. The grunts coming from inside seemed to be from two separate people, and she tugged on Francesca's dress, trying to persuade her from the door.

Outside the ladies' powder room, Ted paused and knocked.

"Gina? Are you in there? It's time for the speeches. Have you seen Tony?"

At the sound of Ted's voice, Francesca swept away from the cubicle door and pretended to adjust the flower in her hair at the wall mirror. Cathy was left standing in the centre of the room as the bolt snapped loose and the cubicle door opened. Tony's wild eyes met with hers, and she backed away.

"What the hell are you up to, little girl? Spying?" He clutched at the opening on his trousers.

"No, I just wanted the toilet. And I don't think you're allowed in here."

"Don't tell me what I'm allowed!"

Francesca gave a sideways smirk. Tony fastened his trousers and stepped out of the cubicle. "Not a word," he warned Cathy.

Ted heard voices and movement coming from inside. He waited a moment, and then started back to the dining room. As he walked away, he heard the powder room door click open behind him, and Tony rushed past on his way back to the wedding guests.

"Out of the way old man," he said, nudging Ted aside. "My presence is required."

Ted watched him disappear into the room with his coat tails half tucked into the back of his trousers. He was about to call after him, and then thought better of it.

Back inside the ladies room, Catherine was aware someone was still hiding inside the toilet cubicle. Francesca was in no hurry to leave, so Cathy made the decision.

"I'm going back to the reception Francesca. Are you coming?"

"You go if you want to," Francesca grinned with mischief. "I'll be there in a minute."

Cathy headed back to the dining room alone.

Tony arrived back at the top table, straightening his tie and buttoning his jacket, with Ted following close behind him.

Joe's forehead creased. "Where's Gina?"

"Haven't seen her," Tony said.

Rosa spotted the trapped coat tails and tugged them discreetly free from his waistband. He picked up a spoon, checked his reflection in the back of it, then tapped it against a wine glass a few times. Joe tossed him a suspicious glance, and checked behind to see if Gina was anywhere in sight.

"Can I have your attention please, ladies, gents?" The room went quiet, and Ted sat back down to Molly's relief. Then Cathy returned to her seat.

"As most of you know," Tony continued, "The late great Bruno Moretti is not around anymore to do the honours, so, as the next best thing, I've been asked to step in and say a few words."

Rosa shook her head, acknowledging the sadness, but glowed with pride as her son continued to speak, and then Gina returned to the table, averting her gaze from Joe. Tony proceeded.

"When we were growing up, Joe and I were excited about the new addition to the family. That is, we hoped for a boy – someone we could enrol into the brotherhood. Instead, we got Wendy..... and she tried to make us play shops, dress up in silly clothes." He paused and stared at Joe. "And I think my brother secretly enjoyed that side of it." There was a pause for some faint laughter, and he carried on. "After we trained her though, she proved kind of useful, even if it was just to keep the Yamaha clean and polished."

"In your dreams, brother!" said Wendy.

Another pause. More laughter.

Francesca returned from the ladies room, and came across to Catherine, watched by Tony as he waited for the laughter to subside. She uncurled her fist just enough and showed Catherine two pound notes rolled up in her palm.

"Look what I got," she whispered.

Catherine wanted to know how she'd got the money, but Tony's stare unsettled her, and she felt a sneeze coming. She closed Francesca's palm inside her own, took two short breaths, covered her face and gave way to the nose tickle.

"Aa...aatchoooo!"

Tony flashed another scowl, as Francesca ran back to her seat.

"Would you like to come up here and have a go yourself, little girl?" he said.

Everyone turned to gawp at Catherine, and her face glowed pink. Ted came to the rescue.

"I'm sure you can manage without the help of a ten-year-old, Tony." He said. "You carry on. We're hangin' on your every word." Tony returned his attention to the captive audience, and one member in particular.

"So, Steven, I hope you know how precious our baby sister is to us. The Moretti name runs through her like a stick of rock, no matter what she calls herself now, or where she lives. We'll be watching out for her, just think on that." Steven smiled, but Tony couldn't have been more serious.

"Wendy, we wish you all the best in your new life, and any time you'd like to pop round and iron my shirts, you'll be more than welcome."

A couple of the guests cheered.

"So, raise your glasses everyone, please, to toast the married couple, Wendy and Steven."

"Wendy and Steven!" sounded the echo, accompanied by the chink of glasses. Tony sat, and the chatter recommenced.

Catherine avoided Tony's gaze for the duration, which wasn't to be for much longer. The Grimshaws felt the atmosphere between the two families deteriorate following Tony's speech, and Molly asked if they could leave. Ted saw Cathy's unhappy face and said, "Aye, let's go. I've had enough too."

***

It was a regular Saturday evening and Steven wore only vest and trousers, with a towel draped around his neck as he tried to steal a corner of the bathroom mirror to shave, while Wendy hogged the lion's share of it testing various pouts with her new shade of lipstick.

"For heaven's sake, Steven, you're putting me right off. Can't you do that in the kitchen?"

He lowered his razor. "Well, thanks for that suggestion. It's plain to see the honeymoon period's over. I don't know why you need all this palaver. It's The Pig 'n' Whistle we're going to, not the ruddy Palladium. Is that more face paint you've been buying?"

Wendy stared at his reflection in the mirror with disappointment. "So you'd rather I took a leaf out of your book and went around like a ragbag would you?"

"Course not. I just wonder who you're trying to impress, that's all."

"There's only you, stupid. Don't start getting suspicious again, I can't bear being around you when you're like that."

Defeated, he picked up his after shave, turned and limped towards the door.

"Right, well I'm off to the kitchen then. If you're sure that's far enough away?"

"Don't tempt me!" she shouted after him.

That was to be the start of many strained evenings out, until Wendy became pregnant with their first child, Louise. She seemed content to be a mother, and Steven sank back into a happy and settled place. Baby Danny arrived less than two years later, and the family seemed complete. But as the children got older, jealousy reared its ugly head again as Wendy flirted with the locals down at the pub, even though Steven would be standing right beside her. Ted would watch from his end of the bar on the nights when Catherine, at age eighteen, chased him from the house to be like normal folk.

But seeing Wendy flirt, and his son's reaction to it was like watching his own life's movie stuck on repeat.

When the kids were eight and nine, Wendy took a barmaid's job despite Steven's protests, and two years down the line in the summer of 1984 he became convinced she was seeing another man. The dog walks were taking longer; she wore perfume and her smartest clothes before leaving the house. Absolute justification in Steven's world, for following her one evening.

It was a warm, airless night, when she set off towards the posh end of Shields. His heavy boots struggled to keep pace with Wendy's clacking heels until she stopped suddenly and glanced behind. Gasping for breath, Steven swung himself into a nearby doorway, betrayed by the squeak from his boot. Seconds later, the clacking started up again. But he had to drop further behind, and by the time she came to a stop at a large house in Tanfield Road he was grateful to rest. Benji wagged his tail expectantly as she tied him to a fence post before going inside. The dog lay with his belly on the cool paving slabs and waited. Watching and waiting also, but from an unlit, stinking back lane for forty five minutes, Steven smoked the first quarter inch of all twenty King Size Players, and his ear glowed scarlet from all the tugging. Maybe he could bang on the door, but what if the bloke took care of himself? He wouldn't stand a chance. Fire raged inside him. He screwed up the empty Players box and tossed it into a nearby skip. He would wait. Talk it out with her.

Wendy's outline appeared in the open doorway, alone. She smoothed out her dress, closed the door behind her, untied the dog and set off in the direction of home. Until Benji tugged her towards a lamp post only feet from where Steven was hidden. Light from the lamp bounced between tiny pearl buttons on the back of her dress, and Steven's eyes settled on those that were done up the wrong way.

A switch flipped inside his head, and he lunged forward, grabbing Wendy by the hair. As he pulled her backwards, she struggled to stay on her feet and let go of the dog's lead. Steven faltered too. She caught a sidelong glance.

"Steven, get off! .... Aagh! You idiot, you're hurting me!"

"Is that right?" he said. "And who might *you* be hurting carrying on like a whore? Your kids maybe? Your husband?" She looked away. Still holding on to her hair, he dragged her higher up the lane out of sight from the street. Only then did he alter his grip and held her by the shoulders, staring her in the face.

"Who the hell is he?"

"Who the hell is who?"

"Don't mess me about." He relaxed his grip and she wriggled her shoulders free.

"You're an arse, Steven Grimshaw. Wait 'til I tell Tony what you did."

"I'm entitled to know. Who have you been with? Or should I just go over there and ask him?"

Wendy leaned into his face, and he saw that the lipstick she wore earlier was gone. “Do what the hell you like! He’s twice your size. And anyway, did you really think I was gonna be the little wifey, at home, content to...vegetate.... with a cripple?” He took a step back. She took one forward. “Can you blame me for looking elsewhere with the pathetic excuse for a husband I’ve been stuck with? Did it ever occur to you why I married you in the first place?”

“Of course it did. I’m no prize, I know that. But you said you didn’t care about any of that.”

“Well, what a surprise, I lied. I felt sorry for you, that’s why.” Her scornful gaze swept over him like a dirty yard brush. “And now? You just repulse me! I deserve better. I deserve a *real* man.”

Steven’s face became distorted. As she turned to leave, he sprang forward and grabbed her by the shoulder, turning her back again to face him. With strength from nowhere, he thrust her up against the brick wall, and as she made impact, a dull crack broke the quiet darkness of the lane. He stood watching her for a few seconds as she slithered down the wall to the cobble stoned ground, panicking at the thought of what he might have done. He leaned across and touched her shoulder again, but more gentle this time. “Wendy?” he said. Her head flopped forward. He stepped back, hesitated for a moment, then turned and limped away at a determined pace.

Casting all moral principles aside, the stupid dog followed Steven back home, trailing its lead all the way, and the next morning when it seemed that Wendy hadn't managed after all to resurrect herself from between the rubbish bins and struggle home, Steven got the kids up and off to school before taking a corporation bus to the police station and handing himself in. The desk sergeant seemed doubtful.

"You think you've killed your wife?"

"I don't think ... I *know* I've killed her."

"I see.... well if you'd just like to take a seat, I'll get someone out here to talk to you." He indicated a row of chairs with his biro.

"Will it take long?" said Steven, "only it's forecast for rain and ... she might get wet."

The officer blinked a few times, glanced around and said, "Well if she's dead, she's not likely to mind, is she?"

Steven leaned into the glass screen between them. "Have some bloody respect!" The officer stepped back, holding up his hands.

"All right, fella. Calm down. I'm ringing through now." He picked up the telephone, still with his eyes fixed on Steven. "Have you hurt your leg?" He pointed with the biro, again.

"No, it's a deformity. I'm a cripple. I've a twisted spine too. Would you like to see?" He began to unbutton his jacket

"That won't .... be necessary."

"Can you just get on with it then please?"

***

They found Wendy's body where he said he'd abandoned it – in a small patch of dried blood, now swarming with flies and surrounded by over flowing waste bins. The indignity of it all, on public display in the raw light of day.

The suggestion of Wendy's involvement with another man was devoured by the press, frowned upon by the church community, and exaggerated by the scandal seekers. Interviewed by police, Butcher admitted to a dalliance with the now notorious Wendy Grimshaw, nee Moretti, but rejected a four figure sum from The Daily Grind for a story. By the same token, Steven didn't want his own brief to delve into his wife's past, even if it led to mitigating circumstances for his defence. He considered that he alone was responsible for the demolition of his family, and without that foundation his sentence was already being served, whether spent behind bars or in the free world.

The Grimshaws' lives were flipped upside down as Steven began a long stretch inside. Recent events proved too much for Molly, and she was readmitted to Cherry Knowles hospital as her grandchildren were taken into care. Ted and Catherine acquired a new pet, Benji the mongrel dog without principles who had lost his family too. But Skipper resented this intrusion into his personal space. The four legged creature irritated him with its barking and fearsome growls when the post arrived. Then there was the whining when any of the humans left the house. In an effort to claw back status, Skipper perfected his own version of Benji's growl, becoming so convincing that Benji would return it, until the back and forth competition was unstoppable. And so, pecking order was reinstated.

***

It was a regular Friday night in the bar at The Fishgutter's. Ted stood at his usual end of the serving counter with his old mate Sam, whom he'd known for a lifetime and then some.

"You're a worry guts, you know that?" Sam picked up his glass and drained it. "Anyway, are the Morettis still doin' all that stuff? They've been in and out of prison more times than I've been barred from the bookies."

"And that's a lot." Ted agreed.

"Maybe they've learned their lesson."

"Well, you know what they say about leopards."

"Do you know why they call Tony, 'nine lives?" Sam smiled, hoping to lift Ted's mood.

"No, but I've a feeling you're about to tell me."

"Well, Tony 'nine lives' Moretti got his nickname from surviving no less *than five* motor bike accidents."

"Well, he's a lucky bugger, isn't he? Anyway, that's only five."

"But I'm not finished...."

Ted showed some mild interest, so Sam continued.

"He also puts it about a bit."

"Well that's nothing new. I've witnessed some of that. At our Steven's wedding."

"But it's not just women he likes, if you know what I mean?"

Ted raised an eyebrow. "Well, I never knew that," he said. "So you're hinting ...... he's also dodged that disease they've just discovered? The AIDS virus?"

"Too right," said Sam. He waved his empty glass at the barmaid. "And there's no cure. He's on borrowed time. You get a diagnosis like that, and you're gone. Nine lives or no nine lives."

Ted and Sam were still deep in idle chatter when the door swung open and in they walked. Tony and Joe Moretti were accompanied by a pair of tattooed heavies. Ted hadn't seen any of Wendy's family since his son's conviction some months prior, and he straightened his stance for the inevitable confrontation.

Tony always walked ahead of his brother with an overly confident gait, stealing the limelight at every opportunity. His trademark herringbone overcoat with turned up collar flapped around his tailored trousers, and a heavy gold chain glistened around his neck. He took a long draw on his cigarette and the bar went quiet as he stopped within feet of Ted's spot, blowing plumes of exhaled smoke through his nostrils.

"Well, if it isn't the murderer's father, out drinking and laughing as though nothing's happened."

"We're all sorry for what happened, Tony," Ted answered, with a sideways glance. "I told you so after the sentencing. No-one regrets more than my son for what went on."

"And yet...that doesn't seem to be the case at all," Tony continued, "or you wouldn't be trying to get access to my niece and nephew now would you?"

"Those kids are my grandchildren. I've no intention of cutting them out of my life."

Tony's face darkened. He stepped closer to Ted and leaned in with a sharp forefinger, prodding at his shoulder.

"If you want what's left of your family to stay safe, Grimshaw, you'd better drop this fucking access idea or you'll regret it, I promise you."

Ted returned his steady gaze. "If you care so much about what happens to your niece and nephew

Moretti, why did you let them go to foster carers? Why not take them in yourself?"

Tony glowered, making a gesture to one of his minders, who stepped forward, grabbing Ted by the throat and pinning his head to the counter as glasses overturned and smashed to the floor. Joe stood at a distance with legs apart and arms folded, while his more confident brother moved in, positioning his face so close that Ted could see into every open pore, track every pulsating blood vessel around Tony's temples.

"Get the hell out of here, or I'll cut off your balls and staple them to your fuckin' earlobes," said Tony with a nod to his minder, who let go of Ted and shoved him towards the door. Ted made for the exit, but just before he left he turned back.

"Better do up your flies Moretti, or you might show everyone how small you really are."

Tony glanced down, and quickly buttoned his coat. He snatched a bottle from the counter and fast-bowled it, overarm, into the doorway, but Ted was already legging it up the road towards home.

***

The children's first visit to the house was for the briefest hour, and Ted had bought coloured balloons of all shapes and sizes to demonstrate how to make a sausage dog with five legs and two heads. Danny was delighted with his grandad's antics and both children made a great fuss of Benji. But Louise, far more mature than her years was quiet and withdrawn, and it would take many weeks of

Ted's efforts to wear down the barriers and get her to smile. But smile she did, eventually.

***

It was a rainy day during the first year of their father's incarceration when Ted and Cathy took the children to a video rental shop in town. Danny insisted his grandad brought the over sized automatic umbrella to shelter all four of them. Louise argued against, but the umbrella came along just the same.

Danny was first inside the shop, spotting the Morettis lurking in Coppola corner. He darted across to say hello. Cathy nudged her father.

"Prepare for trouble."

Ted picked up the first video he could lay hands on and feigned interest as the Morettis came over and hovered either side of him. Eyeing up Ted's impromptu selection, Joe sniggered.

"Like a bit of porn do ya, old man?"

Ted winced as he realised the embarrassing title he held, and shoved it back in its slot.

"Wrong section mate!" Tony snapped, so close to Ted's earlobe he feared leaving the shop without it.

"Too old for all that nonsense," said Joe. "You'd be better off in the *murder* section." At which point they lifted Ted by his elbows and hurled him against a display stand, scattering Rocky sequels across the floor. The shop assistant stood open mouthed behind the counter as Tony brushed imaginary dirt from his sleeves.

"And don't think your cripple of a son is in for an easy time when he gets out. I might just ram his fucking walking stick up his arse until his guts burst out of his fucking nostrils."

Catherine clamped both hands over Danny's ears, but didn't make it in time.

"My son doesn't use a walking stick," said Ted, raising himself up on one elbow.

"No?" said Joe. "Well he'll be needing a wheelchair and a fucking dentist by the time we're done with him."

On his way to the door, Joe lifted his foot to step over Ted. But just as he did, Ted's brolly, still in his hand, shot open like an impatient parachute. Joe went sprawling across the room, cursing more as he fell. Danny's eyes popped at the horizontal chaos spread across the floor.

"Cor Grandad, that was amazing. Can you do it again?"

Cathy's gaze swept to the counter assistant just as a fly buzzed around the gaping entrance to his frozen face.

"You might want to keep that shut," she said.

"Cathy!" Ted threw her a scowl.

Cathy protested. "There was a fly .... I was warning him." Ted shook his doubting head before he stood upright, dusted himself down and ushered his family out of the shop. Louise, silent during the whole episode, resolved to find out the truth for herself the following day by searching archived news at the local library, after which she decided she would not see her father again.

Chapter three : A brief taste of life

On the morning of his landmark birthday, Ted opened his eyes to the back of Molly's sleeping head, encased in rollers she still insisted couldn't be done without. It amused him that despite having reached an age where comfort should be taking precedence, his wife was determined to keep up appearances. With least disturbance, he drew back the covers and sat upright on the edge of the bed, rubbing the shoulder he'd been laying on for the last two hours with a grimace. He heard the milkman's float pull up outside, and realised what day it was. Getting up, he snatched his trousers, hiking them up on his way downstairs, still bare footed. As he pulled open the door, Charlie had his hand poised ready to knock.

"Morning Ted," said the milkman, and tipped his cap. "Looking as delectable as always."

"You can't give me any lip this morning, Charlie. It's my special day."

Charlie's face puzzled. "Special day?" Then his face brightened. "Ah, I remember now. Today's the day the Odeon lets you in for half price."

"You're askin' for a clip round the ear, cheeky bugger."

Catherine appeared from behind her father, dressed for college and holding out a yellow envelope. Ted moved to let her past. "You off, love?"

"Yep." She kissed him on the cheek and thrust the envelope into his hand. "Happy birthday Dad," she said, "I'll do the tea when I get back. Bolognese okay?"

"That'll be grand," called Ted after her as she hurried down the path. "But I'd rather have a meat pie," he confided to Charlie.

"I heard that!" she yelled back, without stopping. "Lucky for you it's your birthday."

Charlie smiled, glancing down at the doorstep. Next to the pint of Gold Top was a plastic ice cream tub with an envelope on top. "Looks like someone else has left you a present."

"Well, I can't think who that could be. Anyway, how much do I owe you this week?" Ted plunged his hand into a trouser pocket and lifted out a handful of loose change.

"One pound sixty five mate. But seeing as it's your special day, we'll call it one fifty."

Ted lifted an eyebrow. "Be careful you don't go over the top, you'll give me a panic attack. Just take the one sixty five and I'll keep a clear conscience .... drinking my cocoa tonight."

"You're a star." Charlie dropped his money into the leather pouch around his waist, tipped his cap a second time and made his way down the path. "I hope it's something nice, by the way," he said, nodding in the direction of the ice cream tub. "See ya."

Ted shoved Catherine's card under his arm as he stooped, picked up the milk in one hand, and the tub in the other. He closed the door with his foot and paused, staring at the writing on the envelope resting on top. It just said 'Grimshaw,' hand written in biro with his address underneath. He placed the milk and the tub on the hall table while he opened the envelope and unfolded the single sheet inside. There was a cartoon-like, yet disturbing drawing made on a local taxi firm's notepaper with a message beneath.

His attention turned to the ice cream tub. Whatever was inside, cast a dark shadow through the thin plastic. He picked it up, gave it a sniff, then quickly opened the door again and dropped the offending article into the bin outside with a clatter. Hurrying back inside with hands aloft, he headed for the kitchen tap. On the table were cooking scales, an upturned bag of flour and an assortment of baking tins. Molly was poised over them, tears rolling down her cheeks. He turned on the tap and rinsed his hands. "What's wrong, love? I thought you were having a lie in."

She wiped her face with a hand, smearing it with more flour. "I can't remember."

"Remember what?" He dried his hands.

"The bloody recipe...."

"What are you making?"

"The ... round things. With the black things inside."

"You mean scones?"

"I can't remember how much ... and I don't ....Where's the ..... hot box?"

Ted whipped the card from his armpit, propped it up on the wall shelf and pulled down a cook book. "The oven's behind you, Moll. And we can find the recipe. It'll be in here."

"But it's in my head ... it's always in my head!"

"Well we can put it back in there ... look, here it is."

She plonked herself on a chair, despondent. Ted grabbed an apron from a door hook and tied it around his middle, inhaling as he did so. He glanced with regret at the sealed birthday card left by Catherine. It would keep for a while longer. At least someone had remembered.

"You're too fat anyway," Molly said. "So it's just as well I can't cook anymore."

"No more of that silly talk." Ted poured flour onto the scales. "We'll make them together."

Her eyes fell onto his bare feet. "You can't cook like that," she said, getting up from the chair. "You need your slippers."

He looked her over, still in her dressing gown with a head full of loose jumbo rollers. But at least she seemed willing. "Okay love. Be back in a jiffy." He kissed her floury cheek and dashed back up the stairs to the sound of Molly's humming. It was a good sign.

***

The taxi firm's notepaper was a dead giveaway. Bigg's Cabs was a small business, operating under the protection of the Morettis and used for deliveries of a pharmaceutical nature. Excrement had to be a more recent sideline. Considering this, the recent threats and with his daughter's best interests at heart, Ted insisted Catherine would be better off completing her education at an unknown college away from home. He'd been a careful saver over the years, and figured by registering as Molly's carer, he could apply for benefits and afford to contribute towards Cathy's living expenses while still working part time on the stall. Always the juggler.

So Cathy was accepted by East Morton College as a student of Hospitality and Catering management, with accommodation on campus.

The rooms were basic, but adequate. Ted gave the shared facilities a once-over, and returned to her room shaking his head.

"How many people are expected to use that shower?"

"Must be four," said Catherine. "There are four rooms anyways, on this floor."

"Looks like mulligatawny soup coming through that spray head. Have a word with the warden. It needs sorting."

"Okay Dad. Don't worry, I'll be fine. Are you sure you'll cope on your own?"

"One of the neighbours, Doris, lives a bit further up on the other side? She's offered to come over and give a hand."

"Is that the one with the hyphenated surname? Just lost her husband?"

"Aye, that's the one." Ted gave a half hearted smile. "I'm sorry, love, I'll have to get back to the van. I've locked your mother inside.

Walk me to the door and I'll give you a spanner from the tool box."

Catherine followed him out. "What do I need a spanner for?"

"To turn the cooker on. There aren't any knobs." He came back from the van holding a pair of pliers in his outstretched hand. "These will do better. You know how to use them."

She tested their action. "You taught me well."

"You don't *have* to cook, I suppose. Or shower, for that matter. Seems like the rest of them don't bother anyway. I've left you some cash on the table."

"Thanks Dad. I've got the toaster, the kettle, and the sink. I'll be fine. You'd best get back. Mam will be running out of oxygen."

"Watch what you're doing, and be careful." He climbed into the van, waved, and drove off.

***

In her second week, two fellow students persuaded Catherine to see a live band at the County Hotel. A perfect opportunity to wear the crazy shoes she'd bought the previous week with saved birthday money.

Students packed the bar that evening, mostly on their feet crowded around the stage. Cathy felt her toes pinching, and wished she'd worn trainers instead of four inch stilettos.

Chapter three : A brief taste of life

An assignment was already overdue, and the guilt nagged at her for most of the evening, despite several snakebites later. Around 10pm she made her excuses, smiled with regret at the protests and headed back to campus.

Approaching the main road, she answered pleas from her throbbing feet and removed the impractical shoes. Then, by the light of a not so far away street lamp, she had to do a double take. A white rabbit appeared to be sitting in the road cleaning its face. Catherine tried to recall how much she'd had to drink, waiting for the mirage to disappear. Then she heard the bus coming and ran out, shooing the rabbit away. But it just sat there, watching her. Without thinking, she waved her shoes at the oncoming vehicle to stop, which it did, but with only inches to spare. The driver stuck a puzzled face out of the cab window.

"What's up love?"

"I'm saving the rabbit." said Catherine. But turning around, it had gone.

"Yeah, so I see. Your name's not Alice, by any chance?"

Catherine still scanned the road. But there was nothing. A passenger yelled from the front of the bus.

"Oi, buggerlugs! Shift yerself!"

Catherine's face burned, and she slunk away towards the halls. As he drove off, the driver shouted after her,

"Stay away from the pickle jar pet. It's not good for you."

The cool, damp grass delighted her throbbing bare feet, and as she turned towards the steps of the building, she saw the rabbit once more, hopping alongside her.

"I reckon you must be Mister Pickles then," she said as she opened the door and watched him hop inside.

Catherine was sure there was a clause in her contract somewhere about pets being barred, but the shower still hadn't been fixed, so she felt justified in keeping Mister Pickles until someone came looking. She tried him with a litter tray and he took to it straight away. No fleas, which was always a plus. Maybe a child somewhere was pining. She'd have to keep her eyes and ears open.

It was about to be another evening of six in total spent with Mister Pickles, several library books and a growing pile of note paper, some of it nibbled around the edges. Rain tapped against the window and a trickle ran down the wall from a crack in the frame. Mister Pickles chased a ping pong ball across the room and Catherine stretched, threw her pen onto the coffee table and got up to fill the kettle. Then there was a knock at her door.

Kenny McGuire stood on the threshold. Behind the gold rimmed spectacles his forehead was moist and he seemed annoyed. He held a pink plastic laundry basket overflowing with female attire, and Catherine's conscience pricked. Without the trademark green duffle coat and college scarf it took a while to recognise him. His perfect English gave the game away.

"Hi, um ... someone told me this could be yours?" He offered up the basket. Cathy felt her face flush. She hated when that happened.

"I'm really sorry. It gets so hot in there. I came back to do some work, and then I ... just forgot." Seconds passed.

Maybe he wants a tip.

Kenny glanced down at Catherine's feet. Her view was blocked by the laundry basket, shoved into her arms. Mister Pickles stood on his back legs, nose twitching as he sniffed the air.

"Graham?"

He's a nut job.

"You found Graham!" he said.

"I did? Oh ..... you mean Mister Pickles. He followed me home from The County. I didn't know he belonged to anyone here."

Bugger it. Shouldn't have answered the flaming door.

Kenny bent down and scooped the rabbit into his arms, nuzzling its head.

"Well, I couldn't put notices up. He's illegal, as you know. And a bit of a wanderer. Thanks for taking care of him." He lifted his gaze from the furry head, scrutinizing her. "Mister Pickles? Really?" With that, Kenny McGuire and Mister Pickles were gone, and Cathy was left holding a lifeless washing basket. No comparable swap by any means.

The following afternoon she returned from classes to find a folded note pushed under her door.

'Graham requests visitation rights. Would it be convenient to call at 7pm this evening for an hour or so?' It was signed 'G & K at number 14.'

Cathy was uncertain. Flattered, of course. Short on romance? No question. But could she handle it? Could *he* handle *her*?

In the end, she tossed a coin before the bathroom was taken or she'd never get in there. An acceptance note was scribbled and shoved under number 14, while her boil-in-the-bag paella heated on the stove. She consumed at speed. As a consequence, G & K from Number 14 were greeted at the door by a severe case of hiccups and a full set of tacky fingernails.

"You need to drink something," said Kenny, holding up a bottle.

Catherine took it from him. "Well I heard you were .... hic .... clever, but I think I could have worked that one ...... hic .... out for myself." She hadn't forgotten the sarcasm in his 'Mister Pickles? Really?' remark.

He let that one go. Stroppy could be a challenge, and he was always up for one of those.

"You coming in? Or are you ...... hic ...... waiting for the rabbit catcher?"

She poured her own glass first and drained it. "That's not bad," she said.

He can pour his own. I'm nobody's slave.

"Have they gone? The hiccups?"

"I...think so. Grab yourself a glass, and come sit. What's that in your pocket?"

"I've come prepared," he said.

I should chuck him out. "In what way?" she said.

He pulled it out, held it aloft. "Carrot. For Graham."

"Good thinking." *Shit, that's a relief.*

And so they talked while Graham / Mr Pickles chewed on his carrot. Cathy spotted the outline of a second carrot in there too, but she wasn't to find out until sometime later, it was nothing of the sort.

Kenny was studying for a B.A. in business with economics. His chestnut brown hair flopped over a pair of grey-green eyes when he lowered his head, and he'd one ear higher than the other, making his spectacles lop sided. Cathy found him easy to be with, and he slid perfectly into the space vacated by her family.

As far as class was concerned, the pair were poles apart. Kenny's parents were high flyers in the corporate world, owned a holiday home in the south of France and even employed a cleaner. But that didn't matter to either of them. For now. However, after only months into her further education and new relationship, events were to scupper Cathy's plans yet again.

Chapter three : A brief taste of life

Chapter four : A leek and a promise

Ted's cheques always arrived promptly and without fail. But back home the problems with Molly had reached a point once again where leaving her alone in the house even when medicated was unthinkable. Her short term memory became poor to almost non-existent, and Ted had to oversee every menial task. Several memory tests later, she was given a second diagnosis of early onset dementia, to run alongside her previous diagnosis of manic depression, which had just been re-classified as bi-polar disorder. It was a lot to come to terms with, and Ted's next letter to Catherine explained his decision to stop work altogether. He told her not to worry, that he still had some savings, and he'd keep on sending the cheques for as long as he could. The money came for a few weeks after that, but then it dwindled. Catherine found an evening job at an all night garage.

***

In the summer of 1985, the college broke up after the first set of exams, so Catherine packed her belongings, kissed Kenny and Graham goodbye and caught the earliest bus, hoping to surprise her dad. Baggage laden students, all with the same idea clogged up the space inside, and after a bumpy two hour ride, Cathy was grateful for a lungful of fresh air as she stepped once again onto terra firma.

She let herself into the kitchen to the sound of laughter and the sight of her mother tossing crunchy nut cornflakes into the air from a family size box, while Benji sat by his dog bowl, puzzled as to why it was filled with frozen peas. Catherine dropped her bags to the floor.

"Come on, Mam," she said. "Cereal's too expensive to chuck around. You used to say that to me when I was a little 'un, remember?"

Molly frowned.

Clearly not.

"I'm waiting for our Joan. She'll be home from school soon. She'll throw you out!"

"Aunty Joan? She died."

Molly held her accusing stare. Catherine continued to clarify.

"Five years ago? We went to the funeral. You liked the cake. *And* the wine." Cathy scooped up some cereal in her hands, put her foot on the bin pedal and dropped it inside. The explanation did nothing for Molly's mood. She swung a kick at the bags on the floor and a rucksack landed with a thud in the hall.

"I don't want you here!"

Can't say I'm thrilled about it myself right now.

"This is my home too, Mam. You won't see me much anyway. Got a job interview at the Co-op on Monday."

Molly glowered. "I hate you. You ruined my life!"

Okay. That was mean.

"...I'm sorry you feel that way, all right?"

"Two fat ladies, dirty Gertie."

Hallelujah! New topic of conversation.

"Should we go for a game of bingo this afternoon? Would you like that?"

"Bingo!" Molly began to sway.

"Let's get you sat down, eh?" Catherine took Molly's arm. "You're a bit too wobbly for my liking, after that hefty kick."

Catherine side stepped the rucksack and led Molly into the sitting room, settling her in front of the television. Skipper woke from his nap and Catherine switched on the TV set.

"Do you know where Dad is?" *One of these days she'll answer and I'll faint.* Her mother was transfixed by Richard and Judy.

"Where's Fred?" said Skipper.

Catherine stared at Skipper. "Dad's name is Ted, Skipper. With a 'Tee'. We don't know who Fred is."

"Where's Fred?" Skipper repeated.

Chapter four : A leek and a promise

Catherine dragged her hair from her face with both hands and turned back to the kitchen.

Place is a madhouse.

After a brief survey of the mess, she went to find her father. Benji still waited by his dinner bowl, and watched with the saddest eyes as she left the room.

The rest of the house was quiet, but as she ventured upstairs, the familiar creak from the second step was masked by a deep groan coming from behind Ted's closed bedroom door.

Turning the handle, she lowered her voice. "Dad ...?" The bed was in disarray but still occupied, and Cathy stared in freeze frame mode.

Oh my God. I'm hallucinating.

Until the realisation hit her. The miscreants gaped at the intruder, and the intruder gaped back. She cleared her throat.

"So, I'll just go and do something downstairs." She made a pointless jab with her thumb in the direction of the door. "No need to get up." Then she left the room.

Catherine's steps quickened as she descended the stairs to the sound of high pitched yelping. Back in the kitchen, she snatched the bread knife from her mother's right hand while Benji pulled his tail free from her left and scampered under the table. Undeterred, Molly pursued him with a pan scourer, utilising it as a grooming tool. Benji rested his head across his outstretched front legs, considering whether to eat the frozen peas and have done with. Ted reappeared in the kitchen doorway. He kept his gaze low, not noticing Molly's menacing stare from under the table.

"Dad?" said Catherine. "Fancy a pot of tea? And your friend too? Kettle's almost boiled."

"No, love I'll be grand. Got some stuff to sort out in the shed." As he made for the back door, Molly let out a scream, rushing at him with fists flailing.

"Bastard! What have you done to him?"

Ted grabbed hold of her arms, but not before she'd landed him a heavy punch. "It's okay, Moll. I'm here. Look, it's me!"

Her brow wrinkled, and she began to cry.

"You're alright now, Moll. Let's go and see what's on TV." He led her into the next room just as Doris appeared at the kitchen door, doing up her cardigan with perfectly varnished red finger nails.

"No tea for me either, pet. I have to get off." She clocked the dog's bowl on the way out. "And Ted might need those frozen peas for his face." With that, Doris slunk through the back door, and as Ted followed her seconds later, the kettle's whistle screamed out from the stove.

Welcome home, our Cathy.

***

Attempted conversations from that point were monosyllabic on Ted's part. Cathy tried telling him that it was okay, that she understood. Hurting Molly's feelings was not an issue any more. Or so she hoped. He deserved some happiness, didn't he? But Ted wasn't receptive to kindness in his current state of mind, and the brick wall response remained every time she broached the subject, so she spoke of it no more.

As the job interview loomed, her concerns escalated. Ted was unrecognisable from the happy go lucky market trader she knew and loved just three years before, and she wondered if anything would be normal again.

A few evenings later, with nothing of male interest on television, she persuaded Ted to take himself off for a pint or three. Molly kept nodding off in the armchair, and snorting herself awake every few seconds, so Catherine put her to bed around seven thirty, and settled herself in front of the television with a bag of cheese and onion and a mug of Horlicks. So absorbing was the Indiana Jones action on screen that she missed the blast of cold air shooting through the gap under the living room door, until her nagging bladder and an ad break came at just the right time to spot the front door swinging in the wind and her mother gone. She grabbed a coat and hurried out onto the street.

Cathy searched around, expecting to spot a candy striped dressing gown and matching slippers without much difficulty. She'd almost reached the main road and desperation point when a friend of Ted's from the same estate meandered across the road towards her.

"If yer lookin' fer yer mother," he said with a slur, "she's entertainin' a crowd outside the pub with a bit of a song and dance..." He started to stagger away, then turned back to shout over his shoulder, "She's not too bad either. Hee hee!"

When Cathy got to The Fish Gutter's, she saw her father on the outer edge of the crowd, watching, expressionless. One or two threw coins at Molly's dancing feet, and someone tried to accompany her on a mouth organ as she attempted to sing 'We'll meet again', though her feet moved to a different rhythm of heaven knows what. The dressing gown formerly described as candy striped, lay discarded in a dirty puddle, and Molly's nightie was splattered with mud along with the slippers.

After some initial resistance from the cabaret performer, followed by gentle persuasion from the minder and cries of 'spoilsport' from the crowd, Catherine got her mother back home in one piece. *Problem : How to prevent future escape attempts. Solution : Fasten her to the bed. Handcuffs, leg irons.* Catherine leaned over her mother and sighed. She tucked in the blankets much tighter than usual, loosened them again, and left the room. Next, she locked the front door and paid a long overdue visit to the toilet. A half hour later, she heard Ted's key in the door, and waited. But he went straight up to bed without a word.

Chapter four : A leek and a promise

***

Weather-wise, the following day was perfect, and Catherine wheeled her mother over to the market square, while Ted stayed behind and do a spot of weeding. The Grimshaws had a large back garden with a high wooden fence, smothered on all sides with ivy, and an oak tree with a complete history of childhood carvings on its gnarled trunk, standing stoic in the corner.

"We're off now, Dad. Give you a few hours to yourself. What about tea? I could do those chicken breasts when I get back."

"Aye, that'll be grand," said Ted. "I'll pull up a couple of leeks to go with it. Take your time. Nowt's spoiling here."

The bright sky and mild breeze lasted well into the afternoon, so after buying some unhealthy cuisine from a mobile van, Cathy pushed Molly's chair along the sea front where there were no cobbles to negotiate. It was after four when they got home, and although there was no sign of Ted in the house, he'd left two leeks on the kitchen table as promised, and a note propped up against the empty teapot.

My beautiful daughter, please forgive me.

Love you always,

Dad xxx

She read the note three times and still didn't understand it. Had he left home or did he just mean sorry about Doris? Juggling these thoughts, she settled Molly in her armchair and crept up the stairs to check her parents' room. His wardrobe was still full of clothes, so he hadn't gone anywhere yet. Feeling less concerned, Catherine returned to the kitchen, carried the leeks to the sink and glanced out of the window. Benji lay on his belly under the tree, next to an overturned set of step ladders. His head turned sideways, gazing upwards. She followed his curious stare ... and then she saw her father hanging there by his blue spotty tie. The tie he saved for special occasions. Adrenalin flooded her body. She raced outside, leek still in hand. Possessed by anger, she took aim.

"What ..WHAT THE BLOODY HELL..... DO YOU THINK YOU'RE DOING?" She choked back sobs as she swung at his legs with the leek.

"YOU.." (bash) "CAN'T" (bash) "DO THIS!" (bigger bash) she yelled, as though it was still possible to change his mind. His body began to sway. Back and forth to the rhythm. Then she let the sobs come, yelled at him again and hit him some more, until she realised the pointlessness of it all; threw down the tattered remains of their intended supper; cried out in frustration and stumbled back into the house to dial 999.

Chapter four : A leek and a promise

The paramedic thought Ted had been dead for at least two hours. Catherine found that hard to believe at first, because she'd heard gurgling sounds coming from his throat. But the medic explained that it could have been stomach gases expelling themselves. She was conscious of her own throat feeling sore, from the unaccustomed shouting rather than empathetic pain, she realised.

Two police officers supported Ted's body as they cut him down, and Catherine spotted something smouldering in the grass at the base of the tree. She bent down and retrieved Ted's pipe, comforter to the end.

Benji took off after the ambulance and didn't turn up until 5 days later, much thinner and very sorry for himself. For months afterwards, he lay at the foot of Ted's armchair, running to the door full of expectation whenever he heard a sound on the path outside, but returned each time, dejected, to his usual spot.

Some of Ted's old market colleagues and best friend Sam showed up to pay their respects at the funeral, and there were long forgotten relatives dressed in sad clothing, making sympathetic noises and ritualistic arm patting gestures. No-one was sure how to be with Molly, as she punctuated the service with random bursts of cackling.

Doris made her peace with Catherine, who hadn't been aware of any war in the first place. At Ted's graveside, Wendy Moretti's brothers, Tony and Joe showed their smug faces and beige suits to mark their total lack of respect. Tony nine lives even sucked on a lolly.

"I was hoping for a knees-up," he said. "But it's all so sad." He exaggerated a frown. "Never mind, though." He twirled the lolly stick protruding from his mouth. "With a bit of luck your murdering brother will be next." Tony removed the lolly and held it in front of her face. "Given up the fags ... my life's sweet now. Pity you can't say the same about yours." Then he inserted the stick back into his mouth and walked off with his grinning brother following behind.

Arsehole. Hope you choke on it.

***

When it arrived, the confirmation of Catherine's success in the first part of her exams did little to raise her sunken spirits following recent events. Any future plans she may have had for university and / or romance with Kenny, were now snookered. They kept in touch for a little while by telephone and the odd letter, but Kenny's student grant didn't stretch to the bus fare, or so he claimed, and Catherine couldn't leave her mother now.

Chapter four : A leek and a promise

Chapter five : The Butcher's dog.

It was a warm evening around eleven p.m., and Mel Butcher lifted his dog's lead from a hook in the hallway. The familiar chink of metal brought Buster running to his master's side with excitement.

"Good boy, Buster. Shall we take a stroll before bed, eh?"

Buster's ears stood to attention. He ran to fetch his ball and within seconds was pacing back and forth by the door. Butcher hesitated at the coat stand, but dismissed the idea.

"All right, I'm coming," he said. "Impatient as ever."

Stepping outside, he was being watched from a blue transit van, parked across the street.

"There he goes, right on schedule," said Tony. "Give him a couple of minutes to get out of sight."

"Powerful looking dog he's got there," said Joe.

"I hate bloody alsations. Still got the scar where one of them bit me on that warehouse job."

"What if he's set the alarm?"

Tony turned on the ignition and manoeuvred the van out if its parking space. "Housekeeper said he never does on the evening walk. He'll only be gone for an hour or so. Should be more than enough time for you to do your magic....or muck it up altogether."

Joe threw him a look.

As they pulled up at the back of the house, all was quiet. A six foot wall separated the row of houses behind, and the nearest street light was some 20 yards down the lane.

"Grab your stuff," said Tony, pulling on leather gloves and a balaclava. "Just gotta get something out the back."

He stepped out of the vehicle, walked to the rear followed by his brother, and pulled open the back doors. He lifted out a ceramic container by the handle. The skull and cross bones label stuck to it was just visible, partly dissolved where the contents had run down the outside.

"What the hell is that?" whispered Joe.

"A strong repellent, Joe. Keeps the enemy away"

"But what is it?"

"Best not to know. You'll start moralizing again. Jimmy the wasp got it for me."

"From the scrap yard?"

Tony wasn't prepared to share any more. He lowered the container onto the ground and hoisted himself up and over the fence bordering

Butcher's back garden. Joe handed the container to him on the other side and clambered over himself, landing with one foot in the dog's water bowl. He cursed, shaking his leg.

"Aw, shit. These are real suede!"

But Tony was already scanning the windows and doors. There was muffled shouting coming from a nearby house, and the creak of a door opening. Light flooded into a garden two doors down. Tony looked at Joe and placed an upright forefinger to his lips. The shouting got louder.

"Your backside must be jealous of all the crap that comes out of your mouth," *she* said.

"I always wondered why you backcomb your hair," *he* said.

"What the hell do you mean by that?"

"Disguises the horns, doesn't it?"

"Sod off!" *she* answered. Something heavy was either dropped or thrown onto the path. "And don't bloody well come back."

"Well don't bloody keep asking me then!" Then a door clashed, followed by a gate, and retreating footsteps.

Tony waited a few seconds until they faded, and turned his attention back to the house windows.

"Those two are single glazed. You could do 'Eeny meeny miny mo?'"

"So it's *me* doing it, then?" said Joe.

"Well you're the one carrying the brick. I've got this thing weighing me down."

Joe dropped the brick onto the grass, and pulled a wide roll of adhesive tape from his jacket. He held out his other arm.

"Hand me the knife Tony."

"Why would I have a knife?"

"Because you always carry a sodding knife."

"Not this time. I've got the other stuff."

"I can't cut the tape with *that*, can I?"

"Use you bloody teeth then. Dick head."

Joe shot him another glance, and struggled to tear lengths from the tape with his teeth, while Tony drummed on the window with his fingers.

Moments later, adhesive strips were laid over an area on the glass pane. Joe scanned his surroundings, removed his jacket, wrapped it around the brick and hit hard against the pane. Two hits and the glass shattered with little noise. He prised off the tape securing the broken glass; extended his arm with care through the hole and loosened the latch. The window swung open.

"In you go then," said Tony. Annoyance flashed across Joe's face.

"Don't look at me like that. You're the smallest," Tony continued.

Without speaking, Joe hoisted himself up onto the sill and through the window, made his way to the back door and opened it from the inside.

"Wasn't so hard, was it Joe?" Tony stepped into the hallway. "Now, where's this over-stuffed safe?"

Upstairs in the study, an obliging street lamp shone a path through the room, illuminating the cabinet described to them and the electronic keypad within. Joe lifted his balaclava.

"This won't take long." With a gloved hand, he keyed in a code. There was a beep. An amber light came on, and he tugged on the handle, but it wouldn't budge.

"What's happening?" said Tony.

"That was the factory reset code. The light should be green."

"Well, duh..."

Meanwhile, Butcher and his dog reached the green at the far end of his road.

"Give me the ball, Buster."

The dog dropped the ball at his master's feet with eyes fixated as Butcher aimed his throw. Legs sprang into action for the chase, kicking back clumps of moist turf Butcher tried to dodge. They were just getting started when it began to rain. Softly at first, but soon it was coming down harder.

"C'mon, Buster. It'll have to be a short one tonight. Should've brought a coat."

***

Joe keyed in the code again. Another beep, and the light turned green. He pulled on the handle, and the door creaked open.

"Second time lucky." Tony pulled a carrier bag from his trouser pocket and began to fill it up. "Not as much as I thought."

"You're kidding. If those bundles are five each, there's a hundred and fifty grand there. Maybe more. We're only owed five."

Tony paused. "You don't think we're just gonna take what we're owed, do you?" He scoffed, then continued bagging up. "We're leaving nothing behind."

"There's something at the back." Joe reached further inside as Tony stuffed the last bundle into the bag. Joe was about to open an oblong velvet box, when there was a crunching noise from the gravel path outside, and then a key in the door. Tony snatched the box and shoved it into a tight space between the cash. He slammed the study door shut as Buster raced up the stairs and leapt at the door, barking ferociously.

"Shit. What now?" said Joe.

"Grab that container." Tony held his hand on the door handle.

Joe did as he was told.

"Get the lid off."

Joe hesitated.

"Do it. Now!"

Joe set the container on the floor, twisted the lid with both hands and removed it.

"Give it here."

Butcher was now outside the door.

"Who's in there?" He shouted above the dog's racket. But no response.

"I've already called the police. Stay there if you like. We can have a chat."

"Control the dog and we'll talk," said Tony, attempting to disguise his voice.

Butcher spoke a command to his dog, and the barking stopped.

"Are you alone?" he asked.

"Yes. I don't want any trouble."

"Do you have a weapon?"

"No."

Butcher paused for a moment, puzzling.

"Is that *Tony Moretti?"*

Joe glared expectantly at his brother. Tony gave him a signal to get ready. His eyes darted back and forth between the container and the door as he counted under his breath. On 'three', he snatched the door open and Buster bolted forward as Tony swung the container at the dog's jaw. Liquid splashed out of it, and Butcher tried to shield his dog with one arm and the side of his torso. There was an acrid stench from the spillage and a deafening squeal from Buster as skin and eyes began to burn. Tony darted past, grasping onto the money and headed for the stairs, with Joe stumbling behind with the container, trying to replace the cover as he went.

Butcher half dragged, half carried the yelping dog towards the bathroom. "It's ok, Buster. We'll have you sorted." He gasped with the effort and coughed as the gas hit the back of his throat. The dog began to fit.

Fumes escaped into the air from the dog's coat, and he continued to squeal in pain. Most of his body and half of his head appeared to be smouldering. Butcher hauled him into the shower and grabbed the spray head, dowsing him with cold water.

"It's all right boy…it's gonna be okay .... Daddy loves you."

It was then that he noticed his own hand and forearm. The skin was raw and blistered, and in parts there were gaps where there was no flesh at all. With the spray still directed at Buster, he glanced up into the long mirror on the wall, and one side of his face appeared to be melting. He played the water onto himself and Buster for some time, before he realised the dog's squealing had stopped, and he lay motionless in the shower tray. Butcher lay beside him and cradled his head close to his chest.

"I'm so sorry Buster, so sorry."

Chapter five : The Butcher's dog

Chapter six : Unlikely friends

It was weeks later, and Catherine cursed as she bleached her mother's knickers at the kitchen sink. Molly sat at the table sporting the Marigolds she'd peeled from her daughter's hands before she'd had a chance to use them. Long narrow strips, torn from The Chronicle's front page formed an erratic heap on the kitchen table while Molly chortled like a blocked drain. Then the hourly beeps sounded on the radio just before the news bulletin started.

"….Local businessman Melvyn Butcher suffered lung damage, second and third degree chemical burns during the attack. Two men have been charged with aggravated burglary, and grievous bodily harm."

Catherine paused at the familiar name. "Butcher? That flaming marriage wrecker?" She glanced over to her mother, in the vague hope she might show some recognition. "I wonder who got to the front of the queue first?"

"Bloody Norah!" screeched Skipper from his cage in the living room.

"You've been teaching Skipper naughty words again, haven't you Mam?"

Molly stood up from the kitchen table, and threw a fist full of paper into the air. Catherine watched as newspaper snowflakes floated down to the floor and sighed.

***

The cost of Ted's funeral set the Grimshaw's finances on a downward spiral, and by the time April of that year arrived, a stack of outstanding bills waved a nagging finger from behind the mantelpiece clock. One of them could be paid by the end of the week, but there was another expense which should really be dealt with that day. Easter eggs for Louise and Danny.

She wheeled her mother to Patel's corner shop and parked the chair outside, next to a toddler's pram adorned with a variety of clip-on toys. Catherine went into the shop, chose two chocolate eggs, and waited for change when her eye caught the front page of the newspaper on the counter. There was a photo of Tony and Joe Moretti being persuaded into a police car by rough handed officers. The headline read,

'EX HENCHMEN OF LOCAL NIGHT CLUB OWNER CONVICTED'

Mister Patel stood holding Catherine's change while she leafed through to the main story. He coughed twice before she glanced up.

"Oh, I am sorry," she said, "Can I pay for this paper as well please?"

By the time she'd gathered up her purchases and got back to her mother outside, Molly was quality testing the baby's rattle against the wheels of the pram with some force, and a passerby attempted to remove it from her clutches.

"Come on now, Molly, that's not yours, is it?"

Doris Fraser-Sour returned the toy to the pram and startled herself on seeing Catherine.

"Oh .... thank God it's you ... and not the mother." she said. "I didn't mean to..."

"Don't be daft," said Catherine. "I'm only too glad you were here. You don't charge for the minding service, do you? Because I'm pretty skint at the moment."

Doris unclenched her shoulders and smiled. "I'd love to pop round and see Molly sometime. I used to be able to make her laugh. But I don't want things to be awkward ... and if you'd rather not ..."

"There's nothing to feel awkward about. What are you doing tomorrow?"

"Just the usual.....you know... polishing the coal scuttle; counting my blessings .... etcetera. I could give you a knock around ten if that's all right?"

"Great. I'll have the kettle on. See you then. Say 'bye bye' to the baby and Doris, mother," she said, releasing the brake and steering Molly towards home.

"Bastard! Bastard!" shouted her mother as she was wheeled away.

Back home with the newspaper, Catherine read how the Morettis were hired by Mel Butcher to burn down one of his clubs for a share of the insurance money, and how Butcher reneged on the deal. After a failed attempt some time ago to use their sister Wendy, now deceased, to seduce the man and take him for every penny, the Moretti brothers burgled his property, ransacked his private safe and caused severe disfigurement using acid as their weapon of defence.

"Oh, my days!" said Catherine out loud.

"Mmmm," said Molly, chomping away on a chocolate egg left unattended on the kitchen work top.

***

The next morning, just after ten, Catherine settled Molly in front of The Open University when there was a knock at the back door.

"Come in, Doris. Take a seat. Kettle's just boiled." Catherine made a quick top to toe study of this lady who had become significant in her father's final months.

"Lovely. Just what I need after the morning I've had," said Doris, stepping into the kitchen.

It was easy to see why Ted had been attracted. Doris was warm, motherly, and took care with her appearance.

"What's been happening? said Catherine.

"That new window cleaner, cheeky blighter. Asked me for four quid. Sherbet used to charge two pound fifty, and he did them properly. This one thinks he's cleaning port holes."

Catherine poured boiling water into the tea pot. "He trampled all over Ted's geraniums a fortnight ago," she said as they sat down.

"Good job he's only temporary."

"Is Sherbet ill or something?"

"A hernia operation, I think." Doris picked up a spoon, lifted the tea pot lid and gave the tea a stir. She paused and looked across at Catherine. "Sorry love. I'm invading your teapot without asking."

Catherine shook her head. "That's okay. I like mine strong too. So ... why do they call him *Sherbet* anyway?"

"Oh, that's good. I think there's some sexual reference? And ... obviously I have no idea what that means ... but many of his lady customers used his extra services. Maybe the hernia was related."

Catherine laughed. "Well, I don't hear much gossip at all, so you're welcome to fill me in on anything you find appropriate. Or *inappropriate*, for that matter."

Doris offered a weak smile. "Catherine, I just have to say this. I feel terrible not coming to see you straight away ... after Ted, you know. I was embarrassed. I didn't know how you saw me. That dreaded woman from up the road who made your father cheat on your mother."

"I didn't see you that way at all," said Catherine. "Dad *was* entitled to some happiness ..... but he was ashamed. And me coming home unannounced like that....well, it made him see it through my eyes...or at least how he thought I might see it. But it wasn't just the guilt that made him take his own life. He was depressed too. It was written all over him. I don't blame you for anything. You gave him some comfort, like his old pipe."

"Well, I've been compared to better things..." Then she thought for a moment, shook her head and said, "No, I'm lying."

"He had one last smoke out there in the garden. It was still smouldering where he dropped it. I carry it with me now. Every time I open my bag, the smell's still there. I love it. Is that weird?"

"I've got my husband's specs. Awful things they are, but never off his face. Still clogged with the same superglue he mended them with. Now that's weird."

"And where would we be without superglue, hmm? Well, I'm glad that's out of the way. And now I need to ask you something."

"Anything," said Doris.

"First question, what biscuits do you like?"

The chocolate digestives on the table caught Doris's eye. "Looks like you already know that answer."

"And ... second question." Catherine pulled an opened brown envelope from her skirt pocket and removed the contents.

"Is that from the council?" said Doris, as a cheque fell out and landed onto an empty plate. "Is it Ted's Poll Tax refund?"

Catherine smiled. "I knew this had to be your doing," she said. "Dad would never think to apply for this all by himself."

"Well, they've taken their time. I'm sure you could find a use for it."

"You're not kidding. Thank you Doris."

"It is payable *to you*, isn't it? You changed the tenancy over?"

"Yes, I did that."

Doris got her eye on the biscuit packet again, and winked at Cathy. "Shall we open these to celebrate? Then I'll pop and say hello to Molly."

***

Within a short time, Doris Fraser-Sour became a valued friend. Catherine was in awe of Doris's ability to breeze through what seemed like unmanageable situations in Catherine's eyes. She listened; shared experiences; offered advice.

Chapter six : Unlikely friends

Autumn was fast approaching and there was a distinct chill in the morning air as Doris polished the outside of her living room window. A block of flats had been built across the way which she thought a bit of an eyesore, and she watched a young woman's reflection in the glass, pegging out smalls on a second floor balcony. She thanked her lucky stars for her own back garden, with its privacy and space, when the young woman let out a squeal, and began flapping her arms.

"Get away! Shoo! You horrible thing!"

Doris turned around. Her eyesight was by no means perfect, but she thought she saw a bird perched on the balcony, its wings flapping in response to the woman's distress. She hurried down the path and crossed the road. As she approached the new building, the woman yelled down to her.

"Have you seen the size of this ruddy thing? It's appeared from nowhere, and it's eating my best knickers!"

"I think I know where it's come from..." Doris shouted back. "If you can stop waving your arms....try to stay calm....I'll pop across and get the owner."

Minutes later, Doris was banging on Catherine's front door. Cathy came quickly. "What's wrong? I thought it was the bloody bailiffs."

Doris was out of breath. "Are you...has Skipper gone walk about?"

"What do you mean, walk about?"

"There's a grey parrot....over there on the second floor..." she pointed in the direction.

"Really? Well it can't be Skipper..."

Doris was now gazing at Cathy's living room window with its opening fully extended, and Cathy felt a pang of dread hit her stomach. "But he can't fly." She stepped outside and peered in to where Skipper was perched ten minutes before. The perch was empty. "Oh God, Doris....will you sit with Mam...I just need to grab a towel or something to wrap him in."

As Catherine approached, a constable stood at the foot of the building, talking with the woman who had ceased flapping, but was still upset. Skipper continued to hold a pair of women's briefs between his beak. The constable saw Catherine approach.

"Oh no, she didn't call the police, did she? I can get him if she'll let me up there."

"He's yours then, I take it?" said the constable.

She narrowed her eyes. "Do I need a lawyer before I answer that?" *He's a bit of all right, under that helmet.*

Switching his gaze back to the woman, he shouted.

"This young lady would like to come up and get her bird, if that's all right, miss?"

"Well get a bloody move on then!" she answered. "It's number seven...with the Rottweiler picture on the door."

"..And is the Rottweiler at home, by any chance?"

"I haven't got a bloody Rottweiler," she said. "And now I've told every burglar in the neighbourhood. So thanks a bunch for that."

The constable led Catherine inside the building and up the staircase. His bottom was right on her eye line.

"I think we know one other, don't we?" he said.

"I'm not sure. It's hard to tell from this angle." *Nice view though.*

When they reached the second floor, she was breathless, but able to walk alongside him. "I can't understand how he got over here. He's had his wings clipped."

"Maybe he's a fast walker?"

"I suppose I'll have to pay for the underwear he's destroyed."

"Well, let's see, shall we?" They approached the door which was already ajar and he knocked. "Hello? Can we come in?"

"Get in here!" shouted the woman. There was a direct view through to where Skipper was perched on the balcony rail.

"Okay. Can I ask you to take your time, step back and let the lady come through?"

Catherine moved along the passage way and stopped at the threshold. "What you doing here, Skipper? Come and see what I've got for you."

Stupid bird. Wait 'til I get you home. She produced a monkey nut from a trouser pocket and held it aloft. Skipper dropped the panties from his beak and extended his neck in anticipation.

"Where's Fred?"

"Oh Skipper, not now...we don't have time for this. You don't want the peanut?" *Stuff you then.* She began to put the nut back in her pocket, just as he gave a loud squawk, sprang forward and landed on her arm, seizing the nut at the same time.

Sodding claws need clipping. She sidled back into the passage way and signalled to the young woman to close the balcony door. Skipper had the shell off the nut in an instant, and Catherine breathed a sigh of relief. She turned to the young woman, spoiling for another rant. The woman grabbed a pack of cigarettes from a coffee table and snatched one out. Her hair was drawn back with a tight scarf, and she'd piercings to one eyebrow and a nostril.

"I'm so sorry about this," said Catherine. "He's not supposed to fly."

"You'd better tell *him* that," she said, lighting the cigarette and sucking on it like it was pain relief in the maternity ward. "I'm guessing he's not supposed to eat Victoria's Secrets either."

"I'll pay for whatever damage..." Catherine began.

"Are you fond of sausage, miss?" The constable interrupted. Cathy's eyeballs popped.

"And what do you mean by that exactly?" said the woman.

"Well, *Catherine* here..." said the constable, "is willing to compensate you with a pound of Sutton's best pork sausages, a whole black pudding and a dozen eggs. How does that sound?"

Catherine frowned. "I'm willing to what?"

"Sutton's sausage? Black pudding?" The woman's face lit up. "My old man can't get enough of the stuff."

"So that's a deal then? I'll bring it round in the morning."

Catherine and the constable descended the stairs with Skipper secured in a towel, head poking out, unfazed. "I've just twigged on how you know my name," said Catherine. "You're the butcher's boy from Sutton's meats. Your black pudding was legendary."

The constable beamed, and she remembered the sparkly eyes. "I *was* the butcher's boy," he said. "And Dad still produces that legendary black pudding, my sister too. I'm Rob Sutton junior. I delivered to your house."

"That's right ... and look at you now."

"Slightly better job prospects, I hope. By the way, what on earth are Victoria's Secrets?"

***

The following day, a leaflet was thrust through the Grimshaws' door with a note. Catherine, already in the hallway, glanced down at the handwriting. She pulled open the door, just as constable Rob was at the end of the path. He swung his head around and stopped.

"I hope you don't mind....it's just a flyer for the carer's group at the church every fortnight. Thought it might be useful....after what you were telling me yesterday?"

"Oh thanks, Rob...that's thoughtful. It's just hard to get away on my own, you know?"

"Okay, well no worries. If things change ... sometime in the future? They'll still be there."

"I'll hang on to it then. You never know." *Come back....please!*

She watched him wave and walk away. *Life's a shit. And then you die.*

Months went by, and then years. Catherine's life belonged in its entirety to her mother. Benji became arthritic, then blind.

Cathy moved the furniture to reduce collision bruises, but as time passed it seemed kindest to put him to sleep.

Neither Louise nor Danny kept up their Sunday visits to the Grimshaws' once Ted was gone. Louise, at nineteen, was still conflicted over which side her loyalties lay, while Danny had no problem. Getting close to Louise was a challenge, but after some healing time and a prod from a wise entity, things would begin to change.

Chapter seven : A view from inside

Steven Grimshaw tossed his book to the end of the bunk and stood to attention. The familiar jangle of warders' keys would have the same effect every time.

"Grimshaw! Fury!" The prison officer barked. "Fit for exercise, lads?"

Winston Fury jolted upright on the top bunk, rubbing an eye with the heel of his hand. "Hey man, give us a minute, yeah?"

"Either come now, or I lock you back in. Your choice."

Steven sat back down and tried pulling on his surgical boot, wincing as he did so.

"What's wrong with your face Grimshaw?" said the officer. "Is the smell from your feet making you sick?"

"It's these new boots. The squeak's gone, thank God. But the measurements can't be right. They're bloody killing me."

"Do you want your old ones back? They've not been chucked yet." Scotty's broad stature and booming voice bounced off the walls of the tiny cell. Qualities that had him hired within the first few minutes of his job interview.

"Anything's better than these. I'm in agony here."

"I'll dig them out for you," said Scotty. "Are you coming out or staying in?"

"I'll give it a miss today if it's all the same. Plenty of reading to do." He pulled the offending boot from his deformed foot and exhaled.

"And what about you, Fury?"

"Ah'm stoppin' here too. Got plenty of sleepin' to do," replied Winston, leaning back on his pillow.

Scotty's chest inflated as he crossed his arms, and his shirt buttons threatened mass evacuation.

"Don't get too settled, Fury. You've got the shower block to scrub out before dinner."

"What? I thought it was Pongo's turn."

"It's the both of you. Check the rota."

"You're a cruel man, Mister Scott. Hands are raw already from muckin' out first thing."

"Aw, stop it., you'll have me in tears in a minute. Just get on with it." He tapped a finger on his watch. "I'll be back in ten, to check."

Winston sighed in acceptance, as Scotty retreated and slammed the door behind him.

Winston peered over his bunk to where Steven had settled, reading.

"Hey Stevie boy, you'll go cross-eyed starin' at that book all day. Fancy a game?"

"Poker? Naa, I've nothing to bet with."

"Your pillow's softer than mine. Ah'll play you for that."

"And what have you got to bet with? Oh I know, those two normal feet will do, or that amazing set of pearly whites. You daft bugger. Nowt gets you down does it?" said Steven.

"You've got to stay cheerful man, or the men in white coats will get you. And you need to talk. Remember ah'm here for you man."

Steven lay back on his bunk and sighed. "It's not so bad for you, Winnie. You're still young. Have you made plans for when you get out? Will you go back to your mother's?"

Winston laid back down. "Well, ah won't be goin' back to Jamaica, that's for sure.... no matter how much the racists in here want me to. My mamma needs me here. Findin' a job will be the hardest thing. How 'bout you? Your son seems like a good boy. You must be proud."

Steven smiled to himself. "Yep, he's a good lad is our Danny. He's old for his age. Keeps telling me he's gonna sort everything. I think he will, too. Young as he is."

"If he was mine ah'd want to believe him. And with all that swattin' you deserve a fresh start. Hard thing is, puttin' the past behind you."

Steven raised himself up on one elbow and plumped up his pillow. "I've had plenty of time sorting all that in my head. From day one, really. And now I'm not in such a bad place."

"Glad to hear it, man. Ah'm still processin' all of that. It goes around and around. At three in the mornin'. Winston paused for thought. "That bastard put her in hospital twice before that, you know. Broken ribs, ruptured spleen. That day when I came home, saw him holdin' her face down in the dog's bowl lashin' out with his free fist. She'd been cuttin' meat and the knife was lyin' right there. Stoppin' him was all I could think of."

"Any son would have done the same. When I lashed out, I was saving myself. And from words. That's pretty pathetic."

Winston was still deep inside his own head. "She blamed herself. She'd over cooked his steak; forgot to wash his pulling shirt."

"My missus didn't cook, or wash many shirts for that matter. Your mother's safe now, thanks to you. All we need to concentrate on now is doing the time and getting out of here in one piece."

"So how many years have you done already, Stevie boy?"

"Nearly eight, I think. Not so sure now you come to mention it.

"Charlesworth wasn't a patch on this. The state of that place ... straight out of a Dickens' novel."

"Yeah? All that Victorian stuff fascinates me. Did you share a cell with Magwitch* then?"

Steven grinned. "I always knew you were an educated boy, despite the front."

"I don't just read smut you know ... that's all I can get in here. Tell me about the Dickensian prison."

Steven blew out his cheeks then let them go. "If you're sure .... or is it just a bedtime story you're after?"

"Never!" Winston said, getting more comfortable.

"Then I'll begin. I got the cell nobody wanted - rising damp, and the most disgusting mattress you ever saw. Stank to high heaven. A patch of fungus on the wall sprouted legs by the time I left. And the characters in there you wouldn't believe...." He left the sentence open ended, testing his audience for consciousness.

A few seconds of silence followed, and then only gentle snores. Steven tried to get back to the book, but his mind wandered.

He remembered the graffiti scrawled on the wall of his first cell. That notorious traveller of

**Magwitch is a character from the novel 'Great Expectations' by Charles Dickens*

men, Kilroy had been there before him, as had Slugger Smith, Biffa Brewis and Flash Harry.

One desperate writer with a yard long telephone number offered his sister's body for fifty pence or nearest offer, and a homosexual requested a rendez-vous inside the lavs with a nice boy.

The move to Finchale Heads was a positive one, and Steven sent out visiting orders to his family. Danny was still only fourteen at the time, and became Steven's first visitor, accompanied by a social worker. Louise was meant to follow two months after, but never showed. The visits from his son made a world of difference to Steven, and he became ready to leave his cell, even socialise. But then came the bad news. Tony and Joe Moretti had been granted a move within weeks from Gartree to Finchale to serve the last few months of their sentences.

Chapter eight : Weapons of destruction

As warned, the Moretti brothers landed and were admitted to 'C' wing. Steven was assured there'd be no mingling between wings and he had no reason to doubt it.

On his second morning at Finchale Heads, Joe Moretti headed for the showers with a towel slung over his shoulder. Approaching the entrance, he picked up his brother's voice from the steam cloud choking the space within. Through the mist, Tony Moretti's slim form, only partially hidden behind a narrow modesty screen, could be seen copulating with an inmate against a tiled wall under running water. Joe hesitated for a moment, turned his back and rubbed his forehead with a grimace. The grunting and vigorous slapping of wet skin against wet skin lasted less than a minute, and Tony moved away from his partner to let the water run over his body. Emerging from the shower, he glanced up at his brother standing by the recess.

"Turn you on did it Joe, watching from afar? That's about as close as you get to sex these days isn't it, you sad man?"

"I can promise you, I wasn't watching," Joe said. "Maybe you can warn me next time."

"No can do I'm afraid. Gotta get it when and where, if you get my drift." He shut off the water and snatched up a towel.

Joe turned to face him. "You've settled in here pretty damn quick."

Tony came over, rubbing at his hair. "We've got to get a plan together......to get that bastard Grimshaw. Make him pay."

Joe's face was doubtful. "We should wait 'til we're out. It won't be long if we keep our heads down."

Tony glared at his brother. "You're fucking pathetic, you know that? Some of the screws here are on the take. It's the perfect opportunity."

"I'm not staying here any longer than I have to," said Joe. "I've done enough time already. It could all go wrong."

"Jesus, Joe. No wonder Gina left you. You need to grow a pair."

Joe grimaced. "Gina left me because you got her pregnant, remember?"

"Oh dear," mocked Tony, "is little brother still upset that he's been firing blanks?"

Joe turned to go back to his cell. "I don't want any part of what you're planning."

"Fucking coward!" shouted Tony after him.

From nowhere, prison officer Eric Nash appeared at the entrance. Compared to the man-mountain that was Mister Scott, Nash was pocket-sized, and forever trying to prove otherwise.

"I've heard quite a bit about you, Moretti," said Nash. "Wasn't sure what to believe, but what I've just witnessed confirms it. You're a faggot, and that boy you've just taken advantage of is only eighteen."

"In the eyes of the law, that's legal," said Tony, turning away.

"Not in here. Read your handbook. This is going on report."

Tony stopped and turned back with a smirk. "I'll just tell them you're homophobic. Nothing happened here. No witnesses. Maybe you're a closet homosexual yourself? Homophobes usually are. Anyway, I'm not homosexual. I just like what I like. And you're lucky I don't like you."

Nash fixed a challenging gaze. "Whatever you're planning, you'd better think again, you disgusting fag. Because it's not gonna happen, not on my watch."

Tony smiled. "We'll see," he said, heading to get dressed.

Nash glanced with irritation at his pocket watch. He still had cell inspections to carry out. Replacing the watch, he strode off towards Tony Moretti's empty cell, pushed open the door, and gave a sardonic smile. He stepped inside, part closing the door behind him and unzipped his trousers.

***

Tony stood brushing his teeth in front of a tiny wall mirror in the wash room. His damp curls flopped onto his forehead as he lowered his head to spit. Two inmates gave sidelong glances as they walked by. Tony had to gain some trust. He would need help for what he had planned.

He picked up his belongings and made his way back to his cell. Pushing open the door, he stepped straight into a warm puddle of urine, seeping through his canvas topped shoes.

"For Christ's sake!" he said, shaking his foot. He turned back into the corridor and swung his head left, then right, sucking in air. "I'll get you back, you fucking wanker!"

***

Days later, Steven Grimshaw stood in the open doorway of his stuffy cell, waiting for Winston. "Come on, Winnie, you must fancy a bit of fresh air today? They'll be back in a minute to lock up if we don't go now."

Winston Fury lay on his top bunk engrossed in a paperback with two pairs of buttocks in active engagement on the crinkled cover.

"Yeah man, ah'll be out as soon as these two finish doin' unspeakable things to one another." He glanced over the page, then back again.

“Three or four more paragraphs man.” The distinctive West Indian drawl was still there, despite several years of broad Geordie being pumped into his ears. Sometimes, when Winston was in full flow, whether in the cell or the sweaty mess hall, Steven imagined he was on a tropical island somewhere in the Bahamas being served by a native waiter, long stemmed triangular cocktail glass complete with mini-parasol in hand, cherry on a stick and maybe a drink in the bottom somewhere.

“Three or four paragraphs? At *your* speed you’ll still be there at Christmas.”

With eyes still on the page, Winston waved his nearest hand in a dismissive gesture, and Steven limped towards the exercise yard alone. The exit to the yard was situated next to the dividing door between B and C wing which was always kept locked, however on this particular day, a support grade officer stood next to it with arms folded. Steven was curious. He’d not seen this officer before.

“What’s up with the extra security?” he said. “You expecting trouble?”

“Hope not,” said the officer, “but the locking system is defective on a couple of the doors, so we’re making sure nobody goes where they’re not supposed to.”

Steven nodded in reply, but all kinds of alarms were sounding in his head. So far he’d been able to avoid the Morettis, but he knew some of the screws could be persuaded to do anything.

Steven was outside only seconds before spotting Tony with another inmate who stopped to light a cigarette. Joe Moretti watched from a distance with Bernie Salter, a convicted drug dealer. Tony and Steven locked eyes briefly, and Steven was the first to lower his glance, tugging hard on an earlobe as he took strides ahead. He couldn't figure out why the yard screws hadn't ordered them back to their wing. He glanced over to the yard officers. Either they were new recruits, or something was about to kick off.

The exercise yard was too small to get lost in, and Steven had no choice but to walk by the brother of the woman he had killed seven years before. He limped on, at a faster pace to catch up with the inmate in front. Safety in numbers. With all senses heightened, he picked up more than one set of quickened footsteps behind him, but kept on moving. And then it came. Moretti's ridiculing tone.

"Let's see how fast you can limp away from me you useless shit!"

Steven's thought processes raced. They were only allowed to walk in twos. Those were the rules. He checked the yard screw's attention, but his eyes were elsewhere. Then, pressure in the small of his back. He turned. A brief flash of sunlight bounced off the blade in Moretti's hand. Another set of running feet moved closer.

Confusion. "Winnie? No!" Winston snatched at Moretti's wrist, but the knife didn't drop.

"What the fuck?" screamed Tony, twisting away from Winston's grip.

"Come on, man," pleaded Winston in his laid back drawl, stepping back with arms outstretched. "Just put it away, man, nobody wants any trouble here."

But Tony's eyes blazed and the yard screw finally paid attention. It took only seconds between Tony's forward lunge and Winston's backward stagger, before he dropped to his knees.

"Don't *man* me, you black bastard." Tony stood victorious over Winston, now bent double. An alarm rang out. Screws came from every direction. Tony made no attempt to move, triumphant he'd been able to skewer at least one of the enemy on the end of his shiny toy. The guards took control of Moretti and the blade. Tony glowered at Steven.

"You can't hide, Grimshaw. Wherever you go, I'll find you."

Entering the building with a guard on each arm, he exchanged glances with his brother who was being ushered back to his wing. The exchange was not a brotherly one.

Winston clutched his stomach. A steady trickle of blood ran over the back of his hand, and Steven got down beside him, pressing his hand on top of Winston's. "Hey Stevie boy," gasped Winston, trying to smile. "I didn't know you cared."

"WE NEED HELP OVER HERE!" someone shouted.

"This is serious, Winnie," said Steven. "You're losing blood."

"Yeah," said Winston, "and I bet you're surprised it's red, huh?"

Steven applied even more pressure with both his hands, toppling the pair of them over onto the tarmac.

"Hey man, not in public, huh?" Winston tried another grin but it melted away as the pain overwhelmed him.

As though prepared, two officers rushed forward with a stretcher, loaded it up and carried the injured party away.

"You might have to cope without me tomorrow," said Winston as he was carried towards the medical wing. "Be careful out there, huh?"

***

Five days passed, and Winston returned to his cell with an angry rash on his backside courtesy of a hospital mattress. Scratching with his one free hand was difficult enough, without threats from a staff nurse to fasten that hand to the bed as well.

"Could that be a secret fantasy of yours, sister?" he said with a wink. "Havin' me handcuffed to the bed, completely at your mercy? Huh?" The nurse was unfazed. She'd heard it all before.

Steven gave up his tapioca pudding and bottom bunk to Winston on his return. Small compensation he said, for jumping into the line of fire. There were two days left before Tony would be out of segregation. In that time, Winston rested and was more subdued than usual, while Steven nursed his own anxieties.

The day after Winston's return, during wake up call, a disturbance two cells down alerted the whole wing. Anguished cries and sounds of furniture being dragged could be heard from behind Pongo's cell door. So called because of his aversion to soap.

"Bastards! You gotta let me out. My brother's dyin'."

"What's happenin' Stevie boy?" said Winston from his bunk.

"Pongo applied for special licence to visit a dying brother," said Steven from the open doorway. "They must have refused him."

Winston grunted as he raised himself up, clutching his stitches. "Not *another* one. He's had two cousins with leprosy .... and a mother needing a heart."

"That's not impossible," said Steven. "I've met one or two heartless people myself."

Chapter eight : Weapons of destruction

Pongo shouted again. “You can’t do this!” More scraping. Pipes clanging.

Steven continued, “.... and he seems convinced he has a dying brother...today, anyway. Bless him. Wups ... here’s a screw... having a peek.”

“Pongo .... You need to calm down,” said the screw. “Don’t make me get the psyche over here again.”

“Fuck off then! Don’t need no psyche. I’ll cut myself.”

“Cut yourself? With what?”

“That’s for me to know and for you to go fuck yourself!”

“Pongo’s got no family,” said Winston. “He was brought up in a children’s home.”

“He just wants attention. No-one visits him, poor sod.”

The screw tried to open the cell with his key, but there was a problem.

“What the hell have you done to the lock? I can’t get the bloody key in.”

“You’re as stuffed as I am then, wanker!”

Steven and Winston watched as the screw radioed for assistance. There followed an exchange of radio speak between colleagues. Conflicting degrees of urgency were expressed, until the attending officer left to seek help.

Pongo continued to make heaving noises, until there was an almighty crash.

"Jesus!" said Steven, "What the hell was that?"

"Could be the porcelain sink. Pongo's is the only cell that doesn't have a metal one."

Steven gave Winston a puzzled look. "How do you know stuff like this?"

"Ah keep ma eyes and ears open," Winston said. "Knowledge is power. 'Especially in a place like this."

The screw returned with just one other officer. He peered through the view panel.

"Christ, there's blood everywhere," he said. "What's this in the lock?"

"Feels like wax or something. You got a lighter?"

The second screw pulled a lighter from his trouser pocket and trained the blue flame onto the lock for what seemed like an age. Then they were in with the key.

Amidst lots of cursing, there was scraping of furniture, shuffling of bodies, until Pongo was dragged out supported by both screws, headed for the medical officer's room.

Winston watched with sharp concentration. Two prison officers went in and two came out. Pongo's cell had to be empty. Winston padded his way along the corridor.

Chapter eight : Weapons of destruction

"What are you doing?" Steven said. "You're meant to be resting." Winston acknowledged Steven with just a backward glance. He paused inside Pongo's doorway, swept his eyes over the chaos. Water leaked from a broken pipe. He bent down, wincing from his wound, picked up two pieces of broken porcelain, tucked them inside his shirt and padded back to his cell.

"What have you taken?" asked Stephen as Winston returned, hugging his ribs. Winston pulled out his contraband.

"Just some broken bits of nothing...could come in handy."

"For what exactly?"

"Toothpicks. What do *you think*, man?"

Chapter nine : Family ties

Another mundane, humid Saturday night in August '92, and Catherine had gone to bed later, but just as exhausted as usual at eleven thirty, put out the light and began to doze off. It was the smell of her father's tobacco that made her lift her head even before she opened her eyes. Trying to focus in the darkness, she puzzled at the fuzzy outline of a figure standing at the foot of her bed. The longer she looked, the clearer the features became. Ted's crumpled face became clearer beneath the shabby old cap, and his broad shoulders supported a familiar gardening coat. But it was grey, as was his skin and hair, and his speech laboured.

"Cathy," he said, "make peace with Louise ... you will need each other, and don't worry ... your father will take care of you."

Catherine lifted herself up on one elbow, and tried to speak.

"Dad ..?" But as she spoke, he raised his hand in a farewell gesture, and began to fade.

Now fully alert, she sat up in bed, snapped on the bedside light, got up and crept around the room. But it was all so very normal. After a few minutes she sat on the edge of the bed and said, just on the off chance he may still be listening,

"Sorry for bashing you with the leek, Dad." Then she climbed back under the covers, turned out the light and went to sleep.

Next morning, no matter how much she tried, Catherine could not dismiss Ted's visit as a dream, nor a figment of her imagination. Ted's gardening jacket still hung buttoned up in his wardrobe, just a she had left it. So it hadn't been worn by an imposter playing a trick. She couldn't wait to settle Molly in front of Richard and Judy, and share her story with Doris over a mug of builders.'

***

Doris stepped into Catherine's kitchen with a jaunty gait. "I'm sure that newsagent on the corner has designs on me."

Cathy closed the door behind her. "Well, lucky you......I think. What makes you so sure?"

"He said I had magnificent cheek bones. The ones on my *face*, I suppose he meant."

"Well I would hope so! And so you do. Hang on a minute. You don't mean that lad behind the counter who looks about twelve?"

Doris pulled an indignant face. "He's twenty three, actually."

"Twenty three? No wonder you're flattered," said Catherine, pouring boiling water into large mugs. "I know the one you mean. He wants to be a sculptor. Maybe he wants you to sit for him."

"I've asked him over for tea on Sunday." Doris sat at the table and opened the biscuits in front of her.

"You've never!"

"Why shouldn't I?"

"Um..... maybe because you're old enough to be his grandmother?" Cathy placed the mugs on the table.

"Well don't go broadcasting that if you don't mind. I've told him I'm only thirty two. Why aren't you using the tea pot?"

Cathy gaped. "And he believed you?"

"Where's the teapot?"

Cathy waved a dismissive hand. "Molly threw it at me yesterday. So, he really thinks you're thirty two?"

Doris tried hard to hold on to her face, but within seconds it crumpled. "You're a wind up's dream, you are. You've spent too much time cooped up in this house. You need to get out there."

Catherine sighed and parked herself on a kitchen chair. "Well, you're not wrong. But that's a bit impossible for the next hundred years, isn't it?"

"We'll have to do something about that. So how come you're calling your mother by her first name now?"

"Because she tells me often enough I don't belong to this family. That she hates me. I've heard it so often now I find I can distance myself by calling her Molly. I think she prefers it anyway."

"I know how it was for you growing up," said Doris. "Ted told me. He did his best to make you feel wanted."

"And he was the best dad, he really was. And the surprising thing is, he's still there for me."

Doris poured milk into the mugs and gave Cathy a puzzled look.

"I had a weird experience last night," said Catherine.

"I'm all ears."

"I think Dad paid me a visit. He told me to make peace with our Louise."

"You didn't fall out with her, did you?"

"Not exactly, but I lost her after my brother killed her mam. Understandable, when you think about it."

"There's been a lot of water under the bridge since then. Anyway, you weren't exactly an accomplice. She'll come round. She's older now. Had time to think about it." Doris screwed up her nose in mid-chew, as she lowered the biscuit from her mouth back down onto the plate. "Eurgh, where on earth did you get these? They're terrible."

Catherine reached across and picked up the packet, checking the ingredients for an obvious poison.

"These are six months out of date. My fault for not wearing my glasses."

"Well, that's your corner shop for you." Doris took a sip from her steaming mug. "No wonder Patel can afford to run around in a Range Rover, with its propeller shafts and rear differentials."

"That's impressive talk."

"Well, you have to take an interest don't you? Besides, I thought he might test me on it later."

Catherine smiled. "Well I don't think he's getting rich on what I paid for these."

There was a thoughtful pause, as both noses and lips disappeared behind tilted cups in a slurp-interrupted silence.

"Well...I think you should go and visit him," said Doris.

"Who? Patel?"

"Noooo! Ted!"

"Dad? ...What do you mean go and visit him? He's dead, remember?"

"What's the date today?" asked Doris.

"Err .... eighteenth, I think."

Doris scolded. "It's the *seventeenth.* And it would have been Ted's seventy seventh birthday. And that's hard to say with stale biscuit crumbs under your dentures."

Catherine hesitated, while Doris continued.

"I'm a firm believer in the spirit world you know," she went on, "My mother was a medium."

"Really?"

"Oh yes. Unlike me, I've always been a *large.*" Then she became serious. "Go and see him. The grave, I mean. It might put your mind at rest."

Catherine hesitated again. "I've not been to the cemetery in years."

Doris got up to rinse the cups. "Go on, before it gets dark and you have an excuse. Call it your first outing. Off you go and explore the world. And take your glasses. You'll need them to find the headstone. I'll watch Molly." She popped her head through the serving hatch to the living room where Molly sat staring at the plate of biscuits in front of her. "We'll manage, won't we love?" Molly snatched up a biscuit, crushed it in her hand and said,

"Fuck orf!"

"Course we will," sighed Doris.

Catherine got up from the table. "She's teaching Skipper swear words. It's a good job the vicar doesn't come calling."

"Well, that's a blessing in disguise."

***

As Catherine walked through the cemetery gates, gazing at the maze of pathways, each with its own row of pigeon-splattered headstones, she wondered why there was no map for first timers. She set off with no plan of action, relying on her intuition and the general pointing direction of her nose, until she spotted someone familiar. Louise crouched over her grandfather's plot, pulling up dandelions, trowel in hand. Catherine slowed her pace as she approached. Louise raised her head.

"Very nutritious are dandelions," said Catherine, offering a smile.

"They make you wet the bed..... or so Grandad used to say." Louise stood, admiring her handiwork.

"He told me that too."

"I do miss him."

"And me. Still mad with him though."

"I thought you might come. He just as good as said so last night."

"You didn't .....you mean you saw him too?"

Louise went across to a nearby waste bin, and dropped inside her handful of weeds.

"Yep... frightened the hell out of me, but he was right. Look Cathy, I don't know what to do ... Danny's run away from home."

The girls sat together on a decrepit wooden bench close by, where Louise explained how Danny had never been best buddies with Gareth, the Martins' eldest son, and how three days earlier they'd had this huge fight over a leather baseball cap which led to one busted lip, two black eyes and an empty bed. The Martins didn't seem worried about it. Danny was almost eighteen and capable, they said, of taking care of himself. He'd likely come back when his money ran out.

"But you're not sure?" asked Catherine.

"Well, I can't pretend I'm not worried. He only had eight quid on him four days ago. He could be sleeping in bus shelters...... scavenging in bins, picking.....dead flies out of his beard."

Catherine peered over her glasses. "I think that last one's a bit over the top. He just started shaving five minutes ago." Louise made a weak attempt to smile.

"What about friends? He could be staying on someone's sofa."

"I don't know much about college friends. Apart from one called George. I think his surname started with a 'W'. Might be Wilson, or was it Winter? And he knew his lecturer quite well."

"You don't know the lecturer's name?"

"No I don't." Louise looked forlorn.

"Would you feel better if we went to the police now and reported him missing?"

Louise shook her head. "No, not the police just yet...I think he could be involved in something to do with the Morettis."

"Involved in what? Something criminal you mean?"

"It's possible. Danny keeps things to himself. But just before Tony was arrested, he gave Danny some stuff to keep safe for him. He had an idea he'd be going away for a long stretch, and I heard him make Danny promise never to let them out of his sight."

"But that was years ago. Danny was *how old* when the Morettis went to prison? Around twelve?"

"I know. I was just a kid myself. At the time I thought it was meaningless junk. But now I'm realising how much they expected of him, and it was madness."

"What did Tony give him? Do you know?"

"It was nothing really. Some trainers and a wallet..... There was a necklace too, I think.... in a velvet box. But Danny was obsessed. No-one was allowed near them. I wouldn't care, but the trainers were awful flashy things and far too big for him."

Catherine chewed her bottom lip. "So this fight with Gareth was over the baseball cap? Is that the cap your dad got him for his fifth birthday? He wouldn't go to sleep without it."

"He still loves that cap," said Louise, "But that's not what started the fight. Gareth said some awful things about our mum. Called her a slag..... Said she deserved all she got for messing about with that Butcher fella. Danny swung a punch....... but missed. Gareth laughed, pulled the cap from under Danny's mattress and teased him with it."

"And when did he leave?"

"That same night. He packed his stuff and just went. He did say *something* to me though, and he'd said it before about six months ago. He didn't want to be here when Tony and Joe were released. Joe's out first. Tony's got a few months longer, because he stabbed another prisoner. Did you see it on the news?"

"Your dad told me about the stabbing. He was the target. But his cell mate got in the way."

"Oh, God," said Louise. "I didn't even know they were in the same prison."

"Well, you've been out of the loop for a bit. Not anymore though." Cathy smiled and placed her hand on Louise's arm. "We Grimshaws have to stick together. How did Danny get to know the release dates anyway?"

"Tony wrote him letters. He phoned him a few times as well. Acting like they were best friends...but Danny was scared of him."

"Do you know if Danny kept those letters?"

"I think they were in a shoe box in his room,"

"And when does Joe Moretti get out?"

"Sometime in December. But a fortnight ago, some baldy thug with a snake on his face turned up looking for Danny. Danny told me later it was one of Tony's crew. He was jumpy after that. Told me not to answer the door next time."

"He had a snake? On his face?"

"Well.... *not a real one.* A tattoo. With a forked tongue poking into the corner of his mouth. Made me wanna puke."

"Sounds a delight. So, this thug.... did he call again?"

"Yeah, last week. Mary....that's my foster mum spoke to him. Danny was out and the snake man wasn't best pleased."

"Hmm," said Catherine. "Do you think we could have a look through Danny's room sometime? If we could find those letters, we might turn something up. If that doesn't work, we'll have to find out this George's surname and see if we can contact him."

Louise pulled back her sleeve and glanced at her watch. "Gareth's playing rugby 'til five. Do you want to come back with me now?"

"Ok, but I'll have to ring Doris and let her know what's happening."

Louise got up from the bench. "Do that from ours if you like."

"I didn't know if you'd still be with your foster parents when you turned eighteen."

"We applied for a 'stay put' order. The Martins suggested it. But now Danny's gone it's not the same. Then to top it all, my foster dad had a stroke and he's still in hospital."

"I'm sorry Louise. I had no idea. Will he be ok?"

Louise exhaled. "It's a waiting game. He's been unresponsive on a ventilator for a week now."

"Are you close?"

"Used to be. Not now. He's a workaholic, hence the big house. My foster mum single parented, mostly."

Louise brushed the back of her skirt and looked with disgust at her hand. A passing seagull screeched above them. "Hee ha," it appeared to say.

"Oh, nooooo." Louise looked skywards.

"Yes!" said Cathy, pulling a tissue from her bag. "We're going to be lucky."

***

Danny's bedroom door was painted in a calm shade of duck egg blue, defying the angry posters within. There were teeth baring animals, erupting volcanoes and lank-haired, pierced individuals straddling motorised contraptions. Louise was the first to find the wardrobe. Danny's shoebox was still on the top shelf. She took it down, but the lack of weight told her it was empty.

"Blasted thing," she said, removing the lid. "What now?"

"We keep going." Catherine tried to sound positive. She began to remove each item searching for clues, and passing to Louise for a double check. The growing pile of Danny's belongings on the single bed began to topple when she lifted out a flashy training shoe complete with cobweb and handed it to Louise.

"That's Tony's."

"Well, where's the other one then?" Catherine reached inside and took out a jacket thrown into another corner. There was the other trainer, sticking out of a side pocket.

"Weird place to keep a shoe," she said, pulling it free, "and there's no sign of wildlife in this one..."

She handed it to Louise, giving the empty wardrobe a quick once over. Louise lifted the tongue and sniffed inside. "No smell - must have used odour eaters."

"No shit, Sherlock?" Cathy was realising the absurdity of what they were doing. "Come on. Let's get this stuff put back before Missus Martin comes up here to check on us."

Louise was more interested in the shoe. "Hang on a minute." She fumbled with the raised edge of the insole until she got a good enough grip and pulled. There, folded once, was the left luggage ticket to a deposit locker. She read out the small print. "The key issued with this ticket is the sole responsibility of the leasee for the period indicated, and remains the property of British Railways, Eastern Region. In the event of the key being lost or stolen, proof of identity must be given by the claimant." She handed the ticket to Cathy.

"It's rubber stamped 'Oldcastle Central station'..."

"Come on, we need to tidy up. Bring the shoe. It could be used as evidence. Then we follow the paper trail," said Louise.

Chapter ten : The Prodigal returns

Catherine couldn't recall her last visit to Oldcastle Central, it had been that long. Back then it was a magnificent piece of architecture, though dismal inside with no-nonsense porters directing passengers and taking a firm stance against bad behaviour. Thick metal turnstiles with lethal spikes guarded the platforms, capable of doing serious damage to fare dodgers. But the new station sported a domed glass roof, intelligent barriers and electronic ticket machines. CCTV cameras watched, and even the toilets were operated by a ticket swipe to prevent misuse. Catherine wondered if the whole place would come to a standstill in the event of a power cut, but this was just the start of massive changes yet to come. British Railways were in the process of being taken over by private corporate concerns, but not quite fully yet.

The Left Luggage Office was still operated by an actual human staff member. She approached the two young ladies chewing on a mouthful of bacon sandwich.

"Yes m'dears, what can I do you for?" she said, placing the half eaten bap on a greasy brown envelope as she came forward.

"Err...hi," said Catherine, presenting the ticket from her coat pocket. "My brother and I have had this locker for some time now...and I wondered if I could check on it please?"

The desk clerk took the ticket and held it at eye level.

"These ruddy bifocals have never worked since I got them. Does that say 898 on there, love?" she asked, thrusting the ticket close to Catherine's nose. Catherine flinched.

"I believe it does."

"Righty o then," said the desk clerk, thumbing through the register in front of her. "897...898, there you are," she said, pointing with the tip of her lead pencil. It snapped as she pressed it against the page. "Bugger it," she uttered, followed by, "Ooo, that's going back a bit. What have you been storing? Proceeds from the great train robbery?" She looked up and chuckled, but the girls' expressions were fixed. The clerk sneaked a covetous glance back at the sandwich, congealing before her eyes and returned her eyes to the register. "Emptied out on Tuesday the fifteenth, by D. Grimshaw. Is that your brother's signature?" She turned the book for Catherine to see and indicated with the broken pencil point.

"I think so, yes," replied Catherine, glancing at Louise who nodded.

"But," said Louise, "if we've got the ticket, how could it have been emptied out?"

The clerk was beginning to get bored, and the sandwich, not fifteen inches away, still beckoned. She sighed.

"As long as someone has the appropriate key and some means of identity, then the ticket need not be produced. It's proof of payment, that's all, and this particular ticket is only proof of the first week's rental. It's years old, as you can see. Someone's spent a fortune keeping this locker going....for some reason." The clerk was beginning to look suspicious.

"So I don't suppose you remember this person calling to empty this box on Tuesday the fifteenth?" asked Catherine. "I just want to make sure *it was* my brother."

The desk clerk took off her glasses, rubbed her eyes and looked up at the girls with freshly polished pupils.

"Well, I normally do the late shift, but the fifteenth was my sister's 49th and they were having a bit of a shindig in the evening, so I swapped with Kevin." She waved her glasses around as she spoke, smiling at the memory.

"So...?" prompted Louise, "did you see who came in and emptied the box?"

"As a matter of fact I did. Mr Grimshaw was a charming young man." She raised an eyebrow and gave a wry smile. "...Late teens to early twenties I'd say, with gorgeous pale blue eyes, brown hair, slight stubble. He had a huge..."

"I think that'll do," confirmed Louise, "that's him all right."

The clerk replaced her glasses. "What I was about to say," she persisted, "was ... he had a huge navy holdall. I don't perv over the fellas, thanks very much. But since you brought up the subject, if I was twenty years younger..."

"Thanks very much for the information," Louise cut in, grabbing Catherine's arm and pointing her towards the door. Catherine turned her head as the pair left the office.

"What's up? Where's the fire?" she said.

"Sorry but I couldn't take much more of that. Lusting after my little brother? That's disgusting."

"Well, he's not so little anymore," said Catherine. "He has a huge ..." Louise hit Catherine's shoulder playfully, and then shuddered.

"... rucksack." finished Catherine.

Outside the luggage office, they paused for a rethink.

"What do we do next Cath? We haven't lost him, have we?"

"No .... course we haven't. That key must've been inside the shoe as well until Danny decided it was time to make his move. Something will turn up...don't worry." She linked Louise's arm and they marched ahead.

***

Two days of excitement seemed to be Catherine's paltry ration for the week, as the tail end of it went by without even a wag. The following Monday morning, Louise went around local newsagents and corner shops, asking if Danny had been seen, while Catherine telephoned his college.

"The only thing I can tell you," said the faculty's secretary, "is Danny Grimshaw dropped out of the course soon after the lecturer left his post for a new business venture. There was another student who left at the same time, so I presume they weren't pleased at having their tutor replaced at such a late stage. Mister Willoughby *was* popular with his students, and it was understandable his son would leave at the same time."

"His son?" said Catherine. "You mean the other student who left was Mister Willoughby's son?"

"Oh... I don't think I said son, did I? No...I said soon....as in *not later*."

"I see .... And his 'soon's' first name wouldn't happen to be George, by any chance?"

"Well .... that's not something I can disclose. Could be Geoffrey, could be Gordon?"

"So, it starts with a 'G' then."

"I didn't say that. I was just suggesting alternatives."

"I don't suppose you can tell me where Mister Willoughby's new business is located?"

"I'm sorry I can't tell you anything further."

"Well, thank you anyway. I do appreciate the information."

"But I haven't given you any."

"You're right. You've given me nothing. Goodbye."

***

By the following Saturday, Catherine hadn't been able to confirm anything at all about Danny's whereabouts, though Louise did seem positive about the name George Willoughby. So it was back to the drawing board, and the mundane chores of cooking, washing and shopping. Speaking of which, if she didn't get to Presto's by 3 o'clock there wouldn't be a slice of Mighty White left on the shelves to make Sunday's French toast.

Saturday afternoon food shopping for the unprepared has been known to cause serious battleground maladies such as post trolley dash stress disorder, pointy elbow combat wounds and shelf shock, to name but a few. Beware the silver haired brigade with sharpened walking aids, out to grab those whoops labelled perishables reduced for a quick sale. Catherine had become wise to their trickery, and matched it by using Molly's chair as a provoker of sympathy. After having her wicked way with a space at the bread counter, she tried to manoeuvre Molly's chair around a tricky corner heading for the tea bags, when she heard a "Pssst..." coming from behind a stone pillar. Dismissing it as a loose cap on a cola bottle, she paid no attention, until there was a second "Pssst..." but accompanied this time by a "Cathy....over here!" She turned towards the pillar, and saw the left side of Danny's face, along with one of his 'gorgeous' pale-blue eyes sticking out from behind it. But something was different.

"Danny, where on earth have you been? You've had us worried sick," she said. "And what's going on with your hair?" Danny came out from behind the pillar and looked around. He smelled of engine oil and wore dirty overalls.

"I know.... I'm sorry. I heard you contacted the college. Just wanted to let our Lou know that I'm fine, and I'll try to keep in touch."

"But where are you staying? And what was in that deposit box?" She had so many questions.

"I'm in a bed and breakfast for now, but I can't tell you where ..... Joe will have my guts for shoelaces when he gets out. I'm sorting something for Dad when he's released and I'm finishing the apprenticeship I started at college..."

Catherine sighed. "That sounds great if it all works out. I'm going to see your dad next week. Does he know about all this? I just hate all this cloak and dagger stuff. And if that ...." She waved a finger at Danny's head. ".. hair thing is meant to be a disguise ... it's not working."

"I'm not convincing as a road sign then?"

"Well in my experience, Belisha beacons are rarely seen in supermarkets."

Molly was meanwhile becoming bored in her stationary chair and tried to rock herself into motion, while the hand basket on her lap began to explore its own freedom.

"If I can help in any way ..... send you some money?" Catherine continued.

"Don't worry about money. I've got enough..." Danny stepped back towards the exit, "and I'll be eighteen next week. Give Dad my best and tell Louise I haven't forgotten her."

As he disappeared through an unmanned check-out, she shouted after him.

"Where shall I send your birthday card?" But by then he was gone.

Then, *smack*! The sound of glass hitting floor tiles brought her down to earth, as the hand basket flew from its launching pad. The odour of pickled garlic was the second offence, while the jam jar rolled into the path of an oncoming trolley and steered it off course towards a pyramid of tinned peas. The avalanche was inevitable, and offence number three. All accusing eyes fell on Catherine.

"What you lot lookin' at?" said Molly. Ugly bastards!"

Chapter eleven : Rescued from the rain

A few days passed, and Louise Grimshaw was about to leave for work when the hall telephone rang.

"Hi Lou. It's Catherine. Have you got two minutes while I tell you what I found out?"

"Did you visit Dad?"

"I did. Brought him up to speed with what's been going on."

"So did you tell him about this Willoughby fella - how he'd left the course at the same time as Danny?"

"Yes, and you'll never guess what he said."

"Tell me."

Well it turns out.... he used to work at Smedleys. That's where Steven, I mean your dad used to work. So they know one other."

"So ... what does that have to do with Danny?"

"Well, Danny mentioned Willoughby to Steven on one of his visits, and Steven told him Willoughby was a good mechanic and a decent bloke, and asked Danny to say hello for him. So, if Danny was already thinking about getting away from here, a new business with a recommended mechanic could be the perfect opportunity.

"I suppose that does kind of make sense. But we still don't know where he is."

"No, we don't. But at least we know he had a proper plan. And he had money...even if it was stolen from a thief. That's gotta be better than what we were thinking."

"No, you're right." Louise glanced up at the clock on the wall. "Damn, I have to dash. We'll talk later, yeah?"

Louise pulled the front door closed behind her, grimaced at the weather and unfastened her umbrella. She made her way down the path just as the postman, with his usual smile approached her house.

"Just one for you today," he said, holding up a postcard with a picture of Marsden Rock on the front, taken before its untimely collapse. Danny had a bunch of these cards in his drawer before he left. So it wasn't evidence he'd posted it locally.

She took the card and attempted to return the smile, despite the ungodly hour on a dark wet morning. She pushed up her umbrella and carried on down the street, reading as she went. It was the first card she'd had from Danny, with no forwarding address and posted from a town some 80 miles away.

Hope you're ok. I'm doing fine...

Danny was no creative writer, but as dull as the words seemed, they persuaded her he was surviving. She'd confirmed her uncles' release dates with the prison and it was lucky Danny had been able to get away in plenty of time. She hoped he'd found a safe enough place. Dropping the card into her open bag, she joined the end of the bus queue and fumbled for her travel pass. Louise was now into the sixth month of her probationary period with Yorkshire Bank. Her adoptive father had just passed away, and she was feeling quite down. Danny was a big miss. Maybe the Morettis, once released, would prevent her brother from coming back at all.

But thanks to a recent transferral from another branch, there was a certain trainee manager who seemed to brighten her days lately. He was always immaculate, drove his own car, and had such a sweet manner, she couldn't help but be smitten. Louise glanced at her watch and craned her neck over the heads in the queue. The bus was already three minutes late. She looked down the end of the road, searching for a red double decker, but approaching instead was Michael's silver grey Montego, which came to a stop just beyond the yellow bus bay markings. He leaned over the passenger seat and opened the door. Louise stepped forward.

Chapter eleven : Rescued from the rain

"Like a lift?" The sight of him lifted her mood.

"Just the job, thanks," she said, sliding gracefully into the passenger side despite the pencil skirt, and hoping she'd think of something more interesting to say on the journey to work. But she needn't have worried.

Chapter twelve : A riot of a time

Eric Nash's point scoring game with Tony Moretti took off on a new level when Tony came out of segregation. Many slumbers were broken for Moretti when Nash was on night duty, swinging a heavy boot at his cell door on passing. He intercepted visiting orders, tipped salt onto Moretti's food and organised too many random cell searches.

At that particular time, relations between prisoners and officers were tense. Unrest over pay and working conditions led to an overtime ban, stretching each shift of officers, who in turn were forced to cut prisoners' recreation periods. There were dirty protests among inmates, weapons fashioned from stones inside socks to use as coshes, loosened chair legs ready to be torn off and used in defence / attack. Tony Moretti had opted for the leg rather than the sock.

It was fast approaching nine in the evening and locking up time when Moretti moved his bed from its regular position, adjusted furniture to hide the missing chair leg, took off his shirt and lay on his bed facing the wall. His cell, at the far end of the corridor was one of the first to be locked, and he listened for the approach of the guard's footsteps and the jangling of keys. The night shift was short staffed, and while three screws took a break in the officers' mess, Nash was locking up on his own. He paused at Moretti's cell and opened the view panel to see furniture had been moved and Tony Moretti lying very still, facing away from the door. He pushed it ajar.

"Moretti! Asleep are you?" he bellowed loud enough to stir cement, but not Tony Moretti on this particular night. "Are you bloody deaf as well as being a filthy faggot?" Nash continued. But Tony nine lives didn't move. Nash pushed the door wide and stepped inside. "Moretti, are you sick?" Leaning over Tony's still frame he felt for his stave, low down on his leg. Inmates hovered in cell doorways on high alert. Within seconds, Moretti was up on his feet and swinging at Nash's head with his hand made weapon. Nash took a swipe back with the stave, his other hand held as a shield. Prisoners were now out of their cells. One grabbed Nash from behind while Moretti whipped blows into Nash's body. Another snatched Nash's belt, swipe cards and keys, and within moments, prisoners had taken control of 'C' wing's upper landings, throwing mops, buckets and furniture at officers and staff scrambling to maintain control.

As the riot progressed, prisoners dislodged ceiling tiles and gained access to the roof through air vents. Despite the darkness and freezing temperature, some balanced themselves on steep sloping roof sections, snatching burning rags and bits of furniture from inmates inside, to throw at the growing crowd of prison administrators and civil police in the yard below.

Every alarm bell and siren screamed out into the night, as housing estates in the distance still slumbered.

Partition walls were broken down in the segregation unit. Windows smashed, and burning material thrown out. All four wings were soon under prisoner control. While the governor sought sanctuary behind a locked office door, the chaplain made his way towards a rowdy mob at the kitchen's entrance in an attempt to negotiate, but was seized by one inmate while another removed his dog collar and made the sign of the cross before pouring cold soup down the neck of his cassock through a plastic funnel. In the senior prison officer's quarters, they smashed furniture and made a bonfire with prisoners' record files in the middle of a plush carpeted floor. They broke open cupboards and drawers searching for alcohol and cigarettes, but by then, what started out as a full scale riot was becoming more of a school boy looting. Some could find nothing better to do than shoot hoops in the exercise yard; amuse themselves dressing up in officers' uniforms; bang out discordant notes on the old grand piano in the officers' mess or smoke as many cigarettes as would fit in their mouths at once.

Meanwhile at the main gate, extra civil police and more prison officers dressed in full riot gear, made their entrance.

Steven and Winston sat side by side on the lower bunk inside their cell listening. Winston got up from time to time and peered out of the door.

"Hey Stevie boy ...... how about we get dressed up too in uniform and sneak out of this place?"

"You're kidding me, right? What with my wobbly leg and your ridiculous dreadlocks we might as well put signs on our backs."

"Hmm, I guess so," said Winston, "but surely we can make use of this somehow."

"Like how? Pinch biscuits from the kitchen?" Steven thought of an alternative. "Have *you* got any contraband hidden away? Got any ginger nuts?"

Winston peered round the door and threw Steven a puzzled look. "Ginger nuts? What ... with my heritage? *Seriously?"*

"Ha bleedin' ha," said Steven. "You're a comedian now?

But there was no response from the other side of the door. Winston had gone exploring.

Back in 'C' wing, Tony Moretti tossed down his weapon and stood over Nash's miniature form. Not quite the majestic trophy he usually went for, but the injuries were impressive all the same. He took in a breath, grabbed Nash by the ankles and dragged him from his own cell to a safe enough distance, then sat for a while in the corridor. He held out each bare arm in turn and attempted to wipe the blood away, then got up and headed for the wash room.

***

Steven peered out from his cell and clocked the time. "Come *on* Winnie, I'm crappin' myself here."

Security doors between wings and floors were all unlocked, and Winston sidled his way to 'C' wing. He paused at the end of each corridor, listening for localised movement. Then he came upon an officer's blood stained torso lying across a cell door's threshold. He glanced up at the bare wires poking out above bracket fixings high up on the wall.

"Thank you, Lord," he whispered to himself.

The sound of running water caught his attention and he felt for the sharp behind his waistband. He continued further on towards the showers. Edging his way along the nearside wall, he stopped outside the entrance where Tony stood over a sink, washing blood from his arms and upper body under a running tap. In the distance there was shouting, hammering and banging of furniture, serving to muffle Winston's approaching footsteps. Seconds later, he'd hooked an arm around Tony's neck from behind and held the porcelain point between bare ribs with his other. Tony grimaced as his head was jerked backwards.

“How does it feel to be on the other end of the blade for a change, Moretti?” said Winston. It wasn’t difficult for Tony to identify the West Indian drawl.

“I should have .... finished you when ...... I had the chance.” He grunted. His head held fast, he couldn’t see the weapon. If there *was* a weapon. Taking a chance, he drew in a quick breath, thrust his upper torso forward, raising Winston from the floor. Then twisted free from Winston’s hold, and grabbed at the offending wrist. But he missed his target as Winston jumped back. The two faced one another, poised for attack. Then a third voice from behind, breaking the tension. Temporarily. Recognition flashed across Tony’s face and Winston’s resolve sank like a stone.

“Drop the weapon and turn around slowly.”

Still with his back to the intruder and eyes fixed on Tony, Winston said, “Whoever you are ... this is not your fight.”

Joe Moretti stepped closer, until Winston felt the mouth of a gun pressed against the back of his head. He loosened his grip on the porcelain sharp and it dropped to the floor, breaking into pieces. Tony watched it fall and grinned.

“You tried to scare me with that? Shoot the bastard, Joe. No-one’s gonna miss this piece of shit.”

Joe remained focussed. “Turn around,” he repeated. Winston slowly turned. Like Tony, his brother was shirtless, a clear sign that bloodshed was premeditated and easily washed away. Winston braced himself for a gunshot. But with a gesture of his hand gun, Joe said, "Now get the hell out of here."

Winston didn't hesitate. He gave Joe a wide berth and made a quick exit, but stopped just outside the entrance and within hearing distance.

"Thanks brother," said Tony. "I knew you'd come around in the end."

"Always there behind you, isn't that the truth?" He lowered the gun to his side.

"I don't know why you didn't shoot the bastard. Where did you get the Glock anyway? You kept that quiet." He turned back to the sink to rinse his face.

"Just like you kept all this quiet." Joe said.

Joe stopped rinsing and gripped the edges of the sink.

"In case you'd forgotten, you said you wanted no part of what I was planning."

"You were planning revenge on Grimshaw at the time. Not this. Not a full scale riot."

Tony turned his head to face his brother. Water dripped from his face onto the concrete floor.

"What's the difference? Anyway, you must have known. Everyone else in here did. It's been all around the mess for days."

"And that's how I found out – In the mess. Not from my own brother. Speaks volumes, doesn't it?"

"What the fuck's got into you? I don't know if I can trust you anymore." Tony turned back to the sink.

"Trust *me*? Oh that's hilarious," said Joe. "I bet you hadn't realised Bernie Salter was banged up in here too, did ya? Bernie and me have had conversations .... about that drug deal we did with him just before we got put away."

Tony stopped washing at the mention of Bernie Salters' name. "What deal was that? I don't remember, it was years ago."

"Bernie said he gave you thirty grand for the cocaine we traded."

"Thirty grand?" Tony attempted a laugh. "He's having you on. I never got thirty."

"How much was it then?"

"I told you, I don't remember."

"Do you remember how much you gave me by any chance?

"No, I don't."

"Well I'll remind you, shall I? Two fucking thousand, that's how much."

"Since you're the one with the foolproof memory, I'll have to take your word for that."

"What did you do with the rest Tony? How *did* you manage all those spending sprees when I was riding around in a beaten up Ford Escort?"

Tony gave Joe a sideways glance. "There are other expenses connected with these deals that you wouldn't understand. I had to pay a bloody fortune for the coke in the first place."

"You paid five grand for it. Or at least Rosa did."

"Don't call her that. She's our mother for chrissakes."

"She's *your* mother. Not so sure she's ever been mine. And don't pretend to have some respect for her. I know she didn't get the money back."

"That's bollocks. She was paid in other ways."

"That coke was cut... one to one with benzo, so that doubled its worth. I know that much."

"I had to pay the cutters, Joe. There wasn't much left after that. I never got thirty grand. Bernie's lying, trust me."

"Your lads were the cutters. That's *one way* to keep the money in the family. And as for trusting you, I won't, thanks. I trusted you with Gina. You knew I was well into her, and still you decided you were gonna have her. You didn't even want her in the end."

"Aargh! " Tony looked for the nearest thing at hand. He picked up a fire bucket and hurled it across the room. Sand flew everywhere.

"Not this again! She didn't take much persuading, did she? So she couldn't have *been into you* could she? You're like a broken fucking record. And what are you gonna do with that gun Joe? Clean your ears out with it? Ram it up your arse and have a fucking wank? Because you're sure as hell not gonna shoot anyone with it."

The remark was all Joe needed to react. He lifted the gun and fired two shots into his brother's chest. Tony's expression was one of disbelief. He jolted backwards and crumpled to the floor.

Winston's insides shook. He backed away, turned and hurried towards his cell.

Joe walked calmly over to the showers. He removed a Ziplock plastic bag from his track suit bottoms, placed the gun inside and sealed the bag. Next, he headed for a wooden bench set against the wall and removed a loose panel. Stretching his arm inside, he felt for a hidden drain cover and lifted it, then he dropped the gun inside and replaced everything as though it hadn't been disturbed. Last of all, he took a hot shower.

Steven gave a sigh of relief on seeing Winston turn the corner and head back towards him. “Where’ve you been? You haven’t done anything, have you Winnie?”

Winston looked disturbed. And breathless. “You’ll never believe what just happened,” he said.

Chapter twelve : A riot of a time

Chapter thirteen : The aftermath, cleanups & investigations

Snow had fallen prematurely for November and frozen hard while he was inside the building. Mel Butcher stepped outside of the double entrance doors to the Pathfinders' Hospital, having undergone electrical stimulus therapy to what remained of the nerves supplying his injured arm. His minder followed close behind.

Butcher was a regular patron of the Pathfinders for various illnesses. Some serious, some minor. His left forearm still hung lifeless inside the sleeve of his coat, after many expensive sessions of treatment. The chemical burns Butcher sustained from the Morettis' attack had been substantial. He'd endured painful skin grafts, and what seemed like endless stays in hospital, to emerge from it all years later still incapable of driving a car, and more importantly, of holding his woman in his arms. He was thankful after the event that she was undergoing treatment in a specialised unit at the time. At least she was spared the ordeal. This was the woman who had stayed tolerant through twenty two years with a philandering partner, suffered four miscarriages and one stillbirth, and who was now living through the final stages of lymphatic cancer.

Chapter thirteen : The aftermath, cleanups & investigations

The gradual awareness of his own selfishness had come too late for the woman he'd taken for granted by course of habit, but always cared for. The loss of cash and jewellery plundered from his private safe seemed inconsequential compared to the loss of a much loved family pet, and this frustrating disability. But collectively, it served as a justifiable reason for seeking redress. Butcher's minder walked ahead, crunching his way through the freezing snow to the car and opened the passenger door of the XJ6 for Butcher, closed it after him, then climbed into the driver's seat. He checked his appearance in the mirror on the back of the sun visor, and adjusted the band at the nape of his neck holding his pony tail.

"Petrol's running a bit low Jack," said Butcher, eyeing the gauge. "Can we get the heater on? It's Baltic in here. And leave your ruddy hair alone – or else get the thing cut off."

"I'll stop off at White Mare Pool boss, on the way back," replied Jack, flicking a switch on the dash and turning on the ignition. The engine purred into life and Butcher pulled up his collar as they drove away.

White Mare Pool service station sold everything from musical horn systems to fresh air by the pound, and while Jack filled up with four star, Butcher bought a morning newspaper and returned to the warmth of the car.

'SEIGE AT JAIL OF FEAR' was the headline, splashed all over the front cover.

Butcher sat back in the passenger seat and read on. 'Finchale Heads prison was under siege last night.....at least two dead, including one prison officer and an inmate. Names have not been released until family members have been contacted. A full investigation is now in progress.'

"Shit!" said Butcher, as Jack got back into the car.

"What's up boss?"

"Take a look for yourself." Butcher handed the paper over to his driver.

"We need to know who's dead first of all. Are you still in contact with that screw, what was his name?"

Jack looked up from the paper. "You mean Frank Stringer? He drinks in the Baker's arms two or three times a week."

"Lucky Baker." Butcher raised an eyebrow. "See what you can coax out of him, will you?"

"You're wondering if someone's got to the Morettis first?" Jack asked.

"Knowing my luck I wouldn't be surprised. Can you pop over there tonight?"

"Sure boss, but it can't be Tony Moretti. He's indestructible. They don't call him Nine Lives for nothing."

"Well maybe he just exceeded his limit," said Butcher, taking back the newspaper and leafing through to the stop press to see if there was an update on the story. As he passed the announcements page, a name caught his eye.

Everly – Grimshaw

The bans are to be read at St. Aloysius Church, Parkend, for six consecutive Sundays commencing 29th November 1992, prior to the marriage of Michael JohnEverly to Louise Ann Grimshaw, which will take place on Saturday 16th January 1993 at 1.30 pm.

"Well here's something interesting," said Butcher. "The Morettis' niece - tying the knot in six weeks." He lowered the paper and gazed ahead. "I'd a brief thing with her mother on the night she died, you know."

Jack looked unmoved. "I didn't know you had that effect on women, boss."

"I could see right through her. The brothers put her up to it and I just played along. If I'd sent her packing that night she'd still be alive. But I was more focused on having some fun. There are always consequences, Jack. For every stupid thing we do." Butcher fell silent for a few seconds, then spoke again.

"Since they were fostered, the Grimshaw kids have been estranged from the Morettis from what I hear. But I bet their grandmother Rosa will want to attend a happy family occasion such as this. Maybe we ought to send her a discreet invitation." He turned to Jack and grinned.

"Sure boss," said Jack. "Tell me what you want me to do."

"Let's get back first. We've got six weeks to set something up."

***

Before the clean up could begin at Finchale Heads, a severe clampdown was imposed on all wings. No visitors were allowed for two weeks. Prisoners had no exercise for days, and prevented from using the showers until damage was repaired. Officers, inmates and even the prison's cat needed medical treatment of some sort. The governor called an urgent meeting of all higher ranking officers and opened investigations on three lower ranking officers for alleged assaults on prisoners. It seemed that prison officers would be taking much of the blame for working to rule, and the governor insisted on having all closed circuit video tapes by the following morning before they were handed over to the police.

It was late into the night shift when Principal Officer Tommy Hunter and his deputy Frank Stringer scrutinized the CCTV footage from the night before. Stringer found it difficult to stay awake, while Hunter fast-forwarded, rewound and played yet another section of tape.

Chapter thirteen : The aftermath, cleanups & investigations

"Look at that one Frank." Hunter alerted Stringer to a scene where Tony Moretti popped up in camera shot, on the fifteen yard stretch of corridor leading up to the wash rooms. He could be seen dragging officer Nash's body along the floor by his feet.

"Holy Mother in heaven," said Stringer. "So much blood .... I may be sick."

Tony then disappeared from view with the body in tow, reappearing a moment or two later without it.

"Look at that bastard! He's done away with Eric Nash. Oh, I think the vomit's comin'up."

Hunter's face threatened. "Not in here it's not."

Stringer continued watching as Tony Moretti came into view and stared into the camera above him.

"Oh, I know what he's about to do." said Hunter, just as Moretti came closer to the camera lens, and disappeared once again beneath it. About thirty seconds of tape passed, during which an officer in the background was hit on the back of the head by a flying chamber pot, and a prisoner tried to either asphyxiate or gas another officer by sitting on his face. Then a hand covered the lens. The officers watched as the image dissolved into fuzziness.

"Pity he didn't think of doing that ten minutes before." Stringer said, now fully alert.

Hunter smiled at the irony of it all.

"Ten minutes before as maybe, but.ten minutes after and we'd have seen *Moretti's* killer. It's pretty clear Moretti murdered Eric Nash. Enjoyed it too. But who's the late comer with the gun?"

"Maybe Nash wasn't dead when he was dragged away," said Stringer. "He could have regained consciousness, there was another struggle, maybe in the washroom – remember there was a fire bucket upset in there. A gun could have been hidden inside it. Nash grabs the gun, shoots Moretti, and before Moretti goes down, he takes a last fatal swipe at Nash before collapsing on the floor himself, bleeding to death."

Hunter looked at Stringer in disbelief. "So how did Nash get out of the wash room to the cell where he was found if he'd already had the fatal blow?"

"Well he must have staggered out of there as he was dying."

"If Nash shot Moretti, what did he do with the weapon, you muppet?"

"All right it's just a theory. Maybe a daft one. The gun might never be found. They've searched everywhere. If someone else was involved, snaffled the murder weapon away, I doubt we'll get to know who it was. The walkway camera was sabotaged as well."

Hunter shook his head and went to turn the video player off.

"We haven't finished yet, what are you doing?" said Stringer.

"We've seen this lot ten times over. There's nothing else to look at."

The deputy was persuaded. "Suppose not. Whoever killed Moretti did us a favour. He wasn't here long, but it was long enough to know he was an evil bastard."

"Well I've met worse, but you're not wrong there," said Hunter. "Something like this could affect our performance rating. Its low enough as it is already. The investigation's out of the governor's hands now anyway. Whatever the police turn up from all these interviews, there's little he can do about it. No doubt he'll be bending the coroner's ear over a game of golf at the weekend."

"Right, let's take a break from this. I could murder a cuppa, I don't know about you," Stringer conceded.

"Better make it coffee," said Hunter, "It might help you stay awake."

***

The following morning back on 'B' wing, prisoners in the mess were just finishing their first meal of the day and not looking forward to their second. In the kitchen, cooking facilities were suspended until a gas engineer could repair a damaged pipe. Steven wondered just how long the monotony of cold corned beef and baked beans could be tolerated before what remained of his hair fell out or his taste buds died of boredom. And who would give a toss anyway? On the plus side, there was no lingering smell of stewed tripe or boiled cabbage in the air, which was the norm.

As Steven prepared to go back to his cell, one of the screws came across with a letter.

"There you go, Grimshaw. You haven't had one of these for a while."

Steven's brows shot up as he double checked his name on the envelope.

With a mouthful of bread, Winston tried to speak.

"Hey, man, don't stand there staring at it. Open the thing for God's sake."

"Don't talk with your mouth full you bloody ignoramus," said Steven, removing the two folded pages from inside. Winston swallowed with a grimace.

"That bread's a bit chewy this morning."

"I didn't try it," said Steven, distracted. "Mine was green and furry. That's why I gave it to you."

Winston faked annoyance. "Bad news is it?"

"No, it's good. For a change. Our Louise is getting married."

Chapter thirteen : The aftermath, cleanups & investigations

"That's your daughter, yeah? That's great news, man." Winston beamed one of his best.

Steven sighed. "It would be ... if the news had come from her. This is from my sister, Cath."

"I've seen your sister," said Winston with a wicked grin. "I love a lady with eye glasses. Single, isn't she?"

"Don't start getting ideas about our Catherine. Far too old for you. Anyway, she's a good girl."

"Hasn't had much choice has she? Keeping what's left of the family together."

Steven shook his head. "I know. I've some bridges to mend when I get out. Louise will be the toughest, I reckon."

"Oh man, now come on. The kid hasn't seen you in how many years?"

Steven hesitated, "Err, eight? Maybe nine? Bloody hell, I must be due for release sooner than I thought."

"Hey man, what's wrong with you? You had your parole board ages ago."

"Oh yeah." Steven started to do some rough calculations, when his mood dropped again. "I'm gonna miss it then. By just weeks. Not that I would have got an invite anyway."

"There you go again," said Winston. "The girl's gonna need a bit of working on, that's all."

"I heard from our Danny last week."

"And? What did he say?"

"He's bought a share in a motor repair outfit. He's offered me a job and a place to live when I get out," said Steven, refolding the letter and putting it back in the envelope.

"But he's just a kid isn't he? Where would he get that kind of money from?"

"That's what worries me. My kids have led separate lives for the last few months. None of the family knows where Danny is, and he won't tell me. His letters are vague, and the postmarks, all different. Maybe he knows Louise is getting married. I'd like to think he'd want to see her on her special day."

***

Two weeks later, and on the first day recreation periods had recommenced, Joe Moretti circled the pool table, weighing up his shot. His opponent, cell mate Teflon, looked worried.

"Scully pulled me up this morning, Joe. He's not hangin' around waiting for his money much longer."

Joe was still setting up his shot, gave an irritated sigh and leaned over the table, cue poised.

"He'll get his money when I have it to give him."

Chapter thirteen : The aftermath, cleanups & investigations

"Oh, that's decent of you, Moretti.....," came a voice from behind. Victor Scully was built like an outhouse with a dark brown voice fit to melt butter. "..... but you'll be out in days, and you need to get me my money before then, because I can't survive on promises."

Joe straightened up and looked Scully in the eye. "You got your property back, didn't you? And sooner than agreed? You can't expect me to find that amount of cash straight away. I'll pay you. You'll just have to wait."

Scully's top lip curled as he snatched the cue out of Joe's hand and pushed him up against a wall. "You seem to be under the impression you call the shots around here Moretti. Don't imagine you can jump straight into your brother's shoes after you ended him."

"All right lads, break it up here." An officer came forward. Scully took three seconds of reluctance before stepping away.

"Give the cue back," said the screw.

Scully did as he was told, never taking his eyes off Joe. "Remember what I said." Then he turned and walked away.

Joe returned to the game, and flashed a smug smile to Teflon.

"He won't let it go, Joe. You don't want Scully as an enemy."

"Well the same applies both ways. Stop your mythering. Let's get on with the game."

Joe poised himself over the table once again, with his cue lined up right on target. A second officer approached, pausing while Joe took his shot. The ball missed its target by a whisper, and bounced off the edge of the pocket, spinning back up the table.

"Bad luck," said the officer.

"Bad smell, you prick!" snapped Joe. He straightened up. "What the hell do you want?"

"There's no need to be offensive, Moretti. The Governor wants to see you."

"About what?"

"Well if I knew that, it would save you a trip wouldn't it?"

Joe threw down his cue, turned and fell into step with the officer.

"Right, let's get it over with."

Outside the governor's office, the screw knocked on the polished wooden door.

"Enter!" The Governor got up from his desk as the men came into the room.

"Ah, Moretti, it's nothing to concern yourself about. I just wanted to have a brief chat to express my condolences regarding your loss, and to discuss the conditions of your release." He looked down at his diary and turned a page. "In twelve days time I believe.

"Yes sir. Thank you sir," said Joe. "My probation officer has already spoken to me about that. I was worried the date might be put back, after the riot. I thought we would all be held responsible sir."

"Well we've had to issue penalties to certain prisoners, but considering your devastating loss and also your exemplary behaviour since you've been here, there's no reason to stop you from being released on the expected date," said the Governor. "Just in time for Christmas."

"That's very good of you sir, I do appreciate that."

"Well, if we don't see you again, and I hope we won't, I want to wish you good luck for the future."

"Thank you, sir."

Joe turned and left the room with an untouchable smugness.

Chapter fourteen : Molly to the rescue

Joe Moretti's release date came and went with nothing untoward happening, apart from the Grimshaw's boiler giving up the ghost. The house was freezing cold, the kettle, worked to death, and the over stretched plumber couldn't call until the following afternoon.

When he arrived, Catherine watched him stagger up the path under the weight of his toolbox.

"That looks heavy," she said at the door.

"Can I, have a sit ... catch my breath?" he gasped.

Catherine opened the door wide. "Course you can. Come on in."

Ten minutes and several squirts from an inhaler later, the kitchen worktop was laden with tools. "Is there any chance of a cuppa, sweetness?" the plumber said.

While Catherine filled the kettle, further up the coast Louise was arriving home from work. Turning the key in her front door, a heavy hand landed on her shoulder and Joe Moretti's menacing tone altered the expression on her face.

"Have you missed me, Louise?

She turned from the half-opened door to force a smile.

"Uncle Joe," she managed to say, "How are you?"

Louise wasn't used to seeing this side of her uncle. Joe looked unkempt and smelled of sweat.

"I'll be fine once I've seen your brother." His heavy hand slapped against the door frame over her head and his eyes fixed themselves on hers. Louise recoiled.

"Oh, er ... he's not here. He's away on a short break, with a friend."

"December's a strange time to take a holiday," he said. "That doesn't sound right to me. You're mistaken, aren't you Louise?"

"No, it's true." Her attempt at calm needed improvement. "It was a ... spur of the moment thing. You know how it is."

"Well now," said Joe, stepping back and staring at a spot on the ground, clenching and unclenching his fist. "I wouldn't like to accuse my niece of lying, but your Missus Martin told me earlier today that no-one's set eyes on Daniel for months." He raised his eyes from the ground and fixed his gaze once more without blinking.

"Oh no, that's not right," she said with another painful swallow. "It's not been months, but I don't know when he's expected back."

Joe slammed his palm into the front door and it swung against the inside wall. "Let's stop with the stupid games," he said, pushing her to one side as he leapt over the threshold. "It's showdown time."

He took the stairs two at a time and shoved open every door until he found Danny's. Louise ran after him, hoping, and then not hoping, her foster mother might be somewhere in the house hearing all of this. She watched from behind as he turned out every cupboard and drawer, lifted the mattress, examined pockets, shoes, wallets, and even Danny's rubbish bin.

With nowhere else to look, he grabbed Louise by the arms. "All right, cards on the table." The words came through gritted teeth. She screwed up her eyes and turned her face away. His breath was sour.

"Where the hell is it?" Joe continued.

"Where's...whaaat?"

"There's a shoe missing...and the goddam necklace, YOU STUPID BITCH!"

Her voice trembled, and she whispered, "I don't know. I *swear* I don't know."

Joe turned towards the open wardrobe, growled, gave the door a departing kick, hurried down the stairs and back out onto the street.

Louise let go a breath she'd held onto and swept her eyes over the mess.

Chapter fourteen : Molly to the rescue

Back at the Grimshaws, the plumber munched his way through the biscuit tin's contents as Catherine refilled his coffee cup. It was a welcome distraction from the masticated swirling mass on full view to her right. With accompanied nasal tunes.

Molly appeared in the doorway wearing a bobble hat, puffa jacket, scarf and slippers.

"You still cold, mother?" asked Catherine. "Do you want another coffee?"

"Biscuits!" she said.

"We're sharing them today. With the plumber. He's going to fix the heating."

"He's a fat twat."

"Well," said the plumber, as clumps of soggy biscuit crumbs leapt from his mouth. "You're a charmer, aren't you Missus?"

"And *you're* a fat twat." Molly turned and went back into the sitting room.

When the telephone rang in the hall, Skipper echoed the ring tone from the living room, and the plumber jumped in his chair.

"What was that? Two telephones?"

Catherine went to pick up the receiver. "No, that's the parrot. He likes to show off in front of the guests."

"I'm hardly a guest."

"I'm pleased *you* said that. I'm just paying you to sit there and annoy me apparently."

Louise sounded distraught at the other end of the line.

"He's been here .... just now. Danny's room looks like a bomb hit it."

"Oh no, Lou, try to calm down. Do you want to come over here? You're not hurt?"

"No, I'm all right. Mary will be back soon...I'll have to tidy up." Her voice began to break. "Cath... he was... vile. And you should get rid of that shoe in case he comes over to yours. We don't want him guessing we found something."

"Ok, I will. Try not to cry love. Make yourself a hot chocolate or something and I'll call you later. It's just that I've got the biscuit eater here at the moment and it's looking like a long job." She swept accusing eyeballs over the plumber. "Don't forget to lock the doors."

The plumber's chewing paused. "She's not got trouble with her waterworks as well, has she?" he said, popping the remainder of yet another wafer into the huge chasm between his lips. Catherine remained silent. "If she's got a leak, locking the doors won't help. You do realise that, don't you?"

I'm kicking his arse in a minute.

***

It was the following morning, and the postcard in her hand pictured a jungle scene. Catherine turned the card over and smiled when she saw the Cullercoats postmark.

Chapter fourteen : Molly to the rescue

Dear Aunty Cath,

I'm still alive, so tell Lou not to worry. Plans are taking shape. Treat this card like the others. Love to all. x

Sometimes, the scantest outline of news was worse than getting no news at all, and Catherine had a hundred more questions. She spooned Molly's egg on automatic pilot, while the buttered soldiers lay in waiting and her own egg went cold. Molly took an age to eat almost anything. But she could suck toasted soldiers to a pulp on her own, as she began to demonstrate when there was a sudden thump on the back door. Catherine got up, still with the spoon in her hand to find Joe Moretti standing outside.

His eyes settled on the utensil. "What are you gonna do with that? Stir me to death?"

"You're interrupting breakfast...what do you want?"

"Have you seen Danny Boy?" he asked.

"No. We lost touch years ago," she said. "What do you want him for?"

Joe gave a dissatisfied grunt. "It's a private matter, and I think I should check for myself. Just to be sure." He shoved her aside.

"Who the hell are *you?* King Ding-a-ling?" she shouted after him.

Joe barged through the kitchen and proceeded to search every room, while Catherine thrust Danny's postcard into her jeans pocket and poured the tea. She heard objects being tossed aside in the bedrooms, glass breaking, and a bookcase tipping over. She waited at the foot of the stairs, arms folded. Then he came down.

"What did you break?" she said, blocking his path.

"I don't know why you're bothered. It's all a pile of crap anyway." He nudged past her.

"Must have been the mirror, then. One look at your nasty face would do it. I'm calling the police."

He turned back. "No you won't, because that would drop your precious Danny boy in the shit." She knew he was right.

Joe headed for the open door again. As he passed Molly sucking on a toast finger, he leaned across and took one from her plate, pushing it all into his mouth. "You're big enough Grandma, you can spare this," he said with mouth full. Molly's face altered from surprise to fury when he reached for a second. She snatched up a fork and stabbed it into the back of his hand.

"Aargh!" He screamed out, and grabbed her wrist.

"Leave her alone!" yelled Catherine. Joe turned, and saw the bread knife in her hand. Catherine didn't recall picking it up, but held it firm. He let go of Molly's arm.

"She bloody well wants locking up."

Catherine picked up a towel and threw it at his bleeding hand. "She's not the only one."

Right on time, Skipper performed his party piece. One ring of the doorbell, two of the telephone, ending with Benji's biggest growl, never forgotten even two years after the dog had passed away. Joe's head darted around in confusion.

"Christ! This is a fucking nut house." Joe wrapped the towel around his injured hand as he made for the door.

"You can keep the towel," said Catherine, following behind him. "......And you're welcome, by the way," she called after him as he hurried down the street.

Molly stuffed all three remaining soldiers possessively into her mouth at once. Catherine hoped she wouldn't have to rely on her mother's fearless responses, nor Skipper's perfect timing again. But she nurtured a secret pride in the capabilities of this newly formed team.

Chapter fifteen : The invitation

Mel Butcher sat behind his executive desk, gasping with impatience as he flicked through a telephone index with his good hand.

“Sod the bloody thing!” He slapped the book shut. “Jack?” he shouted through to the next room. Jack’s bulk filled the doorway.

“Boss?” He approached Butcher’s desk with a John Wayne swagger. Butcher threw the index across the desk.

“Find a number for me will you? It’s Rosa Moretti I’m looking for. She lives in one of those residential care homes....Gusty Corner or something, it’s called.”

Jack’s mouth twitched at one corner. “I think you mean Windy Nook, Boss?” He took the index and sat in the chair opposite. “I have an uncle living there.”

Butcher shrugged. “Whatever.” He watched Jack leafing through the pages, and drummed the fingers of his good hand on the desk. “Just because Tony Moretti’s gone, doesn’t mean his side kick’s gonna get away scot-free. Joe Moretti will pay his dues, make no mistake.

Jack found the number. “Here it is. You want me to ring it?

Butcher picked up the receiver, “Do you mind? It’s this bloody stupid arm. I’m not wasting any more money on that physio, pretty as she is.”

Jack came over to the telephone and pressed the appropriate buttons while Butcher held the handset to his ear. After a short pause, Rosa Moretti answered.

“Hello?” she said.

“Hello, Missus Moretti? George Everly here, your lovely Louise’s future father-in-law.”

“Future father-in-law? You mean our Louise is getting married?”

The surprise in her voice was like music to Butcher’s ears.

“That’s right, Missus Moretti, and don’t fret ...... you’ll be getting your invitation in the post soon.”

“Oh, I’ll look forward to that. I haven’t seen Louise in a long time. Where is it to be?”

“It’s going to be at St Aloysius church...” Butcher began.

“I beg your pardon?” she interjected. “I’m sorry, I don’t hear so well. Just hang on a minute can you? While I get a pencil?”

There was another pause, in which Butcher turned to Jack and rolled his eyes skyward.

“Here I am, back again. What were you saying?”

Butcher exaggerated his pronunciation, "Saturday, sixteenth of January, 1.30pm at St. Aloysius church."

"Right. I think I've got that, but this will be on the invitation when I get it, won't it? Now, the most vital question, what should I wear?"

Butcher sucked in his cheeks with a deep breath. "Something elasticated – the catering will be immense. In a sickly shade of green. And a blue hair rinse."

"I beg your pardon?"

"Missus Moretti, your dear Louise is very upset," continued Butcher with a kinder tone.

"Oh? And why is that?"

"Well this is her special day. She's already lost her mother, your beautiful daughter, some time ago now. Her father's in prison, her uncle Tony just recently passed away..."

Butcher heard the rustle of a Kleenex coming through his earpiece, and Rosa sniffed with the memory of her eldest son's demise. "But I thought she wasn't in touch with Tony. His death almost finished me you know. I may be an old woman but I still have feelings for my boys. He has boys of his own. And so young to lose their father like that."

"And how young are they Rosa?"

"Not even thirty. Poor, poor boys."

Butcher lifted his brows and smiled. "I'm sure many people are feeling a loss with Tony's passing. I feel for you Rosa, I really do. It's OK to call you Rosa is it? We'll be family soon." Butcher's best convincing performance appeared to be working. "So what my wife and I are hoping for, is to gather as many family members as possible, even those who have lost touch, to surprise your lovely Louise and make it the best day possible. And of course another person she hasn't seen so much of late is her Uncle Joe?" Butcher left that statement hanging in mid air for several seconds.

"Oh, Giuseppe? He calls himself Joe, but he was christened Giuseppe you know? I don't think I know where he is at the moment. He travels a lot you see, with his business."

"I see, well that's a shame. It'll be a huge celebration. All of his old friends and family will be there..."

"Maria and Carlo?" Rosa's voice quickened. "Are they going too? He'd be so pleased to see his cousins."

"Of course Maria and Carlo will be there. No good party should be without them." Butcher winked at Jack. He could almost smell victory in the air.

"Yes, er .... leave it with me. I'll see what I can do."

"OK, Rosa, I'll get these invitations off to you. What number do you have on your door there at Windy Nook?"

"It's 16a, but if you just address it to Windy Nook, they'll pass it on so don't worry if you forget the number," she said.

"Hope you find him in time," said Butcher. "Bye bye now."

"I hope so too. Bye bye."

Butcher grinned as he replaced the receiver. "Get a couple of cheap invitations printed up Jack, and put that date in your diary. And while you're at it, get me one of those contraptions they're all using these days with a push button speaker phone. That'll be one less job I have to pay you for."

Chapter fifteen : The invitation

Chapter sixteen : One wedding and an almost funeral

It was a regular morning on C wing at Finchale Heads. Victor Scully plodged through surface water carrying his shoes, on his way out of the showers with a smug look on his face. He stood at the entrance and waited. Two minutes later another inmate arrived, and stopped in his tracks.

“What’s happened here? We’re flooded.”

“Aye, there must be a blocked drain or summat,” said Scully.

The inmate looked down the corridor. “Mister Stringer!” he shouted, “We appear to have a flood.”

At the shower entrance, Frank Stringer groaned. “Oh for God’s sake, I could do without this today. Where’s all this water come from?”

“Well, I’m no Einstein,” said Scully, “but we could have a blocked drain.”

“Clever bugger you are, Scully. So where’s the drain you reckon is blocked?”

“Well since the deepest water is around that bench over there, I reckon there must be one underneath it.

Chapter sixteen: One wedding and an almost funeral

"What kind of a wally fixes a bench on top of a drain? How the hell am I supposed to access that?"

"That bench is loose at one end," said Scully, "I'll show you if you like."

"I might just call the plumber. That'll be the easiest way," said Stringer.

"Not frightened of a bit of water, are you Mister Stringer?"

"It's not the water, so much as where it's been first. And my knees are well-buggered." He shot a glance back at Scully, who offered a sympathetic smile.

"We can give you a hand. Then when you've fixed the problem and saved the prison some money, you can write it up in your incident book. Might get some serious Brownie points for that."

"Oh, what the hell." Stringer pulled off his shoes and socks, rolled up his trousers and paddled across to the bench, followed by Scully.

"The loose bit is down that side," Scully indicated.

"Is this thing screwed to the floor?" He tried to lift the bench. "That's not gonna move," he gasped, "and the legs are too short to reach under." Stringer flashed Scully a warning look. ."Looks like it'll have to be your way."

The end panel came away easily in his hand, which he set aside. Stringer's knees cracked like starting pistols as he knelt down and peered inside. "I can see the drain. Hang on, if I can just get my hand in there, the cover's loose." He withdrew his hand holding the cover. "You'd better be right Scully, because I'm about to get soaked now if I'm gonna reach inside that drain."

Scully and his pal exchanged looks of amusement, as Stringer lowered himself onto the soaking floor and groped inside.

"I can feel ... soggy paper towels. And...holy Mother in a casket! Someone's undercrackers!" Stringer's face contorted in disgust. Scully nudged his pal and silenced a smirk.

Sploshing noises accompanied Stringer as he slid out from the trap and held his catch aloft, before slapping the grey wet drawers onto the bench seat. He gave the lads a warning glance. "This better not be a prank, or there'll be consequences."

Scully frowned. "We'd never dream of doin' that to *you* Mister Stringer. You're one of the good 'uns"

"Hmmm ... butter me up, why don't ya? I'm not finished here yet either. There's more." Bending to floor level again, he slid an arm back inside the gap. "There's something ... like smooth plastic. Hang on. Let me just pull this thing out." Stringer grunted, as he slid out from under the bench and revealed the item grasped in his fist. “Oh glory be, what have we here?” There was a gurgling noise as the water level went down, and Scully tried his best to look surprised.

“Something else to write in your report book, Mister Stringer.”

***

It was the morning of Saturday January 16th. Danny Grimshaw was in the garage, overseeing the final jobs of the week to be finished that day. A Mondeo was mis-firing, a Renault with a steering issue and a Cavalier needed a fuel tank.

George was busy with the Mondeo when Danny appeared from the wash room, suited, booted, and ready to leave.

“Have you got the keys for the Alfa, George? I might as well give it a run – test out all this new gear.”

George raised his head from under the bonnet. “Yeah, they’re on the work bench by the door,” he indicated with a hand-held spanner.

“Will you be all right on your own?” Danny picked up the keys. “I might be gone for an hour or two.”

“I’ll be fine. Just go and enjoy yourself. Press play on the cassette when you go past, will you mate?”

"OK. But keep the volume down, or you won't hear the phone. See you later."

"Yeah, see ya."

***

Eight miles further down the coast, in the more feminine setting of Louise's bedroom, Cathy grappled with the tiny fasteners on the back of her niece's wedding dress. No ordinary white frock was this either, but an original Debenham's creation, altered to fit by a local seamstress just one week before, yet today appeared to have shrunk overnight. There was strain in Cathy's voice.

"It's just these two at the bottom," she gasped. "Can't you breathe in a bit deeper?"

Louise, already holding onto a very deep breath, let it out in a sudden exhale. "Ooh.... that feels better. It's no good ... you'll have to wait until I catch my second wind."

Catherine stepped back. "I don't understand it ... you just tried this on yesterday. What were you eating last night?"

"Just a spoonful of chips, so it can't have been that."

"Who eats just a spoonful of chips? Where's your halo?" said Catherine, fumbling inside her handbag.

"I may have eaten that too."

"I've just the thing in here somewhere. Should be able to fasten them on the inside."

She took safety pins from a tiny sewing kit, climbed under the dress and fought to close the opening while Louise inhaled yet again on Cathy's prompt.

"There! I think that should get you through the ceremony. The veil will hide it anyway." Cathy stepped from under the dress to take in the whole view, while Louise scrutinized her reflection in the long mirror. She held up the hem of her dress and glared at her foot.

"Typical. Look at that. A flaming ladder."

Catherine delved into the handbag again, unscrewed a bottle of clear nail varnish and dabbed the leg concerned.

"How are you feeling Lou? ...apart from nervous, I mean.

"Well, you know I was determined *not* to have anyone give me away?"

"Of course," said Catherine. "You belong to yourself. Why would you need to be given away?"

"I know that, but ….. I wish Dad was here, standing where you are now. No offence."

"I get it," sighed Catherine as she blew on the varnished leg and stood up. "It's a shame he died so soon."

"No, I didn't mean ... this sounds awful, but I was thinking about my real dad. I'm going soft."

Catherine's eyebrows leapt to the edge of her brow. This was the girl who, just a few years ago was adamant she never wanted to set eyes on Steven again.

"Well I have to say I'm surprised." Cathy placed the brush back in the bottle and screwed on the lid. "But if he *was* here, the odds of him carrying nail polish and safety pins would be pretty low."

Louise smiled. "Maybe he'll show up at the christening."

***

It was beginning to cloud over when late arrivals filtered through the heavy Georgian doors of Saint Aloysius' church. Mel Butcher sat next to Jack in the passenger seat of his XJ6, parked half way along an adjacent tree-lined avenue.

"It doesn't look as if he's coming boss," said Jack, peering from the windscreen through a gap in the trees.

"He's got to bloody well come." Butcher was twitchy. "Should have brought the Rover. It's a bit more discreet than this bloody great thing." Jack knew when to keep quiet.

Then a petrol blue Datsun estate pulled into the closest available parking space on Church Street, and Butcher fixed his gaze on Jack, with the clearer view. A grey-suited Joe Moretti emerged from the driver's side and opened the passenger door for his mother. A spindly leg with a white Hush Puppy sandal on the end of it emerged first, followed by a twig like figure, clad in a lavender two-piece topped with a wide brimmed matching hat, set at an angle. Rosa Moretti's hair was blue rinsed.

A smile began to spread across Jack's face, prompting Butcher to lean across.

"Halle-bloody-luyah." said Butcher.

Joe talked and gesticulated as they walked, while Rosa wrinkled her brow and inclined her head. The church doors closed behind them.

"What do you want me to do Boss? Challenge him when he comes out? Or follow him in right now and sit on his lap? Heh heh."

Butcher gave Jack a despondent look. "You know, Jack, sometimes I find it hard to believe you've got letters after your name." He glanced around at the parked cars. "No, is the answer to your question by the way. Too many people around. We'll follow, but he mustn't know we're on his tail. See where he goes. I've waited eight years for this. Another hour or so won't make much difference."

The church doors creaked open and Cathy turned. Joe Moretti grabbed hold of Rosa's sleeve and ushered her into one of the rear pews on the opposite side.

That's all we need. Bloody gatecrashers.

"Why are we sitting back here? I can't see what's going on," said Rosa.

"You can see all the guests Mother. That's what you came for. All those ridiculous outfits. You can tell me how daft they look after."

Catherine sat in the second pew adjusting her outfit. She exchanged glances with Doris, attending to Molly four rows back. Her eyes were drawn to Molly's shocking pink coat with matching hat, chosen to lift her otherwise dour appearance. The effect however, served only to exaggerate it. Then, she farted. Molly, that is. Doris formed an 'o' with her mouth and flapped a hand in front of her nose. There were one or two coughs and a few heads turned. Catherine smiled.

Despite her view being hampered by wide brimmed hats, Catherine caught a glimpse of Danny amidst all the flamboyance at the end of the back row. He wore a blue/grey suit, pale blue tie, with matching pocket handkerchief.

Talk about obvious. Where's the invisibility cloak? Ah, he couldn't find it! Thank heaven the Belisha beacon phase seems to have passed anyway.

The ceremony ran over time. Danny kept an eye on the side exit with the push bar he remembered using on Sunday school days. He had a clear view of it from where he sat, but was it used anymore?

From the opposite pews, Rosa seemed puzzled as she scanned the other side.

"I don't see Maria or Carlo anywhere..." Then she shifted her gaze back to Joe, undoing his jacket buttons. She looked cross.

"That suit doesn't fit you. Tony has...*Tony had* bigger shoulders than you. You shouldn't have worn it."

Joe's gaze swept over the congregation. "Well maybe you shouldn't have chucked all my good clothes. You haven't touched Tony's. And *he's* not coming back."

"And we're sitting on the wrong side," she went on. "This is the groom's side, not the bride's."

His mother's protests were attracting attention. He took a sharp deep breath. "Mother, please...I'm trying to concentrate."

"Into God now, are you? All of a sudden?"

He spotted the woman first, and his expression altered. A sophisticated brunette, mid thirties, in a cream jacket and skirt. From where he sat he had a perfect view of her long, shapely legs. If Looney Tunes was real, red hearts would be springing from his eyes at that moment. Joe glanced at those sitting either side of her. Not that it mattered if she was with a partner. He'd already locked eyes with her once. She was bound to look over again. And then he saw Danny, sitting to her left. It took a few seconds for the penny to drop. Danny was a child the last time he saw him, but this was a mature and confident young man.

"The cheeky bastard," muttered Joe, "with a woman like that."

The woman looked across at Joe Moretti with a grimace and pulled the hem of her skirt over her knees.

'Oh, she wants me...' he said to himself.

"I can't hear you when you mumble like that," said Rosa.

He turned his eyes front ways again, straightened his tie, and decided not only was he having the stash from Danny that afternoon, but he was also having this woman.

The ceremony finished, and after signing the register the couple strolled back up the aisle to a happy organ tune, where they would greet their guests coming out of the church. As the congregation began to move, Danny got up and heaved at the push bar on the side exit, but the door wouldn't budge. His eyes darted from one group of guests to another. Waiting for a clear path, he made a determined stride toward the main doors.

Neither Joe nor Rosa were in the foyer. With a fixed smile on his face, Danny walked across to Louise.

"Danny, how are you?" she said.

He took hold of her forearms and leaned across as if to kiss her. "Lou, it's been great to see you, but I shouldn't have come. Joe's here. I've got to dash." Danny stood back for a long look at his now distraught sister. He shook his head.

"Don't worry, I'll be fine," he said, and hurried outside.

His exit however, was to be delayed. A throng of guests had gathered at the foot of the steps leading down to the path, and there was a makeshift ramp which Doris attempted to negotiate with Molly's chair. Rosa supervised Molly's descent, offering unhelpful instructions which Doris was more than happy to ignore. Danny tried to overtake the wheelchair just as Joe darted out from behind his mother. Both men came to a standstill. Joe leaned forward with his best attempt at intimidation.

"You sneaky bastard," he whispered, to avoid a clout from Rosa standing next to him.

Doris glared at Joe. "Do you mind? There are ladies present, not to mention The Almighty himself," Joe gave Doris a fleeting glance and ignored her. He turned, grasping Danny's arm.

"What have you done with it?" he demanded.

Danny puzzled, and patted his pockets. "Nope, nothin' in there," he said. "But since you're interested, I've invested it, and once it's made a decent return the person you took it from will be getting his money back." He hoped to sound convincing.

Joe scoffed. "Do you think I was born yesterday? You wouldn't do that. And anyway, it belongs to me now." He stood up straight and stuck out his chest. "You got that?" Then he grabbed Danny's jacket lapels and tried to push him against a pillar, but a thumb sucking child already leaning against it steered him into a less imposing shuffle.

Butcher's car moved up the avenue as people dispelled, but the view was poor.

"What's happening over there?"

All Jack could see was a large crowd of fancy clothed individuals encircling the church pillar. He watched the photographer move in closer, as Louise and Michael descended the steps.

"It's just the photographs being taken, boss," said Jack. "They could be ages yet. Might as well relax. Moretti's car's still there."

Butcher sighed and switched on the radio, while Jack continued to gaze out of the window.

"Shouting louder doesn't make it true," said Danny. "Everyone knows that money was stolen. It was all over the papers. You may as well fess up in front of all these people. How much was it you took from Butcher's safe?"

"Fuck all!" said Joe. Rosa Moretti and her defective hearing caught just part of the conversation. She turned to Doris and Catherine standing close by.

Chapter sixteen: One wedding and an almost funeral

“What did he say?” she asked.

“He said, ‘fuck all’,” shouted Doris, right into the old lady’s ear. Rosa stared at her with disbelief.

“That’s funny,” she said, “I could have sworn I saw his lips move.

“I’m not hanging round here while you spoil my sister’s wedding day,” said Danny, pulling away from Joe in the direction of his vehicle. Joe turned to his mother.

“I’ve got to go – you’ll have to get a lift from one of the others.” He hurried towards his car, leaving Rosa with a gaping jaw.

On the main path, he passed the cream-suited brunette and paused in the midst of his pursuit.

“Don’t worry darlin’, I’ll be back.”

She scowled, and kept on walking.

Butcher leaned forward in the passenger seat, and switched off the radio. “Jack,” he said, with his eyes on the street, “he’s on the move ... heading straight for his car.”

Jack sat upright in the driver’s seat and fastened his seat belt. He turned the ignition key and the engine purred into life. “You ready, Boss?”

Butcher watched as Moretti slammed the driver’s door and prepared to move off.

Danny and Joe could each see one another from their separate spots. As Danny attempted two or three tricky manoeuvres of the steering wheel, he knew the day might not end well. With a swift glance in his mirror, he saw Moretti having similar problems moving out. Danny's Alfa was first out by seconds, and the adrenalin pumped as he took another glance at the rear view and saw Moretti's Datsun straighten itself and speed up behind him. He pushed down with his right and sped up through all five gears in a matter of seconds. As he pulled out of Church Street it was beginning to rain, and he thanked heaven but mainly George for fitting the extra wide Firestones. His mind moved faster than the car, planning the next few sharp bends.

Traffic was dense, and it was hard to see past the vehicle behind. Danny drove for two minutes without a sign of Moretti, and almost at the point of self congratulations when he spotted the Datsun's blue nose nudging out from behind a bus, yards away. By stroke of luck, the bus driver was an awkward breed, and for every attempt of Joe's to overtake, the bus indicators would flash, the front wing would protrude, then fall back into place.

Butcher's XJ6 was stuck behind a caravan swaying from side to side in time with the nodding dog on its back window ledge.

"Can you still see him Jack?" Butcher chewed on a finger. Jack leaned further right.

"Yeah boss, he's still trying to get past the bus."

Chapter sixteen: One wedding and an almost funeral

"If Terry and June here would shove off, we'd be laughing."

A roundabout approached, and Danny dropped gears to make a fast turn. The Firestones held on the gravelled road. Moretti's Datsun's performance was yet to be tested.

Joe came at the roundabout with similar speed. Then a low flying seagull defecated across his line of vision. He snapped on the wiper switch and smeared the dropping further. His view obstructed, it took a further two miles of rough surfaced road before the rain cleared his windscreen. The gap between the two vehicles had widened, and Danny's rear view was clear. Confident he'd lost his pursuer, he turned into the slip road leading to Bayliss Park.

He parked the Alfa round the side of the garage, behind a row of vehicles waiting to be serviced. He got out of the car and hurried into the side entrance of the building.

There were petrol fumes in the air. George had changed a damaged fuel tank over the pit, and climbed into the vehicle's driving seat to move it away. The light he'd been working by was clamped to a copper pipe at the top of the inner pit wall and connected to its power source by a long extension, snaking across the floor. Rave music blasted out of the cassette player on the other side, and Danny, having called out twice to George, spotted Joe's Datsun turn into the forecourt. Danny stayed put, and watched him emerge from the car, then Butcher's XJ6 pull up behind him.

Realising for the first time he'd been tailed, Joe ran round to the side entrance where Danny had come in, but was followed by Jack's bulk just inside the doorway. There was a heated exchange of words that Danny couldn't hear. Butcher stepped out of his vehicle and sauntered through the front access towards them. While Danny watched unseen from behind a Jefferson hoist, George, at the far end of the pit, sat back in the Cavalier to enjoy the music, eyes closed.

Rooted to the spot where he stood, Joe sweated inside his heavy suit. His eyeballs swerved from Butcher to Jack, and back again.

"What's goin' on boys? Is there a problem?"

"I think you have something belonging to me, Moretti," said Butcher.

"Who, me? I dunno what you're on about." Joe took a backward step.

"So you've no idea why you've just spent the last seven years in prison?" said Jack in his deepest voice, stepping forward.

"I haven't got your money. Tony had all of it. The cops looked everywhere .... and again after he died. But they didn't find it. It was Danny Grimshaw. He's the one who's had it away."

Butcher exhaled in a long drawn out sigh. "Are there any more suspects you'd like to throw into the mix Moretti, apart from your dead brother and your young nephew? I think he's lying Jack. What do you think?"

Jack kept his eyes fixed on Moretti.

"I think he's been lying for so long, he doesn't know how to stand up straight any more. What shall I do with him, Boss?"

The piercing wail of a siren interrupted, and as it drew near the men stood still. Cars were heard braking in the forecourt, doors slammed, and within seconds three police officers approached. A plain clothes officer held up his badge as he came forward,

"Good afternoon, gentlemen. DCI Martin French." He stopped in front of Joe. "Joe Moretti? I'm arresting you in connection with the murder of Tony Moretti. You don't have to say anything, but if you do it may be used against you in a court of law."

Joe smiled. "You're having a laugh. You think I killed my own brother?"

"If you come with us, sir, we can discuss it at the station."

"I'm going nowhere with you. "You've nothing on me."

"There've been developments, and we need to ask you some questions. Don't make this difficult."

Joe stepped backwards.

"What developments? Tell me ... what bloody developments?"

The uniformed officers came forward. Joe took another two steps back. His heel snagged under the trailing cable and he toppled into the pit, crying out as he fell. The sudden jerk on the cable dislodged the clamp holding the bulb, and it fell crashing into the petrol soaked pit.

A flash of colourful sparks preceded the sudden ignition of petrol fumes and Joe tried to scramble his way out of the pit but panic prevented him.

"Help me for chrissakes!"

The officers were already there, grabbing an arm each and pulling him free of the flames, but his shoes were alight. Out of the shadows came Danny, fire extinguisher in hand, and soon had the pressurised foam trained on Joe's legs.

"Mind the fuckin' suit!" yelled Joe. "It's a Valentino!"

"Beg your pardon. I had this mad thought your skin was more precious." Danny redirected the nozzle into the pit while Joe stamped out the glowing remains of his shoes. He flopped onto the concrete floor with legs bent and hands holding his head.

Butcher watched in silence. The payback he'd come for was unlikely to happen now. The next best thing to hope for was a solid murder conviction.

Chapter sixteen: One wedding and an almost funeral

The pit still burned, and Danny's extinguisher was spent. At last, George sprang from the Cavalier, ran for another extinguisher, and kept the nozzle playing onto the flames until the pit was almost half filled with foam. Danny lowered himself to a sitting position on the ground next to his uncle. Joe sat hyperventilating.

"You need to slow your breathing Uncle Joe."

"Don't tell me how to fucking breathe, alright?"

"And George, turn that bloody awful music off will you? It's driving me nuts," said Danny.

"Mister Moretti, are you able to walk?" said the DCI.

"Shoes .... are knackered .... How can I walk without sodding shoes ..... knob head."

"Would you remove them please, so we can check your feet are ok?"

Joe gave the DCI a fierce look, but did as he was asked. His socks were untouched, and so were his feet.

"Well it looks like your shoes took the brunt," said the DCI. "Are they designer too?"

"Bloody Top Shop," said Joe, pushing his feet back into what remained. He brushed the surplus foam from his trousers, and stood up. "Right, let's get this over with."

The DCI turned to the rest of the group as officers led Moretti away.

"An officer will take your details before you go. You'll be required to make statements at some point. And Mister Grimshaw, it might be wise to give your electrics an overhaul. There could have been a fatality here today."

"I'll see to it Monday morning," said Danny.

Jack, eager to remove his boss from the scene, asked Butcher if he was almost ready to leave.

"No, Jack. I'll wait here. I want to speak to Danny. You can get away if you've given your details."

For Danny Grimshaw, the cost of rewiring was a more than welcome price to pay in exchange for his freedom to walk around in plain sight. So long as Joe was kept in custody, of course.

But a few days later not everyone was rejoicing. Several miles away at Windy Nook, Rosa Moretti sat in her armchair sorting through the contents of an old handbag. A Persian cat lay on the chair beside her, wedged between an arthritic leg and a shabby armrest. Rosa reached into the bag, pulling out a handful of British Rail locker tickets. She threw them onto the table in front of her. Tears coursed along the crevices in her cheeks as she reached into the bag yet again, and pulled out another handful, then another, in a rainbow of colours. She wept for her two dead children, and the injustice of having her least favourite's life spared.

Chapter seventeen : Losses recovered, freedoms gained.

It was growing dusk as Mel Butcher's XJ6 pulled into the car park outside St. Francis' Hospice, and his driver went to unbuckle his seat belt.

"There's no need to get out Jack," said Butcher. "I can take it from here."

"You sure Boss?"

"Take the car round the block. I'll be ten minutes or so."

"Butcher climbed out of the vehicle, patted his inside pocket and headed for the entrance.

Soft, classical music played in the background as he walked through the foyer, past the receptionist.

"Good afternoon, Mister Butcher."

"Afternoon, Carole. How has she been?"

"Elizabeth's rather tired today, but I'm sure she'll be pleased to see you. We'll be round with a late snack around six."

"Okay, I won't stay long."

Chapter seventeen : Losses recovered, freedoms gained

He slowed his footsteps approaching Lizzie's room and peered through the glass. Propped up on two pillows, Lizzie lay with her eyes closed. Butcher eased the door handle and entered the room. With curtains half drawn, light from the corridor exposed the transparency of her skin, stretched beyond limit across hands and face. A clock ticked somewhere. He sat in the armchair by her bed and waited.

"Maybe it's about time you changed that aftershave," she said, without lifting her eyelids.

"You said you liked this one. That's why I've been using it more often."

She opened one eye. "I've changed my mind. I can do that these days. People allow me. It's the entitlement of the dying." He acknowledged her resolute spirit with a grin. "What are you looking so pleased about?" she said. "You normally come here with a face like a slapped backside."

"I've brought you something I think you might be surprised to see." He lifted his good arm and felt for the box inside his coat pocket.

"Is it an overdose of morphine? I've been asking this lot for weeks, but they take no notice. My last request too."

"Well I'm glad you didn't get it, because then you wouldn't have been able to see this." He withdrew the long velvet covered box and placed it on the bed beside her.

"Oh goodness, is that what I think it is?"

"Shall I open it? I'll need to borrow one of your hands."

"I think you'd better."

The baguette cut of the diamonds picked up what little light was available and threw it tenfold back onto her worn out face. Without lifting her head from the pillow, she took the necklace out of its box and ran the cool stones through her fingers.

"How did you get it back? Have you seen the Moretti brothers?"

"Don't worry about that, Lizzie. It was given willingly, I promise you."

"I can't believe it. Did you get any of the money back?"

"It's been invested. My main concern was getting this back for you."

"Can you remember the day you gave it to me?"

"Like it was yesterday. Under a willow tree at Wardley park. We were having a picnic."

"And the would-be thief you managed to distract with a pilchard sandwich?"

He laughed at the memory. "Magpies are born wearing balaclavas. They can't be trusted."

Lizzie held the stones against her cheek. "Oh, thank you. You've made my day."

"Shall I get one of the nurses to put it on for you?"

"No, Mel. You take it home. Keep it somewhere safe."

"You sure?"

"Well, it's not as if I'm going anywhere posh enough to wear it, am I? It's enough to know we've got it back."

She replaced the necklace and closed the box as there was a tap on the door.

"I've brought you a cream horn and a pot of tea Elizabeth, if I can tempt you?" said the nurse.

"I don't think I can manage that, but come in love. Mister Butcher has to get back to his kingdom."

Butcher stood up, placed the jewellery box back in his pocket and kissed Lizzie's hand.

"I do. But I'll see you tomorrow."

"Bye Mister Butcher," said the nurse.

***

Just one week on from Joe Moretti's arrest, Steven gathered his stuff together ready for discharge from HMP Finchale Heads. It was five thirty in the morning, but Winston was wide awake. He lay on his bunk with a new paperback, scanning the text, unable to concentrate.

"You *sure* your Danny is meeting you, Stevie boy?" he said.

"Yep," said Steven. "Don't worry about me. What have you decided about this *other* problem?"

"Well, there's talk goin' around. They're sayin' that even with Moretti's prints on the murder weapon, it doesn't prove he shot his brother. If I don't come forward with what I know, he could be back out on the streets. But if I do, he'll find a way to get at me. Either way it's a bad result."

Steven stopped packing. "You need to speak to your brief. Tell him what happened. Ask his advice. He might be able to give you some odds on how it will go, whatever you decide."

"Yeah, I've been thinkin' that way too. Have you written your address down for me like we talked about? If you've changed your mind, I mean, that's ok, you know?"

Steven smiled, and busied himself again.

"It's on that piece of paper on the table, you silly sod. As if I'd change my mind."

A screw appeared in the open doorway.

"I'll be back in five minutes Grimshaw, to take you to the holding cell. There'll be a strip search, then we'll see about getting you processed at reception and you can be on your way."

"No problem. I'm nearly done here," said Steven, trying to push one of his 'How to' manuals into his holdall. Winston jumped down from his bunk.

"Let me give me you a hand with that, man. You haven't nicked this one from the library, have you?"

"They let me have it for a quid. Worth every penny for the memories."

"Don't know why you'd want to remember this place at all."

Steven stepped back and let him zip up the bag. The sound of it closing was like the end of something important, and although it ought to have been a time for celebration, there was a deep sadness too.

"It wasn't all bad. God knows, I could have had Pongo for a cell mate." He flashed Winston a regretful smile. "You know you can call me. The number's written down there too. Day or night, ok?"

The guard's footsteps approached.

"Give me a hug, man," said Winston.

***

Danny was already parked outside when his father came through the gates wearing blue flares and a striped tank top. Although there'd been visits and calls over the last few months, Steven still felt awkward to be driven away in a B.M.W. by the same son who carried a satchel to school just a short while ago. Or so it seemed to him.

Danny got out of the car.

"It's good to see you, Dad." He took Steven's bag and placed it on the ground, then gave him a big hug.

"What's going on today? I've had no hugs for forty years and then two in the last hour. Strange times we live in," said Steven, trying hard to ignore the tears stinging the back of his eyes. "You haven't ...... got a hanky have you?" His voice trembled. "Got a bit of a cold."

"I've some in the dash." Danny picked up his father's bag, put the other arm around his shoulders, and led him to the car.

"Tell you what Dad, we'll take you down town, get you some decent clothes, then we'll have a bite to eat, take a look around your new place of work...." He paused to sniff the air and wrinkled his nose. "Then back to mine for a shower, and maybe a squirt of Aramis."

"What do you mean by that, cheeky bugger?" said Steven. "I took a shower yesterday."

"It's not you, it's that place. It stinks of bad people," said Danny.

"And I'm one of them, don't forget."

Chapter seventeen : Losses recovered, freedoms gained

"You're a good person who did a bad thing, and you've served your time." said Danny, opening the passenger door for his father.

***

Steven had tasted almost seven months of freedom when daughter Louise gave birth to a baby boy sitting on the toilet while her husband mowed the lawn. She called out, but he couldn't hear above the motor. Five minutes later an ambulance pulled up outside the house, answering her 999 call. "You've got the wrong house," he told them.

"We can't take your word for that sir," said the paramedic. "Do you have a pregnant missus, by any chance?"

"Well, yes .... but ..."

"Then she may have just given birth in your bathroom. Excuse us ..."

Baby Matthew was a heavyweight, otherwise he may have disappeared down the pan altogether. The unsanitary birth made headlines in the local paper, and for a while it seemed everyone knew Louise and Michael's new baby. Everyone that was, except his grandfather.

Establishing family contact again after so many years away was a subject that Steven preferred to put off until tomorrow. He'd telephone Catherine, and she would chat, but he couldn't face walking down his old street again after all that had happened. He may have been able to buy new clothes, but the limp would always betray him. And what of Louise? Would she still hate him?

By December that year, stubbornness and procrastination were still holding firm, so Catherine sent her brother a 'Happy Christmas Grandad' card 'with love from baby Matthew – born 10th August 1995'

Steven already knew about Matthew. Danny now paid regular visits to his sister's new family, but his father always declined to come along. So, all Catherine could do was to wait. And wait. By the time New Year came around, she'd resigned herself to the fact she'd wasted a perfectly good 19p postage stamp.

One Sunday morning in early January, Molly fidgeted in front of the television set with the remote control in her hand. Catherine was upstairs pouring Parazone into the lavatory bowl when the sound volume from Songs of Praise suddenly soared to ear splitting proportions.

Shit! What now?

And to make matters worse, Skipper kept adding to the din with cries of, "***Abandon ship!***" and "***Man the lifeboats!***"

Expecting a mob of purple-faced neighbours on the doorstep at any moment, she ran downstairs to find Molly lying on her side with the remote control wedged between her body and the floor. An empty half bottle of Johnnie Walker's lay next to her, and no amount of tugging would shift either her mother or the remote. Catherine regretted the double whisky given at Doris's suggestion to help Molly sleep two nights earlier. But desperate for sleep herself, she'd given it without a second thought, and Molly had gone out like a light. The following evening Molly was agitated and began emptying the sideboard, so Cathy hid the bottle behind the washing machine. But today, the sleuth had outwitted her.

Payback for wanting some rest. Selfish me.

Cathy began to panic. Questions entered her mind and escaped from her mouth such as, "Where are those purple-faced neighbours when you need them?" and, "Whatever happened to proper knobs on the telly?"

She now found herself with two new problems. Firstly, where to hide future trophies from the hunter, and secondly, how to explain to social services at some point in the future how Molly had slipped into alcoholism unnoticed.

Go to prison. Do not collect two hundred pounds.

Molly lay on the floor chuckling to herself in blissful repose. Her health didn't appear to be under any imminent threat other than from a nasty hangover, which could be hours away.

The rubber plant on top of the television vibrated to the decibels when the inevitable knock on the door happened. The posse from the street must have arrived. When she opened the door, there he stood, a bit balder, a bit late, but nevertheless her very welcome big brother.

"Hi Pipsqueak," he said. "Are you deaf?"

"Steven!" she said, grabbing his arm and half dragging him into the living room. "You've got to help me move mother. She's lying on the remote."

The telly still blasted. The rubber plant, by then, teetered on the edge of suicide. Within seconds, Steven had pulled the plug on the din, rescued the ungrateful plant and saved the whole street from eternal deafness. But aside from all that, his mere presence made his sister very happy indeed.

Returning their mother to an upright position and state of sobriety however, might take a little longer.

Steven leaned over his mother and sniffed the air. "Has she been drinking?"

"That bottle was well hidden."

"So she's not ill then?"

Of course she's not ill. Look at the grin on her face. Happy as a sand boy."

"Right, well, how about you take the legs and I'll grasp her under the arms?"

"That means you get the heavy end. I'm not being funny, but your balance isn't much better than hers."

Chapter seventeen : Losses recovered, freedoms gained

"Well I can't let you take the top end. You're a woman."

Catherine stood up straight and exhaled, loudly. "That caveman attitude is no longer acceptable since you've been inside." She shrugged. "Why don't we just leave her here for a bit? You've rescued the TV. She's content."

Steven raised eyebrows, but didn't argue. His sister seemed to know what she was doing, and who was he but a stranger to all of this?

"Sit yourself down and I'll put the kettle on." Catherine was already in the kitchen, running the tap. He followed her in.

"I can see I've a lot to catch up on. Do you get any help from social services?"

"Would you like a biscuit?" she said, opening a cupboard. "There's chocolate digestives, garibaldis or ginger nuts."

"Yes, anything you've got handy."

"Have a seat then, I'll be through in a minute."

Steven felt like a spare part. He went back into the living room, stepped over his sleeping mother and sat on the couch. Catherine reappeared with tea and biscuits.

"Thanks for the gingers, Pipsqueak," he said. "I didn't think you'd remember."

She sat, smiled at him, pulled down the sleeves of her sweater and picked up her mug.

"Sorry I didn't answer your question. But no, I don't get help. Not official help like you mean anyway. Anyway, Doris helps me loads. I don't know what I'd do without her."

"And..... who's Doris?"

"Oh, that's a story for another time," she said. "I want to know about you. I know we've written a few letters and had a few phone calls, but I wanted a proper conversation about, you know, the elephant in the room."

Steven grinned, glancing across to his mother.

"Yes, ok," laughed Catherine, "I know Molly's gained a bit of weight over the years, but I wouldn't call her an elephant just yet." She pushed her spectacles back to the bridge of her nose. "No, I mean, well, you asked if I get any help, and I'm asking *if you've* had any help .... you know, in coming to terms with what happened, why it happened. And being sure that it would never happen again if you met someone else."

Steven cleared his throat and knitted his brows. "Talk about straight to the point, Pipsqueak. If I tell you everything's fine, you wouldn't buy it, would you?"

"You'd have to make a bit more effort than that, sorry Steven."

He shuffled in his seat, tugged on his ear and took a gulp of tea.

"Well, first off, it's unlikely. That I'll meet someone else, I mean. If it happens sometime in the future we can talk about it then. But I need to get used to just being me in the world, and to keep working on myself. In 1985, and up to '87 in Gartree, I had some talking therapy."

"I'd no idea. How did that go?"

He lowered his head and gazed at the floor. "Bloody hell, Cath, that's the same carpet!"

She followed his gaze. "Course it is. What did you expect? We're not the Rockefellers in case you hadn't noticed. And stop the diversion tactics. I'm on to you." She screwed up her eyes in a menacing stare.

He showed a relenting palm. "Okay, fine! ... Well, first couple of sessions, nothing could be prised out of these lips. Zipped up and locked down. Then they gave me a note book and I had these exercises to do; writing down how I felt about myself in relation to ... well, everyone else around me. I can't blame everything on the disability, but it played a big part in the low self esteem, and the desperation to hold on to Wendy no matter what. So in many ways, even though I hate the coward who threw her against that wall, I understand him better. I never meant for her to die ... I just couldn't listen to all those cruel things she was saying."

"You could have walked away."

"Don't you think I wished I had? A split second is all it takes to ruin a family. I've spent a long time going over all of it, again and again."

"But you've made some sort of peace with yourself? Still dragging on that poor earlobe I see. You'll be able to wear it as a scarf before long."

Steven raised half a smile. "I'm working on that problem too. But seriously, it seems unfair that I had to build confidence. To forgive what I did. And it's selfish .... when I'd taken another life. Why should I deserve to be fixed?" He took another drink.

"But there was no other choice really. Other than doing what Dad did to himself, and that would have been another blow to the family. Or maybe not?" He paused, watching her face.

"I'm not about to stroke your ego just yet. Keep going."

"Well, two funerals within weeks of each other, I mean who could afford that? Unless you stuck me in a freezer indefinitely."

"That could have been an option," she said, "and will continue to be if you don't get on with it."

He'd been away for too long. When did all these changes happen?

"So, I studied, got some qualifications in a subject I already knew a lot about. And now, I'm thinking it was the right thing to do."

Chapter seventeen : Losses recovered, freedoms gained

Catherine put down her mug and sighed. "That's the longest speech I've ever heard you make. I suppose I have to give you a bit of credit now. As long as you continue with that determination, you have my support. You're my big brother remember, and I'm so proud of you right now ... for the speech, especially."

"Thanks Cath. Just don't expect me to do that ever again ... please."

"So it's *Cath* now, is it? What happened to Pipsqueak?"

Steven sighed. "I think Pipsqueak grew up."

She managed a weak smile. "I'm gonna have to ask you to stand up now," she said.

Steven got up from the sofa. "Okay...What now? A good thrashing?"

"I need to give you one of those hugs Danny says you're having trouble with in the modern world."

Steven tried his awkward best to comply, while Skipper paced back and forth on his perch. He'd been quiet for too long.

"Where's Fred?" His rasping voice interrupted the mood.

"I can't believe he's still saying that." said Steven. "Since the first day Dad brought him home. Did you find who Fred might be?"

"Haven't a clue. I thought he was meaning to say 'Ted,' and he'd got it wrong. But he never gets anything wrong. He's such a great mimic. That time Joe was here he did Benji's growl and scared the crap out of him."

The sound of the back door opening made them start.

"Are you decent? Because I'm coming in."

"That's not him too, is it?" said Steven.

Catherine got up. "No, that'll be Doris. She can give us a hand with mother."

Chapter seventeen : Losses recovered, freedoms gained

Chapter eighteen : The cavalry cometh

With Steven back on the family network and making regular visits, it was easier to invite everyone round for Sunday tea. Often, there'd be seven or eight guests at once with four chairs between them. Baby Matthew was happy enough with the floor, and Molly with her wheelchair. Danny's girlfriend at the time was a mental health nurse and so good with Molly, she supervised all of her trips to the little girls' room, thus preserving Catherine's clean hands for making the sandwiches.

"I don't know how you cope with her on your own, Cath," said Danny, during one of Molly's toilet breaks. "She's been good today, but I know she has behaviours." Catherine threw Steven a glance. He'd witnessed a lot over the last few weeks.

"Your dad told you then?"

"I can see your cheek's a bit bruised."

Steven cleared his throat. "No need to cover for me, Danny. Yes, I told him, Cath. It might be your eye next time."

"You can get help," said Danny. "Respite. Hannah knows all about this stuff. She deals with social services all the time. Ask her when she comes out of the bathroom.

Chapter eighteen : The cavalry cometh

"It's been ten years, Cathy," said Louise. "It's time to take something back for yourself."

"Take what back? A few days with my feet up?"

"It's a start. A chance to do something new. Build a life."

***

When Monday morning came around, Catherine telephoned social services requesting a home visit. Doris insisted on being there when the social worker arrived. She'd been through the same process with Ted, weeks before his suicide, and she wanted to make sure Catherine's application would have the right outcome.

On the day, Molly's old dressing gown was banished to the laundry basket, the living room carpet was sprayed with 'shake 'n' vac' and Doris loaned Catherine her lipstick. The television was switched off, and Molly was disgruntled.

Doris kept watch from the window. "Eh up," she said. "Strange car pulling up outside. Young fella with a clipboard. Still wet behind the ears. Oh, and he's got one of those handbags."

Catherine peered over Doris's shoulder. "You mean a man bag. Oh, there's another one. She's got a face on her. Enough to turn milk sour. Look at the size of *her* bag."

"Wonder what she keeps in there."

"Her other face? Handcuffs?"

"Two against two. That's fair."

"We're not planning a fight, are we?"

"Doesn't hurt to be prepared," said Doris.

"I'll get the door."

They introduced themselves as Susan Thom and Gerry Murray, which tickled Doris straight off, though it was clear from their formal introductions they were unaccustomed to humour. Thom was the elder, by at least ten years and appeared to be showing young Gerry the ropes. Catherine offered drinks which they both declined, and a comfortable sofa which Thom examined before perching on the edge. A waft of pine from the carpet permeated the room, and the sofa percher screwed up her nose in a non appreciative way.

"Now, Miss Grimshaw," said Thom, "if you can begin by telling us why you've asked for a new assessment today?"

Do I stand? Feels like a courtroom.

Catherine began. "It's hard to know where to start."

Thom waved her hand. "There are no rules. Just tell us how things have been."

"Right. Well .... I don't know if you can imagine this, but last week I answered the door to the postman. When I came back inside, Molly was conditioning her hair with the contents of her incontinence pad." She took a breath and looked from one to the other, but Thom remained unresponsive, while Gerry began to fill his notebook at speed. She continued. "Everything I do ... shopping, cleaning, going to the toilet is squeezed into the gaps around her. I get up at five in the morning to take a shower before she wakes up. Sorry for the graphic details."

"No need to apologise," said Gerry. "Please continue."

She paused again, and swallowed. "This whole caring thing was sprung on me. Overnight, I swapped business studies for ...toileting business, and having to memorise an endless list of medical conditions..... the drugs she needs..... how much, how often......... and not knowing when she's about to swing a punch. Doris is a great help. She sits with her if I need to collect prescriptions, or have appointments of my own, but I'd like some leisure time, you know. I don't remember the last time I went to the pub, or out with friends." Catherine's face flushed, and she lowered her gaze.

"Where's Fred?" said Skipper. Gerry craned his neck to see who was talking.

Molly's eyes flitted from Thom to Gerry and back again. She pulled a slipper from her foot, hurled it across the room. Thom flinched, and Catherine continued.

"Not that I have any friends, mind you. Not anymore. Sometimes I think if I look hard enough, those bits of myself I misplaced somewhere over the last ten years will turn up. The world moves on without me. Nothing changes. Ever."

Molly leaned forward in her chair. "Eurotrash!" she said. Gerry looked uneasy.

"Well, you sound like you're a little depressed," said Thom.

Bit of an understatement.

"Maybe an appointment with your G.P. will sort that for you."

So that's one problem solved. Go on, tick a box.

"And although I hear what you're saying, that's not quite what I asked, is it? You see, today we're just here to see if your mother's needs have changed, and then we can decide what happens with any package of care she may or may not be entitled to. We'll be asking her some questions, and getting her to perform some tasks."

"Well, good luck with that," said Doris. Catherine looked defeated.

"Take the High Road!" shouted Molly, and removed a second slipper. Gerry's face twitched on one side.

Chapter eighteen : The cavalry cometh

"Perhaps Gerry can start us off with the questions?" Thom continued. "Take it from the top, Gerry."

"Is she all right?" Gerry asked Catherine. "Does she want us to leave?"

"Of course she does," said Catherine. "You've stopped her watching Richard and Judy. Carry on. And get ready to duck."

Remember to bring a crash helmet next time. With a visor.

Gerry gave a nervous cough and shuffled his papers. "Now, Missus Grimshaw... Molly, can I call you Molly? Would that be ok for you?"

Molly stared at Gerry and frowned. "Ted's dead," she said.

"Right," said Gerry, looking at Catherine, then at Doris. "Is that something I need to know?"

"Well, you should know it already if you've read through the case notes," said Doris.

"I see," said Gerry, "but it's not relevant to today's visit." he looked at Thom.

"Where's Fred?"

"Is there something we can get the bird?"

"We'll be here all day," said Thom, snatching the clipboard from Gerry, "I'll do it." She fixed her gaze on Molly, and Molly returned her stare.

"Molly, can I ask how far you can walk without your chair? Can you get to the kitchen perhaps? Holding on to the furniture of course." Thom almost managed a smile at this point.

"He's dead," said Molly with emphasis. "Ted's dead."

"Well, we're not getting far at all are we?" said Thom, looking less smiley by the second.

"As a matter of fact," said Catherine, "I think we've made amazing progress. It's taken a decade to get Molly to say that, and to understand it."

Might give her a Hobnob for that.

Thom looked down at her clipboard and ticked another box. "Of course it's not just Molly's capabilities we're assessing today, there's also a question over her vulnerability. I have a risk assessment to complete with regard to a family member who has recently been released from prison we understand?"

Oo..I'm not having that, cheeky mare!

Cathy stood up. "Vulnerability? You mean you think my brother...who is also her son by the way, would harm his own mother? Is that what you're saying?"

Thom sensed some rattling of cages. "Our job is to assess the current risk, with regard to your mother."

Chapter eighteen : The cavalry cometh

"That idea is just ridiculous!" said Catherine with an incredulous laugh. "She's more likely to kill *him*.....kill the lot of us!"

"Hang on a minute," Doris interjected, "I remember who you are now.... you're Chrissie Logan's daughter aren't you? I used to see you playing hopscotch on the Woodbine Estate when you were meant to be in school back in the day."

"That's highly unlikely."

"You *are* Chrissie Logan's daughter, aren't you?" Doris persisted.

"We don't disclose personal details...."

"Your mother did time herself, didn't she? Benefit fraud, wasn't it? And failing to pay her TV license. How is she doing now?"

Thom gathered her papers together and urged Gerry to do the same. "I think we have all we need now, Miss Grimshaw. When we've typed up the new assessment we'll send you a copy in the post."

"You won't forget, will you," said Doris, "what happened to Ted after you lot refused his request for help last time? This young lady here is desperate for some support. I'd hate to think social services were turning their backs again."

"We'll be in touch," came the response, and with that, they were out of the door faster than a toupee in a hurricane.

"Thanks for saving me, Doris," said Cathy after they'd gone. "I was about to clobber her then."

"You went from Minnie Mouse to Raging Bull in sixty seconds. Mind you, if she doesn't offer you any help after today, I'll happily let you do your worst next time."

Three weeks later, a brown envelope arrived on the mat.

'Following our recent home visit on ..... I am pleased to inform you that funding has been approved for a package of care in favour of your mother, Molly Grimshaw. The respite care providers listed below are informed of the funding award and will be telephoning to arrange visits at your convenience.'

Cathy got all excited. She gave her mother an exuberant hug and a kiss. "You're having a holiday Molly! Can you believe it? After all this time!" She read the letter again, just in case she'd imagined it, then waved it about and laughed. "Woo hoo!" she shrieked, then ran to the telephone to let the world know. Molly grimaced. "Cream crackers!" she said.

There was only one care home on the list that might suit Molly. Haven View said they could accommodate her for seven consecutive days in two weeks time. Catherine could hardly wait.

Chapter eighteen : The cavalry cometh

On the day Molly was collected, Cathy took her breakfast straight back to bed and read the morning paper until she got bored, then had a proper soak in the bath that lasted longer than the usual five minutes. She went clothes shopping in town and treated herself to frothy coffee and a sticky bun. In the evening she watched Coronation Street from start to finish without interruption, and supped two glasses of wine with feet on the sofa before bed. She could not remember a more self indulgent time. But as the week wore on, she did begin to miss her mother.

As the day approached for Molly's return, Catherine took a call from Haven View to say Molly had been admitted to hospital suffering from pains to her abdomen. She wasn't ill as such, and the admission was just a precaution. Cathy wasn't too worried, but rang to inform the family, and Doris, who offered to go with her that evening for visiting.

Molly was sitting up in bed hugging her knees, watching random visitors from behind them.

"Hello Molly, how's the tummy?" said Catherine. "Does it still hurt?"

Molly made no acknowledgement. Cathy looked around.

"Wonder if I can find a nurse to ask."

"Shall I go?" said Doris.

"Would you mind? I'll just put these clean clothes in her locker."

"Don't move. I won't be long."

Doris reappeared minutes later with a large staff nurse. Thighs chafing as she walked.

"Hello, can I help?"

"Hi, sorry to bring you over, when you're busy" said Catherine, "I just wondered what was going on with Molly's stomach. Have you found out what it is?"

"That's not a problem," the nurse said. "Are you familiar with faecal impaction?"

"I've seen that movie," said Doris. "Glen Close was proper scary in that."

Cathy smiled. "You mean she's constipated?"

"That's right," said the nurse, "but badly so. We've tried giving her something orally, but she won't cooperate, so tonight we'll be giving her an enema"

"I've also seen 'Rear Window,' and 'Back Side Story,' continued Doris.

"Right, well she may not take kindly to that," said Catherine. "When she gets constipated at home, I give her Andrews Liver Salts disguised in orange squash. She rather likes that."

"Well that wouldn't look so professional on hospital notes," the nurse said.

Chapter eighteen : The cavalry cometh

"And 'Gone with the Wind,'" Doris chipped in further.

"We'll be sticking with the enema for now," the nurse confirmed, throwing Doris a hostile look.

"Ok, thanks for the update," Catherine gave her mother a look of concern as the nurse returned to her station.

"Have you had an enema before, Doris?" said Catherine.

"Every other Thursday, without fail. No, of course I haven't, but how bad can it be?"

"You're right. It'll all be over by tomorrow."

The following day, Catherine rang Molly's ward to find out how the enema had gone.

"Oh, I was about to ring you," said the nurse, "there's been a slight setback I'm afraid."

"What kind of setback?"

"Your mother fell out of bed in the night and has broken her pelvis. I'm so sorry."

"But I don't understand. How could that happen? She has side rails on the bed doesn't she?"

"Molly was being helped out of bed to go to the toilet," explained the nurse, "that's when the accident happened. She became agitated. The nurse couldn't hold onto her. We've had to move her to Ward 18, where she'll get the appropriate care for her injuries. I'm really sorry."

Molly was out of it when Catherine and Doris visited that evening. In a side room all to herself, she lay completely flat, sedated, with a feeding tube up her nose and IV fluids connected to the back of one hand. It was a shock to see such a difference from the alert people watcher of the night before. Cathy wanted to take her home and make her better, felt guilty for instigating the whole respite process and the way she and Doris had influenced the decision. If she'd sneaked the Andrews Liver Salts into the care home at the right time, this might never have happened.

They didn't stay for the whole visiting hour. No-one at the hospital gave any assurances. It was a case of 'wait and see.'

The only thing Catherine could think of doing with her time at home was to clear the kitchen cupboards of useless junk, something she planned to repeat later with the wardrobes and garden shed.

By the third evening, Molly still hadn't stirred, and by the fourth, she'd suffered a stroke. The nurses assured Catherine it wasn't a bad one, and there was still hope that she could make a full recovery. But by the fifth day, Molly had a relapse. Her pelvic injury showed no sign of healing, and she'd developed an infection. Sepsis followed soon afterwards, and her organs began to fail. As visiting restrictions were lifted, the family filtered in and out of the ward to say goodbye.

It was difficult to know what to say to her mother in those final days, but there was one half hour that Catherine spent with her the day before she died that made her feel, rightly or wrongly, they had somehow connected. She began to tell her mother, event by event, what had been happening with the family since Molly became unwell, as though she could catch up with all the news to take away with her. There was Wendy's murder and Steven's imprisonment, her own exam results, Ted's suicide and Benji's arthritis, Louise's wedding, Matthew's birth, and Danny's business success. She thought it better not to mention the crime which had enabled the latter, and if she had, most of that would have been guesswork anyway. When she got to the bit about Steven's release from prison and how he'd been re-instated into the family as number one granddad, Molly's bottom lip quivered; a tear broke free from the corner of one eye, using a southbound wrinkle path to her ear. It was the first humane response Catherine had witnessed from her mother in over a decade, and an immense sadness came over her for the loss of the person who was, the mother/daughter relationship that might have been, and the life only half lived.

Chapter nineteen : A grand day out at The Purple Dolphin

After the funeral, there were letters to write, phone calls to make and bills to pay. The Benefits Agency was hot on her heels for the return of Molly's attendance allowance which Catherine had failed to stop while her mother was in hospital. The town hall were close behind, since her council tax support had ended, and full payment was now due. Catherine felt lost. There was no structure to her days. Thumb twiddling was fine in small doses, but without something useful to fill the gaps, it kind of lost its appeal. After so many years of acting and dressing middle aged, she'd forgotten she was just thirty three years old. Never mind her mother's wasted life, what about hers? This was her time, and there was to be no more wasting of it.

She needed a job, but the bills wouldn't wait while she updated her skills. The job centre offered a basic course in computing, and though she'd have preferred something more advanced, she had to accept or lose her benefits.

Doris offered a course of her own on the skills of frivolous shopping, which she insisted was vital to counterbalance the seriousness of Catherine's new circumstances. So this became a weekly activity, and while out on one of their expeditions, Doris stopped outside 'House of

Fraser' and grabbed Cathy's arm. "This shop's got my name on it, Cathy," she said, tugging on her sleeve.

"Whaaaat? But we never go in here."

"Well, we do today. I have a hyphenated surname you remember, and we're just as entitled to be in this store as anyone else."

Cathy followed. The make-up counter with all its expensiveness, was the first stop for Doris, and she tested every product there was for the sampling. She'd just tried what she thought was a pan stick on the back of her hand, when an assistant pounced.

"Good afternoon, ladies, is there anything I can help you with today?"

Doris looked up at the made-up face.

"Well, this colour's just the job for covering the liver spots on me hand, but will it make the next man I meet want to plant a smacker on me lips?"

The counter assistant turned down her mouth at the two unclassifiable women before her, who had clearly wandered into the wrong shop. But she wasn't one to resist a challenge from time to time.

"Perhaps you ladies would like to take advantage of our free makeover, which we're offering to selected customers for this afternoon only." She presented a flyer to Doris, flashed a sparkling set of veneers between scarlet lips, and continued. “There‘s no obligation to buy of course, but we do hope you’ll be so impressed with what our wonderful range can do, that you won’t be able to stop yourselves from purchasing at least one of them.” She opened her mouth to flash again, when Doris interrupted.

“Well, I’m always up for a freebie.” She turned to Catherine, “What about you love? Are you game ‘n’ all?”

It was Catherine’s turn to grab a sleeve. “Why have you suddenly gone all broad Geordie?” she whispered to Doris. “Trying to show us up, or what?”

“Not *us*. I’m trying to show *her* up. She’s so far up herself it’s a wonder she doesn’t suffocate. Just smile. You’re with Aunty Doris.

“What d’ya think our Cath? Shall we do it?”

“Oh I don’t think I can spare the time.....it’ll take hours.”

“Don’t be daft.” Doris scolded. “You’ve nothing to rush home for, remember? And it won’t take long to make you look gorgeous. For me, it’ll take beer goggles and a flippin’ time machine.”

Catherine wavered, but the assistant was by now lifting up the counter flap to let them through into a small, screened off area with two high stools, a table top laid with rows of bottles, tubes and scary looking plug in contraptions, surrounded by four huge mirrors to reflect every angle and fault of nature. They were even offered free coffee before the lippy went on.

At the end of their allotted time, Doris and Cathy emerged from the shop like a pair of mannequins escaped from the display window, having spent just six pounds fifty on a mascara between them. Catherine's shoulder length auburn hair was piled up into an elegant French pleat, her pretty green eyes had been emphasised with a subtle shade of shadow, and her bone structure had been brought out with clever strokes from a fat bristled brush. In complete contrast but equally stunning, Doris could have entered an Elizabeth Taylor look-alike competition with Liz herself competing, and won it hands down.

"What shall we do now then?" said Cathy, amused by the absurdity of the day so far.

"Oh, blow it," said Doris. "Let's go to The Purple Dolphin for afternoon tea."

The Dolphin was a mere stone's throw away from the bustle and banter of Oldcastle's Haymarket, but culturally it was in a different world. Maybe it was the confidence boost of House of Fraser's salon treatments, or just plain nosiness, but Doris and Catherine headed down Grainger Street with hair dos held high, in the direction of a new world.

The four star dining experience at the Purple Dolphin, more than lived up to expectations.

Polished oak, to looking glass standard covered the floors in the foyer and corridors. And in the ladies' powder room the golden shag pile was fit to bury a pair of stilettos, with clearance. In the restaurant there were three very grand, tailored bow windows, and the rich walnut dining tables were each laid with a woven cloth of English lace. Fresh strawberries and a fat layer of whipped double cream oozed from Doris's cinnamon scone. Catherine took her first sip of lapsang souchong and decided to keep the taste surprise to herself. But as Doris lifted her own cup to her lips, Cathy smirked and Doris received the alert.

"What's up with you?" she said, "Is it bad?"

"Shall we say it's different?"

Doris took a sip and screwed up her face. "Give me a Tetley's any day of the week. This is a waste of hot water."

On the way out through the foyer, a hand written advertisement pinned to an oak-framed notice board attracted Catherine's attention.

RECEPTIONIST REQUIRED TO HELL WITH CUSTOMERS' REQUIREMENTS. ASK AT RECEPTION FOR DETAILS.

"Oh I say, Doris, look at that."

Doris read the notice. "Oh dear, that might upset the toffs. Do you think one of the urchins from the scullery made that little slip of the pen on purpose?"

Chapter nineteen : A grand day out at The Purple Dolphin

"You know, a job like that could be just what I need. What do you think?"

***

Back home, Catherine dug out her old typewriter from the bottom of Molly's wardrobe, buried beneath bundles of cards and letters. She promised herself Molly's stuff must be sorted through soon, but right now she had just two days to fill out the job application and compose some sort of curriculum vitae. A dash to John Menzies for a new typewriter ribbon brought it to late afternoon when she rolled the paper into the machine and filled it up in minutes. She could do this.

Ted always said that reward came from effort, and as if to prove his point, there she was, ten days after posting her application, sitting in The Purple Dolphin Hotel waiting for her very first proper job interview. An assortment of six other candidates sat in random seats around her. To Catherine's reasoning, all were more suited to the job than herself. An older more matronly type, dressed in navy blue with a pill box hat and a very pink face sat opposite. A stickler no doubt, for punctuality and perfect for biting off the heads of awkward patrons. Sitting next to her, was a life sized Barbie doll complete with Wonderbra cleavage and a vacant stare, who would most likely be hired on the spot. Her analysis of candidate number three was almost underway when Catherine's name was called, and she followed the receptionist along a short corridor leading to the interview room.

Four panel members took turns asking questions apart from an older female who seemed to be snoozing. Catherine took a deep breath before each answer she gave, which helped calm her nerves. It was a tip she'd learned in college for public speaking which had stayed with her. Of course she had to explain the ten year gap in her CV, but she kept her answers clear and concise, and overall she felt she hadn't done too badly. If nothing else, it was a trial run for future interviews. And so she carried on searching.

Dissatisfied with the job centre's offerings, she scanned newspapers and phoned colleges for advice on courses. Then nephew Danny offered to teach her to drive. She'd had two failures already, but at a very young age. Maybe now was the time.

It was two weeks after The Purple Dolphin interview, when Doris popped round one morning, two hours earlier than her usual slot, and rapped on the back door. Cathy abandoned her teeth brushing to let her in. Doris entered the kitchen, brandishing a brown envelope. "You'll never guess what..." she said with a self satisfied grin. "I've got a job." She almost skipped to a kitchen chair. Catherine swallowed a mouthful of toothpaste.

Chapter nineteen : A grand day out at The Purple Dolphin

"What do you mean, you've got a job? It's me who's looking, not you. .... Anyway," she said, "aren't you collecting your old age pension by now?" Catherine closed the door and came over to the table. A splodge of blue foam lingered at the corner of her mouth.

"So what if I am? I've a few good years left in me yet. At least, that's what The Purple Dolphin seems to think...." Doris spoke the hotel's name with a deliberate nonchalant air.

"You've never got that job I went after?"

"Hardly," laughed Doris. "Do I look like a receptionist?"

Catherine considered. "Not in a hotel, maybe.....but a tanning salon...yeah, somewhere like that. Does the Dolphin have a tanning salon?"

"It's got a gym."

"Oh, you'd be all wrong for a gym, Doris. No offence." As Catherine's lips moved, the blue foam splodge became animated.

"Lucky for you, none taken. I've got the chambermaid's job. I didn't tell you about it because I thought you might poke fun ... which is what you've just done if you didn't realise ... and anyway, if you're going to be out at work all day I'll need something to fill in the time."

"Oh, I'm sorry, Doris. Congratulations. I'm glad for you, honestly."

"So you haven't heard anything about the receptionist's job yet?"

"No. But I've been offered a toilet attendant's post for the summer at the top end of Marsden Beach." She tried an optimistic smile, but failed.

"Have you checked this morning's post yet? I just got my letter five minutes since."

Catherine stood up. "Not yet, but...." She left the room and returned with one white and one brown envelope, ripping open the white one. She paused as she read. "Well, this is very nice."

"What is?"

"It's a cheque for Molly's life insurance. What a palaver I've had to get this."

"And the other one?" Doris asked.

Catherine opened the second envelope, went quiet, and lowered the letter onto the table. "I don't believe it," she whispered.

"What?"

"I've got it," said Catherine, "I've bloody well got it!"

Doris stood up. "You do mean you've got the job, and not some fatal illness? You're actually foaming at the mouth."

"C'mon Doris, we share everything don't we?" Cathy wrapped her arms around Doris. "Even rabies."

Chapter nineteen : A grand day out at The Purple Dolphin

Chapter twenty : Personal delivery services

Catherine stood in front of the hall mirror and checked her appearance for the umpteenth time. She wore the navy suit and standard white blouse the hotel had issued her with the week before, and a shade of lipstick she wasn't quite certain about. She watered the cheese plant and hummed a relaxing tune, one of Ted's all time favourites, 'Into the valley of death' or something similar. Then she checked her appearance for a final time, removed the uncertain lipstick with a tissue and went out into the big wide world carrying a zipped leather case under her arm and a swarm of butterflies in her stomach.

***

"...and the third floor... ees favoured by our more affluent guests...phew!" Marcus, the hotel manager caught his breath, along with his broken English accent as they stopped to rest on the third stair landing. Marcus was a thin stick of a man swallowed up by his pin striped suit. As he spoke, his overly large chin bobbed up and down like a piece of headland in an earthquake. But his shoes were beautiful. Catherine always appreciated fine Italian leather. She took a few laboured breaths herself.

Chapter twenty : Personal delivery services

"Not only more affluent," she gasped, "but also ... much fitter. Isn't the lift working?"

"Oh ... the manager prefers the staff to take the stairs .... or the service leeft, which ees over there...." Marcus pointed to a pair of extra wide metal doors at the far end of the corridor.

"But..... I thought *you* were the manager?"

Marcus deliberated. "Ee, yes. That ees so."

As Catherine puzzled, the doors parted and Doris the chambermaid backed out into the hallway, dragging her cleaning trolley into the corridor. Her blue and white striped overall with matching lace trimmed hat was an instant identifier. As was the trolley with its defective wheel.

"The service leeft.... ees being used by the cleaners at the moment, as you can see," Marcus continued, "so eet's best we geeve them space and use the staircase instead. Sorry 'bout that."

As they walked past Doris and her trolley, she straightened its wheels, winked at Catherine and trundled off in the opposite direction.

"I will let you see these rooms, so you can compare them to those on the first floor....and then I have to leave you." Marcus rattled a fat bunch of keys in a nearby lock and pushed open the door. Catherine stepped inside a luxurious suite with every amenity. Velvet window drapes hung in perfectly proportioned folds; there was a remote controlled TV, video and hi-fi at the foot of a king sized bed, framed in polished brass. Persian rugs cushioned the parquet flooring, and for business clientele, a solid oak desk stood in one corner, with telephone, fax machine and word processor. And by the side of it, an upholstered swivel chair.

"We have to be getting along eef you are ready...." Marcus's voice interrupted Catherine's grander thoughts, and made her smile as she turned and hurried back out.

"So what now..? Top floor?" she asked, not welcoming another flight of stairs.

"Oh no," said Marcus, locking the door behind them. "The top floor ees for board meetings, and the director has a suite of rooms up there. I can show you the board room on another day eef you like, but we are a leettle pushed for time at the moment."

She followed Marcus's hurried footsteps to the head of the stairway.

"So, who is the director? Does he or she have anything to do with the staff?"

Marcus spoke as fast as he moved. "No, the CEO Meester Spence oversees all of that. The director ees very private person. He deals only with Meester Spence, but we are like leenks in the chain you understand? Customer complaints, staff problems, pass first through me, then to Meester Spence, and only eef catastrophe, to the director. System work very well."

Chapter twenty : Personal delivery services

Cathy was having trouble keeping up in her heeled shoes as Marcus skipped without effort down the stairs.

"You have met Teresa, my wife on reception?"

"Yes. We introduced ourselves first thing this morning."

"I shall take you back there....She wants to show you one or two procedures, and then thees afternoon, the catering manager shows you the restaurant." He glanced at his watch as they reached the ground floor. "I have a meeting.with Meester Spence ... three minutes ago!"

"Oh, you go on," insisted Catherine, "I can find my own way back to reception."

"Thank you," said Marcus. "He cannot abide lateness." He gave her a polite but hassled look, and was gone.

***

With her styled bouffant and padded shoulders, Teresa's silhouette could have passed for that of Johnny Bravo,* as she sorted the mail behind reception. She looked up from the desk as Catherine reached the bottom stair.

**Johnny Bravo is an animated television series created by Van Partible for Cartoon Network*

"Oh, Catherine, darling ..." she said, "I know you've just come back down, but could you do me a huge favour and take this letter up to 315?"

She's kidding, right?

"Back up to the third floor?" asked Catherine, sounding as weary as her legs.

"Yes, darling. You don't mind, do you? I wouldn't ask but it's marked 'urgent' and the gentleman has been pestering me for an hour since."

Catherine took the letter and headed for the stairway.

"Where are you going? The lift is over there...." Teresa pointed a finger at the guest lift. Catherine turned back.

"But I thought Marcus said we weren't allowed?" "Oh, bugger Marcus darling, think of your poor feet. And if he complains, send him to me."

By lunchtime, Catherine had learned more about staff and marriage politics than the job itself. But maybe that *was* the job.

Although well past the end of the summer season, the hotel was still more than half full, and the foyer seemed never clear of guests, baggage and staff, coming and going.

Chapter twenty : Personal delivery services

Just after 1pm, Teresa's relief, Simon Waterstone came on duty. A slight young man in his twenties, dressed in a mauve suit, lilac shirt and a flamboyant tie with matching handkerchief poking from a breast pocket. He walked across to reception in a mannered way, each step choreographed with precision.

"Hi folks, panic not. Cavalry's here." Everyone paid attention.

"You'll never guess what that stupid dog of mine did last night," he said, resting a hand on Teresa's arm.

"Did you really name her Gaye?"

"Well I wanted to call her Pansy at first but Tristran wouldn't allow it and anyway she answers to neither."

Catherine was all ears. "So what did she do?"

"Well, Tristran and I were having a romantic night .... you know, Chinese followed by a few chardonnays. And after hunting everywhere for a condom, unwrapped it - it flew out of my hand and she flaming well caught it. One swallow ..... and no word of a lie it was gone. Must have been starving, bless her."

"A condom?" said Teresa, "Good heavens darling, did you call a vet?"

Simon shrugged. "I almost did.....she looked as if she might sick it up for a minute. We waited but...nothing."

"Oh darling....Whatever did you do?"

"Well it was fine in the end," said Simon, hanging up his jacket. "Tristran found another one behind the toaster."

Teresa and Catherine exchanged horrified looks, and Teresa tactfully changed the subject.

"Oh Simon darling, this is Catherine. She's our new receptionist, and you have to teach her everything you know."

"Well she may regret that. Does she have a strong heart?"

"Now don't be facetious," said Teresa. "Cathy will be spending some of the afternoon in the restaurant...in fact I'll take her in there on my way out.

Teresa reached over, took her coat down from the stand and draped it around her shoulders. "Phil is a lovely man, darling," she said to Catherine, "Come with me and I'll introduce you."

"Just a minute, Teresa. Is there anything I should know about?"

"Oh yes. There's a convention coming in late this afternoon from Homepride."

"Well I won't be taking any sauce from *them*." said Simon.

"But I should be back by then to help you. Oh, and ..." she lowered her voice and leaned in to Simon's ear. "Keep an eye out for that awful woman .... you know, with the monster size wheelie bag and matching cleavage?" The last few words were mimed.

"Oh, the one who claims she's spreading religion?"

"She's spreading something, that's for sure."

"I wonder what she keeps in the bag?"

"Sex toys would be my guess. I mean she was in here last night. On a Sunday, of all days.......handing out business cards can you believe? Not all of them like it you know."

"It's dreadful." Simon shook his head and straightened his tie. "I'll have her removed straight away. Don't you worry."

***

Catering manager Phil Colman bustled about giving last minute instructions to kitchen staff before joining Catherine at the table where he'd asked her to sit. There were three stragglers left in the small dining room. One, a retired Justice of the Peace and regular guest, frowned as he chewed. His grey goatee and crisply trimmed sideburns moved in sequenced animation. He laid down his knife and fork just as Phil sat down.

"Oh, I'm glad that's over. My poor feet."

"I say young man!" barked the judge.

"Yes Judge? What's the trouble?" said Phil.

"Not wishing to complain, you understand .... but this dish you call vegetarian lasagne is a little bland, is it not?"

"Oh you think so Judge? I'm sorry about that."

"Just because I'm the only vegetarian staying here, doesn't mean you can fob me off with any old Price Chopper's frozen muck."

Phil Colman's nostrils flared. "I can assure you Judge, the lasagne was made here from scratch in our very own kitchens. In fact, I made the sauce myself."

"What did you put in it? Tastes like mashed up dandelion heads and sawdust." He prodded the lasagne with a fork. "Perhaps you could prepare me something this evening I can sink my teeth into, for a change."

Phil turned away, covered his down-turned mouth with nail-bitten fingers, and muttered behind their protective shield. "Like a Steradent cocktail."

Catherine didn't dare look amused.

"What was that, young man?" asked the judge.

Phil put on a smile. "I just wondered if I could get you anything now, Judge."

"Don't bother," he said, rising from his chair. "I have a phone call to make with a far more obliging companion." He screwed up his napkin and threw it into the middle of the table, then marched out of the restaurant.

***

Marcus stood in the foyer waiting for the Homepride party of eleven, when his pager bleeped. He took the pager from his pocket and glanced from the screen to the entrance doors, then hurried for the stairs. Seconds later the Homepride lot burst into the foyer with exuberant chatter and swamped Simon at the desk. The doors opened again and a young woman dressed head to toe in black leather stepped inside pulling a square shaped shopper on wheels behind her. She paused in the doorway, unwrapped a stick of gum, popped it into her mouth, and swaggered past reception, towards the lift.

Marcus came out of Spence's office and ran down one flight of stairs, as the judge rushed from his room, waving a twenty pound note, calling across to the lift "Wait!" But the doors were already closing. Marcus stopped.

"A problem, Judge?"

"Ah, young fellow, I wonder if you could catch the young lady before she leaves."

"Ee...yes Judge? Wheech young lady?"

"She'll be in the foyer by now, dressed in black with a trolley. Perhaps you could give her this for me?"

Marcus hesitated, but took the note. "Now?"

"Chop chop good man! She'll be gone in a minute."

Marcus rushed down the stairs.

Meanwhile in the foyer, Teresa returned from her break and slung up her coat. She attended to one of the group, when her attention was caught by the woman in black coming out of the lift, pulling her trolley towards a group of men in the foyer. Marcus landed at the foot of the staircase and saw her immediately. Glancing from side to side as he walked, he took the money from his trouser pocket.

"Scuse me, madam ..."

She turned towards him, smiling through red lips and a top heavy bosom. "Hello, handsome. Can I give you my card? We can tailor anything to your needs."

Marcus raised the palm of one hand. "No, thank you. I have plenty of suits. The judge, he asked me to geeve you thees." He held out the note.

"Oh jeez, the Judge is such a generous tipper." The woman took the note with one hand, and pushed her business card into Marcus's top pocket with the other. "That's in case you change your mind honey. And we don't make suits by the way." She grinned, swivelled her hips and swayed towards the exit.

Teresa seethed from behind reception. She threw down her biro, abandoned her guest and stepped out to block the woman's path. Marcus backed away slowly. Teresa placed a knuckle on her hip.

"What's going on? Why did he give you money?"

The woman chewed on her gum. She opened a waist pouch, stuffed the note inside and zipped it shut. "Some people tip me well," she said. "I give a good service, what can I say?" Then with a flick of her hair, she wiggled out of the building. Teresa's face blazed, and Marcus stood rooted to a spot halfway between reception and the open restaurant doors. Teresa advanced.

"What the hell have you been up to?" she demanded. Marcus continued to take backward steps.

"Eet wasn't my money," he explained. Chatter from the Homepride guests stopped, as they turned their attention to the floor act.

"That's a pathetic excuse." Teresa stepped further forward. "I saw you with my own eyes!"

Marcus backed up even further, through the open doorway and into the restaurant, where a single diner still remained.

"I swear to you...the judge was too slow...he could not keep up with her."

"So you thought you'd take his place? And for twenty quid, how could you refuse?"

"Whaaat?" By this time, they'd worked their way through to the restaurant, where

Marcus fell backwards into a vacant dining chair. “Of course not,” he insisted. “I would not do that.”

Phil and Catherine watched from behind the serving counter and exchanged grimaces.

“Oh, wouldn’t you?” continued Teresa, “and how could I possibly know that?”

“Because...” said Marcus, lowering his voice, “Because I *love* you. Ee..yes, I do.”

The last remaining diner rose from his table, and left. Phil looked at Catherine.

“And that’s how you clear the dining room after lunch,” he said.

Teresa appeared to be melting at Marcus’s declaration. She sat on his lap, forcing the shoulder pads higher, and gazed into his puzzled face with enough love to tenderise a sirloin. Then she snatched the business card from Marcus’s pocket, just as Simon appeared in the doorway.

“You’ll never believe this Teresa, but she’s not a sex worker after all.”

“No,” said Teresa, gazing at the card. “She’s been delivering flaming stuffed crust pizzas.”

Chapter twenty : Personal delivery services

Chapter twenty one : Wolf number 1 (in sheep's clothing)

Catherine got to know the kitchen staff really well, and began to hang out socially after work. When Phil came along, he made sure he sat next to her, grabbing much of her attention. Catherine enjoyed his company. She'd not had a friendship with a man before. Sex always got in the way. But she sensed they needed to have the talk.

It probably wasn't the right time. Everyone was leaving the pub, and going their separate ways. Phil asked her if she wanted a lift.

"I'm just ... gonna jump on the metro. But thanks for the offer anyway," she said.

"Oh, come on. It's just a lift. Are you worried you won't be able to control yourself?"

"Whaaat?" she attempted a laugh.

"I'm joking. You should see your face."

"Look, Phil. You're a friend. I don't want to hurt your feelings, but those remarks make me uncomfortable."

He held up his hands. "I swear, just joking. But I'll stop if that's what you want."

"Thank you." She turned in the direction of the station. "See you tomorrow."

Chapter twenty one : Wolf number 1 (in sheep's clothing)

***

It was mid-December, and there was to be a small Christmas celebration for staff in a screened off corner of the restaurant between high tea and evening dinner. Staff prepared a table buffet and an alcoholic tipple so long as customer service wasn't compromised. Phil acted out of character, over indulged with the Bordeaux, and his outward reserve of all things emotional, crumbled behind the coat stand. He fixed his eyes on Catherine's, and took her hand in his. Catherine was amused, confident he'd be mortified the next day.

"Cathy," he said with a slur, "if you don't go out with me soon ... I'll bloody kill myself."

Oh no, he's spoiled it again. Why did he have to say that? "Don't be daft," she said. "You're drunk, and you'll be sorry in the morning."

"I mean every word...every word of it."

"Come on, I'll make you some coffee."

He apologised the next day for his drunken behaviour, and asked if he could take her out to make amends. It would have to be a Sunday afternoon because he was working every evening with the run up to Christmas. She hesitated at first.

"I'll come, so long as we go halves with the bill, and you understand this won't be a date."

"He shook his head. "Just two mates going out for a meal. I know all that."

They drove out to a country pub and ate Sunday lunch overlooking a well stocked duck pond. While the duck a l'orange smelled like heaven, they chose traditional fare, in respect for any still surviving relatives swimming past the window. And the drinks this time were alcohol free.

When Phil pulled up outside her home, he leaned across and gave her an affectionate peck on the cheek. She thought they were back on track.

That first Christmas at the hotel turned out to be Catherine's most enjoyable to date. There were celebrity evenings with Tom O'Connor hosting a 'Name that Tune' contest, and someone called Slasher Stevens who could swallow fifteen razor blades in succession, then regurgitate the whole lot threaded on a length of string without a single blood spatter. The festive atmosphere continued on until two weeks into the New Year, and though Phil worked all the way through, he still found a moment at midnight on New Year's Eve to steal another kiss. But this time it was full on the lips, and a tongue was involved. She pulled away.

"Phil, what are you doing?"

"Hey, it's a New Year's kiss, that's all. Look around you. They're all at it."

Chapter twenty one : Wolf number 1 (in sheep's clothing)

He's right. They are. I'm little Miss Prude.

***

It was a weekday evening and a crowd of them had been ten pin bowling followed by something spicy at The Star of India. The curry house was within sniffing distance of Phil's home, so he invited a few back. As they pulled into his cul-de-sac, the street lights flickered. It may have been something to do with the surge of electricity being drawn off to power the hi-fi in Phil's living room. Even old Mister Montague, two hundred yards away and quite deaf since a bomb dropped on his house in 1943, stood on his doorstep and marvelled at the vibrating gravel chips in his driveway.

"What the hell does he think he's playing at?" Phil checked the time on his wristwatch as he pulled up outside the house. "Christ knows what goes on inside his head," he said, climbing from the car.

"Whoa!" said the sous chef, from his car window. "Sounds like your Nat's having a good time."

"Look, guys, I'm gonna have to sort this out. Can we do this another time?"

"Yeah, no worries. Good luck." Two honks of the horn and the sous chef was gone.

Phil headed for the door with his keys, then turned back when he realised Cathy wasn't behind him.

"I'll get away too, Phil," she called from the pavement.

"No you won't. I've invited you and you're coming in," He beckoned, racing up to the door. She followed with hesitation, into the house, along the hallway to the living room. There was a smell of cigarette smoke, and three crumpled beer cans on the fireside rug. A bare footed teenage boy dressed in slashed jeans and an oversized tee shirt with a rude message sprawled across the sofa. He was dark haired with olive skin and rebellious eyes. Phil switched off the music.

"I was listening to that!"

"And so was the whole bloody street," said his father. "This is Catherine by the way. Cathy, this is Nathaniel."

The boy glanced up at Catherine standing in the doorway. "Oh, I get it," he said, adjusting the cushions supporting his back. "Trying to impress the lady friend are we father?"

Phil turned to Catherine. "I'm sorry about this. Nathaniel appears to have lost his mind in the bottom of a beer can."

"Hi Nathaniel," she said. "I hope I'm not disturbing you."

"I'd be less disturbed if you called me Nat. Full names come from Dad when he's annoyed. Why is he annoyed, I wonder?" He picked up another can of beer from behind the arm of the sofa, cracked it open and raised it to his lips.

Chapter twenty one : Wolf number 1 (in sheep's clothing)

"That," attempted Phil in reply, "could have something to do with you getting pissed every time I go out. And where are the cigarette butts I can smell? For God's sake Nathaniel, do you want to be taken into care? Because if someone reports this, we could be in shit up to our eyes. I bet old Montague's on the blower to social services as we speak."

"Sooner the better I say ... couldn't happen fast enough. Get me out of this hell hole."

"You've done no revising for the exams. All the talks we've had. You just go your own sweet way."

"Talks? That would suggest a two way thing, when it's just you making threats.

Catherine had been waiting for the right moment to get a word in.

"I think maybe I should go....leave you two to talk?"

Phil gave Catherine a defeated look. "I'll drive you," he said, then turned back to Nat. "And when I get back, I want to see this place tidied. Or there'll be ... even more ankle biting."

Phil drove most of the way with his lips set in a thin line.

Awkward. Do I speak?

"It must be difficult bringing up a teenager on your own."

He continued to stare at the road in front. "Yeah, tell me about it."

"Well I can't, because I don't have kids. I'm just trying to make you feel better. You got upset back there." They were approaching her street. "Oh, if you turn off here, I'm just round the corner." He turned the car. "Here will be just fine."

As he pulled up, he forced a smile. "You're right, you don't, and there's no reason why you should put up with all that stuff. I apologise."

"A similar thing happened with my mother not long before she died. She fell on the remote after downing a half bottle of whisky and the television was loud enough to wake the dead."

"Bet your mother wasn't a grumpy teenager at the time?"

Catherine smiled. "She may have had dementia but she could sniff out alcohol anywhere. Do you want to come inside? I could make you a drink. Calm you down," she offered.

"That would be nice, thanks."

They stepped inside Catherine's dark hallway. All was quiet, apart from the ticking of the hall clock and a distant wailing of cats. Even Skipper was silent. She took off her jacket.

"Do you have electricity in this house?" asked Phil. "Or is there a meter we have to feed first?"

Chapter twenty one : Wolf number 1 (in sheep's clothing)

"Oh, the bulb's bust, sorry. I keep meaning to get a new one." She hung his coat on top of hers and turned to face him in the dark. "Look Phil," she began, "we do have an understanding, don't we? It's just....you puzzle me sometimes."

"Like...how?"

"Well, you sent the others away. But not me. What do you think we are? Friends? More than friends? Because sometimes it's hard to tell with you." There was a two second silence, and she wished she'd chosen a different place for this conversation.

"I know what you're saying. I feel the same as you," said Phil

Does he really?

The fact she couldn't see his face in the darkness didn't help, and she was about to suggest a coffee when she felt his lips on her cheek, her neck. She gasped for air against his demanding mouth. She pulled away.

"What's going on with you? Remember what we talked about? What we *just* said."

His breathing calmed. "I know what we talked about. I get it.

Do I trust him?

He led her upstairs by the hand.

Not even his house. Need to say something.

Unflattering light from a street lamp bathed the bedcover in a sordid shade of yellow.

"I think we'd be better off downstairs. It's much warmer," she said.

"I'm fine up here."

Maybe I'm not.

He came close and embraced her. "Is that better?"

"You are warm."

Mixed messages. My fault.

With a swift flex of the wrists he pulled the curtains together.

Should have been clearer. Too late to back out now.

He came closer and moved her hair aside to kiss the back of her neck.

That's it, then. I'm stuffed. Or about to be.

Then he saw the single bed. "I don't think we'll manage on that, do you?" he said.

Manage what? Tell him it's gone too far.

She pulled the quilt from her bed, spread it on the floor. He fingered her blouse and began to unbutton it. "You don't mind, do you?"

"Phil, I think...." But she was silenced by his mouth on hers. He removed random pieces of his and her clothing without speaking. His breathing came faster and deeper, and the intensity in his face let her know it would be over soon. Groping hands swept over her body, and he pulled her with him to the floor.

Undignified.

She stiffened beneath him. He forced her legs apart with his thigh and entered her.

Not much longer now. Maybe seconds.

It was beginning to hurt. "Slow down," she said.

But hurry up.

She felt him withdraw, heard him exhale, and knew he was done.

All my fault.

He held her for a short while, then he said he had to go, parental responsibilities and all.

So much for just wanting to hold someone.

He dressed himself, while she put on a dressing gown and reassembled the bedding. He held her to him. "I'm sorry. I spoiled it for you, I was so tense."

"Don't worry about it." *It was always going to be bad.*

He gave a regretful smile, and left.

The following day at work, she had all morning to reflect on the previous night's events, as Phil wasn't due back in until two o'clock. She knew she'd handled it all wrong. Giving him the green light like that. Or not showing him the red one. She should have sent him home.

Chapter twenty one : Wolf number 1 (in sheep's clothing)

Chapter twenty two : Wolf Number 2 (in a leather thong)

A strong hint of lemon fresh bathroom cleaner descended the stairs from the third floor as Doris trundled along with her trolley towards the next room on the rota sheet. She gave her usual two knocks.

"Hello? It's the chambermaid." She waited, then used her pass key.

Inside, she busied herself emptying waste bins, changing bed sheets and having a quiet chuckle at a pair of leather thonged underpants retrieved from the floor. The en suite bathroom door was ajar, and the room was in darkness. Humming a merry tune, she pulled on rubber gloves, went inside carrying cleaning stuff, and snapped on the light. The naked man standing behind the door made her gasp.

"Oh Mister Vincent, I'm so sorry." Doris hurried from the bathroom, but he followed, grabbing hold of her arm.

"Don't apologise lady, I don't mind."

Doris removed his hand. "I need to do my job sir. Perhaps you ought to get dressed now.

His eyes rotated in slow moving circles over her body. She reached for the door handle and just managed to turn it before he grabbed her arm again, pulling her back into the room.

Chapter twenty two : Wolf number 2 (in a leather thong)

"Mister Vincent, *please*!"

He forced her down onto the bed, tugging at her overall. With a grunt, she tucked up her knees and gave him a mighty push backwards with all four of her geriatric limbs, then fled from the room as he bounced off the wardrobe doors. She ran to the service lift panting. Reaching the ground floor, the doors opened and the first faces she saw were those of Marcus and the judge, who was making a new complaint.

"Oh, Mister Capaldi. You've no idea how good it is to see you." Doris's hat hung off her head in a less than jaunty way, her overall ripped, and she was shaking.

"What has happened? Why are you looking so ...."

"Lop sided?" The judge filled in for Marcus.

"Come with me." Marcus ushered her into the empty restaurant out of public view. The judge wasn't one to have his nose pushed out, and followed them in.

"It was that bloke off the telly," she said, "in 302. Oh I've left the bloody cleaning trolley up there."

"Don't worry 'bout the trolley, I'll send someone to get eet," said Marcus, pouring her a cooking sherry.

"Tell us what just happened." said the judge.

"I thought no-one was in. He just grabbed me. Completely starkers he was. Do you think I might have hurt him? Oh God, what if I've killed him?"

"Self defence old girl," assured the judge, "I can get you a good lawyer."

"What? I need a flamin' lawyer?"

"Let's not get ahead of ourselves," said Marcus.

"I'll knock his bloody block off!" said the judge.

"Ee....yes. That wouldn't go down well for a man of your status, would eet Judge? Theenk of what they'd say een the tabloids." Marcus knew he wasn't just speaking about the judge's reputation. "No, we'll keep this low key until I've discussed eet with upstairs. Doris, you go home. I'll get you a taxi. Do not worry. Get some rest. I weel deal with eet somehow."

Phil came into work five minutes early that afternoon with a handful of mail he'd taken from the courier in the lobby. With a spring in his step, he came across to Catherine on reception and placed one letter in her hand, and the rest on the desk.

"Internal mail for you, my darling."

"How are things at home?" said Catherine. *How the hell do I get out of this?*

Chapter twenty two : Wolf number 2 (in a leather thong)

"It's all good," he said with a smile and a wink, then headed off in the direction of the restaurant. "See you later," he called behind him.

You wish. And don't call me darling.

She took the letter from its envelope. It was from the CEO, Mister Spence, congratulating her on being made a permanent member of staff. There was a requirement that she attend a hotel management course at Gateshead college for twenty two Thursday afternoon sessions, all paid for and salary compensated, to commence the following week.

By the time Catherine was done reading, Doris was sitting alone at her kitchen table with notepad and pen, deciding how to word her resignation.

Two days later when Catherine came into work, she barely had time to take off her coat before Teresa appeared before her, bursting to pass on some scandal. Simon Waterstone ended a telephone call, eager to contribute.

"Cathy, darling," Teresa began. "All sorts went on last night after you left."

"So much drama," agreed Simon, replacing the handset. "You couldn't make it up if you tried."

"Ok....." said Cathy with hesitation, "so will someone tell me what happened?"

They both began speaking over one another and not making a lot of sense.

"Just one person speak, please, My eye balls are playing too much ping pong."

Teresa looked at Simon, who gave her the nod.

"Well... you know that Wayne Vincent who was staying on the third floor?"

"Yes. He was opening a care home or something wasn't he?"

"That's right. He made a pass at one of the chambermaids a couple of days ago, and the judge thumped him last night."

"Oh my Lord.

"He *was* opening the care home," Simon said, "but I don't know if he did it or not, because he left here sharpish straight after the punch up."

"Did he pay his bill?"

"Too right he did," said Teresa. "We weren't about to let him leave for free after the trouble he caused."

"So, which chambermaid was it?" asked Catherine,

"It was your mate Doris," said Simon. "She's still off work, poor soul."

"Doris? That's awful. I've neglected her lately........I'll pop over after work; she must be feeling rubbish. Is the judge ok?"

"Fit as a butcher's dog," said Teresa. "It cheered his miserable face up no end. Did him the world of good I reckon."

***

Arriving back home that evening, Catherine dropped off her bag and crossed the road to knock on Doris. But the Doris she expected, was not the one who couldn't stop chuckling as she opened the door.

"Hello, Cathy love. Come in. You've heard what's been going on at work I'm guessing?"

Catherine stepped inside. "From the sound of it, you've had an ordeal."

"Well it was, to be fair," replied Doris, "but it all just melted away when I saw the local news.....I taped it. Come on, I'll rewind it and play it back."

"I also heard a rumour you were thinking of leaving The Dolphin?"

"Well if I was, I'm not anymore. Just take a look at this." Doris pressed the play button.

The TV screen came to life showing the official opening of a day care unit for the elderly, and the celebrity about to cut the ribbon was Wayne Vincent, sex pest extraordinaire.

"What the..?" said Catherine. "Look at the state of his face. His nose is twice the size, and is that a black eye he's got?"

“Well someone’s tried to disguise it, but it’s pretty obvious isn’t it?”

Standing around the new building apart from the public throng, were the Mayor, a number of interior designers, architects, the president of the charity ‘Help the Aged’, and with ribbon cutting scissors in hand, Wayne Vincent, saying a few ceremonial words.

“Ladies and gentlemen, it gives me much pleasure to be a part of this long overdue facility to help our elderly population socialise and remain active. It’s a sad fact that for every breath I take here on this platform, a pensioner dies from neglect somewhere in the world.”

“Well stop feckin’ breathin’ then!” came a heckler’s voice.

Vincent continued. “We all need help from time to time...”

“Looks like *you* need medical help mate!”

“..And so, before we declare this wonderful building open, we must mention some of these talented people who made their valuable contribution. The architect in question is Mister...?”

At this point he turned to the man standing next to him and asked for the architect’s name. The official made a polite hand gesture towards the man standing to his right, and could be heard whispering to Vincent.

Chapter twenty two : Wolf number 2 (in a leather thong)

"My good friend here built it. His name is..." But he hadn't finished speaking when Vincent leapt in with his introduction.

"I give you, ladies and gentlemen, Mister Bill Titt!"

"Dear God," Catherine remarked, "what is wrong with the man? And what happened to his teeth?"

"The judge broke his dentures," said Doris, "No time to get new ones, poor man. I think I'll keep this tape forever. This is justice at its best."

"I do admire you, Doris."

"For what? Doris put down the remote, and sat.

Catherine flopped onto the couch. "A man attacks you in a hotel room. You fight him off, report him. Justice is done. I'm such a wimp."

"How? Has something happened?"

"It was my fault. I thought we were just friends. He had other ideas, and I didn't make it clear enough."

"Is this the restaurant manager you're talking about?"

Catherine gave her a sheepish look.

"Cathy, there are some fellas who will follow their own agenda, no matter how clear you make it. They're the ones you need to kick into touch. You can never be friends with that sort. They don't understand it."

"Well I know that now. I'm just a bit behind."

"You'll catch up, don't worry. And come to your Aunty Doris next time."

"Thanks Doris. You're a gem. I just need to get the message across before this gets a whole lot worse."

"Well, maybe I can help with that," said Doris.

Chapter twenty two : Wolf number 2 (in a leather thong)

Chapter twenty three : Friends reunited?

When Catherine stepped inside Gateshead college doors, she felt rather proud. Here was an opportunity to make something of her life, despite the decade she'd been forced to give up. Surely she still had a chance to salvage some kind of a future.

The security guard on duty tipped his hat as she passed him, clutching the student pack to her chest. Without Molly's chair out in front, she was being acknowledged, and it felt good.

Her first task was to find room G27. Blocks 'A' through to 'E' were no problem, but then the floor-painted lines and arrows changed from black to blue, and after three consecutive left turns she was back where she started. Then she spotted a janitor type in a boiler suit, changing a light bulb. She put on her best helpless look.

"Excuse me, can you tell me where the eff and gee's are please?"

He gave her a disparaging look. "I've a daughter your age, and she'd get a flea in her ear for talking to me like that." He readdressed the light bulb, shaking his head.

Effing hell. Cathy lifted her brows and walked on.

Chapter twenty three : Friends reunited?

By the time she found her way to G27 the class had already started. She opened the door as quietly as she could. The lecturer was writing something on the board with his back to the class, and she was able to creep behind a vacant desk. The heat in the room was unbearable. It was nearing the end of March and the weather was milder, yet the boilers were still cranked up to maximum. Most likely the fault of that rude caretaker she had conversed with earlier on the subject of the English alphabet. She took an exercise book from her bag and fanned her face. The lecturer turned around and caught her eye. She had to do a double take to make sure, but it was definitely Kenny McGuire from East Morton college, all those years ago. His expression didn't alter and she thought he hadn't recognised her. But as she continued to waft the air with her book, he said something which suggested otherwise.

"It's hotter than a laundry room in here, isn't it Catherine Grimshaw?" Her heart skipped about inside her chest as heads turned in search of a guilty face, so she turned as well.

That'll fool 'em.

But she couldn't help feeling rather smug that he remembered their first encounter across a pink laundry basket, and even more that they shared a secret in this room full of strangers.

The next forty five minutes were spent jotting down facts that struck of importance in her shiny new notebook. She began by listing the qualities of kissable Kenny versus foodie Phil. There was no contest. Kenneth J. McGuire, B.A. (Hons), M.Ed., or 'sir' to his students, was still good looking. With tidier hair, stronger jaw line. The spectacles had gone.

Contacts. Ouch. Laser surgery? Even more ouch.

Either way she didn't care, so long as she could see more of his face. His English accent still had a hint of public school about it, and when he leaned across her desk there was a new scent - a vast improvement on the old combined whiff of pork scratchings and cheap cider.

She found herself lingering behind after class, offering to clean the board, which he accepted on condition that she allowed him to run her home.

Their mutual exchange of life histories took much longer than the twenty minute ride, and so they continued on through Blue Peter, dusk falling and a Cantonese take-away. As the hall clock chimed nine, and Skipper chimed midnight, Ken realised his lateness and said he had to go. At the door, he paused.

"You may have heard this one before, but my wife doesn't understand me."

"Doesn't she speak *posh* then?"

"You what?" He gave a confused laugh.

"Doesn't matter," she said. "See you next week."

Chapter twenty three : Friends reunited?

***

"So how did college go yesterday darling?" Teresa was helping Catherine make up the newspaper orders on the office floor. Catherine got up from her knees, gave her ink-stained palms a dirty look and walked to the hand basin in a corner of the room.

"Oh it was good," she said, "But we didn't do much with it being the first session." She turned on the hot tap and soaped her hands, "and as it happened, the lecturer turned out to be an old friend from my college days."

"Really? And is this lecturer a man by any chance?"

Catherine pulled a paper towel from the container on the wall and dried her hands. "Now whatever makes you ask a question like that?"

"Oh, just something about you today that's different that's all. You're brighter than normal. For seven thirty in the morning, anyway." She placed the last tabloid order at the top of her pile and went to wash her hands too.

"Well, whether I like him or not. Lost cause. Married, I'm afraid, with children," said Catherine. "Anyway, I'm there to learn something not make eyes at the teacher."

"That's very true darling," said Teresa, "and to be honest I'm amazed the board agreed to send you on this course, let alone finance it."

She picked up the kettle and filled it from the tap. "Coffee, darling?"

"Yes please. What do you mean you're surprised? Isn't it standard for newly made permanent staff?"

"Heavens, no. As far as I know it's never happened before. Marcus had to pay for his own H.N.D. and attend classes in his own time....I reckon someone upstairs likes you."

As Catherine thought on this, the internal phone rang.

"Hello. News room."

"Hello, gorgeous," said Phil, speaking from the restaurant. "Doing the papers then?"

"Phil? What are you doing in so early?"

"One of the chefs is suffering from Saturday night fever...... or maybe it was exploding head syndrome. Anyway, I'm covering the breakfasts. Listen, I wondered if you fancied the swimming baths on Sunday?"

"Swimming baths?" she hesitated. "I've just had a traumatic flashback. I don't think I've even got a costume."

Lame excuse. Try harder.

"That's all right. We can go to the Metro Centre on Saturday and get you one. What flashback?"

This should sicken him.

Chapter twenty three : Friends reunited?

"I was seven. There was a floating jobbie in Derby Street pool. Right next to me. So you can imagine what everyone thought. Haven't been swimming since."

"That won't happen again," he said. "We'll find you a strong nappy."

Flaming answer for everything.

"Oh well, put like that how can I refuse?" Her tone was flat. One glance at Teresa, and she knew she was fooling no-one.

"I'll pick you up around eleven, ok?"

"Ok, see you then. Bye." She replaced the handset.

"Phil wants to take me shopping for a swimsuit."

"That's nice, darling."

"And we're going swimming."

"I sort of guessed." Teresa held her gaze. "Philip's a decent man, Catherine." It was more of a warning than an observation. "Don't hurt him, will you darling?"

She doesn't know him....

Chapter twenty four : Lesson number one

A busy Saturday lunchtime stuck in a sandwich queue is neither an appropriate time nor place for a serious conversation. Yet here she was, with Phil, trying to do just that. Beneath the shop counter, under glass, a selection of sandwiches were on display.

"How about turkey and beetroot salad on granary?" he suggested. "Or the shrimp cocktail looks good."

Bread and jam would do me.

"Yes, ok," replied Catherine, "either of those will do fine."

"Oh look, they've got Dairylea triangles and jammy dodgers....Nat should have been here"

"How are things between you two?"

Phil shrugged. "It's just a bad case of teenage 'itis'. I went through the rebellious stage myself. I told the cat to bugger off after Newcastle had just lost to Sunderland, and Dad gave me a clip round the ear. Pocket money was stopped for six months and he made me clean the toilet with a toothbrush every morning before school."

Let's turn everything into a joke.

"I can see you doing that."

"I used his toothbrush to clean it with, naturally," he continued.

"Anybody would." *Take control. Swing the conversation around.* "Don't you think Nat resents me taking up what little spare time you've got? Time you could be spending together?"

"Doing what for heaven's sake? Hanging out on street corners? Getting drunk? Because that's all he wants to do."

"Maybe if he was here, like you just said, you could buy him a box full of cheese triangles, and even take him swimming. I bet he'd jump at the chance."

"Why are you being like this?"

"Like what? I'm suggesting you don't exclude him so much. How is that bad?"

Phil looked at her steadily. "All right, I'll ask him. He can come with us next week."

"I didn't mean...I meant just the two of you. Father and son spending quality time together. He may well want you all to himself. That could be the reason he kicks off."

The sandwich queue had moved along, and the assistant was ready to serve them.

"Yes sir?"

"Um, yes thanks. Just a plain tuna salad baguette please."

"Certainly sir. Would you like any dressing on that?"

"No dressing thanks. I'll have it just as it stands," he turned to Catherine, "as plain as you like."

He waited until they were out of the shop before he spoke again, unwrapping his sandwich as they walked.

"Do you want to stop seeing me?" He gazed at his food, then took a savage bite.

"Why do you say that?"

He chewed quickly and swallowed. "Arranging my weekends for me .... away from you." He took another bite.

That's the plan. "I wasn't planning anything at all like that," she said. "I just think it's important for you two to make closer contact, without fighting all the time." She paused for him to fill the gap, but there was nothing. Catherine still held on to her unopened sandwich. Beetroot bled through the wrapper, but she didn't feel hungry. "If I'm not around, you and Nat may just settle your differences a lot easier, and maybe then we could start seeing one another again." *Shouldn't have said that bit. Too much encouragement.*

Chapter twenty four : Lesson number one

He took a while to respond, staring at the ground in front of him. "There's someone else, isn't there?"

Spot on, matey. It's me. She attempted a mocking laugh. "Of course not ..... What gives you that idea?"

He gave a sardonic smile. "I'm not daft enough not to know when I'm being patronised."

That's a double negative, but he's got the right idea. She blinked a lot, but couldn't think of anything else to say.

"We might as well go home. You won't be needing that swimsuit after all."

Am I on the naughty step then?

Without waiting for a response, he headed for the nearest exit, tossing the remainder of his lunch into a waste bin on the way. She watched him gallop ahead for a moment.

Can't believe I did it.

But before he disappeared all together, she hurried after him....

No way am I riding the metro with Newcastle fans.

...only to endure a silent journey home.

The next few days at work were awkward to say the least. Phil had tried ringing several times over the weekend, but she wouldn't pick up.

God bless caller display.

Fun loving Phil was no longer so, and everyone noticed. His colleagues speculated on the reason for his grouchy mood. The last thing she wanted was to be badly thought of, especially by Teresa, so she explained they'd both decided to take a break. She could have made herself more popular by showing regret, but the truth was she never felt more positive. All she could think about were the next twenty odd Thursday afternoons.

On Wednesday evening, she took a long soak in a warm bath, waxed her legs, painted her toe nails and buried her conscience. If Kenny wanted to drive her home it was fine by her. If he wanted to stay and talk, it was fine as well. But if he wanted to kiss her, it would be truly amazing.

She was five minutes early for class that day, and sat with pencil poised as he walked through the door. He wore a classically cut, two piece suit of dark sage green, which brought out the colour in his eyes. And his cream shirt had been laundered and pressed, reminding her of the dutiful wife at home. She kept glancing at her watch, wishing the minutes away, and then not, should he have to go straight home after class.

When class ended, and while other students rushed off, Catherine took her time packing her bag. Kenny waited until they were alone in the room.

Chapter twenty four : Lesson number one

"And how's Miss Grimshaw today?" he asked. She looked up from her over stuffed holdall and beamed.

"Miss Grimshaw's just fine, thank you."

"Oh, that's a pity. I expected she'd be in need of some company."

She does. Desperately.

There was a sharp knock on the open door, and an older female stood on the threshold, dressed in a floral blouse with pussy cat bow and a baggy woollen skirt. Her hair was pulled tightly into a knot at the nape of her neck and she wore Dame Edna spectacles. "Oh Mister McGuire, your wife is on the telephone," she said.

"I'll be there in a minute," said Kenny.

"If you'd like to take it straight away, I'll clear the room for you and lock up once this student has left. You don't mind hurrying along, do you dear?"

I hate her already.

"No, not at all," she said, swinging her bag onto her shoulder.

He threw Catherine a regretful look as he squeezed past the secretary to take his call.

She left the building alone and fed up. She blamed the wife, the telephone, Dame Edna, and the weather in quick succession. It had rained off and on for most of the day, and a looming black cloud right above her head looked fit to burst any minute. She pulled up her scarf against the wind and hurried out of the grounds towards the bus stop.

Finding a secluded seat at the back of the bus, she took out her text book. But she was too distracted by frustration, jealousy, and the odour of wet dog from the intake of passengers. Catherine snapped the book shut, returned it to her bag and watched the droplets of rain weave downward paths outside the window, coming together at the base in wild abandonment. Even raindrops were having more passion than she was. It was no consolation prize, but she promised herself a treat from the corner shop when she got off the bus.

The rain had eased by the time she came out of Patel's Mini Mart with chocolate in hand. She tore the wrapper and devoured the first square. Approaching the house, she spotted *his* car parked outside, and panicked. Her hair was a mess, the rain had destroyed her made up face, and she was shamelessly eating chocolate in the street. There wasn't time to check for her mirror. She pushed what remained of the bar into her handbag, wiped her mouth with the back of her hand and smiled. Kenny leaned out of the car window as she came towards him.

"Sorry I missed you back there," he said.

Chapter twenty four : Lesson number one

"Well, this is a surprise. Do you want to come in while I rub a towel over my hair?"

"Your hair looks fine to me. But I can't refuse an invitation like that."

He stepped out of the car as she fumbled for a door key on her way up the path.

"I thought you must be needed at home when you got the call." Catherine led him into the hall and took his jacket.

"No, it wasn't anything urgent. Just something she forgot to tell me this morning."

Such as? You left your knickers on the floor. Don't bother coming back. Or how much she loves you?

He smiled and followed her into the living room. "What about a coffee? Or tea?" she asked him. He moved a cushion, and sat in the middle of the sofa.

"Anything will do."

Catherine turned as she reached the door. "Or there's wine in the fridge if you'd like?"

No idea how it got in there. Thirteen percent alcohol too. Maybe he'll stay.

"Ok. But just a small one. I'm driving."

Bollocks.

Catherine returned from the kitchen with a chilled bottle of Chardonnay, two long stemmed glasses and a freshly powdered face. He got up and took the wine from her.

"Do you have a corkscrew?"

"I do." She turned to go back out of the room, but he took hold of her wrist.

"You....sit down. I'll get it."

Peel me a grape while you're up. "It's in the cutlery drawer....."

As he headed for the kitchen, Catherine jumped up to switch on the electric fire. He returned with an opened bottle, sat beside her and poured two glasses.

"I took so many notes today..." she said.

"We're getting into the real work now."

She took a sip from her glass. "Look, can I get you a sandwich or something?"

He gazed into her eyes, and smiled. She lifted a hand to smooth her damp hair. "Why are you smiling? Is it the hair? This style's known as the burst mattress effect." He took her hand in his.

Don't look at the chipped nail varnish.

"I already told you," he said. "Your hair's fine. In fact it's beautiful." He took the glass from her hand and placed it on the coffee table. "Just like the rest of you..."

Chapter twenty four : Lesson number one

It's like Shirley Valentine and the stretch marks all over again.*

Leaning across, he kissed the edge of her mouth. She closed her eyes and tried to remember what it was like, kissing him all those years ago. But nothing was the same.

Every movement he made was confident, yet gentle. He stroked the back of her neck, with fingers in her hair, cradling her head with such tenderness.

"Do you know how much I've thought about you this last week?" he said.

"You ... thought about me?"

He just said so, didn't he?

"Never stopped." His words were muffled against her skin, as he teased the neckline of her blouse. He probed between the buttons, and she gasped. As the daylight began to fade, she found herself completely surrendering to him.

All the while he never took his eyes off her. The skinny young man of 1984 had matured. His upper arms and chest were perfectly proportioned, and his skin was just the right shade of tanned.

Shirley Valentine is a character from the comedy film of the same name made in 1989. Screenplay by Willy Russell.

"You're beautiful," he said, and it was easy for her to believe it. Each tender exploration of his hand sent waves of pleasure through her body. "I've wanted you so much." There was no urgency as there'd been with Phil. Every move he made was so considered.

Bet he's had heaps of practice. Bet him and the wife are at it all the time.

Dancing lights from the imitation coals played across their skin as they lay on the rug in front of the fire. He waited, while she guided him. He took in a sharp breath, and let out a soft groan of pleasure. She heard a voice murmuring in the background, and realised it was her own.

Oooh, what's happening to me? There was no turning back. She had no awareness of where she was.

Where the hell am I? It only mattered she was with him.

What day is it?

These waves of pleasure she felt at the start were now building into huge breakers, coming one after the other, until he could last no longer. He withdrew, trembled as she held him, until he finally relaxed. Catherine could hardly believe what just happened.

My God, that was amazing.

Afterwards, they lay together holding one another. The rug was cosy and warm as they lay side by side. She could have fallen asleep right then, but it was still early, and she knew he would be expected home.

"Are you ok?" he whispered, adjusting himself.

He's worried he might have killed me. That's so sweet.

"I'm fine, really," she answered, and then, "Are *you* ok?"

"Never better. But I'll have to be going shortly."

They all say that.

He leaned across, kissed her, and moved a stray lock of hair away from her face, then sat up and got dressed.

She sat upright next to him, and pulled on her blouse and skirt.

"Will I see you again?" she said. He looked amused.

"What a question" he replied, tying his shoes.

Well? My tongue's hanging out here.

"Of course you will." He kissed her again and helped her up.

"I don't just mean...in class," she hesitated. He laughed, and encircled her with his arms.

"Nor me. I love being with you."

“Ok then,” she said.

He’d better mean that!

“I’ll see you to the door.”

Looking down at her bare feet, he smiled. “There’s no need. The neighbours might gossip if they see you standing at the door like that. It’s not dark yet.” There was something about being naked from the ankles down which made her feel vulnerable.

Aren’t these just the most Godawful feet you’ve ever seen?

But she shrugged off the feeling.

“I suppose you could be my foot doctor, on a house call.”

Bunions could do with a trim.

“I think you mean podiatrist,” he said.

I bloody know that!

“You’re the teacher,” she said.

He smiled again, kissed her, and left.

Back in the living room, the scent of him still lingered. She picked up the cushion he’d been laying on and buried her face in it, closed her eyes and inhaled slowly. Then the doorbell rang, jolting her back to the present. She pushed her feet into shoes.

“Window cleaning money,” announced the grubby, middle aged man, otherwise known as

Sherbet. Reaching behind the door for her handbag, she pulled out her purse and opened it. Her secret was safe, she thought. Sherbet's puzzled gawp made her look down. Stuck fast to the pale brown leather of her purse was a half eaten bar of Fry's chocolate cream. She laughed, tugging at the sticky mess.

"Kids, eh? What would you do with them?" she said.

***

Back at work, Catherine's smugness held no bounds. She pitied her work colleagues. Their partners couldn't possibly measure up. At thirty three years old, Catherine was going through the sexual awakenings of someone half her age, and she was hooked. Completely. For two hours of his busy week, he made her feel like the most important person in the whole world. And she walked on clouds.

Chapter twenty five : The driving examiner

Fast forward several weeks of this unchanging routine however, and Catherine began to ask herself questions.

Was she meant to be content with only 0.001% of her man's week? She'd worked it out on a calculator. Sex with no ties. Mutual satisfaction. A convenient arrangement. She added these to her list of positives, but it all looked so cold in black and white. Then she tried a red biro, but it just looked angry. Did he love her? He'd thrown the word at her like it was going out of fashion, but did it mean any kind of future? She had a list as long as her arm, of things she needed to know. Where did he live? He'd given her a street name in a town some twelve miles away, but no house number. She was not to know his telephone number, for obvious reasons. Did he think her stupid enough to use it? They'd not been out in public together. Never met any friends, nor seen any photographs. It was all beginning to look like something dirty. She sometimes wondered if she'd imagined him. Teresa often asked about the mystery man who caused her to be ecstatic one day, miserable the next. She got around it by saying there *was* someone special, but he wasn't a good mixer.

Chapter twenty five : The driving examiner

"The married ones never are darling," Teresa had said.

Because the time they had together was so short, Catherine was reluctant to make it awkward. On average, she'd manage one question a week, and although Kenny's answers were the ones she wanted to hear, there was no way of confirming them. She asked questions about his wife, and he told her of Zoe's accusations of imagined adultery. *Imagined?* Spells of violent behaviour, kitchen knife attacks, etcetera. He stayed, he said, because of the children who were still very young. She believed it all, because to disbelieve was to burst the bubble, and those Thursday afternoons were to remain the highlight of her existence for some time to come.

***

Of all the skills Catherine had mastered in her lifetime, there was one at which she had failed. More than once. Though she found the theory side straightforward, the practical found her wanting. After many lessons given by Danny, and support from colleagues, she was ready to have another go. Coming up soon was the twentieth anniversary of The Dolphin's opening. And, never being one to throw in the steering wheel, Catherine booked another test on the same day. With luck, one party might serve two celebrations.

It was the day before the test, and Danny collected Catherine from the Dolphin for her last lesson. While they were gone, Teresa's identical twin daughters, Jasmine and Stephanie, agreed to decorate the foyer in exchange for a free evening's entertainment. Stephanie was fixing a huge banner across a wide wall overhanging reception.

"Is there any more sticky tape, mum?" she shouted down from the stepladders.

"There may be some in the back office, darling." Teresa pointed behind her with the biro she was holding. "Or there are some drawing pins in the desk drawer."

Stephanie came down from the ladders and entered the back office, while Jasmine inflated balloons with a hand pump.

Catherine returned from her driving lesson, with Danny following behind.

"How was I supposed to know, with all those cones and bulldozers and everything?"

"You could have done what the cop asked, and turned around. Did you not see him waving his arms? You were going the wrong way!

Catherine slapped her bag on the desk.

"I just hope he's not around when I take my test."

"I bet *he* does too." Danny looked away in exasperation, spotting Jasmine standing by a heap of balloons as she attached another to the pump nozzle. His face softened. Teresa, who'd been listening to this heated exchange, raised her head.

"Oh, darling ....You didn't go the wrong way down a one-way street did you?"

Catherine took off her coat. "Well...yes..." she began. "But it was two-way traffic yesterday....before the workmen moved in and set up all those funny little signs. How can I be expected to learn the rules for one particular road when they change them the very next day? I mean, I'm not telepathic." Cathy checked Teresa was still listening, expecting her usual support, but Teresa was watching Danny, gazing at Jasmine. Catherine followed her line of sight as Teresa's eyes came back to meet hers, and she winked.

"Oh Daniel, darling ..."

Danny took seconds to realise his name was being called. "Yes?"

"Daniel, I'd like you to meet my beautiful daughter, Jasmine."

Jasmine squirmed. "Mum always calls me beautiful. But you can call me Jassy if you like." She giggled, and offered her hand for shaking.

"It's a pleasure, Jassy," he said. "Fancy going out tomorrow night?"

Two pairs of eyebrows sprang upwards, as Cathy and Teresa gaped at one other.

Danny threw a sheepish glance in Teresa's direction. "That's if...you don't mind me asking?"

Jasmine gasped. "You don't have to ask my mother," she said. "I *am* a grown up."

"Only just, young lady. You're on a trial period," said Teresa.

"Thing is," said Jasmine, "I have to be here at the party tomorrow. But you're welcome to come too."

"That would be great. What time should I pick you up?"

"Make it six-thirty," said Teresa. "I need her here to set up the tables, and stand around looking attractive." She returned her attention to the paperwork in front of her.

"Six-thirty it is then," said Danny, glancing at his watch. "I'll have to be getting back." He turned to go.

"Hold on," Cathy called after him, "It might be handy to know the address?"

"Sorry, course it would."

Teresa scribbled on paper. "You must wear a tie, Daniel darling," she said as she wrote, "and a shirt with its tail tucked *inside* the trousers." She gave him a meaningful stare, tore the page from her notepad and dangled it, carrot fashion.

He took it. "See you all tomorrow then."

As Danny made his exit, Catherine hung up her outdoor coat and took her place on reception next to Teresa.

"That nephew of mine said I wasn't fit to be on a dodgem ride. Can you believe it?"

"Oh darling, how insulting. I bet that made you feel pretty annoyed."

"Annoyed? Fuming, more like," said Catherine, searching her handbag for face powder.

Stephanie re-emerged from the office. "This took some finding. Someone should tidy that desk."

"Knock yourself out, darling." Teresa twirled the end of her biro between her lips, and bent her head to Catherine's ear. "How about we play a little trick on Danny tomorrow evening?" she whispered.

Catherine lowered the powder compact, followed Teresa's gaze from Stephanie to her twin, and the penny dropped.

"I like it," she said, and snapped the compact shut.

***

The next day dawned dry, calm and bright. Driving conditions were perfect, but as Catherine slid into the driver's seat of the examiner's vehicle, her confidence levels dipped.

Reginald Sayers was overweight and slightly balding. His cheeks were tinged with a purplish-red glow, as was the end of his nose. At intervals he dabbed his sweating brow with a table sized white handkerchief, which dangled from the top pocket of his shirt when not in use. He popped a Rennie into his mouth, chewed, contorted his face into a pained arrangement, and swallowed hard. Catherine began her mirror-signal-manoeuvre routine, thinking perhaps Sayers had been forewarned of her shambolic driving skills, and had come prepared.

They'd been tootling along at a steady pace, when Sayers addressed a prior sticking point.

"Now, Miss Grimshaw, when I slap my hand on the dashboard, I want you to make an emergency stop." He winced once more, rubbed at his chest, and popped another Rennie. "Do you understand?"

"Absolutely," she said, with flitting gaze between the road ahead, and Sayers' hands.

She tried to stay in a low gear to prepare for braking. The road was busy. Up ahead was a single market stall set up on the right side pavement, selling fruit and vegetables. Approaching from the opposite direction was a scrap-loaded cart pulled by a shire horse, which though blinkered, showed clear signs of stress from the volume of traffic. The scrap man jerked at the animal's reins, swore at it as its powerful hooves veered from left to right. There was a road junction coming up on her left, with a black convoy of funeral cars waiting for a break in the traffic. It was then that the Morris in front gave way to the slow moving procession, and she was forced to make an emergency stop right there and then.

Feeling pleased she'd avoided a clash with the Morris, Catherine glanced at the examiner and found him out cold.

"Mister Sayers?" she said. The procession was almost out of the junction, when one of the engines back fired. The horse twisted its head in alarm, reared up on its back legs and detached itself from the cart.

Catherine said again, "Mister Sayers!" and shook his arm. The clip board slid from his knee to the floor with a clatter, just as the horse bolted forwards, collapsing the market stall. King Edward's best scrapers scattered all over the road; potential customers ran to doorways of safety; and still Mister Sayers slept on. The moving tide of juicy carrots brought an instant distraction, and the horse came to an abrupt stop.

Traffic ceased to move in either direction. Impatient drivers either yelled from open windows, or sat fingering their horns.

Catherine opened both front windows, loosened Sayers' tie, and felt for a pulse in his neck as she'd seen on Casualty. Then she got out of the car to ask for help. The motorists close by averted their eyes, wound up their windows, or picked up newspapers. She looked down the road and spotted the flashing blue light of an approaching police car. Muttering something sweary at the don't-involve-me drivers, she reached inside the car for Sayers' white hankie and went running down the centre lane, waving it aloft. The police car braked in the midst of the foray, and the door barely opened when she came rushing forward.

"Please..." she said, breathless. "My examiner's collapsed or something. Can you help?"

The officers exchanged glances. "I'll go with the lady, Bill, said one to the other, "Can you radio for another car?"

"Right, Sarge,"

Though several years had passed, she recognised the figure emerging from the vehicle almost immediately. The twinkling blue eyes gave it away.

On their way back to Sayers, Catherine blurted out the mad sequence of events, and the sergeant radioed for an ambulance, but there was a ten minute wait. At that moment, a second patrol car arrived on the scene.

"If we give you a police escort, can you drive him to hospital? We can be there before the ambulance gets here."

"Well, yes I could..." she began.

"Good," said the officer, and ran back to his vehicle.

"But if I do..." Catherine continued, raising her voice to be heard in the distance, "Won't I be breaking the law...?"

Catherine's stomach did a back flip seeing him again. But it was obvious he hadn't remembered her. Taking a deep breath, she got back into the car, fastened her seat belt and switched on the ignition. The police car ahead moved off, and sergeant familiar face beckoned her out. The examiner groaned, and shifted his head from one side to the other. Catherine gave him a brief sideways glance as she released the hand brake. "All right, Mister Sayers, here we go. Let's hope I can get you there in one piece." Green-eyed motorists flashed dirty looks and hand gestures from the queue as she abandoned them.

Regret it now, don't you? Losers.

Sergeant familiar face shouted over to a paramedic taking a coffee break outside of Accident and Emergency. "Bring a wheelchair or a stretcher, can you? This fella's spark out."

As Sayers was lifted from the car to a trolley, Catherine was told to move the car. On her return, sergeant familiar face was waiting at reception. He took off his cap as she approached, and ran his fingers through thick, dark blonde hair.

"I'm glad you didn't rush off, we'll need to take some details if you don't mind," he said.

"What do you need to know?"

"Is that the examiner's clipboard you have there?"

"Oh, yes.....there you go. He's ticked the first five boxes." Catherine beamed. "That's a good sign, right?"

Taking the board, and a notebook from his pocket, he gave her a considered look. "Depends what your priorities are ... at this moment in time." He dropped his gaze and began writing.

Why the hell did I say that?

"How are you?" he said. "It's been a while."

He remembers me!

"I'm well. Surviving, you know."

"It's good to see you again." He looked up from his notes and smiled, eyes twinkling away. "I was looking back just the other day, at my very first notebook as a constable. Do you still have the parrot? And how's your mother?"

"Mother died. Skipper's still here, but showing his age. I'm indebted to Sutton's black pudding. I still owe you."

Chapter twenty five : The driving examiner

"And the sausage. Don't forget the sausage," said Sergeant Rob. "Sorry to hear about your mother."

The receptionist looked back and forth between these two catch up merchants, waiting for a suitable pause.

"If you don't mind," she said, "we are rather busy here, and I need the patient's details when you're ready?"

What's with these bossy women, hell bent on ruining my chances?

"I'm so sorry," said Catherine.

"Completely my fault," Sergeant Rob insisted.

"Just tell me the gentleman's name."

An announcement came over the P.A. system.

"Would the driver of a dark blue Toyota registration number HG12.."

"Oh no!" said Catherine.

"...please remove the vehicle immediately from parking bay A17."

"I think that's me," Cathy continued. "What do I do with the car now?"

"Well you can't leave it in A17," said the receptionist. "That's our medical director's spot."

Rob pocketed his notes and snatched up his cap. “Come on, we’ll find you a spot and then I’ll ring the examiners and bring them up to date.” The receptionist slapped her pen down on the desk. Loudly.

“I’ll be back to give you the details in five minutes,” he promised.

“I suppose I’ll have to apply for my fourth driving test now,” said Catherine, as they came out of the building.

“You mean you’ve done this before? Three times?”

"Given someone a heart attack? Certainly not.”

“I bet you’ve broken a few hearts in your time, and someone’s got to be waiting for you back home. All I’ve got to go back to is a cold house and a frozen lasagne.”

Catherine thought for a moment. “Would you like to go to a party tonight?” she said.

Chapter twenty five : The driving examiner

Chapter twenty six : Coupling up

Back at the Dolphin, preparations were ahead of schedule for the upcoming Gala celebration. The kitchens were alive with the clatter of saucepans, whirring of blenders and grinding of teeth, while chefs created dishes on a multi-national theme. Phil Colman was in his element, keeping everyone focused on their individual jobs. It hadn't taken him long to recover from Catherine's rejection, as he saw it, and he looked forward to seeing his new love interest later that evening. Relations with his son must have improved, as Nathaniel buzzed about taking instructions from kitchen staff.

The whole of the ground floor was filled with Neapolitan aromas, and Marcus took Teresa's place on reception while she decorated both lounge bars with purple cut outs of smiling dolphins in various dancing poses. Marcus was busy checking in a young couple who couldn't agree on a surname, when the main doors opened and a taxi driver stepped into the foyer with an overnight bag on one arm, and a frail old lady wearing a wide brimmed hat on the other. He dropped her luggage on a seat next to reception with a heavy gasp.

"I'll just leave it there, love, ok?"

"That's fine, thank you," said the lady. "How much do I owe you?"

The taxi driver used the back of his hand to wipe his forehead, and rested it on his hip. "Just three pounds ninety-five love," he said with a sniff.

She handed him a five pound note. "There you are. And keep the change."

"Thanks me darlin'. You'll go to heaven for that." The driver waved the note in appreciation, and left.

Marcus, now customer free, gave the woman a welcoming smile.

"What can I do for you madam?" he said, with all of his Italian charm.

"I have a room booked for this evening," she said, replacing her purse in her handbag.

"And what ees the name please, madam?"

The old lady was having some trouble closing the clasp on her bag with her bony fingers. Marcus leaned over the desk.

"My wife has the same trouble. She never has enough space."

The lady returned his smile, put her hand inside the bag, shifted the contents around, then snapped the bag shut.

"Sorry, you will have to excuse me. I'm a little hard of hearing." She lifted her face from beneath the wide brim of her hat. "The name's Moretti. Rosa Moretti."

***

It was early evening in the Capaldi household. With both of their parents already at the hotel, twin sisters Stephanie and Jasmine were preparing to leave, but not together. Stephanie touched up her mascara at the dressing table, while Jasmine hunted through her wardrobe for a suitable jacket. They were both dressed the same, in strapless black velvet evening gowns, patent leather high heeled shoes, diamante jewellery, and both with their long dark hair piled up in a loose knot. Jasmine took out a three quarter length camel coat and slipped it from its hanger. She gave her sister a disparaging look.

"Stephanie, have you seen the time? Danny will be here soon, and I can't answer the door, remember?"

Stephanie replaced the mascara brush inside its holder and screwed them back together.

"All right, all right. I'm ready now." She stood up and went over to the wardrobe. "Jassy, you can't wear that coat. We're supposed to look the same, or this isn't going to work."

Jasmine looked at the coat with disappointment. "Oh, I don't think we should be doing this. Danny seems like a really nice boy."

Stephanie reached inside the wardrobe and took out a dark green raincoat.

"It's just a little joke, and if he's as nice as you think, then he'll see the funny side."

"But what if he doesn't? Steph, I like him, you know?"

Stephanie put on her raincoat. "I promise you, it won't make any difference."

Jasmine held the camel coat close to her chest. "It's all right for you. You'll be taking my lift ... and I'm left to catch the bus."

The doorbell rang. "That'll be him," said Stephanie, grabbing her bag and heading for the door. Before disappearing, she popped her head back inside the room.

"Oh Jassy..?" she said, "Wear a darker coat ... please?" Then she ran down the stairs. Jasmine hurried to the bedroom door and poked her face through the gap.

"Don't you dare snog him!" she shouted.

Guests were beginning to drift into the main reception rooms. Some had mistakenly chosen to dine first, emerging from the restaurant surrounded by dishes of exotic smelling finger food, both hot and cold, spread out on every available surface. The four piece band arrived at the rear with bulky sound equipment, but no roadies. Catherine and Doris offered to transport a speaker each, from vehicle to stage. With speakers almost as tall as themselves, they stepped blindly through the back door into the lounge with only arms and legs visible. A familiar resident guest was drawn by Doris's glittering purple thigh. He rushed forward.

"Let me assist you with that my dear," he said, taking Doris's load from her arms.

"Why thank you Judge, that's very kind." .

She whispered to Catherine. "Do you think he realises I'm the one who cleaned his lavatory bowl this morning?" Catherine frowned as she struggled with her own speaker up onto the stage, and lowered it to the floor. The judge seemed more sprightly than usual as he deposited his load, flexed his biceps and shot Doris an admiring glance.

"If there's anything else you require madam, you must not hesitate to ask," he said.

"Well, Judge," said Doris with a wry smile, "Now that you come to mention it, a bloody Mary would be most welcome after all that back breaking work." She tilted her head in Catherine's direction. "And a dry white wine for my friend here."

"Of course ladies, of course," said the judge. "Coming up in two shakes."

Doris leaned her head towards Catherine's ear. "What do you reckon? Have I pulled?"

"Well this is the second time he's come to your rescue, Doris. And I don't think he's seeing that hooker anymore."

"So there's a vacancy for me then? Cheers. And you know fine well she wasn't a hooker."

"He's just lonely. That's why he's so grouchy. It's the only way he can get any attention. I think you could be just what he needs."

***

On the third floor, Rosa Moretti emerged from the lift clutching her handbag. She walked the length of the corridor until she found the staircase leading upwards. At that moment, the service lift doors opened and Marcus stepped out, carrying a loaded tea tray. Spotting the old lady disappearing up the stairs, he called after her.

"Oh, excuse me madam, but you can't go up there."

She seemed not to have heard. Marcus set the tray down outside one of the guest room doors and ran after her. She'd reached the top landing just as he caught up.

"Oh madam," he said, placing a hand on her forearm. "Can I help you? Are you lost?"

Rosa gave his hand a look of disapproval, and he removed it instantly.

"I'm sorry..." he said, "but this floor ees not available for guests to use. Were you looking for anyone een particular?"

"I wish to see the owner, if you don't mind."

"Oh madam, I'm afraid that won't be possible. But eef you have a complaint, perhaps I can deal with eet for you?"

She inclined her head. "Did you say *complaint?* It's not a complaint, it's a personal matter."

"I see. Well may I arrange an appointment for you? Eef you remind me of your name, I shall convey your message."

"There will be no need for that," she said, turning back to the staircase. "I shall see to it myself, later." As she descended the stairs, Marcus stared after her for a moment, then went to retrieve his tray.

Downstairs in the main lounge, the band's song choices irritated Stephanie Capaldi to hell. She much preferred a bit of Kylie. Regardless, she dragged Danny onto the dance floor with purpose. She placed his arms around her waist and encircled his neck with hers. As they moved out of earshot, Catherine leaned across to Teresa.

"When is Jasmine going to show herself? If she waits too long, our Danny and your Stephanie will need a crowbar to prise them apart."

"I know," said Teresa, "I just saw her in the doorway speaking to her father. She's giving Stephanie some murderous looks."

Teresa helped herself to a handful of dry roasted peanuts. "It reminds me of when they were six years old and fighting over a rag doll."

Catherine took a sip from her glass. "What happened?"

"Well, Lindy Lou lost one of her pigtails, Steph lost her temper and poor Jassy lost a front tooth."

"Oh God," said Cathy. "Just as well our Danny didn't grow that ponytail he wanted." She glanced around the room. "Speaking of ponytails, who's that big guy over there in the suit? I'm sure I've seen him somewhere before."

"Well, you might have seen him here darling. That's our CEO, Mister Spence...Jack Spence."

"No, it's definitely not from here. Is he famous or something? I'm sure I've seen him in the newspapers."

"Not that I know of, darling." Teresa glanced across the dance floor. "Oh look." she laughed, "there's your little friend Doris, dancing with the judge."

The judge gazed into Doris's eyes, as they quick stepped around the dance floor together.

"You know, Judge," said Doris, "I can't keep calling you 'Judge' all evening....do you happen to have a proper name by any chance?"

The judge waited for a suitable break in his foot work.

"Of course I do my dear ...and I'll tell you what it is if you promise to come upstairs with me for a small nightcap?"

As he twirled her around, Doris clocked the timepiece on the wall. "But it's only quarter past nine," she said, "and besides, I've already had the misfortune of being attacked in a hotel room once before, as you know."

"As a matter of fact my dear, I would not presume you to be that kind of woman. That man was a scoundrel, and he would not dare set foot in here again. No, by *upstairs* I meant upstairs in the lounge bar."

"Oh I see....well in that case..."

"And I shall tell you my name now, without any bribe attached." The judge interjected with an abrupt turn of his head in time with the music. "It is....Ernest Ignatius Wilberforce, J.P."

She lifted both eyebrows. "On second thoughts, I think I'll stick with 'Judge' if it's all the same to you."

Chapter twenty six : Coupling up

Chapter twenty seven : Revenge served cold

Jasmine had been watching her twin sister dancing far too close to Danny Grimshaw for what seemed like hours, trying to pick her moment and becoming more envious by the second. The band played the first few chords of 'Anniversary Waltz' as Stephanie tightened her arms around Danny's neck and rested her cheek on his shoulder. Jasmine seethed in the doorway, thinking he looked like the trapped prey of a widow spider. Teresa came across to her.

"If you're not going to make a move soon darling," she said, "you may as well clear some of these dirty plates away to the kitchen."

Jasmine glared at her mother. She turned and picked up someone's forgotten portion of trifle from a nearby table, "I can find a place to clear this one," and marched across to the dancing couple.

Danny's idle glance across Stephanie's shoulder, developed into a stare of disbelief. As Jasmine reached her sister's turned back, she pulled at the stretch fitting top of Stephanie's dress and tipped fruit, jelly, custard and cream into the narrow space. Stephanie shrieked and turned.

Chapter twenty seven : Revenge served cold

"What on earth ... Jassy! What do you think you're doing?"

Danny stood shocked and still. "Jassy? *You're* Jassy?"

Jasmine set the empty dish down and gesticulated. "Yes! I'm the one you asked out, remember?"

"Then ... then you're twins?" It was so obvious, he knew it sounded ridiculous.

Stephanie was showing increasing discomfort. She reached an arm behind her and eased the back of her dress away from her skin. A dollop of half melted red jelly and cream fell to the polished wood floor with a splat, followed by the clatter of a dessert spoon.

"Jassy....I could kill you!" She forced the words through tight lips before storming off towards the ladies' room. Many pairs of eyes followed her. Jasmine smiled in triumph, and Danny worried what he'd let himself in for.

"Can I cut in here?" Jasmine brushed her sister's face powder residue from his jacket lapel, pressing her body close, and her hands on his shoulders.

"Er, yeah ... I suppose," he said, still confused but grateful for the cease fire.

As the party raged downstairs, Rosa Moretti walked the length of the fourth floor corridor, trying the handle of each door she passed with one hand, holding her handbag close with the other. The first two doors were locked, the third was open, but turned out to be a storage cupboard full of dusty old box files and bundles of yellowing papers. The next door led into an office with a large walnut desk in its far corner, and a soft backed swivel chair behind it. A half cup of black coffee stood next to an open file on the desk top. In the centre of the side wall, there was a heavy wooden door adjoining the next room. Rosa crept across the parquet flooring to the inner door, bent her head and attempted to listen. This exercise of course was quite pointless. Although her right ear was better than her left, it stood no chance of tuning in through four inches of solid oak.

She turned the handle in slow motion, and as she pushed the door forward, the rear view of a middle aged man seated in a burgundy leather chair was just visible through the gap. He spoke quietly on the telephone, and as Rosa's trembling hand took the revolver from her bag, her door key spilled out and landed on the floor. The seated male figure swivelled his chair through 180 degrees until he faced his intruder, and a hand gun pointed straight at him. This was the first time Rosa had come face to face with Melvyn Butcher. He was dressed in a plain light blue shirt, unbuttoned at the neck with a dark blue waistcoat. He spoke into the handset.

"Listen Jack, I have a visitor. I'm going to have to call you back."

Chapter twenty seven : Revenge served cold

In the lounge downstairs, Jack Spence puzzled at his mobile telephone, shrugged, and returned it to an inside jacket pocket .

Rosa continued to glare at Butcher, with the hand gun wavering and her handbag swinging over an outstretched forearm. Butcher spoke first.

"I feel as though I should know you ... but I don't recall when that might have been."

"You may not remember *me*. But I'm sure you'll recall my two sons, and my daughter. My Wendy." She moistened her lips and swallowed.

"You're Rosa Moretti?" said Butcher, straightening the furrows on his brow with the realisation.

"You ... are responsible for the deaths of two of my children, one way or another."

"Now look, Rosa," Butcher began, "I wasn't involved in Tony's death. In fact I heard his brother had been arrested? Is that not so?"

"It was your evidence that put them away in that terrible place. You should have died with your dog in that acid attack."

"Well, that's not very kind, is it? And you do know your daughter Wendy was killed by a jealous husband?"

"After you had her in your bed!" said Rosa, cocking the gun.

"I didn't have to drag her there." As soon as he said the words, he regretted them. She pulled the trigger. There was a loud bang as the bullet hit the back of his chair, inches from his face. The gun shook in her grasp, and she steadied it with both hands, still pointing it directly at him.

"If it helps ... I never intended .... anyone to get hurt ... I swear," he said

It was easier for her now. She cocked the gun a second time and pulled the trigger again. The second shot ripped a hole in his blue serge waistcoat. His body jerked with the impact, yet he tried to speak again.

"Does this make us ... even?" Butcher's gaze upon his assailant remained steady, while his body slipped from chair to floor. Rosa looked furtively around. She stared at the revolver in her hand as though seeing it for the first time, and then returned it to the secrecy of her handbag. She snatched up the hotel key she'd dropped moments before, then turned, and made her exit. The corridor was deserted, and she stepped inside the service lift, descending two floors to the musical accompaniment of 'Tie a Yellow Ribbon,' crackling through speakers.

Meanwhile, Doris and the judge were on their way up to the second floor in the guest lift, giggling at childish witticisms under the influences of Bloody Mary and Jack Daniels. As the lift doors opened, they saw Rosa Moretti shuffling along to her room, choking back sobs and fumbling in her bag for a door key. Doris stepped into the corridor and stared after her.

"I know her, I'm sure," she said. They watched as the old lady found the keyhole through her tears, let herself into the room and closed the door behind her. The judge placed a gentle hand on Doris's shoulder.

"Do you want to ask her to join us? Because if you do, I must confess I'd hoped to have you to myself this evening."

"Oh, come on you flatterer. Let's go and have that drink."

They walked across to the private lounge together, but it looked to be in darkness. The judge pushed open the door and felt on the side wall for a switch.

"Oh dear," he said, as the room filled with light, "It seems we're all alone." He circled a pool table to reach the bar, lifted the wooden flap and stepped behind the counter.

"What are you doing?" asked Doris, following him in.

"Well, there's no ruddy barman." He lifted an apron from a nearby hook and tied it around his waist. "So, I'm going to do the job myself." He grabbed a towel from beneath the counter and draped it, waiter fashion over his arm.

"Now madam, what is your utmost pleasure?"

Doris scowled. "I'm certainly not going to tell you *that*." Then the coffee machine caught her eye. "But I'd kill for a frothy coffee."

***

The bar staff downstairs were finding it difficult to cope. A fourth keg of Best Scotch had just been started as a call came out from the smaller bar for another crate of whisky. Marcus and Phil rushed around doing everyone's job but their own, and Catherine was trying to help Nat keep on top of the dirty glasses. Placing another clutch of schooners on the bar, she stopped for a breather and blew a strand of hair away from her sweating brow. Then she saw Danny coming towards her looking agitated.

"Cath," he said, scanning the room, "I think I'm going to leave."

"What, already?" She looked at her watch. "It's not even ten o'clock."

"I know. But I've seen someone I'm not too keen on meeting again."

She followed his gaze to an area over by the stage, where Jack Spence stood talking with Marcus Capaldi.

"Do you know Jack Spence?"

Chapter twenty seven : Revenge served cold

"Don't you remember me telling you? He was in the garage when Joe fell into the pit."

Catherine was beginning to realise too many coincidences. "You mean Jack Spence is Mel Butcher's minder?"

"I think he's much more than just a minder," he said.

"But I thought that business was all sorted with Butcher."

"With Butcher, it was. I'm just not sure Jack Spence was brought up to speed."

She glanced at the table they'd been sitting at a short while earlier. Jasmine sat talking with Phil Colman and his son Nathaniel.

"Have you been speaking to our catering manager Phil Colman?" said Catherine.

"Oh, yeah. I suggested his son enrol on a youth project we've started. He likes motors." Danny was still distracted. "I've asked Jassy to come with me to a night club. You don't mind, do you?"

"No, no of course not," Cathy said. "You go. But be careful you take the right girl with you this time."

After Danny and Jasmine had left, Catherine kept her eye on Jack Spence, discussing something of importance with Marcus in a far corner of the room. Spence took out his mobile phone, and keyed in a number. He held the phone to his ear for moments, but his lips didn't move. She watched as Spence said something to Marcus, and hurried from the room.

As Jack left, a tall figure in smart but casual dress, passed him in the doorway and entered the room with hesitance, searching around. Cathy waved a gloved arm in his direction, as he excused his way through an alcoholic mist of drinkers.

"Hi there," called Cathy as he came close, "I was starting to think you might not make it."

"It wasn't easy," said Rob, "but I'm here now. What are you drinking?"

Chapter twenty seven : Revenge served cold

Chapter twenty eight : Too many sleuths

Any stranger walking by the open doors of the upstairs lounge that evening might be excused for misinterpreting the conversation going on inside.

"Will you leave my balls alone for heaven's sake?" the judge protested, as Doris straightened her bent back with pool cue in hand.

"Well, what do you expect if you keep sticking them right in front of the hole?" she argued.

The judge sighed. "They're called pockets, my dear....not holes."

"So where does 'a hole in one' come from then?"

The judge beamed. "I think you're having a good tug on my leg, that's what I think."

They started to laugh, until a sudden 'bang,' burst through the muffled music and silenced them both. They looked wide eyed at one another.

"What was that?" said Doris. The judge put down his cue, walked to the door and peered out.

Chapter twenty eight : Too many sleuths

"I'm no expert, but I think that was a gunshot"

Doris came up behind him. "It definitely came from down there," she said, staring down the same stretch of empty corridor.

"Well, there are only two rooms down there, and one of them belongs to your teary friend."

"Do you think we ought to knock or something?" she said. The judge took her arm, and led her towards Rosa Moretti's room.

"Come on, we'll have a listen at the door first."

With both heads close to the door, they heard nothing but their own breathing. Then a clatter from inside. Doris and the judge exchanged anxious looks. She gave three raps on the door.

"Hello? Is anyone in there?" They waited. More seconds ticked by and the judge knocked.

"Hello in there. Do you need any help?" Still no response.

"What do we do now?"

"I think we should open the door."

"It'll be locked."

"Might not be."

"But what if she's asleep?" said Doris.

"Then we come back out again."

Doris turned the handle and eased the door open.

The room was in darkness, apart from the shaft of light pouring through from the corridor. The narrow beam lit up the end of the bed, and the side view of a woman, fully dressed, splayed across it. Doris stood in the doorway and gesticulated to the judge to take a closer look. He tip-toed around the bed and bent over the motionless figure. Rosa Moretti's sightless brown eyes stared at the wall opposite; the bedcover beneath her head had its hotel logo obliterated by a patch of fresh blood; and her blue veined right hand hung over the edge. Beneath it, the gun lay blameless between a pair of mauve slippers.

The judge straightened himself, and glanced across at Doris's silhouette, framed in the doorway.

"I think perhaps we ought to call someone. She's as dead as a door nail."

***

On the ground floor, Marcus hurried from the service lift, beckoning across to Catherine. She followed him outside, where he stood impatiently watching the end of the street.

"What is it Marcus?"

"There's been a shooting upstairs," he said. "Ambulance on eets way." The wailing of a siren and a flashing blue light announced the ambulance. Seconds after, a police car pulled up.

"Who's been shot?" Cathy shouted, as the ambulance doors opened. "Is it one of the guests?"

Two paramedics jumped out of the cab carrying back packs and radios. Another produced a stretcher from the back. Two police officers in armoured vests got out of the patrol car and Marcus walked alongside as they took strides towards the entrance.

"One casualty, one dead. Dead person ees shooter."

"Are you certain there's no-one still armed inside the building, sir?"

"I'm certain. Weapon ees on the floor. I have not touched a thing, and room ees secure.

They entered the building.

Catherine followed behind, still waiting for an answer as party guests were shaken from their alcoholic haze back to reality.

"Catherine," Marcus said, "can you keep thees area clear until we bring heem down?"

He led the police and paramedics to the service lift and they stepped inside.

"But who is it Marcus?" Catherine asked again, as he touched his key against the button marked 'Exec' within.

"Meester Butcher – the boss." The lift doors closed.

Catherine turned around in a daze and almost collided with Doris. Despite the glittering headband having slipped over one eye, she looked the perfect figure of sobriety.

"Cathy," she gasped, straightening her headgear, "someone's dead upstairs, and I know her face. I think it's that Moretti woman from your Louise's wedding.

Catherine looked puzzled. "What? Marcus just said it was Mister Butcher, and there's an ambulance waiting outside, so he can't be dead."

The judge came striding across the foyer towards them with Rob Sutton, just as Doris was about to protest.

"But who called the ambulance? We've only just told Marcus we found her,"

Catherine was getting even more confused. "You found Rosa Moretti?"

"It's definitely her," said the judge.

"We checked the register," said Rob.

"And you say she's dead?"

"Do you want me to go up?" said Rob. "I'm off duty, but I can find out what's been going on."

Chapter twenty eight : Too many sleuths

For the next two hours, scene of crime officers, forensic and ballistic experts bustled back and forth with the immediacy of having something important to do, while party revellers dwindled away for the lack of it. Mel Butcher was rushed from casualty to theatre, where a bullet was removed from his chest cavity. He was then moved to intensive care, while a frail old lady who had led a rather insignificant life in the shadow of her three infamous offspring and notorious husband, was now, in death, being written about and photographed on a par with celebrity status.

Sergeant Rob Sutton stayed around, and Catherine was glad for the ear of confidence he offered to her long, incredulous story. He told her she would have to make a statement of everything she knew, down at the station.

It was well after two in the morning when she crawled into bed, physically and mentally drained. Why would Mel Butcher, after all that had happened, agree to employ her in the first place? She was a dreaded Grimshaw, related by her brother's marriage to the Morettis, who had each made their own contribution towards his demise. Unless he had not made the connection at all? Up until a few years ago, Butcher's name was never out of the tabloids for his calculated and ruthless business methods and he remained a powerful figure. Why had he chosen to hide himself away on the top floor of the hotel for all this time? Surely he hadn't been living in fear of timid old Rosa Moretti? It didn't seem to make any sense.

She reached across to the bedside table and pressed the message rewind button on her answering machine. Kenny McGuire's recording played back.

"Hi, it's only me,"

Why is he whispering?

"I'm guessing you're at work?"

He's disappointed.

"I just wondered how you got on with your driving test this morning."

Long story.

The squeak of a door opening, and his voice speeded up. "Gotta go."

She waited for the 'click' and the subsequent silence. He'd been disturbed. She switched off the machine and turned her body to the wall.

What I wouldn't give, for an uncomplicated life.

She sighed, closed her heavy eyelids to the world and fell instantly asleep.

Chapter twenty eight : Too many sleuths

Chapter twenty nine : Secrets and lies

It took a couple of days this time for the press to hash together some sort of story which was around 90% factual. A freelance photographer had somehow conned his way into the I.C.U. at The Royal Free Hospital and taken a snap of Butcher as he lay unconscious, connected to a functioning existence by tubes and wiring. The photograph made the front page of the Chronicle, but took lower status in the Bugle, somewhere between the TV listings and an advert for cat food.

In return for her overtime worked on that eventful night, Catherine was given a day off in lieu, which she took mid-week for junk clearing purposes.

She donned an overall, tied her hair with a rubber band and took on the task with a rush of enthusiasm. By lunch time, four black sacks had been filled. So the downstairs was sorted. Upstairs would take longer.

Joe had been right about the amount of tat in her parents' room, and she realised how long she'd been ignoring this job. The creation of space felt like a new start. On Molly's top shelf there were bundles of envelopes; a shoe box with letters bound in gardening twine; a collection of newspaper cuttings and a spiral bound note book full of writings. She picked out the note book because there were interesting items sandwiched between the pages.

It was Ted Grimshaw's make-shift diary, recording forty years of eventful days beginning 1944, the year her parents had married. A musty odour rose from its pages as she turned them one by one. Some years had gone by with only two or three entries. Catherine found the day of her own birth, under which he'd written, 'It's a girl. She looks like an angel and has his red hair, but she'll have Grimshaw values, and all of our love.' A dried flower fell out onto the bed. Could have been a rose, but Catherine wasn't sure. She replaced it carefully. Further on, there was a lock of hair from her first hair cut, a postcard from Skegness, sent by Steven on his first trip away from home, and a hospital wrist band, with registration number but no name, from Molly's admission to Cherry Knowles Hospital. Under September 4th 1984 he wrote:

'Visited Moll in the psyche ward. Desperate place. Unclear how much she understands. What might she have said to that nurse who called her an old fool? I should have said something. I'm a coward.'

There was a rhyme, but nothing like the silly ones he'd make up for the market crowd. It was dated six weeks before Ted's suicide.

Watching you fade behind unfeeling eyes,

begging you, take off this awful disguise
Where did you go when there's reason to stay?
Your body's still here, yet your mind far away
Our children are grown, yet I'm still around
clutching at hope someday you will be found
We know that you have only limited time
We once had a life, I've tried to live mine
But now the time's come to call it a day
I'm sorry, my family, I too cannot stay.

Ted Grimshaw

Catherine flopped back onto the candlewick bedspread and swallowed, but the lump wouldn't go down. This was a side to her father she'd not seen before. She remembered how strong he'd always been. Yet here he was, confiding all to a W.H. Smith blue lined note book. He had no-one. Catherine was away from home wrapped up in her own life, her brother Steven had just been imprisoned, and Molly, like he said, not there. Doris had come in at just the right time. To drop off groceries, turn Molly's mattress and lift Ted's heart. It was clear from the dates, Doris had placed his intentions on hold, if only temporarily.

She pulled herself upright on the bed, glanced at her watch and closed the book. The unread parts, along with other papers could be left for another time. But the bundle of letters still intrigued her. Some were fully addressed and post marked, others looked hand delivered with just 'Molly' written on the front. With a pang of conscience she put them back and lifted out the newspaper cuttings.

Separated into two piles, they covered every press story involving the Grimshaw and Moretti families. Butcher's name cropped up in many of the Morettis' news items, but there were also cuttings from his business successes of 1971, 73 &74 included with the Grimshaws' collection.

Dissatisfied at her lack of achievement, she put away the cuttings. The afternoon was almost gone, and she felt annoyed with herself for having wasted so much time. Yet still those private letters of Molly's beckoned to her like a fat cream cake during a bad spell of PMT. She attacked the garden twine with finger nails, teeth, and a pair of pruning shears she found in Ted's old gardening jacket.

Once she began reading, it was impossible to stop. Declarations of love with enough passion to self combust. All dated between June and December of 1961 and she realised the connection. With her own date of birth. For all of her life, she hadn't wanted to know anything about her biological father. Ted Grimshaw was more of a father than she could ever need, but now the Jack was out of the box, she wanted more.

The first four letters were signed, 'Walter.' The fifth envelope included a black and white head and shoulders photograph of a youngish man with a vaguely familiar bearded face, which was presumably her biological father. She only presumed because although the hand writing was the same as all the others, the signature at the bottom had expanded from just 'Walter' to 'W.M.B.' Even more intrigued, she opened the final four letters, placing them in a horizontal row in chronological order across the bedspread. Each one had been signed in full by a man who had seemingly by now, discovered and proudly revealed his own identity, and as Catherine stared disbelievingly at the closing greeting and long winded signature, she began to realise it too.

All my love,

Walter Melvyn Butcher xxx

Catherine's heart pounded against her chest. She hurried from the bedroom and down the stairs to the bins in the garden. It was dark, and the only light available came from the kitchen window. Tossing cans and yoghurt cartons onto the grass, she reached a layer of nasties she preferred not to touch. Then she spotted the corner of it, sticking out from a pile of wet spaghetti, potato peelings and egg shells. And newspapers tended to absorb stuff. With downturned mouth she gave it a gentle tug, until it resurfaced in one piece, and despite a used tea bag stuck to his chest, the remainder of the image was unmarked. She examined his ears and his nose for similarities with her own, but the comparisons were hard to make, mainly because of his horizontal position, facial gravity, and tube installation systems, which formed an effective disguise. And then, she looked at his hair. It was greying of course, but there was no doubt about it. He was, like her, a redhead.

What was she supposed to do now? Carry on like nothing had happened? The pieces with all their misshapen edges were beginning to come together. She'd acquired her job at the hotel, not through merit, but an accident of birth. And the college course – 'Somebody upstairs must like you,' Teresa had said, although 'likes' wasn't quite the right word. How could Melvyn Butcher like her, when he knew nothing about her? Or did he? Perhaps he'd watched her every move without her knowing. She needed to talk to someone, but Doris was working and Kenny was unavailable as always. Then she remembered the scribbled telephone number on a beer mat stuffed into her handbag on the previous Friday, and the offer to call anytime.

She thought at first he wasn't at home, but then she heard a breathless,

"Hello."

"Hello, Rob?"

"That's me."

"Hi, it's Cathy Grimshaw. You probably don't remember me do you?"

He better had.

"How could I forget a woman who attracts mayhem wherever she goes?"

Not exactly the answer I was hoping for.

"I'm not disturbing you, am I?"

"Not really. Why? Is something wrong?"

"I've found something out about your shooting victim, Mel Butcher," she told him. "I don't suppose you could come round?"

Chapter twenty nine : Secrets and lies

Chapter thirty : Discovering Wolf number 3

"So, do you want to go and see him?" asked Rob, when Catherine finished telling her story.

"What would be the point? He's probably going to die anyway...." She picked up the newspaper, pointing at the tea stained photograph of Butcher on the front cover. "Just look at the state of him." Her voice trembled, and she dragged fingers through her hair, throwing the newspaper back down.

"Cathy," he said calmly, "Butcher is conscious. They moved him onto a ward yesterday."

She looked away. "Oh ..... I see."

"If you'd like someone to go with you, I don't mind."

"Thanks," she said, "but I don't think so. If he's going to be all right, there's no real urgency."

"Ok, so if he's going to die, there's no point, and if he's going to live there's no urgency?"

She gave him a brief sideways glance. "I just need time."

"And by the way, your driving examiner's on the mend.

"Oh, that's brilliant news. Thanks for letting me know."

"So, how about a swift half in The Dog and Duck?"

She laughed at his preposterous suggestion.

"Yeah ...... Why not?"

***

If there was one word to describe Sergeant Robert Sutton, it would surely be 'decent.' Now thirty eight years old, Rob, a divorced father of two, with an ex wife and children living in Northern Ireland, appeared to exist for his work. In recent weeks he'd volunteered his dish washing skills to a battered wife, just back from casualty with an arm in plaster, two kids in nappies and a social worker on the doorstep with a child care order. He'd stopped his car on the Coast Road to allow a mummy hedgehog and her baby cross over, ignoring the honking from drivers behind him. And Catherine liked him, which made her scared.

By the end of the evening spent pouring out her soul, Catherine had drunk way too much. Getting through the next morning at work was managed only with the help of over the counter medication. By the afternoon her hangover had lifted, and she went into college as she had done every Thursday afternoon for the last few months, aching for comfort, though this time needing more than just sex. They were using her parents' room by now, and afterwards, they lay together, uncovered. His sweat mingled with hers as they held one another close, and she wished he wouldn't leave.

"Ken," she said with a serious look.

"What?"

"I know that we sort of agreed not to talk about this," she continued, and his brow furrowed. "But are we ever going to be together for more than just Thursday afternoons?"

He smiled. "Of course we will. I told you right at the beginning. I'm only staying until the children are older. Zoe and I can't stand the sight of one other."

"And you really don't sleep together?"

He laughed. "We haven't slept together for over a year now. I mean, she could have grown a third breast and chest hair for all I know." He paused. "Zoe likes to go drinking with her friends most evenings while her mother minds the kids. Do you think I want to sleep next to a human distillery breathing alcoholic fumes all night?"

"Why does her mother look after the kids?"

"What do you mean?"

"I just wondered why you didn't do it. If you were home, that is."

Chapter thirty : Discovering Wolf number 3

"What is this? The Spanish Inquisition? I work in the evenings. I have marking to do, lesson preparation."

She wanted to believe him, and almost as fast as she'd asked the question, she wished she could take it back. She made a pitiful attempt to compensate.

"I see, Mister McGuire." She rubbed her chin in mock concentration. "This sounds like your wife has a case of triple nipple and too much tipple." He smiled, but she sensed his discomfort, and if he had lied, then she must have forced him to do so. It would be safer to keep silly thoughts to herself in future.

A few days went by and news items reported Butcher to be in a stable condition. Catherine still felt the need to do something with the facts recently brought to light, and she began searching for job vacancies. It may have been the wrong course of action, but emotions were high, and something needed to change.

***

On the morning of her interview at the Sea Hotel, she woke with nausea, and put it down to nerves. Her appointment wasn't until 10 o'clock, so she took her time getting dressed in a smart black suit with a straight knee length skirt and a pale yellow blouse beneath, by which time the nausea had passed and she ate her usual digestive biscuit. But this time smeared with a knife load of peanut butter and washed down with a cup of Horlicks. Her period must be due. She checked the calendar to confirm, and then realised it was very overdue. This wasn't normal, but no reason for panic. Things had happened recently which must have affected her hormones or something. Catherine's heart performed somersaults inside her ribcage, and she forced herself to take deep, calming breaths. She thought of questions that might be asked. This distracted her for the bus journey, but hastened her ordeal with the interrogation squad somehow.

The interview began in a small office with two suited and booted executive males, and all seemed to be going well for the first few minutes until she had to excuse herself quickly as a sudden wave of sickness threatened not only her composure but also the hotel's expensive looking carpet.

As she leaned over the toilet bowl in the ladies' powder room, she cursed all men and praised her choice of a yellow blouse that morning. Splashing her face with cold water at the sink, an overalled figure entered the room and scowled at her through the mirror. Catherine pulled a paper towel from a wall mounted container, pressed it to her lips and glanced up at the silent female whose frown lines deepened as she sniffed the air, and squirted a spray can into the cubicle Catherine had just vacated. Feeling too wretched to make a fuss, Catherine lifted up her bag, swung it onto her shoulder and headed for the door. As she passed the cleaner, she paused for a moment.

"If you pride yourself on sterilising all of your female guests, I'm afraid you're a couple of weeks too late in my case." Then she pulled open the door and left the woman trying to solve the cryptic clue.

***

Catherine woke next morning feeling just as rough. She navigated her body to the bathroom and stared nervously at the do-it-yourself pregnancy testing kit she'd bought the previous afternoon. Maybe there was an undo-it-yourself kit she could buy, depending on the outcome of this one. A result within the hour. She glanced at the clock and calculated if she started right now she'd have ten minutes after the verdict to either get over the shock or sigh with relief before leaving for work.

Having done the business, she left the prepared sample on the bathroom sill to develop at its own pace while she washed, dressed, and had half made up her face when the door bell rang. On her way to answer, she glanced at the clock again. It was only eight fifteen and Rob Sutton stood on the door step, uniformed beneath his overcoat and looking serious.

"Rob? What you doing here? Is something wrong?"

"Don't get worried," he said. "It's likely nothing."

"Do you want to come in for a minute?" She opened the door wide and let him through. Rob came straight to the point.

"It's Butcher," he said. "He was taken back into theatre an hour ago. Some sort of internal haemorrhage." Catherine closed the door behind him.

"Do you think it could be serious?"

"They didn't give us any more details than that. I've just come off duty, so I thought I'd let you know."

She shrugged. "I've got to leave for work in a minute. Maybe I can ring the hospital from there."

"Well I'd like to do that for you," he offered, "but I could be asleep for the rest of the day." Then, he suddenly brightened. "Or I could drop you at work now if you like. It's on my way."

"Oh? Well only if it's no bother," she said, with eyes up the staircase to the bathroom door with regret. "I'll get my coat."

It was twelve o'clock lunchtime when she summoned the courage to ring the hospital.

"I'm enquiring about Melvyn Butcher," she said. "I believe he had surgery this morning."

Chapter thirty : Discovering Wolf number 3

"Are you a relative?"

"Yes I am," she said with more confidence. "I'm his daughter."

"Mr. Butcher's surgery was successful, but he will remain in intensive care for the next twenty four hours, as a precautionary measure."

"Oh thank you. That's good news."

"I'll tell him you called," said the nurse. "Goodbye."

There was a click on the line, terminating the conversation.

"Oooh.... please don't do that..."

It may have been due to the optimistic news from the hospital, or else just the simple fact that the sun was shining brightly through the glass fronted doors, but she breezed through the next two hours of her shift without a care. There were, of course, one or two minor in-house crises. An elderly male guest on the first floor had started to run a bath and then fallen asleep with the water left to soak a store cupboard of clean table linen on the floor beneath. Had it not been for the abundance of gravy splashers in the restaurant that lunchtime, the disaster may not have been discovered. Until later, anyway.

In the laundry room, washing machines whirred, tumble driers steamed and Phil Colman made a show of attacking the ironing in person with gusto and spray starch. But they were still short of twelve clean table covers for high tea at 4 p.m. In desperation, Phil begged Marcus to allow a staff member with a slack half hour to buy some new ones. Catherine volunteered.

Nightingale's was the biggest soft furnishing store in town with a decent selection at sufferable prices, and Catherine picked up a dozen white cloths at a good discount. The check out was at the end of the bedding section, through which she began to weave her way, struggling to carry the bundles in her arms. It was the voice she recognised first. That seductively charming Golders Green accent she'd spent so many stolen afternoons alone with. The voice that had told her how special she was, and how much she was loved.

"Aw, Zoe," he spoke with endearment, but this time to another. "Look at this."

Catherine craned her neck past her purchases. Kenny McGuire stood sideways on, facing a cot display with lace trimmed baby quilt and matching pillow from 'The little sleepy heads' range.

"Zoe, come here." He beckoned to a tall willowy brunette, standing with her back to Catherine. Zoe turned towards her husband, and in so doing, revealed a heavily swollen belly of some eight months gestation. Catherine froze. She watched him place an arm around this woman while they swooned over all things miniature. Catherine wanted to laugh, cry and vomit in that order, but she took a deep breath, and swept past the pair of them, excusing her way to the check out. She paid and headed for the exit. As she pushed the door open, she turned briefly and met his gaze for just a second as she stepped out onto the street. Zoe spotted the exchange of looks.

"Do you know that woman?" she said.

He turned to her and shrugged. "I think I may have taught her once."

The counter assistant had tied the brown paper package with very fine nylon twine, and as Catherine arrived back at The Dolphin, Phil, taking the parcel from her, spotted the deeply etched red lines across the palm of Catherine's right hand.

"Whoaa!" he remarked. "I bet that's painful."

She didn't even look at her hands. "Yes, it hurts like hell."

The same bright sun continued to shine through the front doors of the hotel as she sat on reception, but this time it irritated, and she was glad to board the familiar old bus that was to take her back home. She stepped inside her own front door with tired feet and a heavy heart. All those things he'd said were lies. He and Zoe couldn't bear the sight of one another. So what was that bulge inside her coat? He'd already painted her as a knife wielding drunk. Maybe add kleptomania to the list with a preference for scatter cushions. And of course he couldn't bear the sight of her. Could be a test tube creation. Who knows? She hung up her coat and climbed the stairs.

Catherine didn't hate Zoe anymore. If it really wasn't a scatter cushion, Zoe was carrying his third child. For that she was to be pitied. At the top of the stairs, Catherine pushed open the bathroom door, looked at the indicator on the testing kit, and felt even more pity for herself. Her bubble had well and truly burst. Welcome to reality.

***

Catherine was grateful for the next two weeks to study for the exam ahead. Her tuition was over, and she was relieved not to have to face him again. There'd been no telephone calls, no attempt at communication of any sort, so he either felt some sort of guilt, or had erased her name without a second thought from his list of students with 'potential.' Kenny had hinted he might be invigilating for at least part of the exam, but it wasn't certain, and as the time loomed closer she worried more about that than getting through the paper. Cathy's pregnancy was confirmed by her G.P., and a follow up appointment was made for the day after her exam to discuss options, when she could afford the time to be upset.

Chapter thirty : Discovering Wolf number 3

It was the Sunday before exam week, and the family were invited to Louise and Michael's house for lunch. There hadn't been a family get together for a while, and Catherine had missed their company and careless banter. Everyone was dying to know the details surrounding the shootings at the hotel, since nothing of the background story had been printed in the papers. Danny had been questioned by the police about his uncle Joe, but there were still lots of gaps in that story.

While she and Louise washed dishes in the kitchen, Cathy needed answers herself.

"So Lou, I know you and Danny have always been close," she began.

"I think I know what you're going to ask," said Louise.

"You do?"

"Well it's what I'd be wondering in your position. You want to know exactly what Danny told the police about the money and how he got it."

"There are one or two other things as well, like how the conversation went between Butcher and Danny after Joe was arrested? I can't imagine it was a friendly one."

Louise dried another plate, and added it to the pile. She hesitated to answer, so Catherine continued.

"I'm guessing if he was to tell anyone, it would be you,"

Holding a bottle of wine, Steven and Danny appeared on cue in the kitchen doorway.

"My ears are burning," said Danny. The women both turned, and Catherine grabbed a towel for her hands. She looked directly at her brother.

"I expect you know the whole story too, Steven?" she said. "Am I the only one out of the loop here?"

"We had to be careful not to tell you much," said Steven. "You're the one with the copper boyfriend."

"Give me some credit for God's sake. And Rob's not my boyfriend, ok? We're just friends."

Louise looked doubtful. "But you're working on that? It's obvious you like him."

Catherine shrugged. "Maybe I do. But anyway, I wasn't friends with Rob back then."

"You were taking care of Gran," said Louise. "You had enough on your plate."

"Look," said Danny, "I had to tell them the money was freely given by my uncles when they knew they'd be going to prison. And they'd asked me to invest it wisely, so when they got out they'd have some return on it. I wasn't to know it was stolen, was I? I was just a kid at the time." Catherine looked sceptical. "All right, so later, the penny dropped. But I couldn't let the police know that, or it would be admitting I was involved. ....So I bought a share in the garage. I didn't tell them Joe was chasing me that day. I said I was taking him to his new investment, until Mel Butcher showed up looking for Joe, and then the police. They couldn't prove that wasn't how it really happened."

"Danny didn't want to lie to you, Cath," said Steven, "but it was the only way out of the mess. He even offered to sign over his share in the business to Butcher, to make things right, but Butcher told him to keep it. It seemed odd, and we still don't understand why. But until he changes his mind, will you come and have a glass of this wine? Because it's getting warm in my sweaty hand."

Catherine sighed.

"Actually, things are adding up now you've explained. And since we're coming clean, there's something I need to tell you lot as well ..."

***

On the morning of the exam, she was thankful the toast she'd eaten for breakfast remained in place, despite the bumpy bus ride to the venue.

The examination room smelled of sweat. Or rather, fear.

God, help me. Catherine sat down at the isolated desk with her number on it, and a mature female voice addressed the whole room.

"I must ask you all to remain silent from now on. Only writing materials on the desk, please."

Cathy sighed on hearing the invigilator's voice. She turned for confirmation, recognising the spectacle frames, tightly drawn back hair style and sour face of the college secretary who had shooed her out of the classroom months before. The secretary stared back at her.

"Not even God can help you now," she said.

She's a bleeding mind reader.

The secretary licked her thumb from time to time as she placed a question paper on each desk, offering practical advice to selected candidates as she went, such as,

"Would you like a rubber band for your hair problem sir, or is it madam?" and,

"If you can't get your feet under the desk, you'll have to leave your bovver boots by the door, dear."

Crimes against fashion. Off with their heads!

Catherine's paper was about to be lick-thumbed.

Chapter thirty : Discovering Wolf number 3

Go on, say something. I'm just in the mood for a Barney.

The secretary hovered, having placed the paper face down on Catherine's desk.

"Don't you have a black pen?" she said.

"Er, no. Will blue not do?"

"If you'd read your handout from your last class, it says clearly..."

"I missed the last one. I was sick." *Sick of his lies.*

"You should have contacted your department. It's a pity. Your paper could be disqualified."

"Is it worth me staying, then?"

"That's entirely your choice." She carried on down the row.

While Catherine deliberated whether or not to throttle her, a black biro landed at her foot with a clatter. She glanced behind, to see the back of Kenny McGuire slipping out of the door.

Coward with a conscience.

"You can turn over your papers now."

Chapter thirty one : Plan of action

Teresa came into work the next day wearing a grey pin striped tailored suit, not uniform issue, with shoulder pads even higher than normal. She marched up to reception where Catherine sat sorting the mail into piles.

“Marcus is ill, darling,” she explained. “I’m acting up as Manager today.”

Catherine stopped what she was doing.

“Oh, I see. Nothing too serious I hope?”

Teresa scanned the names on the top of each pile of letters and selected a handful for the admin staff upstairs. “No, darling.” She shook her head and waved a hand dismissively. “Just a bit of back ache as far as I can tell, but you know how men are.” She picked up the letters and continued distractedly, “Is everything all right with you, darling?”

“Actually, Teresa. I wondered if I could catch the earlier bus this afternoon. I’ve got a doctor’s appointment.

“Oh, darling!” Teresa pleaded. “You couldn’t have picked a worse day. I was going to ask you to stay a bit later tonight. Simon will be in at five to relieve you. It’s just that I won’t be here to do the middle shift.” She looked around, drumming her scarlet finger nails on the desk.

"What time is your appointment?"

"It's four-thirty," said Catherine, "but I can try to change it if you like."

"Oh could you? Even an hour would make such a difference."

Catherine smiled. "I'll give them a ring."

Teresa squeezed Catherine's letter sorting arm. "You're an absolute angel," she said, turning away, then back again to ask, "It's not a back problem as well is it?"

"No, Teresa, it's definitely not a back problem."

"Well thank goodness for that. Mind you ..." Teresa bent her head closer, "If it *had* been, I might suspect something was going on." She laughed nervously at the absurdity, turned, and headed for the service lift clutching the mail.

Catherine picked up the desk telephone and dialled her doctor's surgery. She waited a few seconds before the receptionist answered.

"Hello, Central Surgery. Maureen speaking, how can I help?" Maureen's squeaky voice made Catherine wince.

"Good morning. My name's Catherine Grimshaw and I have an appointment for four thirty this afternoon." She glanced around the hotel foyer as she spoke, checking for eavesdroppers. "Would it be possible to fit me in a bit later please?"

Maureen made a lot of juvenile sucking noises. "Oh, I don't know about that. Which doctor is it for?"

Catherine checked the foyer again for intrusive ears. A young couple emerged from the guest lift and chattered their way to the dining room.

"It's not the doctor," she said softly. "It's for a counselling session."

"Counselling?" came the squeaky reply, then a little more soprano as she dropped the rising slant. "Oh yes, I've got your notes up on screen now. It's a termination isn't it?"

"Yes, that's right," said Catherine, chewing her bottom lip. She could hear the turning of pages.

"There's a possible cancellation at six this evening, but I'll have to make a call to confirm it."

"Right, and you'll ring me back?"

"Yes I can do that, as soon as I find out," said Maureen, "and the number is?"

Catherine read out the number on the key pad in front of her, and Maureen repeated it back.

"Ok, I'll ring you back soon."

Chapter thirty one : Plan of action

Catherine replaced the handset and massaged her ear. For the last few days she'd noticed an inconvenient urge to empty her bladder more than usual. Some mornings she barely managed the bus journey, and on a regular basis thanked heaven and City Passenger Transport for placing a bus stop right outside her place of work.

Doris came out of the service lift at the opposite end of the foyer with mop and bucket in hand, waved across to Catherine, who beckoned frantically in return. Doris walked over with her tools of the trade.

"What's up love? Did you want me?"

"Would you mind covering for me while I go to the loo?"

"Ok love. You feeling all right? You look a bit peaky."

Catherine came around the other side of the counter, walking uneasily with her thighs pressed together. "Oh, I'm fine." She forced a smile. "Just need a wee that's all."

She hurried off towards the ladies.' "I'll be two minutes," she said, disappearing behind the door. Doris shrugged, walked behind the counter, put down her mop and bucket in a corner, and stared curiously at the computer monitor. The screen displayed icons for 'Windows,' and Doris rested her hand on the mouse, sliding it across the pad until the 'Solitaire' icon was highlighted. She clicked the mouse button and the screen filled with coloured playing cards. Doris's face lit up, and she hitched herself onto the swivel stool, sticking out her tongue in concentration as she manoeuvred the cards around. From across the foyer, the service lift doors re-opened, and Teresa stepped out. She marched across to reception where Doris was totally immersed in the game.

"Pardon me if I'm wrong," she began, leaning on the desk with fingers at full spread, "but aren't you dressed rather inappropriately for a job like this?"

Doris looked up. "Oh, I'm sorry Missus Capaldi," she began to explain, "but young Cathy was desperate for the toilet, and I was the only one handy to relieve her."

Teresa looked from Doris to the bucket, and realised the vessel wasn't necessarily linked to the statement. Doris stifled a laugh, but Teresa wasn't amused.

"This is really most unbecoming for a hotel of our reputation. I'd be grateful if you'd pick up that filthy mop and remove both *it* and yourself from behind that counter."

Doris looked offended. "Oh it's not filthy, Missus Capaldi. I washed it out in the sluice upstairs."

Teresa glared. "Wonderful. So it's clean. But I still neither wish to have *it*, nor a member of cleaning staff out on display behind reception, thank you very much."

Doris got up from her seat and collected her bucket and mop. On her way round to the other side of the desk, she said,

"Will you be taking over here then madam, or shall I go and give Catherine a poke in the toilet?"

Teresa inhaled deeply. "Yes Doris, I will be taking over here," she said, walking slowly around to the other side.

Doris retreated to the storage cupboard, muttering under her breath.

"Stuck up cow. Dress her up in a posh suit and she thinks she owns the flaming place."

Teresa went straight across to the computer screen where the game was set out in front of her.

"Brazen cow," she said. "Stick her in front of a computer screen and she thinks she can play a better game of Solitaire than I can," She seized the mouse and began to click away fiercely. The shrill sound of the telephone interrupted her concentration. Still distracted, Teresa stretched out her hand and picked up the handset in slow motion, with her eyes fixed on the screen and her spare hand on the mouse. The caller had already begun speaking before the receiver met Teresa's ear.

"Sorry to have kept you waiting," said the doctor's receptionist, "but I haven't been able to reschedule your counselling session this evening."

"I beg your pardon?" said Teresa. "Sorry, I didn't quite catch what you said."

"Your termination counselling session?" said Maureen. "I haven't been able to change your appointment, sorry. I *am* speaking to Miss Grimshaw aren't I?" she attempted to confirm, slowing the speed of her voice slightly. Teresa looked across at the door of the ladies' powder room which was just opening, and Catherine stepped out, adjusting her skirt.

Teresa kept her gaze on Catherine as she approached. "Actually, no. I'll just bring her to the telephone." She lowered the handset and pointed it towards Catherine.

"Telephone call for you," Teresa smiled. "Is it a wind-up darling?"

Catherine took the handset. "A wind-up? What do you mean?"

"Well, that awful voice of course. She could double up as a police siren, that one."

Catherine exhaled. "Oh, yeah. Look, if you want to get off, I can take over now." She stared at Teresa, as she held the telephone mouthpiece tightly with the palm of her hand.

"Oh right, darling." Teresa clicked the mouse to exit the game. "I've got a complaint to investigate on the second floor anyway." She slid down from her stool and left the counter, looking back with concern as Catherine began speaking into the telephone.

"Hello, Catherine Grimshaw here."

***

Catherine's decision to terminate her pregnancy was the only practical one to make under the circumstances. She was just finding her way in the world. Without support, she couldn't imagine a future as a single parent. Catherine had only five days until her rescheduled counselling appointment, after which she would have a termination date, and a chance to move on with her life.

It was just after nine in the morning a few days later; the newspaper orders had been made up and dispatched to the guests, and Catherine was relaxing with Doris over a quiet cup of tea in the back office.

"So, where did the judge take you last night then?" asked Catherine, easing herself up onto the desk.

"Oh, you'll never guess." Doris tested the swivel action on her chair. "We went to the amusements and had photos taken in one of those booths they make especially for tiny thin people."

"That's really sweet," said Catherine. "Everyone's noticed how much the judge has changed lately. He's not nearly so grumpy.

That's down to you, no question. I wish I could meet someone like that." She blew onto her tea and took a minute sip.

"Thought you already had," said Doris. "You've been keeping *something* under your hat, that's for sure. I've seen that car bringing you back from college. When are you gonna spill the beans?"

"Oh, *that* car. Honestly Doris, you spend too much time behind those lace curtains."

Doris raised an eyebrow in response.

"Well, there *was* someone. I knew him from way back. Or at least *thought* I knew him.....But it's all over now and good riddance."

"Did he do something awful?"

"You know, Doris, I've never been abroad. I'm well past thirty and hardly been across the doors. How do you fancy going away with me?"

"Well I'm up for anything, you know that. Even if you are just dodging the question."

Catherine adjusted her position in the chair, and seemed suddenly alert.

"No, I mean it. Somewhere like Menorca. You know, one of the quieter islands. When are your summer holidays?"

"Beginning of June. First two weeks I think. Shall I get some brochures?"

"Yes. We can make a night of it. Are you free on Friday?"

"I can be free on Friday. Do you think you might be ready to tell me what happened by then?"

Catherine sighed.

"Can I think about that one?"

"When you're ready then."

"So anyway, has the judge kissed you yet?"

Doris winked. "He's done better than that," she said with a smile.

Catherine almost choked on the edge of her tea cup. "Whaat? You mean he's......"

Doris interrupted. "Yes, that's right. He's asked if he can take my dead husband's place."

"But you've only known him a few minutes. What did you say?"

Doris gave a wicked smile. "I told him it was fine by me," she said, calmly slurping her tea, warming her hands on the cup. "He can take my dead husband's place any time he likes.....so long as the undertaker doesn't mind swapping them over."

The internal telephone line rang out on the desk, and Doris lifted the receiver.

"Halloo. Wishy washy Chinese laundry. How can I help yoooou?"

A serious male voice spoke to her from the fourth floor. "Is Catherine Grimshaw there please? It's Jack Spence here."

Doris gulped, straightened her hat and resumed her self-composure. "Er, yes she is. One moment please." She pressed her hand over the mouthpiece and whispered urgently to Cathy. "It's Jack Spence, for you."

Catherine puzzled as she took the receiver from Doris's vice-like grip.

"Hello? Catherine Grimshaw," she said.

"Catherine. I wondered if you could come up for five minutes and have a chat? It's nothing to worry about, just something we need to discuss."

For a man who kept an ongoing remoteness from his staff, Jack Spence sounded surprisingly human, Catherine thought.

"Um, yes of course, Mister Spence. Do you mean now?"

"Yes, if that's convenient."

"Where do I find you?"

"It's the dark green door with the brass name plate. Just three quarters of the way along the corridor from the service lift. It's impossible to miss," said Spence.

"Right, I'll see you shortly then." She put down the receiver.

Chapter thirty one : Plan of action

"What's up love? Have you been summoned upstairs?"

"I have. And I should have expected it." She got down from the desk and checked her reflection in a tiny six inch mirror stuck on the wall by the door. "And when I get back," she turned to Doris, "I want to know what you really said to the judge."

The fourth floor smelled strongly of wood polish and Brasso. There was a deep red carpet with a fleur-de-lys pattern running the full length of the oak panelled corridor, and there were framed, autographed celebrity photos on the walls. There was a dust-outlined gap where Wayne Vincent's photograph used to be. She'd only been up there two or three times before, but never by invitation.

I'm getting my P45. Feel it in my water. Catherine knocked at the glossy green surface of Jack Spence's office door, already ajar. A man's deep voice could be heard from within.

"Come in."

Catherine eased open the door and stepped inside. Spence got up from behind his desk and came forward offering his hand. The pony tail was gone, transforming his image into something far less thuggish.

"Good morning, Catherine. It's good to meet you finally." For a man of over six feet tall and around seventeen stones, Spence's handshake was untypically gentle.

"Please sit down," he offered with a hand gesture, indicating any one of three leather bound chairs, placed at random around his desk. Catherine chose the chair nearest the exit.

"Mister Spence," she began, "does this meeting have anything to do with my father?" She was surprised at her own outspokenness, but now that it was out there, she had no desire to take it back. Spence's eye to eye contact with Catherine's did not waver, although he managed a smile at her straight question."

He reached across his desk for a small box with a Nokia logo, and handed it to her. "This is yours," he said. She looked confused.

"I don't think I understand."

"All the service staff are being issued with a mobile telephone. It will make life much easier when there's sickness, emergency cover required, and so on. All the numbers you need are in there, and the rental is covered by the company. Just remember to keep it charged." She took it from him.

"Sorry, I thought I'd been called up here for a different reason."

"Well, you have," he said, sitting back down in his chair. "This was just something I had to get out of the way first." She gave him a nervous look. He continued. "Mister Butcher discharged himself from hospital yesterday, against his surgeon's wishes, and he's determined to complete his recovery in the rooms adjoining this office." He indicated an interior door to his left, and noticing her unease he smiled reassuringly. Your father had wished to remain anonymous to you Catherine, and he was coping with the status quo very well, until a recent chain of events rather altered his outlook, and when he came to realise that you knew of his identity."

Catherine interrupted. "Was it the call I made to the hospital?"

"Well, you weren't obvious enough to give your name to the nursing officer, but you did say that you were his daughter, and Mr. Butcher doesn't have any other daughters. In fact, although he may have led, how do I put this, an adventurous life in his youth, I'm afraid you are his only surviving child." He gave her a meaningful stare which she tried to return but failed at the first blink.

"So what happens now? Does he want to speak to me?" she asked.

Spence leaned forward and fingered his biro. "Well that rather depends on you. Mister Butcher would very much like to meet you, but only if you're agreeable."

Catherine thought for a moment. "That's ok…I'll see him."

Jack Spence got up slowly from his seat and walked to the end of his desk.

"And do you feel up to seeing him now?"

Her eyes flitted across the room. She chewed on her bottom lip, and nodded. "Now will be fine."

Spence approached the door leading to Butcher's suite, opened it a fraction, and put his head inside. There was a muffled exchange of words, then he turned back to Catherine. "Would you like to come this way?" he said.

Chapter thirty one : Plan of action

Chapter thirty two : A meeting with father

Mel Butcher sat upright in a wing backed easy chair, supported at each side by soft pillows. A canister of oxygen stood by on the floor, and a transparent mask hung around his chin. His white shirt was only just visible beneath a deep blue silk dressing gown and a brightly coloured patchwork quilt, draped across his lower half. His skin was pallid, stretched tautly across his cheekbones, and Catherine could almost follow the path of blue veins from several feet away.

"Catherine," he spoke softly as she entered the room. "Please... come in and sit down."

As she found herself a seat, Butcher waved a hand at Jack to dismiss him. She heard the door close behind him and looked across at Butcher to see him staring at her.

"You'll have to excuse me," he said, "but .... the medication I'm taking at the moment tends to slow me down a little."

"Is there anything you'd like me to get you? Glass of water?"

He shook his head. "No, no thank you. I have a nurse in attendance ... to do things like that for me." With a pained expression, he shuffled around in the armchair. "Catherine, there are one or two ..... time-sensitive things that I feel we should discuss."

"What does that mean? Time sensitive?"

He gave a sardonic laugh, "I'll get to that in a minute, but in the meantime, is there anything you want to know .... about me?"

"Well, since you're asking, why did you run out on my mother all those years ago when you claimed to have loved her so much?"

Butcher looked at her with regret, then settled his gaze on the floor.

"I don't have a good enough reason for that ..... other than .... not being ready to face up to my responsibilities at the time. .... I ran a market stall. I'd no money, no prospects. I thought I was doing her, and you, a favour. I cared for your mother very much. I wrote to her several times .... telling her why."

"But that doesn't explain why you didn't contact us later on, when you began to make money from your nightclubs, became successful."

"There were only two nightclubs ..... and I did send your mother money when you were three years old. I sent her a cheque, for a hundred pounds." He took a breath. "It may not sound a lot now .... but back then a hundred pounds was worth around six weeks wages. Ted Grimshaw returned it to sender without a stamp." He seemed amused at the memory.

"Yes, well, Ted was always far too proud to accept hand outs of any kind."

"If you've been looking into my past, which I'm sure you have ..... you will know that there was a significant amount of cash stolen from my safe some years ago ..... by a family connected to yours by marriage." Catherine pressed her lips together. He continued. "I should never have got involved with the Moretti brothers. Success seems to make others resentful of it."

She looked directly into Butcher's watchful gaze, and tried to work out what he was thinking. Was this matter really over, like Steven said? He placed the mask over his face and took several breaths, before lowering it again.

"Did you ever wonder ..... why I never tried to get the money back after Joe Moretti was arrested for his brother's murder?"

Catherine shrugged. "Perhaps you didn't know where else to look."

"Well, the police offered to do that for me. But it wasn't difficult to work out once Moretti led me to the prize. Your nephew had suddenly acquired a share in a garage enterprise ...... at a very tender age. I wasn't stupid enough to assume he'd coincidentally come into a huge amount of money ... albeit several years after I'd just suddenly lost one. The Morettis were banged up and they couldn't spend it. It stood to reason that someone was minding it for them."

Chapter thirty two : A meeting with father

She lowered her eyes to the floor. “Danny wasn’t in league with the Morettis. He just took advantage of the fact they trusted him with the safety deposit key. He was a mere child when they gave him that responsibility. He wanted to set something up for his father when he came out of prison. Wanted to make him proud. You can hardly condemn him for that.”

Butcher smiled. “I could never condemn anyone ... for taking care of their own.” He paused briefly to take one or two steady breaths, “... and that’s the reason why I left it where it was, because Danny is a Grimshaw. My daughter’s nephew. If I hurt him, I hurt you.”

“I don’t understand why that would make any difference to you,” she said. “You had the Morettis burn down a night club for the insurance. I’m sure you didn’t concern yourself how many people were inside at the time.”

He looked wounded. “I don’t kill people, Catherine. I may have done some stupid things in my time ... things I regret bitterly now, but I never took lives .... and never used weapons. It’s important to me you understand that.” He paused once again to catch his breath. “There was a genuine purpose for that insurance money.” He hesitated for a moment and diverted his gaze.

“What purpose? If you needed money, why not just sell the business?”

He sighed. "We thought there wasn't time for that."

"Time? What was so urgent?"

Butcher rubbed his forehead. "Lizzie's treatment .... I wanted to take her to the States. They'd done pioneering surgery over there. I thought she'd have ..... a better chance. And ironically, there was no insurance money in the end. The claim failed because the Morettis left evidence behind. Yet they still wanted revenge."

Catherine uncrossed her legs and shuffled about in her seat.

"Who's Lizzie?"

"My wife," he said. "Lizzie ... was my wife. And In the end, I did sell both businesses, and she got her treatment. It bought us a few more years, but her quality of life wasn't good."

She looked down, and began to tug impatiently at a loose thread in her skirt.

"I'm sorry to hear about that."

"They killed my dog, you know."

Catherine raised her head. "Who killed your dog?"

"The Morettis. The money was important at the time, for Lizzie. But my dog. I could never forgive them for that."

"I didn't know. There was nothing in the papers about that. That's a dreadful thing." She paused for a moment. "But why did you really want to see me?"

He pulled himself up in his chair as well as he was able.

"To ask you ... *not* to abort this baby you're carrying."

She stared at him for a moment, then blinked and lowered her eyes. "How do you know about that?"

"Marcus Capaldi is Jack Spence's right hand man. His wife ... heard something she shouldn't have, from your doctor's receptionist, and fortunately for me she tells her husband everything."

"Teresa." Said Catherine accusingly

"Please," he said, "don't be annoyed with Teresa. She's quite innocent in all of this."

She studied Butcher's face thoughtfully. "What is it to you, whether I have an abortion or not?"

His face softened. "I don't have a string of heirs .... to take over from me when I go. My wife suffered miscarriages. I got the news that she had passed away while I was in hospital. So, ... being my only child and surviving family member, I was rather pinning all my hopes on you .... to .... carry on the family lineage."

"Mister Butcher, the father of this baby is already married. I have neither emotional nor financial support to raise this child. It would be madness to even consider it."

"For what it may be worth, Catherine .... I will try to give you as much emotional support .... as I can, and the financial side of things goes without saying. You will have as much as you need, and more .... I own eighty five percent of the shares in this business. There are also two tanning salons, and a bar."

"But why this baby? What if I was to meet someone in say, five years and decide to have a baby then? Wouldn't that be a better start for the child? To have a mother and a father raise it together?"

"Yes," he agreed. "You're absolutely right, and maybe I'm being selfish asking you to keep .... a child you don't feel prepared for. But in five years who knows what will happen? This baby is here now. You can't expect everything to turn out the way you would like. I've learned that the hard way." He gazed out of the window. "I rather like the idea of sitting my grandchild on my knee and making him or her smile. That may sound ... selfish, but it may be the only chance I get. It's a well used cliché, and I apologise for using it, but ... I'm not getting any younger. There could even be another assassin out there .... waiting. We just don't know."

"Do you have other enemies? Is that why you keep such a low profile?"

Chapter thirty two : A meeting with father

"I keep a low profile because ... I'm not the man I was since the acid attack ... and the shooting of course. As far as I'm aware, my only enemies were the Morettis. Since three of them are now dead, while another ... has been charged with murder, I'm fairly confident that threat has gone away, temporarily at least. However, Tony Moretti's two sons are already ... showing their hand in the drugs business. And that's not the kind of business I know anything about, I assure you. But I'll be keeping a close eye on them."

"I should get back to work," she said.

"Your brother should be wary too."

"Steven? You think they'd come after him? After he served his time?"

"The Morettis tend to seek their own justice. I could be wrong .... but he should be made aware."

She stood up to leave.

"Will you think about what I've said before you do anything?"

"Yes," she replied, getting up awkwardly. "I'll think about it."

Butcher reached across and removed a business card from a small desk tidy. "This is my mobile number," he said, handing it to her. "Maybe you'd like to visit again? In a few days or so?"

"I'll have to think about that." She pushed his card into her pocket and held the box given to her by Spence, aloft. "Clever idea – the staff phones."

"Nothing to do with me," he said. "I pay Jack to make those decisions."

Catherine smiled as she went to leave. "Take care, won't you?"

She walked slowly back along the corridor and descended the first flight of stairs when the telephone began to ring from the box in her hand. She opened it hastily and looked at the screen. Doris Fraser-Sour was calling. Catherine pressed the answer button and held it to her ear.

"Hello?"

"Catherine?"

"Doris? You've got one too?"

"Mister Capaldi just gave it to me. I overheard him talking to Missus Capaldi. Is it true?"

Catherine saw the Ladies toilet up ahead, crept silently inside and sat on the lid of a toilet seat. "I was going to tell you Doris. Truly I was. But I've planned a termination, so I thought there was no point."

"A termination? You mean you're pregnant?"

"Is ...that not what you meant?"

Chapter thirty two : A meeting with father

"These phones are damn good. It's like you're in the next cubicle."

Catherine was thinking the same. She stood up and left her cubicle, pushing the cubicle door next to her, to reveal a familiar pair of legs.

"Doris?"

"Jesus!" said Doris, looking up.

"Not quite." Cathy smiled.

"Marcus said that Mister Butcher was your father."

"You don't have to keep talking into the phone, Doris. I'm right here." Doris lowered her phone with a sheepish look and terminated the connection.

"I know that. You gave me a shock, that's all."

"It's true about Butcher. I only found out myself a few days ago. And the baby thing. It's like picking an old scab ..... just when I thought I had it all sorted in my head.

"Are you sure you've thought about this properly?" Doris came out of the cubicle and stood by the mirror. "Was it the mystery man from college?"

Catherine nodded. "He's married. And I've thought about it so much. Butcher....my biological father, wants me to have the baby. He needs an heir with a spare, apparently. Are all men born selfish? He's no ... no right ... to ask."

"Then don't consider him. The decision has to be yours. But please think about it some more before you go ahead."

Catherine sighed. "I don't get why you're so sentimental about a ....a peanut sized foetus neither of us are .... emotionally attached to."

Doris lowered her gaze to the wash basin in front of her. "You only think that's true because of the circumstances. But you can't know how this baby will turn out if you give it a chance. You take that chance away....and you will always wonder."

At that point, the entrance door opened and Teresa appeared on the threshold. "There you are!" she said. "One of the staff said you'd gone upstairs."

"Mister Spence summoned me," said Catherine. "Do you need me on the desk?"

"Have you spoken to him yet? I just wanted to catch you before....in case you didn't know....I wanted to explain. I told Marcus in confidence about the telephone call, I mean."

Catherine shook her head. "It's all fine Teresa, really. There's no point keeping secrets around here. Not anymore."

"Ok, well, if you're sure, then I'll see you downstairs." Teresa stepped out of the room, letting the door close behind her.

Chapter thirty two : A meeting with father

A few seconds went by, and Doris took a deep breath that seemed to catch in her throat.

"I gave my baby away when I was seventeen."

Catherine's gaped. "Whaaat? Oh my God, you never said. Who....who was the father?"

"Tim... my childhood sweetheart." She raised her eyes and looked imploringly into Catherine's through the mirror. "We were far too young. Mother went crazy. She sent me away to an aunt in Devon and I wasn't allowed to go out. When my time came, I moved into a home for wayward mothers.... run by nuns. I kept him for three hours. Then they took him away."

Catherine shook her head. "That's awful. Where did he go?"

"Adopted. They had a waiting list. I don't know where exactly. No-one would tell me. I went back home and carried on as if nothing had happened. Mother never mentioned it again." Silent tears rolled down her cheeks. Catherine had never seen her cry before.

"What happened to Tim? The boyfriend?"

"The family moved away while I was gone. I never saw him again." She wiped her face with the back of her hand. "I thought I'd have another chance when I married Arthur. But it wasn't to be."

Catherine sighed, stepped forwards, wrapped her arms around Doris's shoulders and hugged her close.

***

Catherine went back to work in a daze, and by the time she collected her coat at the end of her shift, she could barely recall the drunken pensioners who'd arrived on a coach, or the dining room search after lunch for a missing set of dentures and a whale bone corset.

She stepped out onto the main street, and instead of heading for the bus stop, she decided to stroll around town. It seemed as though everywhere she looked there were babies babbling in their buggies, toddlers having tantrums and children up to their chins in chocolate. Their mothers were chain smokers, badly dressed and over harassed. She observed them all, thoughtfully rearranging their lives for the better. After minutes, her nose picked up a meaty aroma, reminding her she hadn't eaten since that morning. She followed the trail to the open door of a nearby cafe as a happy patron stepped out onto the street. The room was filled with animated diners, exchanging anecdotes of family, work, and sensitive matters. A waitress with ruby cheeks piled empty plates onto a plastic tray as she swooped from table to table, while another scribbled orders on a pad and skewered the torn off pages on a spike behind.

When Catherine's order came, the plate was a mountain with barely space for salt. She was half way on the descent when her eye caught a familiar face peering through the crook of a diner's elbow. The place was packed, but Sergeant Rob lifted his coffee cup and squeezed between diners' chairs until he reached her table.

"Cathy," he said, as he came forward holding a chair he'd picked up on the way. "I never expected to find you in a place like this".

Catherine chewed and swallowed. "Hi Rob. No, I've never been here before, but the smell as I was passing made me hungry."

He put down the chair but remained standing.

"You don't mind if I join you?" he said. She'd hoped for more thinking time, but she liked Rob, and he'd been so kind to her already.

"Not at all. Sit, please. You can have some of this if you like," she indicated with her fork. "I'm starting to struggle a bit."

"You sure?" He pulled up his chair and picked up an extra fork. She smiled and pushed the plate towards him.

"Please, you'd be helping me out. So aren't you on duty today? Or is this a plain clothes exercise?" She hoped he wouldn't see through her poor attempt at light hearted conversation.

He took hold of his raincoat lapel and lifted it only slightly, revealing his police badge and uniform underneath.

"I've been in court," he said, loading his fork. Her eyes swept over his badge and settled upon a newborn, being cradled by its mother two tables away.

"And can you talk about it, or not?" she asked, still gazing at the infant.

Rob followed her gaze. "Oh, I can talk about it. It's all over now."

"Go on then. Spill..." said Catherine, distractedly.

"There were these two blokes you see. I won't use their real names. Slugger and Les we'll call them." Catherine appeared to show some initial interest.

"Well, they got into this drunken fight," he went on, "and Slugger bit off Les's earlobe, and then made off in a transit van headed down the motorway."

She raised her eyebrows, waiting for the next bit, but her eyes wandered again.

"So the judge says to Les, 'You have caused an affray, and for this you must pay a fine to the court of two hundred pounds.'

So Les protests, 'Yer Honour,' he says, because he wants to get on the judge's good side, 'How can you fine me that much when this man Slugger bit off my earlobe and drove away?'

So then the judge turns to Slugger, pulls a very stern face and says, 'and you, will be bound over to keep the peace for six months.' Well, Slugger was upset. 'Yer Honour,' he says, because he's trying to get in favour as well, 'I can't keep the piece for six months,' he says, 'I spat it out the window half way down the M6.'"

Rob stopped talking, and she realised she'd been rumbled.

"Oh God, I'm sorry. I've had such a day. You were testing me there, weren't you?"

"Maybe," he said. "But you do look like you need cheering up. Is something wrong?"

She screwed up her face. "Do you really want to hear the next episode of the Grimshaw / Butcher saga?"

"You might as well tell me. I can listen and chew at the same time."

He stabbed a piece of meat with his fork and held it aloft. "Is this pig?"

She gave him a wicked look. "To which end of the fork are you referring, officer?"

Rob put down his fork. "I completely gave you that one. It was a gift! Come on then, your turn to spill."

Catherine told him about the meeting with Butcher that morning, the state of his health and what he had asked her not to do. Then, of course she had to explain how she came to be pregnant in the first place, and that meant telling him all about Ken.

"Can I get you a coffee?" he asked, when she'd finished, "or a glass of milk might be better. Build up the stocks, so to speak." As soon as the words came out, he cringed. Cathy attempted a smile, but stayed quiet.

"Sorry, that wasn't the right thing to say."

"Don't worry about it. Things happen. I'll get over it."

"Whatever you decide to do," he continued, "if you need to talk, well, you've got my number."

"Thanks, Rob. That's appreciated."

The middle aged couple at the next table began to raise their voices, and people stared.

"I suppose when you die," shouted the man, "you'll be just as cold as you've always been." He stabbed at his egg and thrust it into his mouth. The woman leaned across and wiped a trickle of yolk from the side of his mouth with the edge of her sleeve.

"And when you snuff it," she said, "I expect you'll be as stiff as a poker.... for a change."

Catherine coughed. "I've got to go," she said with sucked in cheeks.

"Maybe we could go out sometime? I have to repay you for the pig chop."

Chapter thirty two : A meeting with father

Chapter thirty three : The decision is made

The following morning she phoned in sick. It was the last Saturday of the month, the day for updating the accounts. But Catherine couldn't focus. Ticking away at the back of her mind were the next forty eight hours of thinking time, and she wanted each moment uncorrupted by outside influence. Washing up the breakfast dishes she was reminded of the height of the grass outside and resolved to tackle it.

Ted's prehistoric lawnmower roared into action once its creaky joints were oiled. But as she turned the mower around, there was a different kind of squeak. It continued even after the blades had stopped. She left the mower, peering into the narrow space between tool shed and garden fence, where she found the towel she'd hung on the washing line weeks before. Lying on the surface, was a litter of kittens. Three dead, and two others protesting loudly, necks outstretched. Their tiny bodies were emaciated. Catherine looked around the garden and up into the tree, but there was no sign of a mother, and from the plight of the kittens, she'd been gone some time.

Catherine squatted by the end of the shed and stretched her arm as far as she could until she felt the edge of the towel connect with her finger tips. Several grunts later, she'd dragged them clear.

"You're ok, little ones. You're safe now." The squeaks got louder as she scooped them up. One had the bluest eyes she'd ever seen on an animal, and the other had four white socks with necklace to match.

Catherine dug out a high sided pressure cooker and placed the two kittens inside it on the kitchen floor while she warmed some milk and hunted for a suitable drinking vessel. She'd left the back door ajar, and didn't see Doris come in behind her.

"Why aren't you at work young lady?" said Doris.

Catherine turned and gasped. "Doris! Don't do that. I nearly had kittens."

Doris looked down at the writhing balls of fur struggling to climb the cooker walls.

"Looks like you already have. And if I were you I'd chuck an onion and a stock cube in there as well."

"Aw, Doris, aren't they sweet? I found them at the back of the shed. How do I get this milk into them? Will this work?" She held up a glass eye dropper.

Doris shook her head. "They're too young for cow's milk. Water will do better, and you can get kitten food in cans these days. I'll nip to

Patel's if you like. I've a couple of envelopes to push into the neighbours' doors anyway."

"Would you, Doris? That would be great," said Cathy, "because I'd hate for the poor things to die on me."

"I thought you hated cats. How come you've gone soft over these? Are you sure it wouldn't be kindest to drown them?"

Catherine already had her purse in her hand. "Here's ten pounds. See what you can do with that. If you can get a baby's bottle with the smallest teet, that would be great." She gave Doris a distracted look. "Did you come round for anything in particular?"

"Oh yes," said Doris, pulling an envelope from her apron. "I've brought your invitation." Handing over the envelope, Doris peered inside the pressure cooker. "Aah, diddums. Does mummy not want you anymore then?" She straightened up and grinned at Catherine. "Can I have him please?" she said, pointing to blue eyes. "He looks like mischief. That's a good name, don't you think?"

"You're getting married?" said Catherine, reading the card. "That's our holiday out of the window then."

"Well you can't go abroad in your condition, can you? So I have to do something to fill my time."

"I haven't decided what to do yet."

Chapter thirty three : The decision is made

"Can't I have him then?" Doris repeated.

"You can have Mischief, so long as I can have a plus one added to this invitation, and you promise not to drown him – that's the cat, obviously. Not my plus one."

"Do you mean that copper? So it's official then?"

"We're officially friends. Good ones. So what do you say?"

Doris looked down at the cooking pot again. "Go on then. And of course I won't drown him. That would be a terrible waste. I'm gonna make a casserole, just like you."

After Doris returned with the food, the kittens had been fed and settled in a cardboard box, Catherine put the lawnmower away and went inside to write herself a note. First thing Monday she'd telephone the council about collecting unclaimed dead bodies, but for now she needed a warm soak. As she lay relaxing in the water for a few moments, happy for Doris's good fortune in finding someone to love but sad because things would be changing, she looked down at her belly, and thought she saw a tiny movement. *Could that be?* She lay there watching until it happened again. It was just a gentle ripple that could have been wind. A trickle of condensed steam ran down her nose and she wiped it away with her already wet hand. *Bloody hell.*

For the rest of Saturday and much of Sunday, Catherine, with the help of Doris, fed those tiny mouths on demand around the clock. At four in the afternoon she rang Butcher's mobile.

"Mister Butcher, it's Catherine."

"Catherine. I heard you weren't feeling well yesterday."

"I'm fine. I just needed some time to myself. I'm taking care of kittens I found in the garden, and I was wondering what to do with them tomorrow when I have to come to work." *See how you deal with that one.*

"How old are they?"

"Difficult to tell. They're really skinny."

"We'll think of somewhere to put them," said Butcher. "I'll get Jack to pick you up."

"No, that's ok," she said. "We can manage on the bus."

"I have a pet carrier," he said. "Jack can help you with it. Please let me do this."

"Ok, I suppose that makes sense. This is just one of the negatives of being a parent. Losing independence, juggling things so you can go to work..."

Chapter thirty three : The decision is made

"Catherine," he said, "I'll build a ruddy crèche for you if you want to come to work." He paused, and she could hear his laboured breathing. "I'll do anything. Please."

Right answer. "Thanks, Mister Butcher. I start work at eight thirty. Tell Jack he needs to be here around ten past."

***

It was four forty five and her thoughts were back in the doctor's waiting room on this Monday afternoon. The annoying child sitting behind her was long gone; the tropical fish were swimming undisturbed in their tank and Catherine's apprehension had mysteriously vanished. Her eyes settled upon a grey haired old man sitting diagonally opposite. His broad shoulders were slightly bent and he wore a heavy grey overcoat. Far too heavy for the time of year, and haphazardly buttoned. His wiry moustache curled up at the edges, and he had an anchor tattoo on his hand. A small boy, tired of exploring the children's toy corner, came across to the man and stared into the old timer's watery eyes. His heavily pregnant mother, who sat two places away from Catherine, watched him, eagle eyed. The boy pointed down to the man's shoes.

"Your laces are loose, Mister. Do you want me to tie them for you?" The old man's face crinkled up into a smile.

"Why thank you, young man. Are you sure you can do it?"

The boy bent down, taking hold of the dangling laces, and systematically went through the looping, wrapping around and pulling through, until the shoe was tied.

"I learned how to do it last week," the boy said, "and sometimes I do Richard's. He's my best friend. My name's Ben, what's yours?"

"My name's Fred, and I'm very pleased to meet you,"

Ben smiled. "Do you have any pets? I used to have a puppy, but he died. I've got a canary now. His name's Custard."

"That's a good name," said Fred. "A long time ago I had a parrot called Skipper, but someone took him."

Cathy's ears pricked up.

Ben's mother still watched with concern. The old man put his hand in his pocket and pulled out a bag of sweets.

"Skipper was *my* best friend," he said, opening up the seal on the bag, "and because you've tied my shoelace so well, I'd like to offer you one of my jelly babies." He held the packet out to the boy, and Ben was about to plunge his hand inside.

"Ben!" shouted his mother. Ben turned. "I told you never to take things from strangers. Come here to me now."

Chapter thirty three : The decision is made

Love the Irish accent. Don't like her so much.

The boy went back to his mother, who examined his clothing carefully, brushed away a speck of imaginary contamination, and started a conversation about wayward men with the woman sitting beside her. Ben sat on the floor next to her chair, and untied his own shoe laces. Catherine watched the old man's smile disappear as he replaced the packet of sweets and resumed his solitary gaze through the window.

Poor Fred.

Snippets of the conversation going on beside her were becoming hard to ignore.

"So what happened to the father then?" said the female to Ben's mother.

"Oh, he beggared off as soon as he found out, so."

"The very same thing happened to me," recalled the woman. "Twenty five years ago now." She leaned toward the expectant mother and patted her arm.

"One thing I've learned," she said. "Never trust a coal man. Once their sacks are emptied, they're off like a shot."

Not only coal men.

Catherine got up from her seat and moved across next to where Fred was sitting.

"I hope you don't mind, but I couldn't help overhearing your conversation," she said.

Fred smiled. "That's all right. It relieves the boredom sometimes, doesn't it?"

"What kind of parrot did you have, if you don't mind me asking?"

Fred's eyes twinkled. Almost as much as Rob's. "I don't mind at all. He was an African grey."

"And how long ago did you lose him?"

"Oh, let's see. It was almost Christmas, I remember that. It'll be some thirty odd years ago now. I was burgled." His brow furrowed at the recollection. "Damn blighters. If only I'd got my hands on them."

"You might not believe this," she said. "But I think I may have your Skipper."

He looked at her in disbelief. "Why would you think that?"

"Because everything you've said fits. He still speaks your name, his name, and he has all these phrases."

Fred became quite animated. "Man Overboard? Full of surprises?"

"Yes, and yes!"

"That's incredible. Where did you get him from?"

Chapter thirty three : The decision is made

"My dad bought him from a man in a pub. The Christmas before I was born. It was 1961. Look, you should come round and see him. He'll remember you, I'm sure of it."

Fred scratched his head. "After all these years ...."

Catherine opened her handbag and pulled out a note pad. "I'm going to give you my address and telephone number," she said while writing, "and I want you and Skipper to be reunited." She tore out the page and handed it to him. He glanced at it and pushed it into his pocket.

"I'll do that, I promise."

At that moment, everyone straightened up as a uniformed police officer entered the waiting room and walked over to where Catherine was seated.

"Rob, what are you doing here?" she whispered loudly.

"I didn't like the thought of you being on your own."

"But I thought you were on duty," said Catherine. He leaned towards her ear and whispered.

"I am. On my way to the cells with an arsonist in the back of the car."

Catherine gave him an impatient look. "You're doing it again, aren't you?"

"Doing what?"

"Making sure I'm listening."

The receptionist's voice sounded over the P.A. system, "Catherine Grimshaw for Doctor Hyde," it said.

"Doctor Hyde?" whispered Rob, "I can't let you go in there alone. Anything could happen."

Catherine got up. "Don't be silly. I've got to go."

Rob followed her into the corridor. "I'll pick you up from the hotel. I'd better get back to the car. He might have burned it out by now."

Catherine shouted after him. "See you around six."

***

The doctor's room smelled fruity, and made Catherine want to retch. On the desk, without its screw top lid was a jar of traffic light lollies.

The doctor looked up from his written notes as she entered the room.

That's a first.

"Take a seat. I'm just catching up here, and I can see you cancelled the counselling session. Does this mean you've changed your mind?"

She glanced at the lolly jar on his desk and pulled a face. "Sorry, but would you mind if I put the lid on this?"

"Of course. They're a bit pungent, aren't they?"

"I never thought I'd say this a few days ago," she said, tightening the lid. "But I've decided to go ahead and have this baby."

Chapter thirty four : The reunion

Fred came by just two days after their meeting and brought younger brother Charlie. As Catherine opened the door, Fred whipped off his woolly hat, and nudged Charlie to do the same, though his was a deerstalker, tied in a bow beneath the chin. He gave Fred a martyred look, and then for Catherine, a charming smile.

"Hope you don't mind me bringing my brother," said Fred. "He's really well behaved, and best of all, he provides the transport."

Charlie shrugged. "And I have to be nice to him, because he lets me live in his house."

Cathy smiled. "Please, come in. I'm hoping you'll have a pleasant surprise."

She led them into the living room, where Skipper was poised to receive visitors. With head cocked, he leaned forwards on his perch. Fred walked slowly towards the cage.

"Hello, Skipper old boy. Do you remember your old mate Fred?"

Skipper tilted his head to the other side, bobbed up and down, followed by sideways pacing to the end of his perch and back again.

"He's looking much paler around the ears," said Fred.

Catherine went over to a drawer in the sideboard and opened it. “I’ve some photos here, taken in the early days by my dad. He was a bit darker then.”

Fred felt in his coat pocket. “Blast, forgotten my specs again.”

“Here you go old man. Take mine. It’s one of the few things we have in common - bad eyesight.”

“Yes we do Charlie, thanks. Of course it’s me that was blessed with the good looks.” Fred put on his brother’s spectacles and scanned the photographs. “Skipper was only two years old when I got him,” he said. “He must be forty years old now.” Fred looked up. “Practically a lifetime. I can hardly believe it.”

“Well, you know the ultimate test,” said Charlie. “The decider.”

“He could’ve forgotten,” said Fred.

Catherine puzzled. “What’s the ultimate test?”

Fred turned his full attention to Skipper, and began to chant.

“Fifteen men on a dead man’s chest...”

Skipper tilted his head again and opened his beak.

“Yo-ho-ho..... and a bottle of rum,” he rasped, pacing from side to side with excitement. ***“Fred’s here! Fred’s here!”***

Fred grinned, placed his forefinger inside the bars and Skipper came close, brushing his head against it.

"That's my boy."

Tears spilled down Catherine's cheeks. "I've never heard him say that before. I'm gobsmacked."

"Skipper used to play the part of Captain Flint in our local production of Treasure Island," said Fred. "And he hasn't forgotten his lines."

"That's a relief," said Cathy. "I thought you were a real life pirate."

"Well, I can't say it wasn't an ambition of mine."

Catherine didn't know whether to make the offer or not, but before she could decide, the words were out of her mouth.

"Do you want to take him home with you?"

Fred hesitated, and when he looked up he had tears in his eyes too. "I think it rather depends on Skipper," he said. "It's been such a long time, he may not settle."

"Would you like to try? We could keep tabs on the situation and stay in touch."

"Wouldn't you miss him?"

"Of course I would," she said, wiping her wet cheeks with the back of her hand. "But life around here is about to change so much, he may not be too happy here either."

"If you're sure, we'd love to give it a go." He turned to Charlie. "Wouldn't we?"

Charlie looked at Catherine. "We have an aviary at home. There's nothing Fred doesn't know about birds. Skipper was part of our family. He and Fred were very close."

"That's settled then."

***

For the next few weeks, Catherine was syringed of blood; extracted of urine; internally examined and dietetically advised. At ante natal classes they praised her for gaining a pound, yet scolded her for gaining two. Medical students took turns in prodding her swollen abdomen; shook their heads at her disadvantaged pelvic bones, and argued over how many heads they could feel attached to just the one torso. By the time of Doris's wedding, she was rather swollen, but resisting tent style fashion.

It may have been a small gathering at the church, but the occasion was romantically huge, with a surprise horse drawn carriage waiting outside. Doris looked delectable, to use the judge's own description, in a pale turquoise organza dress and jacket, with a wide brimmed hat adorned with decorative fruit. During the photo shoot, the judge passed an unfortunate remark about saggy plums, and took a sharp elbow to the ribs just as the camera shutter clicked.

At the reception, wedding gifts and cards bagged their own table. The judge's mother, still very much alive at ninety seven, kept shifting the coffee percolator she'd bought to the front of the display. The booze was a free for all, and since Catherine couldn't indulge, those who did, sprang to her notice.

"You know Rob, I should have asked Doris for a copy of the seating plan. There's barely a handful of people I know here. And most of *them* live in my street."

"Well, you're better off than me," said Rob. "I can't even claim a handful."

"Sorry, I should have thought about that" said Catherine. "I didn't want to come on my own. Like Billy no mates, propping up the wall. Tell you what though, that one over there's having a good time." Cathy pointed her tomato juice at an Annie Lennox look alike, with close cropped hair, a dark trouser suit, shirt and tie.

Rob cleared his throat and gave Catherine a sideways glance. "And there's a story I should tell you about her."

Catherine puzzled. "Oh yes? Did you arrest her once?"

"Used to go out with her."

Shit.

"Oh? When was this? Recently?"

Rob twirled the stem of his glass between forefinger and thumb, watching the liquid pirouette inside. "It was about four years ago now. Her name's Babs. I knew she had a great uncle, a Justice of the Peace, but didn't connect her with the judge until I spotted her in the church."

Catherine scrutinized Babs more closely.

Strong jawline. A bit masculine. Is that his type?

Babs was packing the booze away like it was about to be outlawed, grabbing the woman she was with around her waist and pulling her close.

"So, who broke up with who? Catherine continued.

"It was me who finished it. She wasn't cut up about it, if that's what you're wondering."

"No, I can see that. Looks like she's still celebrating."

Rob began to laugh. "You're a hard woman, Grimshaw."

"Oh my God, it's you. You're the one who's cut up! I can tell by your face."

"Shall I tell you what I'm cut up about? And it's not because I liked her that much."

"Don't tell me. I think I can work it out." Catherine glanced across at the two companions again, and a broad smile spread across her face. "You think you turned her gay."

"Not only that, but her girlfriend. That's my sister, Diane."

Catherine gaped. "Is this … the sister who works in your dad's butcher shop?"

Rob nodded. "She makes all the sausage, ironically. And they don't talk to me."

"Why ever not?"

Rob shrugged. "Guilt, I suppose, on their part. Humiliation on mine. I was the laugh of the cop shop for months. No-one took the piss out of *her*."

"She's a police officer too?"

Rob gave her an affirmative look.

"You should have said something. We don't have to stay."

"It really doesn't bother me. The only thing that upsets me is my sister doesn't want to be my sister anymore."

"I can't believe that. It's mad. Has all this put you off relationships for good?"

Rob took a sip from his glass and pulled a face. "Oh that's gone warm."

"I'll get you another, and don't avoid the question."

Rob considered. "Not for good, exactly."

"What does that mean? Is there someone on your radar?"

"You could say that."

Tell me who and I'll scratch her eyes out.

"You're not going to tell me, are you? I shouldn't have dragged you here when you don't like weddings. I'm sorry."

Rob locked eyes with Catherine's. "I never said I didn't like weddings."

"It's just.....well, you never talk about your marriage. I assumed the whole thing was a sore topic."

"I miss my kids. That's why I don't talk about it. Anyway, never mind Babs....looks like Doris has had a few too many as well."

Catherine followed his gaze towards the happy couple. Doris did look rather dishevelled.

The judge grabbed her attention. "My dear, are you sure you still want to do the speech? You've had nearly that whole bottle of sherry to yourself."

"Of course I'm doing the ....hic.....speech. Is there anything .....hic......you'd like me to avoid saying, my sweet?"

"If you were sober, you wouldn't have to ask that. But if you could mention how much we adore mother's gift ...you know, the percolator she's so proud of? I think she'd love you forever."

"I'll add it to my ... hic ... serviette." She picked up her spectacles from the table, aimed them several times at her ears while scrawling on a paper serviette. Standing up with the support of the dining table, she lifted the silver bell provided and shook it. It gave a fairy-like tinkle.

"Ladies, gentlemen, and those … who remain undiagnosed ….."

Catherine grimaced. *Way to go, Doris. Foot straight in it.*

"I'm overwhelmed … hic …. with indifference …. at the turn out …. for our little …. hic …. shindig. Such … thoughtful gifts … most of them. Cannot thank you all …. Hic … enough. But special thanks … to my mother in law in particular ... for the most … hic ... precious gift of all ... and that is, my wonderful .... perky .... copulator."

Whaat? She never just said that.

The room went silent. A single titter, followed by a much larger roar of laughter came from the guests. Unfortunately, neither the gift giver nor the grateful recipient could quite understand why.

***

The kittens, in company with Catherine, grew larger and were soon ready to be re-homed. Socks, despite being the smallest of the litter was typically a man's cat. Outwardly he appeared to be independent, showing a great interest in the outside world and its wildlife through any glass pane he was able to leave a nose smear on. Yet he showed a special sensitivity to human infirmity, which made him the perfect companion for Mel Butcher. Butcher's recovery from the bullet wound was slow, and on his weaker days Socks would curl up close on his bed, nuzzling his head against his master's neck.

Having already taken a strong liking to Mischief, Doris convinced the judge they needed a feline addition to the household in order to complete their marital bliss. Mischief, however, was a bit of a wanderer, and while Doris went scrambling about in a neighbour's privet hedge at midnight one evening, she innocently admitted to two patrolling policemen who pulled over beside her, that she was looking for Mischief.

Despite the unsettling events surrounding her latest exam, Catherine received confirmation that she had passed. Even then, she wondered if Ken had marked the papers and given her extra points to compensate for his unforgivable lies.

Rob became such a trustworthy friend and willing DIY enthusiast, that she gave him a front door key for convenience, especially since he offered his wallpaper hanging skills in the new nursery. This small room hadn't been used since Steven left home more than twenty years since, and had needed a complete re-plaster.

***

Rob was up to his armpits in rolls of Peter rabbit when Catherine came home from work with Chinese takeaways. She dropped her keys into a bowl on the hall table and shouted up the stairs.

"Rob? You still up there?" She took off her coat and went through to the kitchen.

"You can't stop me now, I'm on the last lap," he shouted back.

Catherine had the plates out and lids off the containers. "Oh, that's a pity. I'll just have to eat all this food myself then."

Rob came out of the bedroom, paste brush in hand and stood at the top of the stairs. "Is that chicken chow mein I can smell?"

"Might be," she teased, scooping the contents onto both plates and taking two bottles of flavoured water from the fridge. "But you just keep working. I can finish this lot, no problem."

"Did ... did you get crispy noodles?"

Catherine fished another bag from the larger bag and opened it. "Oo, they're still warm and crunchy. Lovely!"

Rob ran down the stairs and gaped in the kitchen doorway. She looked up from the table and grinned. "I knew you'd cave."

"Just ten minutes. Then I must get back upstairs." He took a bottle opener from the drawer and sat down. “Didn’t get here ‘til half three. Then I had to go out for more paste.”

“I need to pay you for more than paste,” said Catherine, taking her seat. “It’s Friday night. You could be out partying.”

He took a forkful and closed his eyes as he chewed. “There’s a party going on in my mouth right now. Didn’t realise how hungry I was. How was your day, anyway?”

“I’ve been upstairs in admin, doing the wages. Butcher wants me to learn all aspects of the job.” Catherine opened the bag of crispy noodles. “Shall I pour these on top for you?”

“Just half for now, thanks.....So you’re ok with all that? Is bellhopping on the programme too?”

“I don’t mind doing that either. Marcus does it, and he’s the manager. Not sure about valet parking though.”

“No, best give that one a swerve.”

“I will pass my test you know, eventually.”

Rob was staring and smiling. “What have you got on?”

“Oh, this?” She tugged at the skirt of the baggy pinafore she was wearing. “Well...I had to give in at some point. I know it’s ugly...I know *I’m* ugly. But I might be half way presentable again by February. As long as I don't eat too many of these." She held up another forkful of noodles.

"Don't call yourself ugly....because you're not, and never could be." As her eyes met his, he returned his attention quickly to his food.

"You're a sweet man, you know that, right? You should be out there, finding someone. Not hanging out here, doing me favours all the time. I ask too much of you."

"Believe me," he said, "I wouldn't give up my time if I'd something better to do with it."

"Oh cheers, that makes me feel a whole lot better. Anyway....What happened to that woman you hinted about at the wedding? Did you ask her out yet?"

"I'm waiting for the right moment."

"What's keeping you? Is she married or something?"

"Nope."

"Could you be any more vague? Is it worth me asking any more questions?"

"Nope."

"God, you're stubborn."

"Erm .... the words pot and kettle spring to mind." Rob picked up his empty plate and carried it to the sink.

"Fair point."

He turned on the tap. "Thought I'd take the ferry over to see the kids before Christmas. Have to swap a couple of shifts around, but it'll work out ok."

Catherine finished her food and got up from the table. "Oh, that'll be nice. Will you be staying with them?" *Bed and Breakfast. Much better idea. No temptation.*

"May as well. Adam's got a double bed. He won't mind his old dad bunking in with him." He took her empty plate.

Double bed? He's only ten.

"Lucky Adam," she said.

"He wants me to watch him play in the under fourteens five a side."

Family day out then.

"And Sarah wants a new keyboard....three hundred quid's worth."

"Absent parents can't say no, can they?"

"Truth is....I'd happily give her three hundred to stop playing."

"Well...it's not like you're there much to hear it. Think of her poor mother."

I really don't give a toss about her mother.

"Do you want me to come up stairs with you?"

"Well, there's an offer I haven't had in a long time. You can mix me some more paste if you like."

That's all I'm good for these days.

***

As Catherine took time to get to know her father, she discovered a wise yet vulnerable man with a desperate need to recover thirty three lost parenting years in whatever time remained. In complete contrast to his former distant self, he displayed a genuine affection for her, and an eagerness to teach every business skill he knew, in preparation for the time when she would have to take over his position.

"I've every confidence in you Catherine," he said. "But I must warn you that I'll turn in my grave if you ever sell out to one of these obnoxious chains. We've turned them all down up to now, and I expect you to keep this place independent."

"Oh, so that's why you wanted me on board," she said, "and here's me thinking you had a sentimental streak hidden somewhere inside you."

Butcher smiled. "Well if I had, I couldn't *possibly* reveal it."

***

Rob was due home from Northern Ireland on Christmas Eve, and Catherine planned to finish work at noon, exactly three weeks before her due date. However, a seasonal crisis would not only delay the time of her departure, but also downgrade the style in which she was to make it. There was a small Christmas party being held for the guests' children in the hotel's downstairs lounge. Marcus had poached the services of a popular Santa Claus from a local store's grotto, to speak kindly to the children and hand out a few gifts. One of the hotel's service cars was poorly disguised as a sleigh, complete with jingling bells, inflatable reindeer and liberal quantities of cotton wool randomly stuck to its bodywork. But Santa had a party of his own to attend prior to the Dolphin engagement, at which he over indulged on festive spirit, tripped over a raised paving stone in the street and was knocked unconscious. A stand-in was urgently required, and based on her own portly appearance, Catherine was elected.

It was only meant to be a thirty minute appearance. The red and white outfit could have been made to measure, or so Simon said with a snigger, and the kids seemed enraptured by the whole event. Though there was one little girl who'd been giving Catherine evils from beneath her tasselled party hat ever since Santa had waddled into the room. When it came to Alice's turn with Santa, she approached in slow motion and attempted to sit on Catherine's knee two or three times, but due to stomach overlap, space was limited.

"This is hopeless," said Alice, jumping back down to the floor with arms crossed.

"Oh, I'm sorry Alice," said Santa. "Is there anything you'd like for Christmas that I can bring you on the big day?"

"You've forgotten already?" Alice frowned. "I told you what I wanted last week. I sat on that very same knee in Toys 'R' Us and there was plenty of room.

Rumbled by an eight year old. Catherine searched for a believable explanation. "Sometimes … those treats your mummies leave out for me are just too tempting."

"Well, I don't know whose mince pies you've been eating," said Alice, "but one of them just kicked me."

Catherine winced and clutched her belly. "Me too … ouch!" She called across to Teresa, who was speaking with a party helper in a corner of the room.

"Teresa! Teresa! Something's happening!"

***

The medical staff at A&E were accustomed to unusual admissions, but never before had they seen a heavily pregnant Father Christmas arrive in a chauffeur driven motorised sleigh, about to give birth. But as Santa's gender and medical condition were being established and she was allocated a bed in the delivery suite, her father, back at the Dolphin was having problems of his own.

Chapter thirty four : The reunion

Being Christmas Eve, Butcher allowed his nurse to leave early, feeling sure he'd manage alone until Jack returned from a meeting in the next room. Socks the cat paced back and forth in front of the refrigerator, mewing occasionally and throwing the odd glance from his empty saucer to Butcher, resting in an armchair next to his oxygen cylinder, listening to a music album. He returned a tired smile to his feline friend, and slowly raised himself up and out of the chair.

"All right, Socks." He lifted his hot water bottle and oxygen mask to one side. "I'll get you a drink." Butcher shuffled across to the fridge in his carpet slippers as an icy December blast brushed by him from the slightly open window. The cold fresh air kept him alert. As he opened the fridge, Socks licked his lips and sniffed the air.

Butcher bent over to lift a carton of single cream with his functioning hand, when his breathing became more laboured, and as he straightened, he found himself gasping for air. Still holding on to the cream, he clutched at his chest and dropped the carton in the process. Socks jumped clear as Butcher struggled to draw air into his lungs, sinking to his knees, then flat out onto his front. He drew short, frantic gasps as the cream □ran at first around his face before travelling the grouting grooves in the tiled floor. Socks came forward and lapped at the cream from the puddle's edge before circling his master with curiosity. Then the open window caught his attention, and he took a short run followed by a leap, squeezing his tiny body through the gap. Perching on the narrow balcony rail separating the two rooms, the cat began to wail. Deep male voices filtered through from the next room, and a thin band of light streamed out from the gap where the curtains didn't quite meet. The window was closed, and Socks continued to wail until Spence's guest became distracted.

"That sounds like a cat," he said.

Jack Spence rose from his chair, drawing back the curtain. Initially puzzled by what he saw, he eased open the French windows. "Excuse me for a second," he said to his guest, as he stepped onto the balcony and edged slowly towards the feline, making a carefully timed grab with both hands. No sooner had he placed Socks on the floor inside the room, than the cat hurried to the door, mewing loudly. Jack excused himself once again.

Butcher's door wasn't locked, and while Spence hurried to his boss's aid with the oxygen, Socks mopped up the remainder of spilled cream with an eager tongue.

Meanwhile, back in the delivery suite, Catherine strained and pushed while a midwife and junior doctor made encouraging noises at the business end. She still sported the cotton wool eyebrows and rosy cheeks of her alter ego, but there were no more 'ho-ho-hos' left in her.

"Come on Catherine. You're doing really well. Just one more big push and baby's head will be out."

"I'm trying. Just really ……. tired." Catherine closed her eyes.

"No sleeping on the job Catherine." Said the doctor, "Not 'til it's done."

"You gave me the flaming morphine and now you tell me I can't sleep." She picked up the gas and air nozzle, wrapped her lips around it and sucked deeply.

"Yes, we're cruel like that," the midwife said, "but you'll thank us in the end when you have your little reward. Now, just once more. Give it everything you've got."

By this time, Rob Sutton had arrived at the hospital and was directed to the waiting area. Still carrying his luggage, he looked an oddity, but was soon chatting with an expectant father of twins.

"So, are these your first babies?" asked Rob.

"Oh no," said the man. "We have two sets of twins already."

"That's amazing. So you get twins every time?"

The man gave Rob a look he might have saved for a village idiot. "Not every time," he said. "Sometimes, we don't get anything at all."

Catherine eventually gave birth to a healthy baby girl weighing just over seven pounds at 00.10 hours on Christmas morning. By 00.45 hours she'd been stitched, cleaned up, and handed a cup of tea. Rob, who'd waited all this time grasping a bunch of now sad looking flowers, was allowed to see Catherine just as she was transferred from delivery to a side room off the mother and baby ward. At the ward entrance, he dropped the flowers into a nearby waste bin.

Catherine winced as she raised herself higher up the bed. Rob gave her a weary smile and her stomach growled. "So, what was it?" he said, pulling up a chair.

Catherine lifted the bed cover slightly, peered down into the darkness and said with pained expression, "Just hunger, I think."

"No, I meant the baby. What variety?"

She stared at the suitcase. "Did you come straight off the train? Is the case full of all my presents? And how come they let you stay?"

"Just dirty laundry in there … mostly. They must have assumed I was your husband. I didn't put them straight. Everything's ok, isn't it? Are you going to tell me what you had?"

"Pretty sure it was an elephant on the way out, but amazingly it turned out to be an actual human. Of the female variety."

"That's.... brilliant news. I brought you flowers earlier, but they lost the will to live while I was waiting."

"Oh, that's a shame. I'm starved. Could have eaten a few flower heads." She raised a hand to her face, and picked at the cotton wool still stuck to her eyebrows.

"I think *my* flowers might have poisoned you. But ... I do have throat lozenges." He patted his jacket pocket to make sure.

"Give 'em here then."

Rob thrust a hand into his pocket. "How are you feeling?"

"Like I've been trampled by a herd of angry wildebeest." She unwrapped the lozenges and popped three at once. "Don't let my state of euphoria fool you. I could be waiting at the door."

"What door?"

"Death's door," she closed her eyes and groaned with pleasure as she chewed.

"You feel that bad?"

"I do." She glanced through to the corridor where two white coated medics were deep in conversation.

"But there's a doctor over there, threatening to pull me through."

Rob didn't laugh. "What have they got you on? *I'm* the bad joke merchant, not you. Anyway, I got you something." He opened his case and took out a red drawstring pouch. "I saw a sign in the shop window and thought of you."

"Really? That looks like jewellery. What did the sign say? How many words, how many letters?"

He looked at his watch. "You seriously want to play guessing games at one o'clock in the morning?"

"And Christmas morning too. Just humour me, before I go to sleep."

Rob sighed. "Ok then, one word, four letters."

She felt her lids drooping. "Was it L-O-V-E by any chance?" Then she opened her eyes wide.

What the hell just came out of my mouth? Must be the drugs.

It was the first time she'd given any hint of romance. But he'd led her straight into it.

His face flushed. "Where *is* the baby?"

"She's in the Special Care Baby Unit because she came early. It's just a precaution."

He nodded in reply.

Well I've done it now. May as well be hung for a sheep as a lamb. "So go on then, what was the four letter word?"

"I'm embarrassed to say now."

"Go on, I'm still drugged up to the eyeballs. I'll never remember anyway."

"Ok, it was S-A-L-E," he confessed.

"Cheapskate." She attempted a laugh, grimaced at the effort, and opened the jewellery pouch. It was a silver bracelet with a single charm of a baby's bootee attached. She took it out and held it up. "It's beautiful, Rob, and so thoughtful. Thank you. Could you keep it for us until I get home?" It felt strange saying 'us' for the first time. She would have to find a name for baby Grimshaw, and soon.

They looked across the room as a nurse poked her head inside the door.

"Excuse me, Catherine," she said. "Just to let you know about a few phone calls. Your brother, and someone called Doris phoned to ask how you are."

"Ok, thanks for letting me know."

"And there's something else. A message from Mister Spence?"

"Oh? Does he want me at work today? Because I might have to decline."

"He wanted you to know that your father was admitted to ICU earlier this evening."

Cathy tried to get herself up from the bed and winced.

"My father? Is he all right?"

Chapter thirty four : The reunion

Chapter thirty five : One in, one out

Baby Grimshaw was back on the ward with her mother by the afternoon. Catherine had already been out of bed and suffered the initial pain of visiting the toilet on the arm of a nurse, eaten a long awaited breakfast, and fed her baby successfully at the second attempt. The addictive scent of her new baby's head quickly became the object of her existence. And it was legal.

A visit to see Butcher in ICU was scheduled for later that afternoon, and a male nurse duly arrived at her bedside with a wheelchair. Despite dark circles beneath bloodshot eyes, he forced a smile.

"Catherine Grimshaw?"

Catherine looked up expectantly, though for what she was never sure these days. "That's me."

The nurse gestured with a hand towards the mobile chair. "I'm here to take you to ICU. Your carriage awaits."

Catherine pulled back the frayed cotton bedcover, and swung her legs out of bed at normal speed, but was reminded on standing of that dragging sensation in the nether regions which slowed her to a snail's pace.

"Let me help," said the nurse, placing an arm around her back and easing her slowly into the chair. "Not as easy as you think, is it? Not after all that heavy work last night and those painful repairs." He lifted a blanket from the back of the chair and handed it to her.

"Ooh," she said, breathing more heavily than usual. "I've turned into an old woman overnight." The blanket across her legs was the nearest to a hug she was likely to get, and she tucked it tightly into the sides of the chair.

The nurse nodded. "That's what it feels like. And you're thinking you can squeeze into your old size ten jeans now that your bump's gone down. But you'd be wrong."

"Well thanks for the vote of confidence." She gave the nurse a worn look as he steered the chair towards the exit.

"Hang on a minute." Catherine looked anxiously over her shoulder. "I can't leave my baby behind."

He stopped abruptly, and made a 180 degree turn with the buckled wheels.

"That's what you say now. But a week with no sleep will change your mind."

"Sounds like someone left their bedside manner behind this morning," she said.

He strode across to the clear plastic cot labelled 'Baby Grimshaw' and lifted out the grouchy infant, rudely woken from slumber. Her mop of spiky fair hair and disgruntled face made Catherine melt yet again as the child was placed in her arms. Then, and only then, did they set off.

The journey to Intensive Care was through a maze of bright corridors, down two floors in a lift that smelled of bananas, and through a glass tunnel leading to an annex. She resisted the urge to ask, 'Are we there yet?'

The nurse pulled up and parked Catherine's chair outside a pair of glass panelled doors sign posted 'ICU'. The baby girl resting in her lap stretched out her tiny fists and puckered her eyelids as Cathy tried to peer through the glass. Melvyn Butcher lay on his back with his head supported by two pillows. An oxygen cylinder stood close to the bed connected to a transparent mask covering half of his face, and electrodes and wires hooked him to a bleeping heart monitor.

"I'll take you in, give you ten minutes or so, then I'll pop back." The nurse pressed the intercom access, announced their presence, pushed open the doors and wheeled her to Butcher's bedside, directed by another nurse. Then with a squeak of tennis shoe soles against linoleum, he was gone. Butcher turned his head as much as the mask would allow, blinked at his daughter and raised three purple-tinged fingers into the air. Catherine looked down at her waking child, scooped her gently upwards in both arms and placed her tiny body on the bed next to Butcher's reaching hand.

"It's a baby girl," she said. "I'm thinking of calling her Madison." Butcher's hand found the child's tiny head, and his eyes crinkled. Catherine squeezed his forearm. "You must get better. Madison needs her Grandad." Butcher looked straight into Catherine's eyes and lifted his good hand from the baby's head to lower his oxygen mask.

"Sorry," he gasped. "I should have told you." Catherine manoeuvred her chair closer, and used both arms to encircle her child and also to grasp her father's hand. She felt his fingers squeeze hers, and then relax. His eyes became still as the continuous tone of the heart monitor kicked in. Footsteps came running, and she seemed unable to move.

"Excuse me miss," came the urgent voice of a medic from behind, who scooped up the child, placed it back into Cathy's arms and dragged her chair clear of the bed. Bustling staff surrounded the bed, barking instructions at one another. She felt her chair being manipulated from behind, and suddenly she was outside the room, listening. They shocked him, garbled something about output, and shocked him again. Someone asked for adrenaline, and a moment later they began CPR. Catherine held her baby close. For ten long minutes she listened to orders being shouted, more running footsteps and the humming of electrical equipment. Then gradually, the panic subsided and all was quiet again. A medical man wearing scrubs emerged from the room, pulled off his hair covering and sighed. He looked across at Catherine.

"Are you…are you a relative?" Cathy wasn't sure she wanted to hear what he was about to say.

"Yes." She swallowed. "He's my father."

The man in scrubs walked awkwardly towards her, pulled up a chair from close by and sat facing her.

"I'm Doctor Novaccs."

"That's an odd name for a doctor," she said. "I'm Catherine Grimshaw, and this is....." she glanced down at her sleeping child, "Madison .... his granddaughter."

The doctor nodded. "Catherine, were you aware how advanced your father's condition was?"

She felt confused. "He was shot in the chest a few months ago. What do you mean? He was supposed to be recovering."

"Your father was terminally ill. His lung cancer was end stage. I'm so sorry."

She shook her head. "But he begged me to have this baby. He wanted to be a grandfather, and why are you talking as if he's already dead?"

"I'm so sorry, but you father died just a few minutes ago. We did everything we could."

Chapter thirty five : One in, one out

Chapter thirty six : Driving test number 4

She had come to expect tragedy of course, but was it really too much to ask that all the secrets and lies had been done with by now? The disappointment she felt for her child, exaggerated by her plummeting post natal oestrogen levels, went deeper than the thoughts of Chairman Mao. This infant, having already started out in life without a father figure, would now never know any of her natural grandparents either.

When Rob came to visit that afternoon, he held a sprightly bunch of daffodils. He stood over Madison's cot with a gentle smile on his face. "Just look what you made, Cathy. Isn't she amazing?"

"Yes, she is rather perfect. Though I say so myself." The words were the right ones, but her tone was flat.

Rob sat next to her bed. "What's up? Are you still sore? I brought you edible flowers." He held up the daffs, and she attempted a smile.

"Would you mind.....giving me a hug?"

He placed the flowers on the bed and carefully put his arms around her. She held on tight. And then came the tears.

Chapter thirty six : Driving test number 4

In the immediate weeks that followed Butcher's funeral, Catherine's work diary was so crammed full of meetings with legal advisors, probate solicitors and paperwork to complete, that she had little time to spend on emotions, let alone quality time with her new baby. But as she signed legal documents dealing with financial provisions made in advance by her father for both hers and Madison's future, she remembered the words spoken by Ted's apparition all those years ago, 'Your father will take care of you," and finally understood what they meant.

Jack Spence, who had been Butcher's right hand man, advised and accompanied Catherine in the early stages of her newly imposed employer status, and became one of her most valued members of staff.

Catherine now had her father's top floor hotel suite in which to live, but that didn't make it any easier to give up the council house which held so many memories. In the procrastinating weeks before the decision was made, the rooms at The Dolphin were used as a private nursery for Madison in the day time, and Socks the cat made it clear he was never going to move, so eventually she gave up her house, albeit with a heavy heart.

In January, Doris retired from the hotel at her husband's request, but this plan was soon sabotaged by baby Madison's requirement for a day time nanny come granny. The judge was used to having his carefully made plans crushed by the dominant females who seemed to organise his life, and Doris was happy to carry on the tradition, as his mother's role began to fade.

***

There continued to be never a dull moment at The Purple Dolphin Hotel, as a group of government officials from local constituencies checked in for a meeting to be held in one of the conference rooms. The meeting began at 11 a.m., while restaurant staff prepared a lavish lunch for the recess at 12.30, and took delivery of four crates of Australian wine, all paid for by Tory party funds. Sir Bernard Austin-Briggs, an M.P. of wide spread notoriety and waistline, known for his love of expensive cars, was seen after lunch walking unsteadily to his vehicle in the hotel's rear car park carrying a surplus bottle of wine which he placed on the back seat of his Porsche, intending to share it at an alternative address with a female associate.

Simultaneously, outside the city's driving test centre, Catherine slid into the driver's seat of her examination vehicle. After a few simple manoeuvres, her confidence grew despite heavy traffic, and the examiner proceeded to give her directions. Coincidentally, Sir Bernard's Porsche was headed in the same direction, although his erratic control of the steering alerted several motorists to give him a wide berth. Eventually, Catherine found herself on the same stretch of coastal road, and she spotted his haphazard control from some distance behind.

Then he widely misjudged a gentle bend in the road, and at the moment of impact with the front right wing of an oncoming Escort, Catherine realised she'd seen the same Porsche being parked at the hotel earlier that morning. The examiner asked her to slow up behind, and then stop. She wound down her window. Shards of broken glass lay scattered in the road, presumably from the Porsche's headlight while the Escort, in company with its driver, looked severely distressed.

Sir Bernard got out of his car, and examined his vehicle. The Escort driver climbed out of his vehicle rubbing his shoulder with a pained expression. He was middle to late thirties, dressed in dusty work clothes with a pencil behind his ear. After surveying the damage to his wing, he came nervously across to Sir Bernard,

"Are you ok, fella?"

Sir Bernard gave him his politically rehearsed look of empathy.

"I appear to be unharmed, but you look dreadful, young man," he said. "Look, I accept this was completely my fault. Probably need to get the steering checked on this bloody awful car."

Catherine's driving examiner, a much younger and healthier version of his predecessor, wanted to get out of the car and offer assistance, but Catherine persuaded him to wait.

"Well, that's all very well," said the crash victim. "But I can't work without my car. We'll have to exchange insurance details." He studied Sir Bernard's face and demeanor for a long moment, pulling out a mobile telephone from his trouser pocket. "And ... perhaps we should phone the police."

Sir Bernard laughed nervously. "Oh, come on now, we can settle this between ourselves, can't we? No need to get the police involved." But the young man was already searching for a number, just as Sir Bernard lunged forward, trying to knock the phone to the ground. His aim was useless, and stumbling with the momentum he turned back to his car, dived into the driver's seat and sped away, just as erratically as before.

Catherine seethed. "Can you believe that? Should we go after him?"

"What?" said the examiner. "We're not bleeding Starsky and Hutch!" He looked at her thoughtfully. "Don't make me …"

"I was kidding..." she said, in a much lighter tone.

Then her face lit up as she recognised the figure in the passenger seat of the approaching police vehicle. Sergeant Rob Sutton got out of his patrol car and approached the battered car at the head of a long queue of honking vehicles, while his colleague attempted to rescue the situation by directing traffic away from the scene. It wasn't until he questioned the unfortunate crash victim, that he glanced across and recognised Catherine's smiling face staring out through her open window. Rob strolled across looking puzzled. Nodding politely to the examiner, he turned to Catherine.

"What on earth are you doing here Catherine? You didn't tell me you were taking lessons again."

"I'm not," she answered, "This is my driving test. I wanted to surprise everyone."

Rob looked anxiously back at the crash scene as another patrol car pulled up alongside.

"How do you always manage to show up in the middle of these kinds of accidents?"

"Oh, I see. So this must be my fault then, just because I've failed three times before. You'd better be careful what you say Rob Sutton. I think you may be needing me as a valuable witness."

"Well it all seems a pretty straightforward case of hit and run as far as I can see. I'm just about to breathalyse this one."

"Of course you are," said Cathy rather smugly, "but all is not what it seems. I watched and heard the whole episode. It's the other guy you need to breathalyse."

Rob looked thoughtful. "And how do you propose we find him?"

"I can assist you with that," she said. "His name .... where he's staying, his profession. Even his registration number."

"Right then. Well in that case, can you jump out and tell constable Dixon in the second car I want him to take your statement?"

"That's fine by me." Cathy stepped out of the test vehicle and took a walked towards the second patrol car, before Rob touched her forearm to slow her down. She looked up into his face, slightly puzzled. "What is it?"

"I need to tell you something. Something important."

"Ok," she said. "Do you need to tell me now, or can it wait?"

"I don't think it can wait much longer," he said.

"Shall I guess? You're going back to your wife, aren't you?"

His brows strained to meet in the middle, only prevented by the deep furrow between them. "Not at all. I want to marry you."

She gaped. "No kidding?"

"Absolutely not."

"Right. I'll just .... do the statement then, and ….we can talk about this …. tonight?"

"Absolutely."

Chapter thirty six : Driving test number 4

Catherine walked slowly across to the second patrol car, paused and looked back at him still watching her intently. As she climbed inside the police car, Rob leaned into the test vehicle and spoke to the examiner.

"This is a bit of a nuisance, isn't it sir?" he said, glancing over his shoulder at Catherine yet again, now giving her statement. He turned back to the examiner.

"She'll be booking another test in the near future, no doubt. So be prepared." Rob smiled and began to withdraw his chauvinistic head from the car when the examiner set him straight.

"Oh, there won't be any need for that," he said, returning the smile. "I just gave Miss Grimshaw the good news a few minutes ago. She's passed."

***

Rob Sutton's mind was elsewhere as he drove to the Dolphin that evening. A tense face reflected back from his polished shoes, and he sniffed himself several times on the journey, thinking he'd overdone the aftershave. 'Concentrate, Robert,' he said to himself. 'You're no bloody good to her under a lorry.' The flowers on the back seat were considerably fresher, and more expensive than the ones he's turned up with at the maternity ward a few months prior. He parked the car and made his way to the front entrance. His mouth was dry, but he resisted the urge to order a drink from the bar. Simon Waterstone was on reception, speaking on the phone. He acknowledged Rob with a raised forefinger and one eyebrow, before replacing the handset.

"Good evening, Sergeant. I see you've brought gifts." His eyes rested on the flowers in Rob's hand.

"Evening Simon. You don't think they're too much, do you?"

"Well that rather depends on the occasion, doesn't it?"

"So she hasn't said anything? I know how much you lot gossip, don't forget."

"Oh, you mean passing her driving test? Well that's not really gossip, is it?"

Rob was grateful for the misunderstanding. "Of course it's not. Bad choice of words." He looked casually around. "So ... where do I find her?"

"She's down in the cellar. One of the circuit breakers needed resetting."

"She's what? Where's that handyman of yours?"

"It's just a circuit breaker. The cat could do it." He looked at his watch. "Although, *she has* been down there about ten minutes already.....do you want to check on her?"

"Well, I think someone should!" Rob lifted the counter flap and made his way to the cellar door. At the foot of the steps his eyes were drawn to the pool of light from Catherine's torch surrounding the fuse box.

"Rob?" she said, looking up. "I'm nearly done. Just had to replace this fuse wire."

"Simon said you just had to reset the switch. Where did you learn to replace fuse wire?"

"You learn lots of things when you have to. ...There! Let's see if it works now." She flipped the switch, and the lights came back on in the cellar. "Let's see if they're on in the lounge." She started to make her way towards the steps, but he caught her arm.

"Just before you do that ... have you thought about what I said?"

She smiled and looked at the flowers, still in his hand. "I've thought of nothing else."

"And? Have you ... is there a conclusion?" A torturous three second pause forced his gaze downwards to an old beer stain on the floorboards.

Catherine's face remained neutral. "The flowers are beautiful. Are they for me?"

Rob's awkward gaze flitted around the room as he spoke. "I just want to take care of the two of you .... and you have to know ... this isn't something .... I mean ... from the first time I met you … met you properly, that is .... and that was eleven years ago….you've been stuck there, in my head. Anyway.."

"Like dandruff. Or nits."

He stared at her properly now. "You're determined to milk this, aren't you? Just ... put me out of my misery, for Godsake."

"I would love to marry you, Rob Sutton."

"I'm sensing a 'but'..."

She took the flowers from his hand, setting them down on the steps, then came towards him and hooked her arms around his neck. "There are no buts. I love you, you daft lump."

Rob's eyes almost popped. "Oh, my Lord, that is such a relief!" He picked her up and swung her around.

She laughed. "I think you're meant to kiss me now."

A raucous cheer erupted from the top of the cellar steps. Simon burst into a rendition of 'Congratulations', and Teresa, Marcus and Doris followed his lead. Then the lights went out again. There was a distant groan from the lounge, but no-one cared.

------ End ------

* Footnotes - in order of appearance

**Magwitch is a character from the novel 'Great Expectations' by Charles Dickens*

**Johnny Bravo is an animated television series created by Van Partible for Cartoon Network*

**Shirley Valentine is a character from the comedy film of the same name made in 1989. Screenplay by Willy Russell.*

Note from the author & acknowledgements

Thank you for choosing to read The Purple Dolphin. As this is my first novel, it would be great if you could leave an honest review online at Amazon which you can do whether you purchased from there or not.

Thanks also to Jericho Writers for granting me a bursary to join their Summer Festival of Writing, which taught me loads.

<u>Other books by M. S Saxon</u>

<u>Cheese on Wheels – A recipe for Trouble, starring Bubble & Squeak</u>

Children's book of illustrated rhyming jokes.

<u>Dinner's in the dog and other sod's law stories – starring Bubble & Squeak</u>

Adults' collection of illustrated rhyming jokes & stories. Book 2 is coming soon.

Printed in Great Britain
by Amazon

32251523R00263